SHADOW ON THE SUN

SHADOW ON THE SUN

The Mound Builders, Book 1

ZOE SAADIA

ISBN-13: 978-1096147497

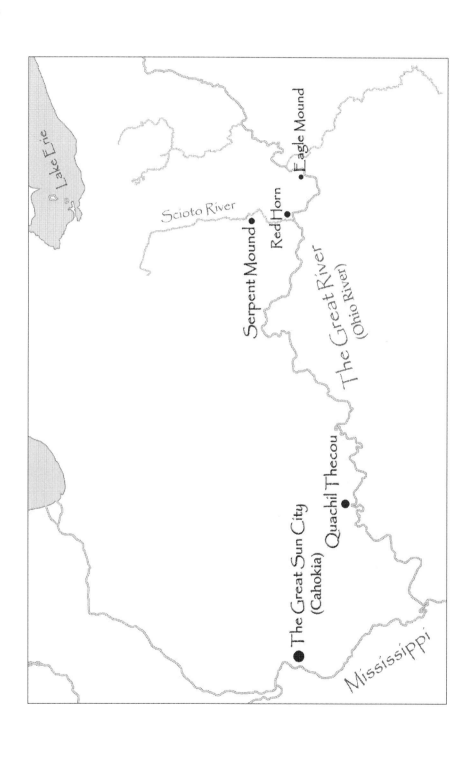

Lake Erie

Eagle Mound

Scioto River

Red Horn

Serpent Mound

The Great River
(Ohio River)

Quachil Thecou

The Great Sun City
(Cahokia)

Mississippi

CHAPTER 1

Ohio River valley,
Late summer, 1205 AD

The bear was huge and ugly, clearly an old hunter, with little patience for petty creatures that stood in its way. Iciwata felt his heart pounding, racing unseemly fast, thundering against his chest, sending waves of primitive fear down his stomach and into his limbs.

Wait here, he motioned at his companions, two more youths of rebellious enough nature, ready to defy the elders by embarking on this unauthorized hunt. Good for them. He didn't feel rebellious, not at all. Just too good to waste another day out there in the fields, carrying buckets all the way from the creek's shore, watering crops that no rain bothered to water throughout the unusually hot, dry summer moons. So near the harvest time, what was there to water anyway? When the crops were ready to be picked, he would be there, working as hard as anyone. But for now, a hunter of his skill could be spared silly running around or splashing in the clay pit up to his shins, carrying its thick, disgustingly sticky contents to the pottery workshop that their village was famous for. Boring! And unnecessary.

Still, to encounter the old sticky-mouth, the ugly grizzled bear out to get to his and other people's traps in the shallow water of the river's bend was not something he had expected. Not in the least.

For another few heartbeats, he hesitated, chewing his lips,

fighting the temptation. The traps may not have been in real danger, and if the bear did not make it a habit of coming here, so close to the village's water hunting, then there was no need to disturb the old forest giant, no need whatsoever. And yet...

He bit his lips until they hurt, his bow clutched too tightly, his palms sweating profusely. To challenge the forest giant face to face was dreadfully tempting. He could best it, he could. With all his arrows still in his quiver, flint-tipped and in the best of shape, checked only this morning, ready for a hunt—oh, but he could do much with such lethal missiles, enough to take down a worthy adversary without getting killed in the process. Not many men could shoot several arrows simultaneously. No one was as good as he was. It was as simple as that.

One of his companions was shaking his head vigorously, not daring to speak in such close proximity to the monster but eager to relate his opinion. It was risky, and moreover, unnecessary, unhelpful. At this time of the season, bears weren't for hunting, certainly not an old specimen, not as fat or as meaty as a female bear after her winter sleep. Giant and lethal as the old ruler of the forest was, he did not offer much besides the fame of besting it alone and unaided. Some meat for cooking, yes, some fat, but mostly its fur and the necklace of giant claws to spread the word of his bravery. Iciwata rolled his eyes then motioned them to stay behind and keep quiet.

Deciding against the bow after all, the arrows too fragile, not likely to penetrate deep enough to hurt the forest giant for real, he let it slip into the grass along with the quiver, clutching his spear yet tighter. It got in his way as he dropped to his knees, crawling closer, guided by the noisy splashing near the shore, untroubled by dilemmas, not anymore. The opportunity was too good to let it go unheeded. The best hunter of their village and the surrounding hamlets, he could not be expected to shy away from the challenge, could he? No man in his right mind did this, oh yes, attacked the old monster, the man-eater, all alone. Not unless having fasted and prayed to one's guiding spirit, preparing for the outstanding feat of bravery. People of their village were no warriors.

The familiar wave of disdain came and went, pushed away by

the bear's sight that he now managed to glimpse from closer up, still crouching on his hands and knees, hidden by the tall grass but not very well now. It was a blessing that the wind was blowing toward him and not away. If not that, the bear might have sensed him and grown curious or alarmed. And then, he would stand less chance than ever against the good runner that all vicious grizzled giants were despite their size and their seeming clumsiness. When on the hunt, a grizzly behaved like light-footed deer, leaping and speeding, not tiring at all.

Again, the unwelcome wave of fear splashed, unworthy of the best hunter and the bravest of men. If afraid of the old sticky-mouth, he should have gone fishing with the rest of his fellow villagers or into the fields, to toil between the stalks of maize or crawl around the unripe squash, pulling stupid weeds out, good for nothing but this sort of activity.

Narrowing his eyes, he forced them to focus on the monster that now straightened into an upright position, alarmingly huge, standing on its hind legs in the shallow water, its forepaws raised high, the massive head turning this or that way, clearly watching the surface of the stream, waylaying its inhabitants, wholly immersed. Good! The effect of surprise would be on his side, even if his hiding place was unsatisfactory, with not that many avenues to escape should he misplace his throw, not wound the beast as badly as needed be.

The thought of coming back, carrying the hide and the claws and the fame those brought pushed his limbs into careful movement, his fingers taking hold of the spear, bettering their grip on the familiar sturdy shaft. Its tip was wide and lovingly carved out, ragged with sharpest of edges, fastened with plenty of fiber and sap. Should be enough, unless the wind was against him. Or something else interfered, influencing the course of its flight. *Oh mighty spirits, please don't let it happen.*

If coming back after besting the forest monster, challenging it alone and nearly face to face, he would be respected more than ever, allowed to make a warrior's tattoo maybe. Not the markings everyone could carve out, a form of this or that animal, nothing special about those, but real warriors' markings, like those of the tribute collectors who were rumored to arrive once in a while in the towns further up the Great River, the filthy lowlifes that they were, taking everything they fancied. The dwellers of those villages and towns claimed that the snotty intruders were after pottery utensils and pearls, the prettily shiny pellets and other pearly fragments made into necklaces everyone loved but couldn't afford to keep. Even without the menace of the mysterious tribute collectors, pearls were traded for the important, necessary goods, to be taken to the huge mounds and cities somewhere down the river and then another one, where the waters were so wide one couldn't always see the other side of it, many days of sail away, many days and many nights. None of his fellow villagers had ever undertaken such a journey, but the people further down the Great River claimed that it was so.

Back on the shore, the bear turned sharply, making Iciwata nearly jump out of his skin, his heart bursting into too wild of a tempo. Something swift popped out of the water, a nimble river dweller, quick to dive back into the safety of the muddy depths but for the reaction of the predator stalking it. The heavy monster whirled in the air like a creature half of its size, then came down on all fours, pawing the shallows viciously, relentless in its single-minded determination, sensing the proximity of its prey. When it growled and lunged again, a round fat body of a beaver was fluttering in its mouth, the massive legs already pushing ashore, wasting no time.

Iciwata felt his heart freezing for a moment, then beginning to pound again. To crawl back and away was still an option, with the bear occupied with its catch, less attentive to its surroundings, busy. Its prey was still struggling, weakly, but it did, which made the mighty hunter growl and turn around, trying to better its grip on the slipping catch, presenting Iciwata with a sight of its broad backside, such a perfect opportunity. To crawl away or to shoot? He didn't hesitate, not this time.

Straightening in one leap, he brought his javelin up in the same movement, his instincts taking over, causing his body to shift in the right way, to achieve maximum drive, aiming as he did, sending his missile flying in a beautiful arc. Not wasting his time on watching it burying itself in the muddied fur, trusting his throw as he always did, he spun around, breaking into a wild run, aiming to reach the grove to his right, the roar of the wounded beast resounding in his ears, the hint of pain and not only anger in it encouraging. He must have wounded it badly enough, he must have!

With no time to glance backwards, daring not to slow his step, he heard the bear coming after him, smashing bushes with its every leap, closing the distance. The cluster of the nearest trees was still a few tens of paces away, even when Iciwata leapt over the shrubs the monster trampled with such gusto, roaring deafeningly, nearing with every step.

Letting his instincts decide once again, Iciwata tore at his sash, crumpling it into a ball before tossing it over his shoulder, hoping his pursuer would take the bait. A few precious heartbeats of distraction for the monster to sink his claws in should give him the advantage he needed desperately. The lucid thinking was back, like always in such situations, with no other consideration than survival clouding his judgment.

The wheezing breath of the creature let him know that his "offering" was received with enthusiasm. Good! With a few more desperate leaps, he reached the nearest tree, clawing his way up it like a squirrel that ate a wrong plant, in a clumsy rush.

Clinging to the sturdy, satisfactorily high branch, he shot a wild glance around, rewarded with a view of the bear – so monstrously big, larger-looking than from his previous unsatisfactory vantage point in the grass – tearing and clawing at his embroidered sash, marring it with mud and blood, so much of it. It was streaming from the wide-open mouth, red and frothy, promising victory. Forest creatures that sported that did not last for long enough to get away from their hunters, or to hunt those who dared to shoot at them.

The wild thundering of his heart calming gradually, leaving his limbs almost empty, strangely light, he clung to his precarious perch with all he had, struggling to remain still. However, by that time, the bear, done wrecking the meaningless sash, leapt as though about to resume his chase, then dropped onto the ground with loudest of thuds, to lie there motionless, harmless all of a sudden, wonderfully lifeless – a victory.

His whole body trembling, limbs out of control, Iciwata jumped down with the same lack of grace the fallen giant had displayed, staggering back to his feet, his mind in a momentary haze. The sounds all around, even the voices of his companions registered in his mind but barely. He was too busy forcing his step, the whoop of victory forming on his lips, impossible to suppress. It made his head spin.

Momentarily at a loss, he just stood there, staring, aware that he must pick up the remnants of his sash, then... what? Skin that thing, yes. But in what way? The hunters who went after bears did so in groups and in a proper manner, hunting a deer to mix the meat and fat, and... He shook his head forcefully, trying to make it work.

By the time his companions reached him, he was in better shape, not shaking like a leaf in the wind and not as hopelessly lost. To spread the sprawling giant turned out to be a challenge. He was smeared in too much mud, blood, and worse, still struggling and with not much to show for his efforts.

"Help me," he groaned toward the apprehensive shadows that fell upon him rather than the messed-up fur. "Don't stand there all useless."

Hikua, a tall, stringy youth, closemouthed and awkward at times, knelt beside him obediently, reaching for one of the giant paws with obvious hesitation.

Trapped under the same aforementioned paw, Iciwata cursed. "Go get my sash and see if my knife didn't get damaged," he hissed. "Bring it here!"

The tall youth scampered away, this time annoying in his readiness. Pushing the dangling limb aside, Iciwata glared at the other one, Nara, a sturdy fellow, not as irritatingly meek, trailing along out of a wish to prove himself. Still, the way he stood there now, undecided, openly troubled and wary, annoyed him as well.

"Give me your knife." With his free hand, he motioned angrily when his words alone did not generate a quick enough reaction. "Don't look like a scared forest rabbit. It's dead, you know. Won't get up to crunch on your worthless bones."

The sharpened bone attached to the nicely polished wooden handle made its way into his spread palm. "You can't start cutting the old forest giant without saying proper words to his spirit."

Iciwata stifled another curse. "I did it already," he grunted, the lie coming easily, like it always did. "When you two were busy strolling out of your hiding."

His companion tightened his lips and said nothing, glancing at Hikua, who was hurrying back, carrying Iciwata's sash, or what remained of it. Not much when it came to the material and its pretty embroidery. Still, the bag with his personal amulet and other items of value seemed to be whole, torn but not badly, and best of all, his knife was glittering in the youth's fist, a precious flint and not a simple bone, the most costly among his possessions. How reckless he was to leave it in its sheath, attached to the sash while setting out to challenge the forest giant.

"I'll cut the claws, then we'll skin him," he said briskly, in the best of spirits once again. "We'll work on it together, so it won't take us half a day to do that. We'll be back home well before dusk, richer on all this fat and meat, eh? Come on, let's get on with it."

Some of the elders made faces, which was to be expected. Iciwata didn't pay it much attention, basking in the glory his deed brought to him otherwise. Word made it quickly all around the village, so even those who were in the fields or at the river came back agog with curiosity, wishing to see the magnificent pelt, so large it could cover an entire floor of a middle-size dwelling.

It didn't look that magnificent, still dripping fat and other meat juices that were yet to be scraped off clean, then dried, then worked on some more. Still, a huge brown bear's pelt was something people did not see every day. Or every moon, for that matter. It had been some time since hunting parties brought home something like that, and certainly not a lone hunter. Iciwata tried to look less smug than he felt.

"You just came up to the old sticky-mouth and threw your spear at it?" Uruna, her skirt and hands still dripping water, her baskets piled with the catch of the day, mainly mussels and shallow water treasures, the usual target of the women spending their day at the river, bestowed him with a taunting smile. "You are making it up!" Her eyes sparkled nicely, relaying a challenge.

"Ask Hikua," he tossed, indifferent to her barbs. Nothing new about that, her spunk and allure an old story, belonging to the past, even though she tried to bring it back every now and then. "The old sticky-mouth did not go down without a fight, though. It made me race it some."

His eyes swept over the rest of the women, plenty of young girls among them, all wet from their daily activities, their baskets round and dripping as well. Kayina's was half full, looking too large and heavy even so against the girl's slender form. She was thin but wonderfully pliant, and her eyes avoided his gaze, dropping hastily, as though finding something extremely interesting down there on the bark-covered ground.

Uruna's laughter rolled over the poles of the palisade and the open ground spreading behind those. "You raced after him or he raced after you?"

"What do you think?" He made a face at her, beginning to be annoyed. She was pushing him into either lying and risking to look stupid, or coming out less brave than his deed testified for, running away from a wounded bear.

"He did quite a race," contributed Hikua, snickering happily. "The sticky-mouth was bleeding all over, but it ran as though it was not, in huge leaps."

Iciwata blessed every deity and forest spirit that their second companion Nara wasn't around to back up that story, or rather, add more juicy details. That one had rushed off upon their arrival, to pacify his angered father most probably, or to do something equally silly. As though fathers angered with their sons absent in the fields and at the pressing time of an unusually dry summer could be pacified just like that.

"Did you see it? Where from? The top of the tree?" he inquired of his friend most disdainfully. "Where you hid, I'm sure the view was enchanting."

That shut the annoying snitcher up, but he could see Kayina edging away, the distress upon her face reflecting on the clouding expressions of the older women.

"Come, girls! Stop crowding like that. Go about your business." One of the matrons waved her free hand, shooing her lightheaded charges away, to the open approval of her older companions. "You have plenty to do. Take your baskets to the square and start sorting the mussels."

"Yes, hurry before the dusk is upon us." Another one, his great aunt's closest of companions, bestowed Iciwata with a reproachful glance. "You too, young man. I'm sure you have better things to do with this pelt and all this meat and fat than to brag about it and idle around."

Out of politeness, he let his gaze drop, not showing his real feelings, not wishing to get in more trouble than he was already. The monotonous chanting coming from behind the large square on the other side of the village reminded him that he would have to face his father sooner or later, providing no good excuse for his absence in the fields or at the river where some of the men went fishing since before midday. The fresh meat of several deer might have made up for the unauthorized absence. Some fat and less edible flesh of an old bear, with its pelt and claws being a personal prize, were not. Oh well.

He glanced at the several other young men who stayed to linger around, fascinated with the rare sight of the slain monster. "Help me take this thing to the storage house." The pelt needed to be attended to, still serving as a carrier for all the meat that had already been scraped off – not a proper use for the magnificent treasure it was. "The women will make use of all this fat and some of the meat."

"You threw it from truly close, eh?" One of the older men bent to examine the mangled fur. "The spear cut in deeply here."

Iciwata nodded happily, satisfied. "It did. Although I didn't have time to see if it went in properly. The old sticky-mouth was getting angry for real. Left me with no time to stay around and check on its injuries."

They all stared at him, some taken aback, some openly impressed, a few nearly hostile, jealous.

"Did you see it all?" asked one of the more spirited youngsters, addressing Hikua, who was hovering quiet and wary, trying to live down the previous telling off. Good! What bad taste it was to start badmouthing him, undermining his victory and in front of the girls too. Come to think of it, that one used to eye the willowy Kayina with the stupid staring of a bashful buck before he, Iciwata, began showing interest. Was that why he was so busy marring his big moment? He shot a furious glance at the youth, who in the meantime shrugged with obvious discomfort, as though trying to escape the attention. Good for him.

"He didn't see much of it, neither he nor Nara. They were busy lazing around at the safety of the grove. Far enough to walk back to the village leisurely had the old bear decided to chase them."

The ensuing chuckles cleared the air. "Have your sisters stretch this hide with no delays," one of the men said, lifting the lifeless paw. "What size!"

"They won't be bothered." Iciwata grinned in his turn. "Not them. But get your womenfolk here with their pots. Spread the word. My sisters, then his." Briefly, he motioned at his faithful follower, over his previous resentment again. "Hikua's womenfolk deserve the first helping. He earned them that. Then all of yours. There should be enough fat and meat for everyone who gets here fast. I need to start stretching this thing, so they all better hurry."

With a grateful look, Hikua and a few of the others disappeared in the direction of the main square, where the girls' chattering still splattered loudly, busy sorting their catch. He let his mind's eye dwell on the image of Kayina squatting with her typical fragile grace, as though not utterly comfortable, less belonging, picking through piles of mussels, knowing which ones would contain dimly glimmering pearls without even opening them first. She was the one to work those treasures into pretty necklaces and beads. One didn't find her among the rest of the girls by the river or at the fields, not often.

"The elders won't be pleased with you, feats of bravery or not."

Tcumu, the oldest among the young hunters, studied him through irritatingly narrowed eyes, as though hard to see against the strong midday sun. Which of course wasn't there, not even near. "The old forest giant is a personal thing. Nothing to do with the community, to make it up for your absence at the mutual works."

"Nothing to do?" exclaimed Iciwata, nearly gasping at such effrontery. "All this fat and meat are nothing, eh? Well, don't let your family women touch any of it. How about that? They can cook without any fat, can't they?"

"They can do without your largess, yes!" The man drew a deep breath, visibly trying to calm down. "But that's not what I said. Bear meat is not like regular hunting fare. Not everyone will eat it, and anyway, it's not as much as a few deer would yield. That's what I meant when I said this hunt was personal. At such a pressing time, it's not appropriate to go on personal hunts."

"Oh yes?" The others' expressions made Iciwata wish to break something, Tcumu's skull preferably. "Look who's talking. A man who didn't hunt anything but stupid deer his entire life. What an achievement!"

The older man's eyes flashed dangerously. "Careful with your tongue, young buck!" His jaw jutted as though pushed out by an outside force. "Take that well-meaning advice along with the previous one and use it, both of them. You don't deserve this largess, but I'm being generous with you."

A heartbeat of mutual staring brought dead silence into their corner of the square, the others holding their breath, not daring to move. However, more voices were filling the open space now, clearly heading back, the clacking of women's pottery and the shrill of their voices confirming the assumption. Iciwata's mind raged impotently, the thought that he might have been in the wrong here nagging, hateful, and annoyingly familiar. He was rude to the man older than himself, and although he was better than all of them put together, politeness dictated that one wasn't to show any such inkling or awareness. Not openly and in front of everyone. Damn them all!

"With the first star, there will be a gathering by the Sacred Eagle Mound." The women burst into their staring contest, oblivious of the tension or indifferent to it. "So much fat!"

He nodded stiffly at his eldest of sisters, a beefy matron, mother of too many children, a respectable member of the village, appreciated by the elders. Being a daughter of the spiritual elder of the Eagle Clan was surely of help, reflected Iciwata grudgingly, not ready to admit that he himself enjoyed extra privileges due to this simple yet undeniable fact. Oh yes, Father was an impeccable elder, in charge of the ancient rituals connected to the Sacred Mound of the Ancestors, the strange-looking hill in the form of a bird of prey, or so the elders claimed, even though no one knew when it was built or why. Or how, for that matter. How could people construct a hill or a mountain? But the ancestors did this. With the help of divine spirits, of course, leaving a legacy to their descendants to follow and revere, and live accordingly. The giant Eagle Mound kept them fed and protected. It made the crops grow and the game stay abound. It kept their village thriving and safe.

The thought of his father made Iciwata uncomfortable once again. The Eagle Priest was always preoccupied, too busy to pay his son, his latest of children, much attention. Still, if the village's elders complained, Father would have to look into his frequent transgressions, would have to do something about it. Bother this!

"You killed that giant all by yourself, little brother?" Another of his sisters was fussing around, jumping with excitement, her pottery vessel in the danger of cracking from all this bouncing. "I can't believe it!"

"You can believe it, you know," he said, forcing a smile, liking this sibling of his more than the rest, all females, five in all, too many girls for anyone's taste, a certain thought he was careful to keep to himself even when being a mere child. He was the youngest, the fruit of much praying on Father's part, or so he suspected. Not a disappointing addition, not as the summers went by. "It's all here for you, the proof."

"You!" She beamed at him, then her eyes crinkled a conspiratorial smile. "They should send you fight off the tribute collectors from the south, or those scary northern savages. When you beat them all, they won't be mad at you for not attending the

SHADOW ON THE SUN

fields, will they?"

The warmth of her grin made his mood improve once again. "They will be mad all the same. They'll want me to fight and fish at the same time." Then her words sank in. "What did you hear about the greedy lowlifes from the south?"

As she bettered her grip on her cargo, her neatly done braids jumped. "They say they are coming here. In a huge array of boats too. And when I say huge, I mean huge! Dozens of boats, they said. All full of warriors!"

He caught his breath, trying to pay no attention to the commotion around his pelt, excited more than perturbed. Real fighting, at long last! "Who told you that?"

"A woman from the town down the river. She came here this morning, trading some goods. With those double-bottomed basket of theirs. That's how she managed to deceive the greedy southerners. They didn't know any better, stupid foreigners!"

"What did she say? Where is she?"

Her unpainted jars jumped together with her shrug, but by then, more women, their vessels overflowing as well, paid their conversation due heed. "She didn't come from the Red Horn Mound town down the river. She came from further south. All the way where our river flows into another one."

"Not from so far away!" exclaimed one of the younger hunters, who, like Iciwata, had stayed around, indifferent to his own womenfolk and their wish to get some of the precious fat. "Why would she travel so far?"

"Ask her!" was the indignant reply, shouted in too many high-pitched panting voices. The fat was truly plentiful, and those who had enough vessels helped themselves to the meat as well. So much for "bears' meat is not as good as deer's." Vengefully, Iciwata sought his previous antagonist with his gaze.

"No greedy lowlifes from the south came here for summers!"

"Maybe they won't bother to row all the way here," someone suggested.

Iciwata felt his sister's nudge, discreet but insistent. "Come to the gathering by the Sacred Mound when you are done with this pelt. Father will be pleased, you know. He is readying for the harvest ceremonies."

He nodded. "Of course."

But it took him a long time to stretch the pelt at the open space between their dwelling and the neighboring one, the stalks used for deer skins too small, not sturdy enough, forcing him to improvise with addition of ropes, the annoyance with the need to do it alleviated when some of the youths came to help on their way to the gathering. Never lacking in following and actually fond of company, the more the merrier, he made them come along to the river, needing to wash up after splashing in bear juices for half a day, the drumming coming from the direction of the Scared Mound promising, suggesting a pleasant evening of ritual dancing and then socializing no young hunters were ready to miss. Girls dressed their best for such occasions and there were plenty of opportunities to talk with them, to flirt a little and get to interest those who would catch one's eye. Plenty of different opportunities, oh yes, to laugh and to talk with, to dance in the non-ritual circles, to stroll by the river later on. The girls were usually willing, accommodating, most of them, even if angered later on, after one tired of their company. But not Kayina. When being honest with himself, he suspected that maybe it was what drew him to her in the first place, that shy if not humble indifference. There was more to her than the eye met and the rest of the girls were so easy and there.

"Will you be getting another marking?" Nara was asking as they made their way toward the Sacred Mound, silhouetted clearly against the glimmering sky. The intensified drumming and soft but most distinct chanting suggested the way as readily. "I would accost the elders for permission to get a real warriors' marking if I had such a battle with the old forest giant to claim."

Iciwata grinned to himself, in the best of spirits and feeling better by the moment, the thought occurring to him as well. The real warriors' tattoo, and why-ever not? "Maybe I'll get one of those, yes. The last time, it was such a pain, though."

"What? Why?" demanded several of his followers.

"He was sick like a coyote bitten by a mad wolf." Hikua, trailing along as always, allowed to be the closest and speak for him on occasions, laughed softly. "Not a dawn or two of feeling bad like always. Worse than that."

"It wasn't that bad." Iciwata rolled his eyes, not as amused by the memory as he tried to pretend. It was bad, those three dawns of sickness, the bridge of his nose where the pretty new red and black marking was made inflamed and hurting worse than anything he had experienced before, his mind wandering, body bathed in sweat. A bad memory.

Still, it all would be worth it if he was allowed to make a real warriors' marking, a tattoo of those who faced an enemy on a battlefield and came out victorious. A few boasted that, unlike in the Red Horn Mound town, two dawns of sail along the current of the Great River, at the mouth of another large watershed. Over there, the snotty townsfolk strolled all around, looking down upon their villager visitors, annoying lowlifes that they were.

The drums were upon them, and the crowding people. Politely, they tried to push their way in. Father must see him somewhere around, realized Iciwata, suddenly anxious to minimize the damage of his recent behavior, from going on unauthorized hunts to missing half of the ceremony without a good reason, to plenty of smaller transgressions of his; oh, but he was pushing it, wasn't he? Yet, if Father saw him somewhere near the pontificating elders just now, he might assume that he had been around all along, mightn't he?

"Make your way to where your uncle is standing," he whispered to Hikua urgently, motioning with his head. "Tell people you must be there or something."

It didn't ease their progress, not by much, so by the time they were entrenched not far away from the chanting elders, his father in their lead, those seemed to finish with the fragrant tobacco smoke they were spreading in all directions, nourishing the Sacred Eagle Mound, revering it and those who had built it many generations ago, their prayer feathers still out, their singing addressing the ancestors' spirits. The story of cycles and the great creation were clearly over by now, so the builders of the giant wonder were honored, and to the highest degree.

Dressed in fine deerskin clothes daubed with red and black

designs referring to the nearing Harvest Moon, his leggings stripped red, his loincloth adorned with weasel tails, a bag of medicine thrown over his shoulder, within easy reach, Father led the ceremony with accustomed ease, an impressive elder, full of authority. In the proximity of the Sacred Mound, he was always like that, not a reserved, soft-spoken, close-mouthed person of the rest of the earthly occasions, impartial and uninvolved, as though above petty activities of the daily life. A good turn for Iciwata at times, and yet sometimes, he wished to have a father like any other elderly or even younger sort of a man, like fathers of his friends and followers, just men like everybody else, approachable, easy to talk to, even if tougher and more difficult to deceive. He pushed the silly musings away.

By the time the ground maize powder was spread over the mound and the last prayers sung, the aroma of cooking meals began spreading like the sacred tobacco smoke, bringing an inevitable stirring among the crowding people, like a gust of spring wind.

"So you've called the fight upon the forest giant, young man," one of the elders who wasn't praying at the foot of the mound stated, confronting Iciwata with not an entirely unfriendly stare. There was a hint of admiration in the old man's voice. He breathed with relief, lowering his head with the right amount of humility one was expected to display. "I trust you have made offerings to the forest giant's spirit."

"Yes, I have, Honorable Elder. I wouldn't dare to take his life and his treasures otherwise." The lie made him slightly uncomfortable, as though the bear's spirit could have told on him. It was all so uplifting, so hectic and frightening and exciting. Who could have remembered prayers and offerings? "It was an honor to be allowed to fight the forest giant. Its fur would make a worthy decoration to the House of the Elders, I hope."

Awed by his own brilliance, he lowered his gaze once again, mainly to hide his thoughts this time. A bearskin was a nice thing to line one's bed with, inarguably; still, as long as the necklace of claws, his rightful spoil, were his, he could do without such softer bedding, while the elders of the village would be pacified with his offering, praising him to the skies instead of admonishing. Brilliant!

The elder was nodding thoughtfully, seemingly unperturbed, yet obviously pleased, and other respectable people surrounded them, talking with less restraint. Women were making their way through, bringing food to the dignified part of the gathering, the pontificating elders. The rest of the village was expected to fend for themselves by picking up edible offerings where those were warmed up or cooked.

His stomach growled at the mere thought, reminding him that he hadn't eaten since the hasty morning meal before setting off to do feats of bravery. To retreat from the elderly circle became a necessity. He did so with as much politeness as the occasion required, anxious to reach the informal part of the gathering, the youngsters like him making a less dignified crowd, a vividly agitated throng, interested in the non-ritual part of the ceremony when intensified drumming would allow everyone to join in the circle of dancers, massaging the earth, making it feel people's gratitude. Or so Father would say. The old man said that the sacred earth needed this stroking and kneading of bare people's feet, this connection between itself and the grateful creatures walking it.

"Someone deigned to leave the dignified part of the gathering!" exclaimed Uruna, blocking his way, her dress decorated with fragments of pearly shells, her braids neat and oily unlike earlier when coming back from the day at the river. A lovely sight many eyes followed, still he found himself glancing elsewhere, seeking the fires and the large pots upon them, knowing who would be helping the older women in distributing food offerings. "Have you eaten already?"

"No, not yet."

"I'll get you some."

"No need. I'll get it myself." He forced a smile, then shrugged, motioning toward the intensified drumming pouring from the mound's base. "Go join the circle."

She gave him a scowling glance, then tossed her head high, making her braids jump with their message. "You think too much of yourself!"

As the unadorned fringe of her skirt swished, enhancing her demonstratively angered walk, he noticed a few of the youths scowling, clearly not pleased with the attention this girl was paying to him. Good for them. They could go and enjoy this whiny ball of spunk and demands. For himself, he had had enough of this.

Not amused, he motioned at Hikua and some others to accompany him to the fires with food, where sweating women of the Eel Clan were doling out plain pottery plates, with plenty of helping hands speeding the process along, Kayina, among those, as expected.

She didn't look flustered or perspiring, not even in these sultry surroundings, with the night being anything but cool, with not a breath of a breeze making its way through the crowded darkness. Her eyes avoided his gaze even when handing him the plate, somehow managing to keep their focus on the milling around fellow villagers. A feat in itself, as the plate was wavering precariously, threatening to tip over, pieces of deer meat floating in a generous amount of its own juice.

He felt the budding sparks of anger returning, noting the shy smile she bestowed on Hikua, not avoiding this one's foolishly timid stare.

"They are forming the circle already," he said more curtly than intended, addressing her forcefully, not letting her escape into the protective shell of the ground-staring. Like the pearls she was working with so much skill, she was hiding inside the clam of her shyness whenever she could, a strange realization. "Why don't you go and dance with the others?"

Her eyes turned round with panic, staring at him as though he was the bear he had slain this morning, not daring to blink. Amused, even if still slightly bitter, he watched her nicely folded mouth opening several times before sounds came out. "I... I must help here," she squeaked in the end. "I must." Her gaze darted toward the pile of empty plates, as though seeking help there.

He didn't fight his grin from showing, his mood improving immeasurably. She was just shy, bashful, self-conscious. She didn't know what to do with the attention of a man of his caliber. "They can do without you. Come along."

The hasty step back she took made her bump into one of the women, the one who minded the ceramic pot. "Careful, young one!" Then the older matron's gaze focused on him, assessing. "You got your plate, young man. Move away. Let the others enjoy the food. And also," her eyes sparkled nastily, in the unbearable manner of older females, "let our girls work without bothering them, will you?"

He ground his teeth at the chuckles of the others, women and men alike, some aware of the embarrassing telling off, some just in a good enough mood to enjoy irrelevant laughs.

"Iciwata, come." Hikua touched his elbow, still there, as always, trying to be helpful. This shadow of a real man, this slim piece of worthless river slime, enjoying her open smiles. Unable to control his fury, Iciwata pushed the youth away with more power than he might have intended, making him crash into the pressing people, then topple over and straight into the stones supporting the boiling pot.

A woman cried out, several such. The pottery vessel tilted and but for him catching his friend's upper arm and pulling hard while stabilizing the wavering vessel with his leg, somehow managing to do that against all odds, again acting his best while out of instinct rather than a conscious decision, it would have been bad. As it was, Hikua was still upright, if wavering, the half fallen pot in the same condition, the women who hastily jumped away and into the darkness where no hungry crowd was pressing, in no danger of being scourged.

Another heartbeat of stunned silence, then too many voices broke out at once, talking in a rush, yelling something. His anger still blinding him, refusing to analyze what just happened, Iciwata let his friend's shoulder go, disgusted by this whole incident as much as by the entire happening, his plate gone, probably fallen over, his fury soaring. To storm away seemed like the best of solutions. If he stayed, he would harm someone badly, he knew, with his fists or his words, or maybe even his knife. To run into the darkness felt safer.

CHAPTER 2

Not enough that the news from the glorious Sun City far down the Great River kept coming with less encouragement from one cluster of trading canoes to the next, now their own Revered Sun's health was failing. Or so said the rumors, worrisome in their persistence.

The outbreak of the deadly fever shook Quachil Thecou, Lesser Sun City, never failing to reappear, the wrath of the deities manifested every now and then, not always with the same vengeance. Yet, through the last awakening moons, it had fallen upon the Royal Mound, not satisfied with the deadly toll it was taking among the outlying neighborhoods and the outside villages, endangering the lives of the Sacred Sun Family, the great sky deity's direct offspring, setting every mound with its important priests to work, praying and offering goods in unheard of quantities. Due to so many pleading and offerings, the great ruler himself didn't die, but the rumors kept spreading, claiming that without special brews, the fever kept returning to torment Quachil Thecou's sovereign, to endanger his sacred life again and again. A certain cause to worry.

Wielding his paddle with more vigor now that the busy wharves were upon them, just beyond the bend of the river, the steady hum of the city reaching their ears for some time by now, Ahal doubled his efforts, glad to finish yet another successful journey. More than a dozen other vessels trailed after him, sitting low in the water, proclaiming their abundant cargo. The tribute collector of his status was expected to bring a considerable amount of goods every time he returned to the city, and this was as good a foray as any, even though the lands to the south and the west were in a certain strain these days, the late summer moons not yielding the fruits as usual, not abundant as of yore. The villages scattered along smaller rivers and lakes of the region concentrated solely on food-growing in the face of the prophesized dry winter, worried about their most necessary supplies, pretty items for the privileged rich of the important cities to wear being not among those, hence a certain lack of clay jars full with powdered colors, well dried and already ground tobacco, and pearls, the precious moon-colored drops, pitifully little compared to what had been demanded by the royal house and the priestly colleges alike.

Shrugging the nagging worry away, Ahal motioned the men of his own lead boat to start rowing on their own, tossing his paddle to the vessel's bottom. Not above contributing to the rowing efforts while on the journey, he could not enter the city paddling like a simple working *miche-quipy*. There was no telling who could have been there, touring the busy shores, wellborn *considerates* like himself or even more privileged elements, warriors and priests who served the Royal Mound, allowed to ascend its hallowed stairs.

Pushing one of the jars out of his way, a heavy thing full of neatly folded pieces of cloth packed with seeds, the bulk of their cargo, he made his way toward the prow of his boat, spreading his legs wide to counter its sways. In time, as it turned out. The busy shore was upon them, cluttered with vessels, people, and goods. So many of them! The inevitable wave of pride welled. Nothing compared to Quachil Thecou, no town and no clusters of larger settlements spread along the Great River and its tributaries. No place and no settlement, save the Great Sun City, of course. That one was beyond human measure, truly the seat of the direct gods' descendants.

Shielding his eyes, he watched the silhouette of the nearby mound boring down on them, casting its shadow upon the water, challenging the mighty current. Other similar sacred constructions spread farther away, their flat or terraced tops pleasing the eye, the temples upon them unmistakable, their conical roofs easy to tell apart from regular dwellings.

Straightening his back, Ahal motioned at his men to hasten their progress. They were late to return as it was, and closer to the busy shore, it wouldn't be as easy to maneuver their way and make a fast landing.

"Tribute Collector!"

The sun was still forcing its way up the sky, when his lead canoe managed to worm its way near the dry land. Too busy to seek where the call originated from, Ahal leapt out of it and into the shallow water, yelling at the milling around crowds to clear the way, gesturing with both hands. The javelin that a man of his status was allowed to carry helped to make a certain impression, not enough to cause but a few dozen of the nearby *miche-quipy* swarming their own overloaded vessels to move out of the way. He cursed under his breath, knowing that escorting warriors that he refused to take whenever offered would have done a better job out of it.

"Move your canoes further up, toward the bend of the shore."

The man who had called him did not deign to enter the water but was standing at the edge of the artificially laid stones, gesticulating widely. Clad in a decorated leather shirt and leggings, he presented a respectable enough image to accept his direction without demanding clarification of his actual status. No barely dressed *miche-quipy*, not this one. Ahal nodded curtly, then turned to gesture to the rowers in the rest of his boats.

"Lead the way toward that bend," he shouted at the man on his main vessel's prow. "I'll meet you there on the shore."

The official waited patiently, standing on the slippery stones, his shoes' decorations fluttering with the wind, looking as though they didn't see much of the outside, certainly no muddy shores. It made Ahal aware of his own travel-stained looks. They had been rowing since the dawn-break, and for quite a few more days. Careful to keep the scowl off his face, he jumped up the slippery stones himself.

"Greetings, Honorable Tribute Collector." The official eyed him with the correct amount of deference, murmuring additional greetings. "I trust your journey was fulfilling."

"It was, Honorable Official." Not bothering with more acknowledgements than that, he turned toward the remaining among his boats, motioning them to follow the lead of the first. "Send your men to report to the official in charge of the goods destined for the Royal Mound. Notify the head of the Royal Mound's guarding warriors as well. Also send for at least a dozen of your own men. Our cargo is plentiful and most of it has to be distributed between the warehouses with no delays."

"Of course, Honorable Tribute Collector!" The man hurried after him as Ahal began forcing his way toward the pebbled shore and the nearest sheltered construction of erected poles supporting a thatched roof, as always crowded badly, surrounded by throngs of swarming people fighting for every measure of space, pushing and yelling at each other, cursing in general directions. Still, on the firm ground, the crowds moved out of his way more readily, forcing him only every now and then to shove away those who bumped into him using his javelin's handle, his patience wearing thin.

"I'll have my men bring a few dozen carriers to take the edible goods to the storage houses."

"Do that," grunted Ahal, not pleased with the time wasted on purposeless talk. The man should have been gone already, summoning the required help, sending messengers. But for him being a relatively important official, clearly someone responsible for the boats' activities of today, he would have yelled at this one by now or rather kicked him into a more efficient attitude. "The foodstuff is plentiful. Bring two dozen men."

"And the rest?"

The effort to control his temper came less easily with each passing word. "The rest will be taken care of by my own men. As I have stated before, the non-edible goods are to reach the Royal Mound's stores and those of the various priestly mounds."

To which no help might be needed, with the pitifully few containers and baskets, he reflected gloomily, heading toward his lead boat, which already kissed the sandier shore, hauled out by his men promptly, without being dragged over the slick pebbles or upsetting the goods in it otherwise. Oh, yes, his men were adept and efficient, already out and engaged, unlike the local officials. He did not tolerate any less in those who worked for him. Still, the lack of luxury goods did not let his mood sour. It wasn't a failure, this last expedition, but a great success it could not be called however he chose to look at it. Two canoe-loads of clay jars full of powdered colors, well-dried and already ground tobacco, a single bucket of pearls, so pitifully little compared to what had been demanded. Revered Sun's officials were clear while requesting considerable amounts of pearly jewelry for the Royal Mound's dwellers and the priests serving them. Not to mention the canoe-loads their city was expected to send to the Great Sun City itself every other full moon. The cooler and drier awakening moons and the lack of rains that had followed were of no concern to the descendants of the sacred sky deity and the priests serving them, even though those were the priests themselves who had warned against the upcoming moons-of-no-rain.

As though one didn't have eyes and other senses to assess the situation all by oneself, thought Ahal bitterly, willing his welling worry away. It wasn't he who made rains delay their coming, and it wasn't he who neglected to produce enough pottery and pretty items; but it very well might be he who would be blamed for the lack of them. Someone had to! And what would be a better person than the leading tribute collector sent in the head of the delegation to collect the aforementioned goods, spending more time on the journey than it usually took, bringing in less than of yore?

As though eager to reinforce his worrisome thoughts, a figure wearing nothing but a loincloth, his body painted in dark clay, dotted with red and white symbols of an open palm, appeared from behind the bend of the shore, where the stockade wall separated the busy shore from the city and its more respectable parts, as busy at times but better regulated.

"What is the meaning of this?" The priest of the Vulture Mound was difficult to mistake, not the largest cult in the city but an important one, occupying one of the central earthworks, with several dozen stairs and a terrace for additional rites and special ceremonies to conduct.

The official straightened abruptly, his breath clearly caught, and Ahal felt a small ripple of uneasiness sliding down his spine, making his stomach twist. Bad timing to face servants of gods, any of them. Not when one is out of breath, covered with sweat, and other signs of prolonged journey, carrying inadequate amounts of requested goods for the priests to enjoy.

"We came from the valleys of the Great River, our regular route of tribute collecting, Honorable Divine Servant," he said as calmly as he could, pleased with the way the words were coming out, measured, unhurried. "We bring goods requested by our Revered Sun, the great ruler of our city."

The priest nodded slowly, his forehead, disproportionally high, painted in red and white as well, either shaved or actually deformed, furrowing like a wrinkled blanket. "Why do you land on this patch of land, Tribute Collector? Why so near the city walls? No vessels are allowed to do that." The expansive gesture of the painted hand indicated not only the hubbub they had left behind, but the rest of the river as well, rolling by calmly, dotted by plenty of boats, fishermen mostly, but sprinkled with enough trading vessels loaded with basket and jugs. "Don't you know where the arriving canoes are expected to unburden their cargo?"

"Our cargo is important and to be brought to the Royal Mound with no delay." He didn't add any title this time, and his tone had a stony quality to it, beyond his ability to control. Divine servant or not, he was no common worker to question him in such manner.

"The Honorable Tribute Collector is in a hurry, Revered Priest," offered the official, finding his tongue apparently, even if not controlling it too well, his words pouring out in a frantic rush. "I shall make certain no disorder is left behind when the boats are unburdened and taken away, oh Revered Priest."

The painted man reacted with his eyes narrowing and his eyebrows climbing ever so slightly, contemptuously. "Send the cargo destined for the priestly college with no delay. Have a contingent of your men deliver it along with the Royal Mound's goods. Do not make servants of our revered gods wait. Honorable Tribute Collector," he added with pronounced delay.

Ahal nodded curtly, slightly pacified with the added title.

Priests could get away with all matter of impoliteness. "I shall do that, Revered Priest."

His remaining boats were crowding the vacant patch of the land, threatening to turn it into as messy a landing as back on the crowded piers. He tried not to show his impatience, willing the nosy servant of gods to go away.

"I shall send a representative of our temple to guide and supervise your men."

Not to roll his eyes turned into a difficult business. "My men will find no difficulty bringing the goods designated for the Vulture Mound temple," he began, then thought better of it. Priests were a law unto themselves and this one was clearly after something. To motion the official and some of his men toward the nearest vessels seemed like the best course of action. Let them start sorting his vessels out, because he wasn't about to do that, not under the watchful eye of the nosy priest. What was that one after?

"When you visit your brother, our Revered Sun's Adviser, give him our temple's special regards." The priest shifted from one sandaled foot to another, the decoration of his fancy footwear clacking. All those prettily polished stones. Ahal suppressed a shrug, reminded of the inadequate amount of jewelry his boats were carrying. Less than ten necklaces of good undamaged pearls, and some less quality pearly ornaments of drilled pieces, with a small jar of red-blood stones popular with the Royal Mound. A pitiful result as far as the refined elements of the city were concerned.

"I shall do that." No title for no title again. Childish, but he couldn't help it.

"The honor your admired brother's household was awarded with pleased our temple and its servants. As it certainly pleased our patron deity and the one who watches over Quachil Thecou."

What honor? he wondered, then glimpsed a group of impressively clad figures heading down the incline, emerging from behind the shadow the stockade wall cast. Dressed as though for a journey, the prideful bearing of the Royal Mound's guards was impossible to mistake. Another "welcoming committee"?

Ahal glanced at his crowded boats. Would the Royal Mound appreciate the foodstuff he brought instead of fanciful pearls? He had covered a dozen of villages in barely a moon, visited three regional centers, all covered in a hurry, with no leisurely stops to enjoy a day of rest in this or that blissfully forsaken location, the smaller hamlets surrounded by thick woods, full of accommodating village girls, not beatified or sophisticated but pretty, delightfully uncomplicated, enchanting in their own natural way. But not this span of seasons. This journey was nothing but strenuous rowing and difficult confrontations. A veteran of enough seasons of tribute collecting, he didn't like the necessity to use force or even bother to bring warriors along. He and his men were skilled in the use of weaponry, able to defend themselves and their cargo, yet there were always other ways of making the villages pay what was due. And what could one do when there was not much to offer in payment? No one dared to argue with the tribute collectors of Quachil Thecou that ruled this part of the land on behalf of the Great Sun in the Sacred Sun City far, far away from here. Still, the resentment of the surrounding settlements was tangible. They didn't like paying more than they could afford, and at times, he couldn't help but sympathize with them and their plight.

"Back already, Tribute Collector?"

Their faces glistening with sweat, glowing in distinct coloring, the newcomers neared, their torsos covered, revealing nothing but their arms, the leather of their shirts well-tanned and lavishly decorated, covered with an intricate layer of woven material, unlike his own practical wear, fitting for the journey. If only he was allowed to go home and change!

"It took you time to return this time. Your name was mentioned only this morning in certain sacred halls." The man at the lead motioned at him while changing his own direction, not bothering to coordinate his action with the rest of his peers. But of course. The personal guards of Revered Sun could do as their please while outside the boundaries of the largest mound in the entire region. "What are your boats doing on these moors?"

"We have just arrived, Honorable Leader. It was too crowded at the regular moors and I saw it fit to unburden my cargo here. I hope it doesn't create a problem, my boats' presence here." The head of the Royal Mound's guard was no sniffing-around priest.

The clever, deeply set eyes measured him briefly. "What is your purpose here, Tribute Collector?"

Another trait of the great mound's nobility—a direct way of speaking, of asking questions one wished to be answered. Ahal didn't mind. After the rudeness of the priest, it felt good to speak to a person of much higher rank but with much lower presumption.

"The Vulture Clan's divine servants wished to have their goods delivered straight to their temple, Honorable Leader."

"Come along. " The broad palm motioned him toward the edge of the water and away from the avidly listening ears, those of the lingering priest and Ahal's men as well. The rest of the man's entourage was gestured to proceed along the shore, complying with surprising readiness, considering their own obviously important status.

"This journey took you longer than usual, Ahal. Why?" Halting by the protruding pole of the old wharf, the man leaned against it, seemingly unconcerned with the unfitting state of their surroundings. His name was Anksheah, a spectacular enough alias, his status among the leading guards of the city impressive. "Is the situation bad out there in the west? Unsatisfactory? Do our tributaries need to be reminded of their expected loyalty and servitude to our great city or the Sun Sanctuary beyond our Great River?"

Ahal gathered his thoughts hastily. "The situation is not entirely favorable, yes, Honorable Leader. This is why the journey took longer to complete. The harvest expected in the outlying villages isn't good, so the villagers are spending their time in the woods, gathering everything edible or clearing more fields. And the situation down the Great River is the same if not worse. Some of the settlements managed to harvest half of the regular amount of edible goods. At some places, it is the second summer of such happenings." He took a deep breath, then forced his eyes to stand the hardening gaze of his interrogator. The man demanded the truth, didn't he? "I took what is lacking in food through other goods, tools, and ornaments. The villages that produce salt stood the new demand with no trouble. And so did the villages near quarries of cutting stones."

The older man was nodding thoughtfully, absorbed in his thoughts. To slow the unsatisfactory racing of his heart, Ahal let his eyes wander, the view of the busy river calming his nerves, as it always did, even though after the long journey, it was good to be home, back in Quachil Thecou, the beautiful cultured and refined center of their region, the leading among those who paid and supported the Sacred Sun City.

His gaze slipped over the towering wall, craving to be inside already, free to walk the Grand Plaza in the shadow of the sacred two-tiered Royal Mound, where Revered Sun and his family dwelled, overlooking the better side of the town, with another inner enclosure and many clusters of neat houses parted by alleys and green patches of gardens and groves, his own house among those. Or the further part of the town, with squares of simpler traders and their neighborhoods, with Lallak's neat little house among those, not far away from the second market square.

His chest warmed with anticipation. This very evening, he promised himself. Somehow. Against the displeasure and open complaints of his satisfactorily aristocratic but unsatisfactorily cold and not-very-good-looking wife, the daughter of an important *considerate*, a necessary match. The children she bore him were good, a pair of healthy twins and another baby. Well, he provided them all well, moved up the ladder of positions, kept his family in style higher than that of his father-in-law, if not as high as his own elder brother, one of the great ruler's advisers. The woman complained about that too. She had ambition, this one, but men in his position kept mistresses. The trouble was that Lallak was of a good family too, a widow of a prominent trader, eligible to be taken as a minor wife, if he wished to do so. Which he didn't, despite her insistent hints on the matter. Women! Still, he would make certain to visit her tonight, he decided, his mood lightening at the mere thought. The rumor of his arrival would make it around the town by that time and she better be waiting, ready with her mats covered in furs and every delicious snack she might hunt around several market squares.

"I suppose it is proper to take other goods when the villages cannot produce the correct amount of foodstuff." The sharp voice snapped him back from his reverie, reminding him that the free-of-duties evening did not arrive yet. "I trust you to be not too lenient, or easy to deceive." The gaze boring at Ahal turned piercing. "It is surprising how much goods a village that is afraid of our warriors can produce despite the claims that it couldn't otherwise."

"I did my best to impress it on our tributaries, Honorable Leader." He pushed the new wave of welling resentment away, hardened against protesting villagers but not to the extent of wishing to bring warriors along. If people couldn't eat and sustain themselves, they would produce no tribute at all. "The villages we visited did not hide their resources from us. I have seen to that."

The feathers upon the important man's headpiece rustled with the thoughtful nod of his head. "Good." Then the pursed lips twisted in a lighter grimace. "Good, but not good enough. Our own storage rooms are not groaning with goods. Which only means more traveling for you, Tribute Collector. Double the same amount of men you took on your previous journey, then add three dozen warriors out of our Royal Mound's guard. They would be under your command. Let them know that it is my word, my personal word. Is that clear to you?"

He tried to conceal his irritation with a polite nod, seeking words that would refute the unwelcome suggestion decisively if still cordially. Another journey to the regions he had already visited? There was no logic in it. And with warriors who, of course, would not put up with his allegedly more senior status but would only mess up his arrangements with the already-resentful locals. No, he could think of no worse prospects, not at the moment.

"Where will this delegation be heading?"

An appreciative nod was his answer. "You will sail against the current this time. The towns up our Great River are paying us tribute but sporadically, or so I'm told. Our Revered Sun and his divine servants deserve to enjoy those eastern settlement's riches. Pearls are getting scarcer in Quachil Thecou, for one. It's time the far east paid us a more regulated tribute." A half grin blossomed, then disappeared. "Examine what they have, the goods they boast. Then determine the amount they owe us. Rare foods, rare ornaments. Pearls in particular, pearly jewelry. The dwellers of the east should be able to serve our Revered Sun in this way and thus make the Great Sun in his faraway Sun City of Gods happy as well."

Forgetting his initial resentment, Ahal tried not to stare. "How far do I progress? What sort of settlements do I seek out? Is it left to my consideration as well, Honorable Leader?" Against his will, the possibilities swamped his mind, the temptation to sail the far east temping, to see those faraway lands and in the head of a well-armed, well-protected delegation. Traders sailed there, of course, and some priests were reported to travel against the current. At times, Quachil Thecou did send demands of payment, but sporadically, once in a few summers, and never further than half a dozen or so days of rowing upriver.

"It is." The smile was back, satisfied, almost fatherly. "It will be left to your consideration alone. You do well in your travels, Ahal. You prove yourself a worthy member of your noble family. Make this journey fruitful and you will not regret the effort put into rowing against the current." A curt nod completed the words. "The Adviser, your noble brother, is advised of these plans."

He tried to restrain his welling excitement. "I will do my best, Honorable Leader."

"Good. Spend no more than a few dawns recruiting your men, the *miche-quipy* who load your canoes. The warriors will be waiting for you with the dawn of the third day. Be ready by then." The man was turning as he spoke. "Bring back serving hands. Several dozen men. As many as you can gather. Our Master of the Ceremony complained of lack of manpower. The new mound flanking our Grand Plaza is not rising as quickly as it should be. The eastern villagers who do not obey your command would serve us in this way. Our warriors would see to it."

Ahal nodded stiffly. Still, the excitement was there, splashing against his will. To sail at the head of three dozen warriors was a promising prospect, to see what the far east had to offer. If he managed to bring back a satisfactory amount of tribute, a promotion to a position of a higher official might be his, a chief inspector, a chief supervisor of rituals, even a minor adviser. To step outside the shadow of his prominent brother at long last was tempting.

He tried to slow the mad racing of his thoughts. So much to do! Round up the necessary amount of helping hands. How many would he need? How many canoes? Then to inspect the boats, to replace the leaking or damaged vessels. Then to gather necessary provisions. How many of those?

"This journey will be completed to your satisfaction, Honorable Leader," he said, trying not to let his sudden enthusiasm as opposed to the previous mere politeness show. "The goods of the far east will reach Quachil Thecou. Our Revered Sun will enjoy rare jewelry and beautiful adornments and his advisers and guards will not find themselves wanting as well."

"Good." The man nodded without turning back, his lips twisting in a conspiratorial manner. "Our Revered Sun will enjoy more than rare jewelry and beautiful adornments in the end of this moon. Or rather, he would be requiring more of such items upon your return. Having enriched his collection of wives with the beautiful daughter of the adviser, he might certainly wish to decorate his new spouse. They say the girl is a beauty. Is she?" The deeply set eyes narrowed, questioning. "I'm certain your family must be thrilled with this honor."

He knew who the girl was even before the last words left his converser's lips. Sele! The sparkly, vital, dazzling jewel from his important brother's collection of offspring, her beauty delighting the eye, her vitality and quickness of mind even more so. Or so he felt. It had been in the works for some time. There was talk about it. His ambitious brother, apparently not satisfied with his position as one of Revered Sun's main advisers, certainly craved additional honors. Still, he hoped it would not come to this. Sele was so young and radiant, and the ruler of Quachil Thecou was middle-aged and sick for some time, having recovered but not fully from the deadly fever that took so many lives around the Great River's valley before summer moons came. And what if he died soon? The girl might face a challenging fate if it happened, required to follow her master into his afterlife journey.

He forced the worry away, concentrating on the leading men who deigned to gossip with him in such surprisingly open fashion.

"It is a great honor to our family, yes," he said, pretending to be in the know, not surprised and not dubious, promising himself to visit his brother's household this very afternoon, no matter what.

Revered Sun's Adviser's household was in a state of an unbecoming turmoil; only to be expected, given the news. Still, he didn't anticipate stumbling on such a hubbub, his mind preoccupied, busy with plans and developments of his own.

To lead an expedition to the unknown north, against the current and not alongside it, accompanied by two war canoes with a dozen of warriors each to keep them and the collected goods safe, was an interesting challenge, with the hint of the anticipated promotion adding the spice like a salt to the otherwise familiar meal; an honor to live up to, even if that meant rushing from one journey to another, with not even a single day of rest spent in the city. A demanding prospect, certainly. But not the one that left him desolate. Not even close! While traveling, besting the currents, forging rapids and difficult trails, pitting his strength and his wits against those who were supposed to pay his city a tribute, not always eager or willing to do so, he felt more alive than in his impeccably aristocratic and therefore flawlessly prim and cold home near the Grand Plaza, not far away from where city officials and leading warriors lived. Between his distinguished oldest of siblings, the Adviser, and his ambitious socially-aspiring wife he was ready to take the life of the traveling in the head of the tribute-collecting delegations any day; or any night, for that matter. The city offered cold comfort and aloof, chilling security; the outside offered challenges and fulfillment, and leadership, something he could not enjoy in the city. Or so he admitted strictly between himself on those rare instances when there was nothing but a night forest around him, a steady hum of this or that river or stream, and the tranquility that demanded nothing but honesty with oneself. Rare moments, but priceless, bitter-sweet, to be cherished and tucked deep inside his mind again, to be forgotten.

"Uncle Ahal!"

The girl intercepted him as he crossed the spacious, meticulously arranged courtyard, preparing to lower his head in order to pass the threshold of the prominent slanted-roof building, the main house of his brother's estate. Honored with an immediate admission, not always the case in the realm of the important adviser, escorted by a rigid, dignified servant, Ahal halted abruptly.

"Sele."

She looked changed, not thinner but more willowy, taller than he remembered, more gracious than ever. A nimble little thing, quick-witted and bold, cheeky at times, sparkling with life, eager to pounce on it, the favorite among his brother's numerous offspring, yet now suddenly a woman and not a sweet little thing to chase around the courtyard and spoil with forbidden treats.

"You are back in the city! I knew it. I knew you would not forget visiting me." Beaming, she rushed toward him, causing the dignified steward to frown dourly, disapprovingly. "Have you heard the news?"

Ahal waved the servant away. "Yes, I have." His eyes traveled her face, anxious to detect signs of possible distress. To be accepted into the household of the great ruler was an outstanding honor, even for an adviser's daughter by the most prominent of his brother's wives. A great honor, oh yes. Still, she was so young and innocent. "Are you happy about it?"

"Of course I am!" Her eyes, prettily spaced and nicely tilted, looking larger than ever, outlined by a darker shade of some delicate color – another new facet – widened at him. "How could I not? It's such an honor, such a privilege. Think about it! Aren't you pleased, Uncle?"

"Yes, I am." He nodded hurriedly, not wishing to put her off this happy state of mind, the implications of being given to the great ruler in a proper marriage huge, not all of them positive. Revered Sun was not in the best of health, unless the rumors were not true. Someone like him, a person not permitted to ascend the Royal Mound, not even its lower terrace, Ahal could only assume that his brother, the important adviser and allowed to do all of that and more – even to address the sacred ruler in person – knew what he had been doing.

"Then why do you look so gloomy?" The girl's husky voice rang with pronounced mischief. "You are jealous that I'll be living up there on the Sacred Mound, aren't you? You would have rather lived there yourself. Admit it!"

"As the newest wife to our Revered Sun? I'm not certain either of us would be sorely tempted."

She giggled in a familiar fashion, just a child yet, despite her new looks. The clothes, he noticed now. It was her clothes. A grown woman's attire of white garb covering her from neck to feet, fastened with an intricate net of threads and strings, some hanging up to her covered knees, adorned with claws of a large bird. Symbolic wear, a virgin about to be given in marriage. A clear statement.

"Silly you!" she chirruped, turning whichever way, making her bird decorations clank. "I can't believe you came only now. It's been almost half a moon since Father told us, my mother and me. I was afraid I wouldn't see you at all before it happens. What if I'm not allowed to leave the Scared Mound, ever? Not even to see my family…"

There was no distress behind her frown, only a practical question. He shrugged. "Some wives who lived up there with the Sun Family are allowed to descend the Royal Mound when Revered Sun travels. Or maybe even without him. *Quachilli-Tamailli*, his revered sister, and her son, the heir, have been certainly seen around the city. I recall seeing the royal palanquins quite often, and who could those be but the Sun's family members."

She nodded thoughtfully, her thinly plucked eyebrows knitting. Another change. Her eyebrows used to be decisive and wide, matching the thick richness of her hair, but now she was not just one of the children, not anymore. How old was she? He tried to recall. Fifteen summers maybe, or sixteen. Not too young to be given the treatment of grownups, from plucking body hair or offered pretty clothes to be given in marriage, yes, but definitely too young to chance the fate of Revered Sun's wives upon the great ruler's possible death. Not all wives followed their master into his new beginning; only the favorite chosen ones were offered this honor. He shuddered at the very thought, then grew angry with himself.

"I want to still visit my mother and my sisters. And some of my brothers too. And you! I want to visit you and tell you all about the life up there."

He found himself swallowing hastily. "You will, little one. I'll try to make sure of that."

"How?" she asked, echoing his thoughts. He had no means to make it happen, no means at all. Her forehead creased again, with decided practicality. "If you are not allowed up there on the Sacred Mound and I can't come down into the city whenever I want to, how will I manage to let you know that I need to see you?" Her small, delightfully even teeth clutched at her lower lip in a familiar gesture. She was always chewing her lips or her fingernails, no matter how her aristocratic mother or servants assigned to it tried to make her quit an inappropriate habit. "You must find ways to send me word. Through Father maybe. Or through servants who go down and up. Find a person you trust."

Against his will, he grunted. "Stop talking nonsense, Sele. You are not that little anymore. You are to be given in marriage and to a great ruler of this city. Think he will be pleased with his new wife sending clandestine messages to the denizens of this city?"

Her eyes sparkled with a familiar flash of anger. Even when little, she didn't cope well with being corrected or put in her place. "You are not just any denizen of this city. You are my uncle! Am I not allowed to see my family?" Now even her plucked eyebrows related her mounting fury, challenging him, demanding an answer.

"You don't have to ask me *that*," he retorted, put out with her spoiled streak, as always, yet wishing to help or shelter her all the same. "I'm not the one to make rules of the Royal Mound. Stop being a spoiled little brat."

However, his heart was going out to her already, the sight of the trembling corners of her mouth, pressing tighter before his eyes, determined not to cry, tearing at his chest. She was just a child, and they were sending her off to a demanding future at best, indefinite or maybe even tragic at worst.

"I don't know if you will be allowed to meet with every member of your family, little one," he said tiredly, wishing she was a child once again, to be picked up and tossed in the air until she squealed and forgot all about her troubled fears. "I'm certain it will be nice up there, in all this sacredness and luxury. Think about it." His gaze held hers, willing her into listening. "All this delicious food and pretty clothes like the ones you are wearing now. I bet you won't even remember your previous life with all the joys of being one of the celestial family. Your children will be great nobles. Even in the Great Sun City, the family of our Revered Sun is regarded with respect. Think about it."

"The Sacred Sun of the Great Sun City is greater than ours," she muttered, scowling dourly, her lips pursed in a funny way, set on being obtuse, the little beast. "He does not regard our Revered Sun but as a son, a lesser being." Her hands flailed up in a gesture of pronounced triumph. "We send them canoe-loads of goods every full moon because our Revered Sun is not equal to their Sacred Great Sun."

Sharp little Sele, always curious and asking too many questions, remembering it all, plaguing him with more demands; the demands he was usually more than happy to withstand. It was amusing to talk to her with a measure of seriousness, to explain her things and tell about his journeys. Through the recent few summers, he was looking forward to his visits in his brother's household because of that.

"No one is equal to the Great Sun who rules the Great Sun City, yes," he said, not rolling his eyes but wishing to do so. "Every important settlement sends goods there. Their Great Sun is our direct connection to the gods up there, and his duty is to keep us all safe and our crops plentiful. But!" He raised his hand when she tried to interrupt, demanding her undivided attention. "Our Revered Sun is of the sacred family as well. He has the same duty of keeping our ways and traditions, petitioning for our wellbeing before the sky deities. His connection to the Great Sun is direct, and so his connection to the Great Sky God. You couldn't be given in marriage to a greater person that walks the earth we walk, Sele. You have nothing to complain about."

"Unless offered to the Great Sun of the Sacred Sun City," she stated smugly, pleased with herself.

He didn't fight an outburst of laughter, even though other dwellers of this estate were spilling out of a lower house to their left, the lesser women's quarters. "Oh, go away, you little pest. Go and make life difficult to your revered great husband. Tell him that he is not good enough for you. Tell him to send you to the Sacred Sun City among the tribute of the next moon, between all those baskets and jars."

She snickered, then tossed her head high. "I'll find ways of letting you know how it is up there. You'll see!"

Again he wished to have her back all small and giggly, liable to be tossed in the air or comforted if she cried, not grown up and respectful. It would have been easier to protect her that way.

The dignified steward reappeared at the doorway of the main house, beckoning Ahal with just the right amount of humbleness, aware of his status in this household, even though that of the guest was infinitely higher. Some servants thought the world of themselves.

"Do that," he told her lightly, unwilling to relay his earlier misgivings. It was silly of him to worry about something as irrelevant as her private happiness. The honor of being given to the ruler of Quachil Thecou, Revered Sun second only to the Great Sun of the Sacred City was huge, unparallel, bringing honor to their entire family, himself, and his own offspring included. "Let me know how it is. Send me word anyway, even if you just need someone to talk to. I'll find the means to see you. Don't worry on that count."

More abruptly than intended, he whirled around, diving into the dimness of the entrance, his chest tightening with misgivings concerning her and his own impending journey. But why was he sent to the east where the tribute was collected but sporadically, not systematically like in the south, in richer, more important areas, with civilized settlements dotting the river banks. And why at the head of so many warriors, who would surely prove difficult to control like all warriors were.

Shrugging, he lowered his head to pass the threshold. Maybe Revered Sun's adviser would know.

CHAPTER 3

Word of the tribute collectors reached them in a timely manner, just as they had run out of excuses to stay around, not doing one sensible thing, namely heading out and back to their village. A journey of two dawns of sailing against the current, and still Iciwata stalled as long as he could, prevailing upon those who came with him, making them back him up.

Half a dozen men, and a few women with their double-bottomed baskets, had traveled here, to the place where two great rivers crossed, bringing goods to trade and news to exchange. Or rather, to gather. There was no news to deliver from their side of the Great River, to Iciwata's secret chagrin. How was one to become a warrior if one's village was never attacked or never sent out a party to attack someone? The west or the north, it didn't matter. There were warlike people in both directions, either those who thought the local settlements should pay them in goods, or those who just raided places, the mysterious northerners. But their village was too far removed from everyone's path, and evidently liking it this way. A bother!

Still, this time, it wasn't difficult to talk the elders into letting him and a few others take some goods for trading. Everyone wished to know about the western people in their rumored war canoes, even though their village was never accosted with any demands but only heard about them. Yet now, thanks to the tales of the woman from one of the downstream settlements brought on the evening of the ceremony, the elders suspected that there might be a cause to worry, wishing at least to try and find out what it was all about.

A delegation that was organized hastily carried baskets loaded with edible goods and some blankets and pretty items of pearly jewelry, instructed to trade those off for as many jars of salt and other western rarities as possible, while fishing for information. Did the tribute collectors visit, and if yes, what were their demands?

The question Iciwata echoed eagerly, in addition to some others, like the amount of warriors those canoes brought, their weaponry, their gear. So many questions, none of them to be shared while talking the elders into letting him go with the delegation, required to keep it safe. Slaying that bear with the single spear throw did earn him more than just fame, didn't it? The status of a warrior, oh yes. Even Father did not object to his going. The Priest of the Sacred Eagle Mound was surely as concerned with the possible menace from the west, even though he did not talk about any such earthly matters. Father had his divine responsibilities to attend to; still, it was easy to notice that he wasn't his usual tranquil self through the days following the great ceremony, creases of worry furrowing his high, partly shaved forehead, shadows lurking in the veiled eyes. Often when those rested on him, Iciwata, admittedly. Still, he brushed his misgivings aside, convincing himself that Father's perpetual frown had to do with the unsettling news, more important developments than his own misconduct or transgressions. Had to be.

Pushing the unpleasant memories away, the anger they brought making his stomach cramp, he concentrated on the harpoon he held, scanning the muddy water that flickered all around, splashing up to his waist, offering opportunities. The people of the town that hosted them did not object to their guests' wish to stay for another day, especially when such a wish was reinforced with the offer to join regular daily chores. The basket he made to perch on the nearby flat stone was not about to have the townsfolk disappointed, half full with the fluttering fish already as opposed to the locals' baskets and nets, mostly empty as yet. Apparently not only in their village was he the best with a harpoon. A warming realization.

"You don't plan on splashing in this stream until nightfall, do you?" Balancing his still largely empty basket, Nara trod the slippery stones, edging closer as though not trusting their foreign company, with quite a few locals dotting the narrow stream, busy with their fishing business. "We should be heading back home. They will be furious if we stay out for so long, and the women will tell on us. Ciki made faces when you made us all stay for another day."

Iciwata grimaced offhandedly, eyes tracing the current, seeking the movement among the bright muddiness. "Who cares for the faces my sister is making? She is lazing around now, I bet, chattering with the local women." He shrugged, then took his mind off the rippling surface. "We came to collect news, learn of the western scum. We can't go back without finding out what is happening with those who visited that village further down the stream."

"Well, those people don't seem to know much."

"They may receive word yet." He shrugged again. "Get busy with your harpoon. They are looking at us as though we were children that try to laze around. Annoying skunks!" The nearest fishermen indeed seemed to glance their way somewhat repeatedly, their baskets not even half as full as his, stupid rats. "Where is Tcumu?"

"Stayed in the town. On that square they were crowding this morning when we arrived."

Iciwata snorted, then put his attention back to the glimmering surface, not happy with the older man who was in charge of their expedition. Without Tcumu, always up and ready to criticize, to put him in "his rightful place" as the man was heard often enough saying, not daring to do so in his face, he might have managed to talk the rest of their fellow travelers into staying for yet another day, or maybe even traveling further downstream. The locals didn't seem to mind, as did the remaining members of their delegation, all young enough and under his spell, even the women. Ciki never said "no" to his ideas, older sibling that she was. Among the rest of his sisters, she was the best, and the most understanding, always amused and affectionate, ready to cover his numerous slips.

"The western collectors, they are coming!" The excited words preceded their bearer but not by much as the man appeared at the muddy bank, panting, having evidently run his hardest, losing no time. Doubling over, leaning his hands against his own knees for support, he paused at the slippery slope, then encircled his audience with his gaze, his face glowing healthy red, eyes wild. "They are sailing against the current, in those huge things, the war canoes!"

The hum carrying above the stream died abruptly, then erupted in agitated shouting.

"Who saw them? Where?"

"How many?"

"When?"

The questions burst from all around, like a coordinated volley of arrows on a cornered herd of deer. Iciwata grabbed his basket on his dash toward the shore.

"They are on their way here. Our elders, they already sent out a delegation to greet them in."

"War canoes? How many? What do they look like?" The questions burst out of his mouth on their own, with no regard to his will, his heart beating fast, the excitement mixed with something he didn't wish to admit sliding down his spine, making his stomach cramp. Like back with the old bear, that tickling in his hands and feet. "Who was the one to see them?"

The men crowding the slippery bank looked at him, surprised. He didn't care. Outsider that he was, he needed to know, the urge to run back into the settlement, then make his way out and toward the Great River's banks overwhelming. The warring boats! But what sort of boats they were? How many people did they carry? And what people?

"Our youths who were working near the Twisted Island saw them." The man who had brought the news managed to catch his breath and was looking at his fellow townsfolk, hopping with impatience. "They'll be escorted into the town shortly."

"All of them? How many were they? How many boats? War vessels and otherwise?" A tall man with a scar crossing his chin in an intricate manner pushed his way up the slope, balancing his basket upon his simple one-sided harpoon. His head swayed lightly toward Iciwata, in no unfriendly fashion. "The villager has good questions."

Iciwata let the "villager" bit go unchallenged, pushing his way upwards as well, needing to know.

"I don't know. Many. War boats, they said. Those long things, with plenty of warriors in it. Go and see for yourself!"

"Maybe I will," drawled the tall man, evidently not pleased with an uninformative answer. "My brother is working out there by the river. I'll know more about those foreigners before they step in the town square. Who is coming with me?" The words generated quite an exodus, making the shallow stream's waters boil from too many feet leaping out of it.

Iciwata pushed his way through. "I'll be coming with you."

The man measured him with a brief gaze, then shrugged. "Why not? You've been asking questions about the westerners, haven't you? Come along."

Racing all the way back to the town, passing by the thick fence that separated it from the forest behind – a novelty to their villagers' eyes – they hurried to drop their catch at the care of the women in the large, spacious square surrounding a pair of impressive earthworks that did not resemble the Eagle Mound back home, not even in their shape. Higher by far, curving as though trying to outline the square they had guarded, mirrored by puzzlingly prolonged earthwork on the other side of the enclosure, this one adorned with a set of polished wooden slabs leading up to its flat top and a low construction poised upon it, they made their village's ancient mound look dwarfed, insignificant, even dismal.

However, this time, Iciwata had no time to fume about such earthworks' obvious superiority. Pushing the wandering thoughts away, he concentrated on the news from the Good River's shore, more important by far, as well as more exciting. The sense of urgency his new companions seemed to reflect, in a hurry to rush on, only to be stopped by the loud protests of too many female voices shrilling at once. No one fancied the task of smoking

freshly caught fish being pushed onto them. The argument that
ensued reminded Iciwata of home, and as he stuck an elbow into
his friend's side, he could see Nara snickering, evidently seeing
the semblance as well. An altercation they, of course, could not
contribute to, being outsiders themselves, even though he could
see his sister huddling with a cluster of older women, chuckling
with healthy amusement. Of course they did!

A very pretty girl, tall and pliant, better looking than Kayina
and evidently surer of herself, stood next to them but somewhat
apart, watching the spectacle, her lips twisting with light but
pronounced amusement. Iciwata let his eyes linger on her for
another heartbeat, then motioned at his friend. "Come."

"Where to?" Nara seemed to be watching the same pleasing
sight.

"The river. They can argue with their women until the next
dawn comes. But we owe them nothing. So let's go."

Across the square, the shadow of another lower mound
provided a much welcome touch of coolness, a flat row of wooden
slabs towering one above another at even intervals puzzling,
inviting to climb them like rocks on a river bank. A strange
arrangement. Why would someone wish to climb a sacred mound,
even though this one also sported a conical construction upon its
top? He made a mental note to ask his sister about it. After all the
chatting up done to the town's womenfolk, Ciki was bound to
know.

"Here is your archenemy, flirting with pretty-looking birds."
Nara's nod indicated the detestable figure of Tcumu, the would-
be leader of their delegation, standing where the women were,
talking to the tall girl now, looking as amused as she was.

Iciwata ground his teeth, then motioned his friend to keep
going. "That dirty skunk. I'll have it out with him one day. In the
not-so-far-away future too!"

Nara just shrugged, evidently more interested in finding the
shortest way out of the town and toward the riverbank. A much
better companion than Hikua, reflected Iciwata bitterly, a
traitorous piece of meat that Hikua turned out to be, one moment
a meek follower, annoying in his readiness to do as he was told,

the other, a silent slab of stone, keeping away but with no displayed fear, dancing attendance to Kayina, the filthy skunk that he was. And the girl as well, all quiet and bashful, busy with her pearly beads, but now less ground-staring, flashing occasional smiles at the filthy skunk, talkative all of a sudden.

The sounds of the river overcame the clamor of the town as they reached the intricate fence of a sort he had never seen before arriving in this settlement. As solid as a riverbank at times and as muddy, it towered twice as high as the palisade back in their village, presenting a solid obstacle, not something one might count on climbing over in case of need. Slowing his step, Iciwata glanced around, tempted to touch this thing, to feel it out, wishing to know what it was made of and how. But for all those rushing around people. There were so many living here.

"We'll go down the shore and check our boats," he said for the benefit of those who rushed past them, giving them curious glances. Maybe from the outside or on their way back, it would be easier to sneak a peek without everyone gawking at them.

"What do you think—"

"Let us pass!" The loud words cut Nara's question short, as did the rapid footsteps, a group of men bearing upon them, clearing its way toward the opening in the wall, causing the rest of the rushing around people to lurch aside. Armed with javelins of an enviable quality, the flint of their spearheads glittering in the sunlight, relaying a dangerous message, their clothes elaborate if spare, they bore upon the wide path, a few colorfully dressed elders in their midst.

Iciwata found himself staring. They looked so determined, so sure of themselves, so warlike. Escorting the elders, no doubt. And the elders, so colorfully dressed, with such elaborate decorations adorning their well-tanned shirts and leggings. Those put even Father's most festive attire to shame, him and the rest of their elders, sporting a few colored pieces of leather sewn with some fur, unlike these people, with the glitter of their flint and those ornaments…

"Come, quickly," he tossed at Nara, hurrying toward the same gaping entrance between fortified poles through which the important group was already pouring out, followed by curiosity-filled gazes and no attempts to do likewise. "They are going to meet the western scum."

His friend's palm fastened around his elbow, not arresting his progress but as though trying to do that. "No one is going after them, no one is following."

He pushed the restraining grip away. "I can see *that*." The sharpened poles on both sides of the opening towered uncompromisingly, blocking the idea of a roundabout way. Still, he edged closer, glancing around. The people were talking agitatedly, some waving their hands, reinforcing their words. All eyes were upon the disappearing backs of the elders.

"We'll wait. Then we'll sneak out as well."

Nara's eyes were gaping at him, unusually round for a change. "We can't!"

Iciwata turned his attention back to the crowding townsfolk, the opening between the poles already vacant, with only the wind bursting through, bringing the heavy aroma of the great river.

"Yes, we can. No one will notice. We'll find a good place to see it all without drawing attention. Just need to sneak out without making them all stare."

Again, he scanned their surroundings, then the wall itself, a strange thing indeed from this closer proximity, like the palisade back home but so much more massive, coated with a thick layer of what looked like a mixture from a clay pit. An impressive construction, come to think of it, suggesting real solidness.

"Now!" The crowd seemed to be dispersing, most people drifting up the main road leading back toward the square and its mound with stairs, others spreading along smaller pathways.

He didn't wait for his friend to react, but dashed toward the breeze of the outside, his breath caught, heart pumping like on a dangerous hunt. As though one wasn't allowed to walk out of the town if one wished to do so.

Darting into the shadow the fortified wall cast generously on this side of the sloping incline, Iciwata paused, trying to force his thoughts into a semblance of reason. To run on like a mad buck in heat wouldn't do, would it? The plan was to follow the elders discreetly, without making everyone aware of his prying into their hosts' affairs, a sure way to land himself in trouble with everyone, here as much as back home. Oh well.

A quick glance around let him know that thick clusters of surprisingly high bushes separated him from the river, concealing the view he was eager to observe. Another brief scan of the surroundings he just left apprised him of a few other figures evidently following his example of sneaking out unobtrusively, heading in the opposite direction, darting toward the right of the wide path and not the well-shadowed left. Three more men, none of them looking like Nara. Cursing under his breath, annoyed with the cowardly skunk who didn't have enough guts to follow – Hikua wouldn't have lagged behind – Iciwata watched their silhouettes disappearing in the cluster of loosely planted trees. To follow them seemed like a good idea. They were after the same thing he was.

The incline straightened, then twisted upwards, ending on a bank significantly higher and drier than the shore that hosted the town's boats. All three men, youths of his own age or maybe a little older, already crouched behind sparse bushes, observing the happenings upon the shore eagerly, wholly immersed. No one protested his uninvited and unasked-for presence. They paid no heed at all.

"Look at the size of them!" one of the observers muttered while Iciwata hesitated, seeking a good observation point for himself. "Bigger than the last time."

"No, they aren't. You just can't see well from up here." The youth who said that turned his head ever so slightly, appraising Iciwata with a brief glance. "Who are you?"

Iciwata forced a shrug, annoyed with such impolite questioning. Just who did this skunk think he was? "We are here to trade things."

"With them?" Grimacing, the youth motioned with his head, indicating the river they were observing.

Iciwata pushed his way closer, dropping between the prickly bushes, eager to see, but also to let them know that he did not need their permission to do so.

"No, they are bigger, they are!" insisted the first one, oblivious to the changed subject, still immersed in his observations. "It's easy to see. Look at their sides! Or count those lowlifes in that one. Twelve! That's more than a regular war boat." His jittery movements made the bushes rustle quite wildly, annoyingly prickly even when not disturbed.

However, by now, Iciwata managed to glimpse the happenings down upon the shore, which made him forget all his previous irritation or other such petty concerns. But how could such things even float? So long and narrow!

From closer proximity, the spacious strip of shore looked like a stream where herds of animals came to drink, plenty of herds all at once. His gaze darted toward the men who were securing a monstrous boat, carrying it out of the water instead of dragging like one might do to a regular canoe. But of course! Who could drag out such a monstrosity? There were plenty of people milling around, plenty of other floating vessels being secured upon the shore, all normal-looking, some impressively large, some regular-size dugout, all made to look ordinary beside those ridiculously narrow water snakes. Oh yes, that's what those warring vessels were – water serpents! Straight away from the worst stories too.

"How do they sail it without turning over?" he asked, forgetting his previous irritation with the inhospitable locals, needing to know.

The rustling bushes beside him related a shrug as an answer. "They are good at it, villager."

He let the "villager" bit go unchallenged again. "How many are sailing each one?"

"Twelve; I just told you that." The first youth was still shifting agitatedly, all nerves. "I counted. Twelve armed lowlifes got out of the one they are dragging up now."

"Armed?" Iciwata's eyes slid over the working men, their shirts outlandish but not overly so, wet enough to cling to their bodies, their exposed limbs glistening with water or sweat. There was no weaponry in their burdened arms and there were only six of them. "They aren't warriors, are they?"

"Yes, they are. Who do you think sails in war canoes but

warriors?" The second youth snorted, but his eyes were fixed on the shore, suggesting less composure than he evidently tried to relate.

"Their weapons are inside the boat," commented the third man, who had kept quiet until now, studying the shore through dourly narrowed eyes. "Spears and shields and whatever else they fancy bringing along."

Iciwata caught his breath, trying to see better. The men upon the shallow sands were strolling about, the elders of their hosting town easy to tell apart, neatly dressed and so very presentable compared to the newcomers' wet outfits. Some of them were already engaged in conversations, but the dignified elders among the locals kept themselves apart, squatting upon the mats clearly placed for them there in a special order, forming half a circle, all dignity and good manners, an island of tranquility as opposed to the hubbub of the waterline. A few of the newcomers were already squatting among them as well, again easy to tell apart, and this time not because of their outfits only. There was something about the way they held themselves, so arrogant and self-assured, so straight-backed, no humble visitors those. Iciwata strained his eyes.

"Can we sneak down there, take a closer look?" The words came out on their own, before he could contemplate them. "I want to know what they are saying."

"Everyone wants to know that." One of his companions snickered, this time with no obvious malice. "Too risky. The elders will spot us, and if not them, then their escorts will. Awiti has eyes of an eagle. There is a reason why he is always escorting."

"Look at this one!" The first youth was pointing in quite a reckless fashion, leaning out too far from the protective prickliness of their bushes. "That filth eater. Strutting out here, by the other boat."

The commotion around the second vessel still appeared to be considerable; even on their prickly bank it was easy to hear the shouting of those who struggled with their monster of a vessel. Iciwata's eyes rested on the man who was indeed strutting

between the boats, pointing every now and then, evidently
haranguing his fellow travelers, or rather, ordering them about. It
was easy to guess that.

"I'm off to see what is happening down there."

Daring to stick his head out, he measured another bushy
incline with his gaze, not a bad descent, leading straight toward
the bend of the river, away from the hubbub of the shore and
seemingly possible to best without rolling into the thorns or
giving his presence away. Just a few careful leaps.

"Do they speak like we do?" The thought never occurred to
him before, even though some people who came to their village to
trade goods did speak in strange ways at times, twisting familiar
words in a different manner, understandable but not perfectly.
And what if those faraway foreigners did not use familiar words
at all?

"Yes, they do. Not like us, but you can understand them. Well,
the ones who had been here before the last rains. Maybe these
lowlifes do speak differently. Like those traders, eh?" Turning
toward his crouching peers, the second youth hesitated, then
looked back at Iciwata with a hint of solemnity that wasn't there
before. "You will never get close enough to eavesdrop. They'll
spot you easily, our men or those warriors."

"They can try." It came out well, with just the right amount of
confidence he didn't feel. In so much disorder and running
around, someone was bound to discover him if he crept too close
to the conversing elders, weren't they? Still, he couldn't help it. To
crouch above the gathering, barely seeing and not hearing a thing
was pointless. He could have stayed in the town like his cowardly
friend did.

"Come back and tell us what they said."

"If I'm not too busy." He made a face, not pleased with them
not volunteering to come along. Cowardly rats! He didn't know
these surroundings, and they were evidently as curious, weren't
they?

Another glance at the hubbub of the shore and some of the
figures strolling it, armed with spears now, glancing whichever
way, made him regret his previous openness concerning his

intentions. It wouldn't be easy to get close to them, and if discovered, he might be in trouble and with the authorities of the important settlement he was a mere guest at.

"Come along unless you are good for nothing but huddling safely away and gossiping."

They didn't take it well, if three darkened faces that now stared at him were any indication. Briefly, he regretted his last words as well. They were useful so far, forthcoming with information and not as obtuse as in the beginning. Also, they were no youths of his village, healthily wary of him and his temper, knowing their place. Oh well.

Turning around, he glimpsed an opening between the shrubs to his left, a new idea occurring, encouraging in its simplicity. There must be plenty of reeds beyond the river bend and the strip of a shore, enough to provide cover, to let him observe the happenings without chancing being discovered even if he didn't manage to overhear what had been said. The cowardly youths up the bank wouldn't be able to know if he didn't, stupid skunks.

A few obstacles and a much steeper incline hindered his progress, forcing him to jump into the shallow swamp, worried that the splash he made would alert not only the people rushing upon the shore but the natural inhabitants of the marshy shallows as well. No big-mouthed monsters hopefully. His stomach constricted painfully at the very thought.

The clamor of the shore just beyond the reeds was promising, taking his attention away from the water splashing around his waist, putting him into quite a helpless position should some river predator decide to see his worth as a snack. Not a high probability. Too close to the clamor of the settlement, or so he hoped. He waded his way carefully, the reeds surprisingly tall, thicker than back home, providing a satisfactory cover. Good! A hesitant peek rewarded him with a view of another cluster of boats. No monstrous war canoes, but clearly no local dugouts as well. A few men loitered by them, squatting beside an overturned vessel, nibbling on what looked like slices of dried meat. Iciwata held his breath.

"Who cares if we aren't invited in?" one of the loiterers was saying, kicking at a dry twig with the tip of his foot clad in a strange shoe, looking like a bunch of interlaced strings. "I just wish we turned around already. The river is getting strange, too narrow and twisted to my taste. And those villages are annoying, living worse than in our slums."

"You tell me!" another exclaimed. "The last one was so dirty and tiny. One single mound, imagine that. A dozen steps with nothing on it. No wonder they had nothing but stupid cakes and ugly necklaces to offer."

"And ugly women, straight from the mud of their fields. Disgusting!"

For another heartbeat, or maybe several such, brief silence prevailed. Iciwata's heart was thumping in his chest, his blood boiling, wishing he did not understand their words, the clamor upon the shoreline beyond the bend reminding him that he came to take a closer look at the war boats. Not to eavesdrop on the gossiping pieces of animal excrement who twisted their words in an ugly way and who thought these locals to be nothing but dirt. But how dared they?

"This village looks bigger, though." A man who perched upon the edge of the overturned boat reached for another piece of meat. Or was it a slice of dried bread? It was difficult to tell, not that Iciwata cared, his mind busy coping with their foul hints. Did they claim that the people who lived down the Great River were worthless, beggars with nothing to offer? What was wrong with having only one sacred mound, not that this large important town didn't have several towering earthworks of puzzling forms.

"Maybe they'll offer enough goods to make us turn back now. How many more pearls and necklaces the tribute collector is after?"

"They'll have us all rowing against the current for many more dawns." Gloomily, one of the men kicked at the driftwood that dotted the tiny strip of a shore. "It's not Honorable Ahal who is after collecting the stupid locals who can work. It's the head of the warriors, and he gives our leader a hard time in case you didn't notice." Shaking his head, he got up, then strolled closer to the reeds, causing Iciwata to contemplate a hasty retreat, noise or not.

As long as he wished to listen, he couldn't take one single step without alerting these people to sounds of his wading. "He is after glory and captives. Wants to fight the local savages. I heard him saying that just a few dawns ago, when we left that stupid settlement of Curving Mounds. They are yielding too easily, he said. Just give us what we ask; argue some, then give in. It's always like that with Honorable Ahal, but that leader Utawah isn't happy about it."

"Well, the locals are wise enough to give us what we want." One of the men shrugged, then tossed the half eaten piece straight into the reeds, causing Iciwata to almost jump out of his skin. "Revered Sun's guards can look for their fights elsewhere."

"Go and tell them that."

Amidst an outburst of merry chuckling, Iciwata dared to move backwards and along the reeds, not wishing to hear a word of what the filthy invaders of the overturned boat were saying. But to lay his hands on them one by one! How dared they call his people savages and unworthy, meek givers of whatever was to be taken from them. The mere thought made his stomach tighten so painfully it felt as though he would not be able to draw in any breath at all. Filthy lowlifes!

The shore with the war boats was calming down, his ears reported to him, with less shouting and loud talking coming out of it. With the reeds turning taller and denser, he dared to wade into their midst, getting a glimpse of the flat piece of sand he was observing from the higher bank such a short time ago. For a moment, he wondered if the youths up there saw him nearing their mutual target.

"You two! Bring the paddles here."

The loudly yelled order erupted so close it made him jump, then freeze in his tracks, eyes glued to the silhouettes beyond the reeds, blurry but visible. As was one of the monstrous vessels, lying on its side, darker than the rest of the shadows.

"Hurry!"

Again the words rang too close, as though there was no rustling obstacle between him and these people, no distance of many paces, or so he hoped. Were they plodding in the water as he did?

He strained his ears, trying to determine their proximity as well as their amount, anything really, his hand on his sash and the knife hanging there, ready. Oh, but to be able to engage one of them in an actual fight, to hurt the presumptuous skunks. Yet not now, not while creeping around, splashing in the slough.

"Honorable Utawah said to stay by the boats." This voice came out satisfactorily removed, muffled by the canes' rustling. "Even if the tribute collector stays for the night, the spoiled pieces of meat he and his men are." The last phrase carried on the wind somehow quieter, like a late addition and not for everyone's ears.

"You two stay. The rest of us will go to that filth-infested hamlet up there." The voice that distributed orders rang as uncompromisingly as before. "Keep an eye on our vessels, both of them. The tribute collector's water craft is his to safeguard." Again, a quieter addition, like in the case of the previous speaker.

"Bring us something good to chew on."

"And a pretty fowl or two." This came with roars of laughter. "Send the lustiest ones here. The most hungry among them."

Iciwata ground his teeth, thinking of his own sister up there in the town, or other women who came with them. And the locals too, snotty maybe at times, yes, but not hungry animals in heat. The filthy collectors wanted to take the women like they took the rest of the goods. What beasts!

For a while, the voices of those who remained carried in the wind, following him as he moved along the reeds, keeping to his previous course, hoping to circumvent the shore. The boats, he must see them. And the lowlifes who safeguarded them but not the "water craft of the tribute collector." But what did these men mean by that?

The wind strengthened or maybe it was his soaked loincloth that clung to his body unpleasantly as he climbed out as soundlessly as he could, glad that he came here straight from the fishing in the other stream, with no leggings or better walking shoes to ruin. To make his way through the reeds was challenging enough. He chanced a quick peek, the thick canes still there, still providing a cover.

Heart racing, his eyes took in the sight of the shore, different from what he observed from above such a short time ago, abandoned. The boats were all there, scattered in seeming disarray, but no elders sat in half a circle and no richly clad newcomers faced them or strolled about. Gone into the town, of course, oh yes, but where were the two men who didn't want to guard but the war boats? Weren't they ordered to stay and keep a watch?

Carefully, still as jumpy as a deer coming down to drink from a stream, Iciwata edged closer, his senses reaching out, seeking danger, his eyes drifting toward the nearest monstrous boat, so huge, lying on its side, not looking defeated. So long! A dozen men could have crammed themselves in and not feel too uncomfortable to row or navigate, couldn't they? But how would they keep such a monster afloat, not turning upside down with every gust of wind, or even just a rough rowing? It looked so unstable.

His senses focused on the marvel ahead, eyes noticing the weaponry piling inside the wonder – round objects with leather strips, quite a few of those, the javelins with their flint tips gleaming dangerously, so well-polished, so massive, nothing like his favorite spear with its thin brittle tip – he didn't notice the change until a frantic rustling in the canes to his left heralded danger, let him know that he wasn't alone in his hideaway of the reeds anymore. A blurry figure lashed out, throwing something at him. A stone, a missile?

He didn't spend his time trying to find answers to that. Darting aside, still in the water up to his thighs, helplessly clumsy because of that, he threw his body aside and into the thickest of the reeds, acting out of instinct that told him that there might be more attackers around, more missiles heading his way. Indeed, additional splashing erupted to his right and in the direction he was trying to escape, another swish that this time ended with a forceful push that he didn't understand at first, finding himself landing into the worst of the swamp, desperate to escape its revolting grip. Strong hands were grabbing his arms, twisting them backwards as though trying to wrench them out of his shoulders, with the muddy water getting into his eyes, interfering with his ability to breathe, not helping the panicked sensation.

Never before having been confronted with such outright deadly violence and still beyond understanding, Iciwata squirmed wildly, kicking and pushing with everything he had, one of his feet connecting with this or that limb of his attackers, shoving again, encouraged at its success. In another heartbeat, his left arm was free to lash out as well.

Someone was cursing above, more than one voice. Disregarding the pain in his right shoulder, not as unbearable as before when he was held more firmly, he managed to roll over, the reversed situation promising, his attacker now under him and in the muddy shallows, his head going momentarily under, to be kept this way. His instincts guiding him, he let his legs kick at someone else's renewed charge, seemingly as successful.

The man underneath him was pushing strongly, shoving him backwards and away, making his grip slip, not helped by another pair of arms that was dragging him off his prey, the sturdy reeds everywhere, sharp and hurtful, some of them broken by their thrashing about. The memory of the weaponry those canes served to make, temporary knifes and even durable enough spears for a single use, surfaced, popping up like his body did, now again in the water and eager to get out of it before his attackers managed to trap him underneath the marshy shallows again.

They tried to do that, indeed, but just as he fought frantically against their united assault this time, their bodies heavy, hands like stony traps, impossible to escape, his palm fastened around a wide enough cane that gave way with a loud enough creak to overcome the commotion they were creating, not giving him the support he counted on but remaining in his hand instead, a good sturdy stick, hopefully sharpened at its broken edge.

He didn't have leisure to check if it was. Acting out of an instinct rather than a thoughtful reaction again, he gave way under their pressure, backing away and into the muddy water that actually made it easier to squirm free, to throw himself backwards while driving his improvised new weaponry into the man who rushed after him, eager to recapture his prey. From such close proximity and with the drive of the body descending on him with much determination and speed, it went in like a proper knife slicing the fat of hunted game, his own back hitting the uneven surface, fighting not to let the marshy slough close above his face. The body of his attacker was weighing him down, struggling, but this time not in order to pin him to the river pebbles. It was easy to tell the difference.

Kicking it away with everything he had, the improvised weapon not there anymore, trapped in his enemy hopefully but of no use against his other assailant, Iciwata writhed madly, somehow managing to roll over, pushing his groaning, contorting rival onto his peer and thus gaining himself a precious heartbeat of respite.

The thickest of the reeds were there, offering possibilities, a route of escape. He plunged into them without thinking, oblivious of their hurtful welcome, knowing that if needing to swim his way out with or against the current, he had better attempt that. These people were worse than a wounded bear, or at least as bad in their relentless fury, their determination to kill him off, or make him drown, or capture, or whatever else they wanted to do with him.

CHAPTER 4

Word of the wounded was brought into the town just as they were settling around the stone-edged hearth in the middle of a relatively spacious house, its wall benches and floor covered with prettily patterned mats but empty of other furniture one might expect to see in a house. A place of gathering for the town's authorities, no doubt. Ahal looked around with curiosity.

Compared to the several villages they had visited since leaving the familiar shores of the Great River and its relatively mild current, this town was large, almost impressive. Several mounds of a puzzling shape, a few with staircases and temples upon them, looked like a certain achievement compared to the mound-less hamlets or villages centered around unimpressively low earthworks with no stairs and no purpose. This other stretch of the river abounded with settlements of this sort, not as sparsely inhabited as he expected. The traders going against the current were apparently a close-mouthed lot. He made a mental note to talk to his brother about it, or maybe the head of Revered Sun's guards. It was a mistake to neglect this side of their river, the reasonable tribute its settlements could and should contribute.

Focusing back on the locals, not such a dignified lot, dressed in plain leather, their decorations of the simplest kind, more polished bones than pearly wonders, he refrained from shaking his head, unimpressed. He needed to bring back pearls, and half a dozen canoes loaded with edible goods and considerable amount of manpower were already sent back to Quachil Thecou only on the day before this one. Was there a point in a continued journey against the current if no precious items of wear were to be found further upstream?

"We trust your travels were pleasant, honorable guests," one of the elders was saying, his words strangely twisted but understandable, pleasant on the ear. "We are thrilled to welcome our western neighbors, to share what we have with you, to extend our humble hospitality."

Oh yes, you are bursting with excitement, aren't you? reflected Ahal briefly, careful to keep a frivolous thought off his face but detecting it lurking in the derisive half-grin playing upon his lead warrior's lips. A prominent man and a personal appointee from the head of the Royal Mound's guards, Utawah was responsible for the three dozen fighters assigned to his expedition, now sitting there straight-backed, exuding stiff, uncompromising importance, a sense of danger that was impossible to overlook. Not a bad man, all in all, a reasonable person when not argued with. The trouble was that they did have to argue, too often for Ahal's taste. He was the head of their expedition, an appointed leader, a man expected to make it into a success. However, and as expected, the lead warrior saw it in a different way, appropriately tractable when inside the settlements, offering neither argument nor counsel, yet uncomfortably adamant when on the move, argumentative, offensive in his derisiveness, his assumption that when on the move, no one counted but warriors and their prowess whether in fighting if need be or when just rowing in an unreasonable speed. The long warring boats carried nothing but warriors, manned by at least half a dozen of rowers, moving much faster than the heavily weighted canoes of his men, loaded with goods and only two men with paddles each.

"We thank you for your hospitality," he heard himself replying, repeating the same phrases he used throughout this journey, the basic politeness being the same everywhere, even if moderated according to the location and the size of the settlement. This town needed more flowery greetings than the village they had left two dawns ago. The amount of their mounds and their height dictated that. "Your forests are beautiful and well-tended, and your side of the Good River," deliberately, he used the name mentioned in other villages, careful to pronounce each sound just as it had been spoken, "is impressively large and strong, evidently rich in its benevolence toward its people. The tale of your hospitality will reach the ears of our Revered Sun and will be praised and rewarded."

Hiding his frown, he could see Utawah twisting his lips in yet another crooked grin. How unsubtle. These elders were no simpletons, no primitive villagers to understand little if at all. There was no cause to assume they weren't shrewd people, receiving his message, understanding it well enough without the need to rub their inferior position into their faces. Tributaries or not, all people had their pride and if it was hurt, the mission would suffer, yielding lesser results in goods, not paying off for all this rowing against the current. It was as simple as that, but apparently, the lead warrior did not understand it or couldn't be bothered with such subtlety. A pity. For the hundredth time, he wished he hadn't been bestowed with warriors and their war canoes at all.

The clamor of the square outside the surprisingly cool building, its walls well-protected, plastered with clay like back home, grew considerably, and he could see some of their hosts glancing at the opening, their frowns light but pronounced. Ahal held his peace.

"Revered Sun of Quachil Thecou is honoring us greatly," one of the dignitaries was saying, nodding monotonously as though in agreement with his own words. "We haven't been honored with the visit of your glorious city's representatives for a long while, and it is a pleasure to greet you even in such difficult times. A blessing from the offspring of the celestial family of sacred suns will bring a good harvest our town did not enjoy for several summers in a row."

Two at the most, thought Ahal, and even this might be called an exaggeration. Back home and down the Great River's current all the way to the Great Sun City, only the last harvests were truly poor, while the tales of the villages along this eastern side of their so-called Good River talked of only one rainless summer.

"Our Revered Sun would certainly petition for you before our great celestial deity who is his direct ancestor, Elder," he said more coldly than before, not hiding his mounting displeasure.

"His goodwill concerning your settlement and all the lands of your Good River will shelter you from any divine displeasure."

A shadow fell across the strangely high opening, which was an additional novelty beside such an important building standing on the flat ground and not upon this or that mound like in civilized cities back home. Ahal forced his head to turn slowly, regally. It was unseemly to have their conversation interrupted like that, but maybe the warriors' leader was right and these people were truly nothing but savages.

"Honorable Leader!"

No wayward local but apparently their very own warrior hesitated in the doorway, standing there uncertainly, blinking in the windowless semidarkness after the brightness of the outside, the afternoon sun still strong, flowing in through the doorway alone.

"What is it?" Utawah was on his feet in the same heartbeat, as though welcoming the opportunity to engage in something more invigorating than sitting through long, flowery talks. It wasn't the first time the hardened warrior found excuses to retreat, leaving Ahal to deal with the locals. Not something Ahal was opposed to. If he could, he would have made the warriors stay by the boats at all times.

"One of our men..." began the newcomer, then swallowed hastily. "Would you please come outside, Honorable Leader?"

What happened? wondered Ahal, suddenly perturbed. The elders were craning their necks as well, reflecting the same worried sentiment. He forced his expression to remain unperturbed, his ears reporting him that the commotion all around the vast enclosure grew yet louder. But what could that be?

Nothing good, apparently. The meeting didn't progress beyond a few additional veiled messages when Utawah stormed back, his mouth pressed tight, eyes shooting thunderbolts, burning the elders with his accusing glare. Appalled with such a coarse interruption of procedures that were his sole responsibility to conduct, Ahal tried to remain calm, until the news broke upon them, causing even the elders to gasp.

The wounded warrior, one of those who were raiding the second war vessel, a cheerful man alternating rowing and shield-holding duties – the warriors were always prepared in the case of attack, or so Ahal had learned, each rower having his neighbor holding out his shield, protecting from the possibility of a sudden shower of arrows – was in terrible pain and dying, a makeshift spear, nothing but a broken stick made of the sturdy cane sticking out of his torso, planted there deeply, impossible to even attempt to pull out without killing the man off right away. His peer, another warrior who had been left guarding the boats, and two more men out of Ahal's team carriers, also left loitering on the shore, keeping an eye on his vessels, were frantic, their story gushing out like a current in too narrow a channel, spitting a dozen words per heartbeat, unable to stop. They had gone after the filthy piece of a traitorous meat, the sly local who had pounced from behind the cover of the reeds, mounting his cowardly attack, but the filthy snake managed to get away, plunging into the river and swimming like a fish, like the sleazy water creature that he was. They had no chance of apprehending him, no chance whatsoever.

The frantic story did not make much sense, each speaker contradicting the other, confusing in their version of what happened while the wounded writhed upon the sand, screaming in a high-pitched, terrifying voice.

"Is this your hospitality?" roared Utawah, kneeling beside the hurt man, supporting his head while trying to restrain the mad contorting of his limbs that brought forward more of the vividly crimson sprinkles, washing the dry sand, marring its brightness.

A surprising reaction in the man Ahal came to know as nothing but a tough brute with a quick temper. It wasn't easy to control this one, to make him accept his, Ahal's, leadership that was still semi-contested after so many dawns of their journey. Yet none of that seemed to matter now that one of the warriors was dying and their leader's features twisted in a frightening grimace, promising no good for the villagers who dared to challenge his authority in such a way.

"Oh, you will pay for this, you all will!" The roaring voice shook, then dropped to a growl, sounding as out of place as the agonized shrieking of the wounded, whose mind seemed to wander realms of terrible suffering.

Hurriedly, Ahal stepped forward, placing himself between the enraged warriors crowding their kneeling leader and the huddling villagers, the dignified elders from the negotiations as well as the rest of the locals, at least half of the town or so it seemed, old and young, men, women, even gaping children. Evidently, no one wished to miss the terrible happenings. Dozens upon dozens of them. Not a serious challenge for the armed and trained warriors of Quachil Thecou, but still a possible danger. There was no need to escalate the situation that was difficult enough as it was. They were here to collect substantial tribute, to establish procedure of future payments. Killing locals out of mindless rage was not a part of their mission. The culprit and maybe a few of his associates would be more than enough.

"Healer!" he shouted, trying to overcome the general clamor and anxious to have their attention on him before Utawah burst into more blood-curdling threats and promises that clearly hovered at the tip of the warrior's tongue. "Bring here a healer in a hurry. The best medicine man or woman your town can produce!"

A moment of silence seemed to stretch to several heartbeats. He let his eyes focus on the elders and their spokesman, the man he had conversed with back at the strange house with no mound underneath it. For another heartbeat, their gazes locked, but there was no hostility in the calm, washed-out depths, and when the man nodded then spoke quietly for a few heartbeats, addressing the nearest of his companions and thus setting a hurried movement among the crowding locals, he didn't feel surprised in the least.

"Our healers will see to your wounded." Another elder, his face wrinkled like an old drum made of hide, round and weathered, nodded solemnly, acknowledging their right to demand treatment. "Our men will find out who did this. The culprit will not escape or hide from his deeds."

"Our warriors should know what he looks like." Satisfied with such openly displayed support from the people on whose willing cooperation he didn't count, not without considerable pressure, Ahal motioned at the tousled pair who had been a part of the attacked group, standing next to their leader, still dripping water, their stance anything but a proud straightness. No wonder, of course. If the warriors' leader decided to transfer his anger from the treacherous locals, there was nothing they could say in their own defense, unable to apprehend a simple villager armed with a broken cane. "Tell the honorable elders about this man—what he looked like, what he wore. Everything that you remember."

A rising commotion at the back of the crowd produced a squat, broad-shouldered man carrying a basket loaded with frightening-looking tools. A healer, at least! Ahal moved away hurriedly, his hopes not high. Stomach wounds were nasty business, their owners suffering much yet not living to tell their stories, not usually. The amount of blood soaking into the crispy sand promised nothing but a nearing end. Still, the locals owed them an attempt to relief the suffering.

"When you are done entertaining our tribute collector and those elders," Utawah was back on his feet, his face a frightful mask but his voice calm enough, dripping disdain, eyes boring into the dispirited warriors, "spread around with the rest of our men and hope you are the ones to put your hands on the treacherous lowlife before the others braver fighters did this. There will be no other way to redeem your names."

With that, the furious leader stalked off, shouting orders at the rest of his men, gesturing broadly.

Ahal shrugged, then concentrated back on the humbled warriors and the crowd of locals. "Tell us what he looked like, then you may go."

The shore fell significantly quieter once again.

"He was young, Honorable Leader," muttered the taller of the pair, his features pleasing the eye but for the bruises covering them. From the thrashing about with the violent local? There was little reason to assume otherwise.

"How young? A young man, a boy?"

The townsfolk were listening with what seemed like bated

breath.

"A young man. And a strong one! There were the two of us, and then the two of your men came running. He had no chance against us, but..." The fervently flickering gaze dropped down abruptly, boring at the crispy sand. "He was exceptionally strong."

Good for carrying buckets of earth, reflected Ahal, remembering the request to bring working hands upon his return as well as other goods. A wild killer would not be the best choice to take back to Quachil Thecou, but if manageable, he may prove to be of use, along with other strong men he would have to collect from this settlement. Another topic to bring up with the elders of the town, a topic they were certain not to like. However, in the current situation and if eager to appease, to prevent Utawah from burning half of this settlement in revenge...

Glad that the angered warriors' leader had gone with his fellow warriors, eager to lay his hands on the culprit personally in most probability, he let his eyes wander, traveling their faces, mostly the men in the front of the crowd, curiosity filled or foreboding, some glaring openly, not displeased with what happened. "Who saw any of it? Do you know who is responsible for the murderous attack?"

A hardened tone as well as the piercing stare focused on several faces yielded results. Less open glares, more shifting gazes. The women were hushing the children up.

"The inquiries will be made, Honorable Visitor." The spokesman among the elders was still busy shooting hushed-up instructions, so it was another important-looking elder who nodded at Ahal solemnly, not attempting to avert his gaze. "If any of our men were involved —"

"Who else could be responsible?" demanded Ahal, judging the moment correct to press this particular point. "Are your shores frequented by people from other settlements? Do you share this part of the river with others?" A vital piece of information to extract under the coverage of the pressing problem. The traders talked of settlements setting wide apart from each other.

"It was one of your snakes and your entire town will pay for this cowardly deed!" cried out one of the warriors, who had evidently been told to remain on the shore, guarding the wounded and the rest of them.

Ahal shut him up with a fierce glare, wishing Utawah had taken the most eager part of his forces along and away from here. The locals were frightened enough, evidently appalled by what happened. There was no need to threaten them into silence and lack of cooperation.

"Your inquiries will have to bring results before the sun leaves our world tonight, Elder," he said mildly, holding his previous converser's gaze. "This incident must be addressed before our conversation continues."

One of the younger men stepped forward, his gaze brushing past the healer, who was kneeling by the wounded in exactly the same way Utawah did before, his features screwed in as troubled scowl, eyes squinted into slits.

"The man came from the river, your warriors said. He could be someone from out there. He doesn't have to be one of our town."

"Who could it be, then?" demanded Ahal harshly, glad to have someone besides the elders to question. The town's people, hunters and fishermen, were bound to know plenty, come to think of it. "Do the people of nearby settlements fish on your shores, hunt the game of your forests?"

"No, they don't!" cried out several voices, offended. "Our shores and forests are ours."

"However, we do receive visitors," said one of the elders, his frown dour. "Just like you western guests, people of the north and the east are coming to visit us, bringing goods to trade."

"The men from the village of Eagle Mound are still here!" exclaimed someone, a woman at the edge of the crowd, clutching a child in her arms. "They didn't leave on the day before like they wanted to."

"Yes, yes, they were fishing with us today." More excited voices joined in. "Their young men were right there at the spring."

"And their women were in the square." A young girl waved her hands wildly, then brought them to her forehead, shielding her eyes against the afternoon light like a scout in a warring canoe, observing. "They were here. I just saw…"

Additional commotion produced a round-faced, pleasant-looking young woman, openly frightened, resisting the hands that were pushing her forward.

Ahal frowned. "Who are you?" Stepping closer, in case she tried to dive back into the protection of the milling around locals, he tried to look as calm as he could, not willing to frighten her into silence or tears. "What do you know?"

"I… I know nothing. Why should I… How could I know anything? It wasn't any of us!" Desperate, she turned back toward the pressing people, bringing her hands forward, palms up, openly pleading. "None of us is involved in this. We were all back in the town, and our men are out there at the woods, fishing. Ask anyone!" Two more women, older and less good-looking, were huddling close to her, as though supporting her claims.

"Where do you come from?" inquired Ahal mildly, the resumed shrieks of the wounded, who had been quiet for some time, fraying his nerves. It was better for the man to die already. Couldn't their healer do something to that effect, ease the suffering?

"The Eagle Mound village," said one of the older women, while the young one burst into noisy tears. "We came from there. But none of us is involved in this. You can ask anyone. Our men, they are all here, ready to testify."

Ahal suppressed a shrug. "Bring them for questioning. How many men came here with you?"

"Three!" burst out the younger one again, her sobs subdued, temporary most likely. She was truly a treat to the eye, round-faced and dimpled, very fresh to look at. Ahal nodded at her encouragingly. "We came here with goods. On the day before the previous one. We were supposed to leave on the evening before." Again, the sobs. She was clearly regretting the decision to stick around for another day, poor thing. "But we stayed. My brother, he was anxious to learn the news, the news of—" Her expression turned yet more frightened and the flow of words stopped.

He put his attention back to the elders. "Where are those visitors? Send the word to bring them to me. I wish to talk to them, all of them." He hesitated, knowing that his wish to escape the screams was not admirable or brave. "Make a carrier to take the wounded back into the town. In the meanwhile, let the crowds disperse and let us return to our business, Elders. There are important matters we need to discuss. Our warriors will comb the shores and your men will help them. And the rest of you, work on the carrier or help the warriors." He encircled the pressing mass of people with his gaze, trying to look encouraging, valuing their good will and cooperation. It all might still come to a peaceful gathering of the goods due for collecting. A half a dozen working men would be a more difficult thing to squeeze out of the wary locals, but he would have to. "Let us go."

The elders did not hesitate, clearly welcoming the idea of retreating from the troublesome shore and into the familiarity of the town to deal with the trouble. The round-faced woman edged closer, as though intending to fall into his step and keep it that way. For some reason, it pleased him. It wasn't her fault the men of her village were suspected and had to prove their innocence. There was no harm in sheltering her from the distrust of the townsfolk.

"Who are the women who are visiting here with you? Those two?" he asked affably, glad to be heading away from the troublesome shore as well. To witness the death of the wounded was something he could do without. He wasn't a medicine man or a priest to see the dead into their new beginning, and the man was not someone he knew or was responsible for.

She nodded readily, her frown clearing, revealing that she was even prettier up close and when not troubled, all dimples and spark. Like Lallak, but a simple, unsophisticated peasant version of his mistress. Briefly, he wondered what was happening back in the city, or how his niece was doing up there in the sacredness of the Royal Mound, in the bed of the ailing deity-on-earth.

"We came here together, and but for my brother, we would have left already." Her words gushed out lightly, uninhibited, chatty; with no appropriate titles either, as though she was talking to her fellow family member. A refreshing change. In small villages, it was often like that, those delightfully simple, fresh,

natural women. "He talked us all into staying, and now I wish
that he hadn't."

"If he is here in the town and the rest of your fellow villagers
are as well, then you have nothing to fear or regret. Is your
brother the leader of that delegation? Do your men listen to him?"

Her chuckle trilled the air, delightfully light. "My brother? No!
He is a youngster. No one listens to him yet but other youngsters.
He is the strongest, the best hunter and all that, but he has some
summers to pass before people start listening to him the way he
wishes."

The strongest, the best... He pondered her words, not liking
where they led. "Run ahead and find him with no delay. Bring
him to me wherever I—"

The shouts broke from the shore once again, overcoming the
steady hum of too many people moving at once, talking loudly,
unconcerned, with no need to keep their voices or the noise of
their movements down, on their home ground. Still the voices of
the returning warriors fragmented the steadiness of the hum,
invading the shore once again, clearly visible from the beginning
of the incline, dragging a few terrified-looking figures between
them, shoving them ahead violently, with little consideration to
none.

Frozen in surprise, Ahal stared for longer than a heartbeat,
before bursting into a run, clearing his way through the throngs
filling the trail now, his heart beating fast. So soon? But those
warriors *were* efficient.

"What happened?"

"They were hiding up there on the cliff," tossed Utawah,
shoving the man he partly dragged partly pushed ahead so
violently his prisoner went crashing down upon the blood-stained
sand. "Filthy pieces of human excrement!" His sandaled foot
frustrated the panicked attempt to get back up again. "What is
happening with the wounded?"

"They are constructing a carrier to take him up and into the
town."

The warrior nodded grimly. "Any hope?"

Ahal shook his head, then glanced at the prostrated youth, who didn't attempt to get up again but just stared at them from the ground, his face bruised and terrified, lacking in coloring. Another two culprits were still upright, kept between quite a few warriors, powerless and as aghast as their fallen peer.

"Will you question them here or up there in the town?"

The lead warrior scowled in reply, wiping his hands with the edge of his shirt as though they got dirtied. "The filthy pieces of human waste were hiding up there like mice under a basket of maize!" Another kick made the youth upon the ground whimper with fright.

"What is the meaning of this?" A few respectable-looking men charged toward them, followed closely by the town's elders who, like Ahal, seemed to reverse their course. Better they had time to reach the town and leave the warriors to deal with it on their own, reflected Ahal, studying the captured youths once again, finding no evidence of exceptional strength or bravery the murderer should have possessed according to the account of the warriors and the evidence of his deed as much as to what the young woman said. Briefly, he sought her with his gaze, pleased to find out that she had followed him back here, lingering by the edge of the pouring back crowd, her eyes wide with fright.

He motioned her to come closer. "Is one of these youths your brother?"

She shook her head vigorously, not moving from the protective circle of her country-folk, daring not to venture a word.

"Go away, villagers," tossed Utawah curtly, glaring at the pressing people with so much ferociousness the crowd swayed backwards like one man.

"What do you accuse these youths of?" demanded one of the elders, drawing closer but carefully so.

One of the warriors, a man always closest to Utawah, a businesslike person Ahal appreciated and liked, glanced at his leader, who was busy contemplating the prisoners with a frighteningly menacing gaze.

"They did the crime, or were accomplices to it," he said when no reaction seemed to be forthcoming.

"No, no, we have nothing to do... we know nothing!" cried out one of the youths, resisting a less violent push, struggling to stay on his feet. "We have nothing to do with what happened!"

Forgetting all about the round-faced woman, Ahal leaned toward the sprawling youth. "What did you see? Do you know who attacked the warriors? Did you see it? Answer quickly!"

As opposed to the rough treatment at the hands of his capturers, mere words with no physical violence seemed to have an encouraging effect. The youth upon the ground perked up, straightening, even if not daring to get to his feet as yet. "We saw, yes... From up there. On that cliff..."

"What were you doing there?" roared Utawah, but the rising murmur among the watching locals made even the fierce warrior moderate his tone. They were in no position to beat up answers out of local culprits. This town was no humble village. "Speak up."

"What did you see?" repeated Ahal, motioning the youth to get up. "Who did this?"

"The foreign youth, the villager. He was the one to go down there, sneak around the boats. None of us—"

"What foreign youth?"

The silence around deepened, and he wanted to sneak a glance at the round-faced woman but was too busy concentrating on the interrogation. "Talk!"

The youth swallowed loudly. "The villager... one of the villagers... He said he wanted to take a closer look, hear what you were saying. He went down and into the reeds!" The words were spilling faster and faster, the last phrase shouted as though it proved their own innocence beyond doubt. "He wanted to know what was happening, to hear what's been said. We told him he would be discovered. Impok told him. But he went on all the same."

"And then what happened?" The silence around was wearing on his nerves, the crowding locals listening as intently as the warriors did. Even Utawah volunteered no violent or threatening comments. A wonder. "Tell us everything you saw."

But as the accented words began spilling out again, pouring anxiously, eager to convince, he wished he could get it over with soon, knowing that they were wasting their time with this unfortunate incident, that they should head back to the town, back to negotiations, loading the canoes with the requested goods first thing in the morning, sending them back home, to follow the previous load of five dawns ago. Then on to another settlement; a few more dawns, and he would be able to head back home, satisfied, his mission accomplished. This shore and the pitifully frightened local youths, those people watching intently, with reproachful eyes, the girl with a violent brother who was to be hunted down and then pay for his crimes, oh but they were all unimportant, not worthy of his time, not even valuable to bring back as a working force, not these whimpering creatures intimidated by mere yelling at. The violent villager was the one proving most valuable, come to think of it, a useful person to capture and put to good use, seeing how he bested a warrior with a stupid piece of a broken cane. Oh yes, warriors should have had better sense than to loiter about, getting beaten or impaled on stupid sticks.

"Bring here the men who had fought the lowlife in the reeds," Utawah was shouting, sending a few of his men on the run and back around the bend of the river. "Go and find them and bring them here with no delay."

To question them again along with the locals who saw it? Shrugging to himself, Ahal turned back to the elders. "Let us proceed back to the town in the meanwhile." His eyes brushed past the hovering locals, slightly disappointed to see that the woman who reminded him of Lallak was not anywhere in sight anymore.

CHAPTER 5

The sun was painting pretty pictures, sneaking in through the strange openings gaping at her from far away under the ceiling. Suppressing a yawn, Sele studied them, finding nothing better to do. Back home, in the children's quarters of the other secondary house, they didn't have any wall openings at all, while in the main house where Father lived with Mother and sometimes this or that minor wife, there were additional means of letting the light in besides the entrance, but not like here. The temple upon the Royal Mound and the spacious hall adjacent to it was a wonder to behold.

Leaning on her elbow, she raised her head to look around with more comfort, never tired of studying her new home, seeking yet undiscovered wonders, intricate decorations she might have overlooked, vases of fascinating patterns, mats that concealed both the inner and the outer walls. The under-roof openings poured the light with exquisite softness, themselves a wonder, covered in some transparent sheets that let the sun or the moon in but not the wind or the rain. A magical place, her new home.

A temporary home, maybe, yes. Only Revered Sun's chief wife was allowed to share the sacredness of the royal hall adjacent to the main temple atop the Royal Mound with the Quachil Thecou sovereign. However, her husband's chief wife had been dead for quite a few moons, having left on the afterlife journey during the spring of the deadly fever, while his other wives did not please him, not like his new favorite addition. So for now, this was her home, and she intended to keep it this way.

Stretching under the softest of wraps, a hide so delicate it felt like a skin of a baby, Sele yawned again but didn't dare to move, listening to the uneven breathing of the man beside her. Revered Sun, she thought, the master of the entire valley of the Great River, ruling their beautiful Quachil Thecou and all other towns and villages who paid tribute to Uncle Ahal and did as they were told, a person not many were privileged to see through their entire lives, not allowed to look the sacred person in the eye even if happening to cross his path when he toured the city. Only people like Father, important warriors and advisers, could address the great ruler when bidden. But here she was, sleeping beside the powerful man, the descendant of the Great Sky Deity that he was, curled under his covers and upon his intricately padded and decorated mats, allowed to talk to him and laugh and please, feeling sure of herself, at home, not frightened by the unparalleled honor in the least. Wonder of wonders.

His breathing was again fast and uneven, but undisturbed by the shaking that would sometimes take him and leave him drained of strength, soaked in sweat, frighteningly weak. It happened to him only a few dawns ago and it frightened the life out of her, even though the servants were there in swarms, hectic and frenzied, with healers by almost the same amount, bringing foul-smelling brews, helping the shaking to subdue gradually, leaving the great ruler fragile and frighteningly feeble, sleeping like a dead man for so long it looked as though he had truly died.

Through all that, she had huddled in the corner, shivering and unnerved, afraid that she might be blamed for what happened, somehow, because the great ruler had kept her by his side since her arrival and against the light frowns and hinted reproach in the glances of those privileged to visit or serve this hallowed place. And what if it was truly her fault? He had spent plenty of time with her, performing his husbandly duties sometimes but mostly talking and cuddling. It was easy to amuse him, to make him laugh quietly or just smile. The sacred sovereign of Quachil Thecou turned out to be surprisingly nice and approachable, easy to please.

A grin of smugness threatened to sneak out, bidden in the privacy of her bed. A summers-old habit and vast experience of

manipulating her elders and betters, even Father himself, turned
out unnecessary here on the Royal Mound.

Shaking her head, she reminded herself not to grow too
pleased with herself, not in these surroundings. Not since
returning to the hallowed hall from the lesser women's quarters
where she had been hushed when the healers were busy fighting
the violent shaking that racked her sweat-soaked husband
between spells of frightful heat and most terrible chills. Revered
Sun needed to rest and sleep, recovering his strength, the maids
had told her, looking at her kindly, as though understanding her
plight. When he felt better, he would surely summon her back.

A prediction that made her wish it was true the moment she
had descended to the lower terrace and stepped through the
doorway of another vast construction that housed wives and other
female relatives of lesser importance, various cousins and nieces
of the Sun Family, those who were not sent elsewhere, offered in
marriage alliances, a hubbub of noise and forked-tongued
exchanges, and nasty looks. Not entirely helpless, having grown
up with plenty of siblings of her own, some older than herself and
therefore better armed for verbal attacks and offenses, she still
didn't expect to encounter so many snakes with such intense
venom, caught momentarily unprepared. They were supposed to
be the highest of the nobility, weren't they? Living on the lower
terrace of the Royal Mound, old and young hags each and every
one of them, even the quiet ones, those who didn't say a word
through her brief stay in these quarters, but who would surely
reveal their nasty faces when an occasion presented itself.

Luckily, she had been summoned back to the royal quarters as
the next dawn came, retrieved from the shocked misery, relieved
to learn that the great ruler didn't hold his sudden illness against
her. Because another day in the women's quarters and she would
have done something stupid, like running away and back home
maybe, a silly thing to even consider.

A light rustling outside the low doorway pulled her from her
musings, heralding the advance of this or that personal servant, or
maybe even someone of importance. Very few were allowed to
near Revered Sun or even look in his direction, let alone address

or disturb his sleep. Sele made sure the exquisite covers concealed sights destined for her husband's eyes alone.

What is it? she motioned, raising higher on her elbow, taking in the sight of the dignified official, a middle-aged man who oversaw the activity around the main side of the royal hall, yielding his authority to the relevant high-ranking priests when it came to the ornamented partition that separated the insides of the great temple from it. Not a person to wave away, not even at the hands of the favorite new wife occupying the sleeping ruler's bed. There were several officials like that on the top of the Royal Mound and at the lower terrace's temples, their word uncontested, obeyed with no delay. Even the wives were wary of such men, even the less important relatives. Everyone but the great ruler's elder sister whose son was to inherit the throne upon his uncle's death, may all powerful deities keep him from such possibility.

The royal sister, *Quachilli Tamailli*, Revered Lady Female Sun, was herself scaring the life out of the Royal Mound's dwellers, worse than any official or adviser. Sele preferred not to think of this woman at all. Not if she could help it. In the glory of Revered Sun's personal favor, it was easy to do that. Nothing could touch her as long as he cherished her, and the man seemed to be enthralled just as he should have been. She smiled to herself, then focused on the invader, not hiding her displeasure with his insolent interruption, wise course of action or not.

Wake the master, motioned the official, not taken aback at all, paying respect only to the sleep of his sovereign. It was as though she was a maid caught in the ruler's bed. Sele ground her teeth, then spent another heartbeat burning the insolent man with her gaze. Just who did he think he was, nothing but a privileged *honorable,* a servant to the Sun Family, of which she was now a part. Not an integral part, yes, not even through the children she hoped to bore to the great ruler – that privilege belonged to the females of the Sun Family alone – still, she was Revered Sun's favorite wife and an important adviser's daughter. They had no right to look at her as though she was just a concubine, a new toy for the revered ruler to enjoy. The gall!

Another heartbeat of staring did not make the insolent man's steady gaze waver. Wake *the master*, he motioned again, his face a stony mask, unreadable and as cold as a winter night. Defeated, she turned toward her sleeping husband. "Revered Sun."

Her whisper was as gentle as her touch, like a breath of fresh air, to enter his sleep and lull him out of it softly and pleasantly. Again she blessed her mother and a special female teacher the older woman had brought into their house even before learning of Sele's impending fate. The most promising among the adviser's daughters was certainly worthy of such investment, Mother said once. One didn't hold the position of a favorite wife by the virtue of one's birthright alone. A wife had to be gentle and pleasing, and not only beautiful. She had to become indispensable, better than her peers of the same position and rights, and better than any pretty *miche-quipy* who were always around and eager to get into powerful men's beds, to please and sometimes stay there for a long time, the pushy concubines bearing children.

Oh, but did Mother love to harp on this subject. And yet, the teaching did prove itself now that she had to compete not only with possible lusty peasants but with women of her rank and higher. Her gentleness and just the right amount of playfulness did keep her in the Royal Hall near the temple. After more than half a moon there, it came almost naturally, the fragile man's reactions and patterns known almost by heart; this and her own responses to him. Apparently, being married was an easily managed business, great rulers no more difficult to understand and therefore to manipulate than various brothers and cousins and even servants who were supposed to tell on her when she did something bad as a child but never did. From tears to playfulness to calculated insolence at times and all in between, it had been easy to fulfill all her wishes, now armed with an additional weapon of marriage, the lovemaking, apparently a mighty weapon in itself.

Pleased with herself, she slid her palm along the bony chest, all skin and sharp angles, the tattoo encircling it not hiding its angularity, a magnificent image of a massive half circle of a sun, with wide rays extending from it. The Sun! Such fitting marking for the glorious descendant of the Sky Deity to carry. Even though she couldn't help thinking that such tattoo would look more magnificent on Uncle Ahal's well-muscled chest. He looked like a warrior, Uncle Ahal, and Father said that he was something of a warrior indeed, adept with weapons, the best at the spear-throwing game, fighting sometimes when the people he led were attacked. Uncle Ahal, the epitome of a perfect man. When she was too small to know better, she remembered wishing to be given to him in marriage. A silly thought, of course. With all his good looks and fascinating conversations, his rare but delightfully crinkling smile and deep contemplative eyes, Uncle Ahal was beneath her father's status and she, a favorite and most promising daughter, was destined to be given to the most powerful man in the land.

"Revered Sun."

He stirred uneasily, as though unwilling to escape the dream. The calm drained off his features, sharpened them into unhealthy lines. His eyes, when opened, looked sunken in the darkness of the wrinkled skin surrounding them. Not an old man, her husband looked terribly old at such times. She pushed a slight wave of revulsion away.

"Revered Sun. The Master of the Ceremony wished me to wake you up." A demure whisper, a calculated smile. Playful or concerned? He looked sicker today, so the concern it should be. And what if he started to shake once again? She reached for his cheek, as though daring to caress but in fact feeling it out. Was he hot? Feverish? "Revered Sun?"

He nodded slowly, his gaze focused, but not on her or her words. It was as though he was peering into himself with his mind-eyes, seeking answers to the same questions that worried her.

"Are you feeling well, Revered Sun? Can I bring you something?"

His lips stretched into a colorless line. "Tell the servants to bring a cup of water before my morning beverage." The smile widened. "Be quick as a wind, little wife. Instruct them as to the food and the clothing. Tell the Master of the Ceremony to summon the advisers if they have not yet come to pay their respects. Let him inform our Female Sun that I shall receive her after I've seen my advisers." The sunken eyes softened. "Then come back and busy yourself with your weaving by the far hearth. I do not wish you to listen, little wife, but I do wish you to stay."

Sele made sure her smile reflected none of her inner smug satisfaction. "You honor me greatly, oh Revered Sun. It will be done as you wish." Another smile, this one more intimate, hinting at the night spent under exquisite wraps, the laughter shared together and not only the dutiful copulation – not an exciting affair in itself, a hurried business to get over with without him turning ill again or suspecting that she could do without any of it – and she snatched her prettily embroidered, brilliant-white, spotless robe, then rushed off, stepping with vigor and care, knowing he would be watching her going.

Another smile threatened, this one of self-satisfaction, unobserved and thus needn't be suppressed. Oh yes, the powerful master of Quachil Thecou and all its surroundings was honoring her to the highest degree, and there was no need for it not to remain so. He loved her vigor, he had said often, her youthful energies, her vitality and spunk, displayed in just the right amount, as always, carefully calculated, truth be told. That gentleness her mother talked about was not always that handy, and there was no need to worry about her in the first place, as apparently, to handle a powerful husband was the easiest thing, and not much different than when handling one's own father, a power noble in himself, a willful man that was used to his word being law inside his home and plenty of other places, but not when it came to her. Among her numerous siblings and Father's wives, she knew better than anyone how to get her way without turning outright rebellious and demanding. Women saw through her sometimes, her mother and the older among Father's wives, but men were incredibly gullible, even the most powerful among those. A good state of affairs, certainly. Most comfortable. Among the men in her life, only Uncle Ahal could see through her at times, she suspected. But he loved her all the same, just like they all did, even though if her childhood wish would have come true and she would have been given to her uncle in marriage, he might have turned out to be more difficult to handle.

Well, the powerful descendant of the celestial deity turned out to be as easy as everyone else, with only one wrinkle on this happy state of affairs – his health. If Revered Sun died while overtaken with that dreadful fever, she would be reduced to the pitiful status of former wives unless made to accompany her powerful master into his afterlife journey. A true honor that would elevate her and her family even higher, the children she might have bear to this man; and yet, to think of death, even as honorable as this one, proved to be shamefully frightening, may all powerful deities keep Quachil Thecou's sovereign healthy and safe. She pushed the disquieting thoughts away.

The Master of the Ceremony was still there, hovering near the doorway, as foreboding as a figurine carved out of stone.

"Have the servants bring Revered Sun some water before they serve his medicine and his food," she told him curtly, holding her head high. "He will have his drink before the advisers came in. If they are not here, summon them. His sister, Revered Female Sun, he will receive after them." A sway of her hand was imperious enough, at least to her taste.

The man measured her with a veiled gaze. "The Revered Lady expressed the wish to see her exalted brother not long after the dawn broke," he retaliated in the end, his tone matching hers in coldness and cheek. "Revered Female Sun mustn't be made waiting. Certainly not until after the meeting with the advisers."

Sele fought the uneasiness that was forming at the pit of her stomach, not liking to be reminded of the haughtiest lady in the land, the mother of the next Revered Sun, afraid of her like they all were but unwilling to admit that. "The Revered Lady will have to wait. Our Revered Master was clear about that."

The glance the older man bestowed on her made her wish to flee back into the safety of the ruler's bed. She made sure to toss her head higher than before. "Have your men hurry. Our Master is the one who must not be made waiting. And have my maids sent for as well. I need to break my fast too, then to dress properly. Revered Sun wishes me to be present at his meetings."

As you must know, she added with the flicker of her eyes alone, pleased at having this man put in his place, his brief but unmistakable expression of angered frustration everything she was hoping for. Fancy taking the powerful sister's side or some other jealous hag. Pah!

The open seat carried on the shoulders of two sturdy men made her victorious feeling dim. Heading in the direction of the towering temple with its high, typically round roof, it still passed in too close proximity to the entrance into the Royal Hall to leave Sele feeling safe. Only the true members of the Sun Family, those who carried the divine blood, used such palanquins while traveling the sacred mound itself, refraining from marring their feet by the carefully flattened and daily swept earth of the Royal Mound's spaciously flat top.

Her stomach twisting uneasily, she watched the woman upon the cushioned platform reclining royally, one shoulder thrust forward, the other supported by the ornamented bolster, the draperies of her brilliant blue wear fluttering with the breeze, the transparently glittering crystals adorning it ringing with delightful yet unsettling clearness. The proud head that turned toward them did so slowly, reluctantly, as though unwilling to mar its sight.

"Master of the Ceremony." The sway of the royal palm summoned Sele's converser into a hurried near-run. "Is my exalted brother awake?"

Contemplating a quick dive back into the dimness of the doorway and the safety of the ruler's protection there, her stomach as tight as a wooden ball, Sele watched the richly dressed apparition, unable to take her eyes away, never before having seen Revered Female Sun but from a safely respectable distance. The divine family was above conferring with lesser human beings, *honorables* as they might be considered outside the sacredness of the towering mound. No common *miche-quipy*, oh yes, none of the Sacred Mound dwellers were, not even the servants, but not as divine as the royal family was.

The cold eyes shifted, resting on her for a brief moment, turning chillier. Even from the distance of several tens of paces, it was easy to see that. The arm loaded with softly glittering bracelets beckoned her closer.

"Is it not my divine brother's new toy?" The words rang loudly enough, chilling in their freezing amusement. "Come here, girl."

Despite the icy wave gripping her stomach, Sele kept her head high, putting her entire attention upon her step, striving to walk as proudly as she could. A new toy? But what did the woman mean by that?

"Greetings, Revered Lady." Her voice rang with satisfactory firmness and it pleased her, despite the wild fluttering of her heart. There were too many people around, and she wasn't even dressed properly, wrapped in a morning robe, with no comb applied to her hair and no warmed wet cloths to her face. Didn't she tell the annoying official to summon her maids? The haughty woman's entourage was vast, including several important-looking men, all staring at her with varying degree of curiosity and familiar healthily male appreciation, all of them beside the fleshy and exceptionally clad man that somehow resembled her powerful husband, a healthier and considerably fatter version of the same prolonged face and long limbs, sitting straight-backed in the second carried chair, the look in his eyes intense, even piercing, full of open desire. It made her shiver and wish to run back into the safety of the Royal Hall.

"So you've been making our Revered Sun's days into happier affairs, adviser's little daughter?" From closer proximity, it was easy to see that the exalted Female Sun was older than her divine sibling, indeed, her cheeks glittering under the generous layer of oily substance, successful at hiding its dry, wrinkled state but only partially. Father's wives used such creams in great quantities, and with better success.

Sele forced her own gaze down once again, not liking the squinted eyes and the equally thin smile playing upon the woman's lips. "I'm doing my best, Revered Lady."

"Master of the Ceremony, attend to my brother's needs." The woman's attention was back on the hapless official, who looked as though he might wish to be elsewhere, so fidgety and ill-at-ease, his eyes darting up and down. "When I'm through with my temple duties, have me escorted into his revered presence along with my son, his favorite nephew and successor. Have an ample escort waiting for us at the temple's entrance."

"Oh, Revered Lady," began the Master of the Ceremony haltingly, but the flash of the bracelets upon the woman's dry hand cut the forming words short.

"Do as you are told, mortal."

Mortal? thought Sele, incredulous. Having spent nearly half a moon on the Sacred Mound, she hadn't heard any such words before, not in regular conversations. Her powerful husband did not call anyone mortals, and he was more divine than anyone besides Great Sun of the Sacred Sun City out there in the west.

"It will be done as you wish, Revered Lady."

The pudgy man in the second palanquin – the famous nephew, apparently, the successor – took his eyes off her, glancing at the speaking woman, his forehead furrowing slightly, in a thoughtful rather than troubled expression.

"Have my brother's new little toy escorted to the women's quarters where she belongs." The necklace of glowing pearls upon the woman's scrawny neck, a beautiful jewelry in itself, sparkled dully as did the rest of her pearly wristlets, encircling the lean arm up to its bony elbow.

Forgetting the man with the piercing gaze, Sele gasped, not prepared for her safe haven to be shattered in such cruel way.

"But, Revered Lady." The official, now reinforced by equally dignified-looking servants preceding a procession carrying trays and appetizingly smelling bowls, seemed to be struggling with his words. "Our divine master, Revered Sun, he wishes—"

The neatly plucked eyebrows climbed high, arresting the rest of the man's mumbling, but by then, Sele found her tongue as well. "Revered Sun wishes me to remain by his side. He said so himself many times, and he repeated it just now, before I came out!" Her voice rang stridently, annoyingly high-pitched and climbing higher with every word. She didn't care. "You can ask him yourself. He will tell you. He told me to be as quick as a wind, to come back and stay, and I won't—"

"Halt your insolent speech, you ill-mannered brat!" The

bolstered platform shuddered with the sharp movement of its rider's free arm. "Do not dare to answer Revered Female Sun and the mother of the next Revered Sun, or to speak without being spoken to! A lowly person like yourself should not even dare to raise your gaze, you insolent thing, or think of words of reply inside that empty little head of yours. It is not a minor wife's place to skulk around important meetings. Pretty toys like you have their time of use." A wave of the bejeweled hand completed the order. "Off with you, girl. Do as you are told."

"I will not!" The words came out on their own, but it pleased her, the clarity of their ring, their decisiveness. "I will follow our Revered Sun's orders and no one else's. I belong to him, not to you!"

In the disturbingly deep silence that prevailed, the noises of the city below reached them but barely, gushing somewhere away, outside the sudden quietness around them. Other signs of life emanated from houses spread along the well-swept surface of the Royal Mound's top, but even the chirping of the unconcerned birds and day-insects seemed to dim in their immediate proximity.

Sele licked her lips against the bitter taste in her mouth that became suddenly dry, needing a gulp of water, anything that would bring relief. Her heart was making strange leaps inside her chest, but her blood was boiling, rejoicing in her momentary victory, such an uplifting feeling. She didn't dare pause in order to take a breath. "I will follow the orders of our divine master and no one else's."

Then her instinct of self-preservation took over, making her head shoot yet higher while her body whirled around, charging back toward the protection of the Royal Hall, the dimness of its entrance beckoning, promising safety. Another decision made by her inner self, with no regard to her mind that kept staring at the proceedings, stunned. Did she just flare at the divine family's most prominent member after her husband, his sister and the mother of the one who would be taking the burden of the reign upon his divine uncle's death? There was no point to even think about it. The dead silence behind her back said it all.

CHAPTER 6

The rain intensified after the dusk fell, beating against the greenery of the trees, displeased and showing it freely. Tiredly, Iciwata pressed closer to the rough bark, pulling his legs to his chest but daring not to close his eyes and try to sleep. In such weather, no one would be out and about, no animals and no people, even those who were busy looking for criminals.

Still, with the filthy westerners, those surprisingly violent, relentless, determined warriors, one never knew. May the bad forest spirits take them and their ferociousness, and their multitude of canoes, and the way they had gone into this large important town as though it was theirs to stroll and order the locals about. Not a village of barely a few hundred people like theirs was.

He shivered and hoped it was from the cold. The wind was blowing strongly, mercilessly, his loincloth soaking wet from his afternoon adventures, clinging to his body in most unpleasant of manners, not helping against the chill of the night. That was the only reason. Nothing to do with the danger he was in, the helplessness of his situation. Or was it? He ground his teeth, then pushed the nagging doubts away. He would find the solution, he would. He had to. But what would it be?

The question hovered since the beginning of the rain, since that blissful moment when the drops began falling heavily, out of nowhere, with no warning, like they sometimes did. He had been huddling in the thickest of the bushes, down the shore and far enough down the troublesome river bend, the same spot that had gotten him into trouble in the first place, such a stupid impulse.

But what had possessed him to do what he did?

Scratched all over, panicked, confused, on the run, and not liking the sensation, not in the least, he had huddled in the worst of the undergrowth, trusting his senses that warned him against going up the slope and into the forested banks, closer to the town, to the people that might be searching for him. Which turned out to be a correct decision. While lying in the prickly underbrush, half buried in the mud, disgusting as it felt and uncomfortable to defend himself should he be discovered, he could hear the voices coming and going, people cursing and shouting, climbing up and down the banks, the shore back beyond the bend humming with steady but obviously fierce agitation.

At some point, more voices had broken out in frantic then violent shouting, up the bank this time and closer to his hideaway than the shore. Frightened, he had listened to the yelling and whimpering, his senses telling him that those might be the youths from the vantage point he had enjoyed briefly before plunging into adventures that brought him no good, blessing his decision to stick to the unfriendly welcome of bushes and reeds.

When it grew quiet once again, he had clawed his way deeper into the river brush, staying there until the voices of the shore died down. By then, the rain began in earnest and he knew he might have a chance. They wouldn't chase him through the stormy night, would they? He had had enough of running like a spooked deer. It was a novelty to run from anyone, and not a novelty he enjoyed.

And now, here he was, not far away from the town, able to see its flickering lights, the sheltered fires people would make on such nights, to keep nicely warm, to enjoy a good meal and lightened evening while the forest spirits raged or vented their tempers out. Speaking of tempers! He cursed between his teeth, then contemplated his next step for the thousandth time since the darkness fell.

The most sensible thing was to sneak into the town, sniff around, and find someone to ask questions. Did the warrior he stabbed die? Where they in trouble on account of it? No one knew it was him who did the deed, did they? Unless the other warriors, the ones he had managed to escape, remembered his looks, but he was not proposing to stroll among those foreigners. The people of the town were not the ones who should know or care. Unless…

Shivering with cold, he remembered that moment when the sounds of a violent struggle up the higher bank had reached him in his hiding place, suggesting that the youths with whom he had observed the boats at first might have been discovered and probably dragged out, the cowards that they were. If caught by the warriors and suspected of something, a true possibility judging by their yelling and whimpering, then everyone might know who he was by now and not only the stupid foreigners. From their vantage point, those youths must have seen everything that had happened, and if the answers were to be beaten from them…

He ground his teeth, then tried to think lucidly once again, to count his possibilities in the light of the new suspicion. If the entire town was after him and not only the foreigners, then he was better off heading back home and in a hurry. The rainy night was on his side.

The heavy rapping on the greenery all around him intensified, as though suggesting rethinking the matter. To grab a canoe, unobserved and unfollowed, would be easier than to proceed with navigating it. Not a night to paddle the waters he wasn't familiar with. But he would be careful, and he would pause when just a little away from here, wait for the storm to subdue. Then it would be an easy sail, to reach home in just a few dawns, three at the most. To face his father and other elders and explain. Explain what? His arrival in a stolen boat, with no supplies and no decent clothing? And worst of all, with no people he had left with, his own sister among them! The people who would still be here, in this gods-accursed town, detained maybe, held against their will, facing the wrath of the locals and the invaders alike because of his crimes from stealing a boat to harming a foreign warrior; all because of him.

A punch he landed against the trunk of the helpless tree hurt his entire arm. He didn't attempt another one, his muttered curses not overcoming the cacophony of the outside, pitifully weak

compared to the raging rain deity. He was nothing, nothing but a
stupid, mindless buck with bad temper, and they were all out
now, eager to show him just that, even the deities. Another punch
against the rough bark had him groaning aloud. As though he
hadn't collected enough bruises as it was!

By the time the rain lessened to let the moonlight sneak in, he
had run plenty of plans, all coming to nothing, a dead end every
time it came to the problem of his own fellow villagers stuck in
this town like helpless hostages. If only there was a way of
contacting them, letting them know that they must escape as well,
sneak under the cover of the darkness. With no one he knew left
inside the stinking palisade, he could go away, free and proud,
never to set his foot here again, the stupid things he did here
forgotten, at least in his mind. If only there was a way to convince
Nara and Ciki and the rest of them not to let any of it out, to forget
all about it as well. Tcumu would turn a problem, of course, but
he would deal with the foul-mouthed man somehow.

Encouraged, he peered at the brightening darkness, taking in
the muddy ground, all slough of puddles, the water still dripping,
drops ricocheting off leaves and branches. A pretty sight. He
listened intently, trying to remember where the womenfolk of
their delegation slept on the previous night. Conveniently close to
that impressively fortified fence of theirs, but from what side? His
soaked moccasins made plopping sounds, sinking into the mud,
resisting each pull. Curse them all! He pulled them off, but it
didn't help. It only made his feet prey for every piece of bark or
pebble eager to stab them. Was everything against him in this?

When the dark silhouette of the unfamiliar mass of the fence
materialized to his left, he was shaking with cold, clenching his
teeth against their rattling. Enough that his steps weren't as quiet
as they should be. To attempt scaling this wall was out of the
question, but one of the entrances should be near if he
remembered the outlay of the hill surrounding it correctly, close to
the stream they had fished in this afternoon, before he went out to
do stupid things. From there, it should be close enough to the
dwelling his sister and the other two women slept at last night,
just across the square and away from those strange double-

layered mounds of theirs.

Voices poured from the chaparral surrounding what looked like a maize field to his right. Freezing dead on his tracks, he listened, unable to make their words out but still curious, needing to know. Maybe he could talk to these people, ask them about what happened? A stupid idea, of course. They would wish to know who he was, a mud-smeared apparition, half naked and wild-looking, proclaiming his guilt. And what if everyone was looking for him now?

Another outburst of voices assaulted his ears a few paces later, coming from a different direction, louder and surer of themselves.

"Stupid to sneak out on such a night," one of the speakers complained. "I'm soaked and what would we say if those lowlifes run into us on our way back, eh? They wouldn't sleep like normal travelers would. Not them!"

"So what? We can wander around, enjoy the night," another voice countered, sounding calmer than the first, in control.

"Outside in the woods? Who would do that?"

"All sorts of people. The stupid foreigners for one. That brute with the spear that yells at everyone, he went to sniff around the river, didn't he?"

"Or the violent villager they are after." This time, the first speaker sounded more cheerful, his chuckle intermingling with the drizzle. "He must be out there too, swimming against the current."

An outburst of soft laughter answered this claim, causing Iciwata to clench his teeth until they felt like cracking.

"He better swim fast."

Through the glimpses of moonlight, he could see their figures drifting away, carrying baskets, more than one piled upon each straining arm. An evidently heavy burden, but they didn't seem to pant or look uncomfortable otherwise. Where were they going?

Puzzled, he was about resume as silent a progress as he could manage, when another group heralded its approach, this one larger but quieter, concentrated on the burden they carried, in an obvious hurry. They didn't talk at all, passing so close he could hear the rustling of their steps, the familiar plopping.

Hurriedly, he slipped into a gaping split in the nearby trunk, just in case. Were they searching the woods in order to find him? It didn't seem the case. Grinding his teeth, he waited, annoyed with the clouds of mosquitoes that buzzed around him but unable to do something about it, not even knowing what he had been waiting for. They were acting strange, the dwellers of this town. Why?

After being feasted on by the greedy night insects for some time, he forced his way through the bushes, seeking a better vantage point. The moon grew stronger and he needed to know what was going on. Maybe no one was interested in him at all. But for this to turn out a true possibility!

Careful to keep in the soaking wet yet helpful protection of the greenery, he surveyed the partially clear view of the hilly countryside, the stream he had fished with the locals glimmering darkly, the path toward the town twisting like a black snake. A few clusters of people were walking it, returning from the woods, it seemed, unburdened, the baskets he had glimpsed before nowhere in sight, their paces light even from such a distance, skipping between the multitude of roots and bedrocks, in a hurry to return, obviously. The darker mass of the town's fence was even more visible now, a permanent presence. Yet the figures that lingered near the darker gap of the opening did not look like a part of it, moving as though pacing back and forth, carrying long sticks. Spears? His stomach heaved painfully.

Diving back into the protection of the thick vegetation, he tried to make his thoughts organize, his mind running amok again, limbs ready to break into wildest of runs. Did those warriors know? Were they expecting him? Another peek came as an effort, his instincts urging him to run somewhere, anywhere.

The silhouettes were still there, waiting patiently, not about to go anywhere. It was hard to determine how many they were or how well armed in the once-again dimming moonlight. As opposed to them, the people with no baskets made good progress, a quick side-glance told him, reaching the incline he had climbed, clearly in a hurry to approach the town. Were the warriors waiting for them? Oh, every powerful deity of these woods, please let it be so!

He felt his stomach constricting once again, then heaving with relief. The locals coming out with baskets, then going back without them. Were they hiding something out there in the woods? Something they didn't wish to share with the greedy foreigners?

His instincts pushed him backwards and through the shrubs, to make his way hurriedly, careful to create little noise but not overly so. The warriors did not look as though about to leave the wall opening, did they? He pondered about it briefly, remembering what the first pair with baskets he overheard said, that there were some still sniffing around the river. Well, he was far enough from the river now, and those locals, they might appreciate a warning, mightn't they? A timely word about the waiting warriors should make them grateful enough to wish to repay him in this or that way. Bound to!

Skidding upon the slippery mud, he nearly burst into the trail the burdened locals walked earlier, arresting his own progress barely, catching a branch of a tree to do that. It was eerily quiet again and, but for the buzzing of night insects and an occasional distant howling of coyotes, one might have thought that the world froze like in stories told by the winter fire. Had he imagined people moving all over these woods?

Once again, his instincts of a hunter warned him before his mind had time to arrive at conclusions. No branch creaked, but he threw himself sideways all the same, sensing the attack even if not seeing it. Somehow managing to stay upright, twigs of a sprawling tree helpful if cruelly thorny to touch, he glimpsed a silhouette of his attacker wavering, trying to change his direction without going down, unsuccessful on this count. Just a man and not a forest predator. The realization sent a wave of relief down his spine, while his body threw itself once again, this time attacking his assailant, not wishing to let the initiative stay with the enemy.

The collision made them both go down and into the worst of the mud. A nearby puddle splashed them with its revolting substance, but his rival was caught under him and, but for additional hands and feet that joined the fray, he knew he was winning, about to hurt the filthy piece of excrement, to make him pay for attacking him like that.

However, strong hands grabbed him from behind, pulling hard, frustrating his attempts to stay where he was, making his fingers slip from the comfortable hold it got on his rival's throat. To fight them didn't help. In another heartbeat, he was caught in the same puddle, pinned there firmly, with too many limbs to struggle against, just like back in the reeds of the river.

His panicked senses reacted to the recollection with the same degree of madness, throwing every bit of his strength into renewed struggle to break free, oblivious of reason. An entirely new sensation, twice on the same day. Oh, but he had had enough of people attacking him all at once. Back home, no one ever dared to do that.

Careless of his own hurting limbs, he kicked them away, shoving his way back to his feet with the strength he did not suspect himself capable of, his hands clutching a broken log they managed to grab somehow, ready to use it. The echoes of the fighting back in the reeds? He didn't have time to think about it. Their silhouettes were still there, surrounding him, breathing heavily, some still on the ground, groaning.

"Who are you?" breathed someone, the figure nearest to him, leaning forward but as though out of exhaustion, grabbing a sprawling branch with one hand, clearly for support.

"And you?" he rasped, his breathing as heavy, tearing the night, his heart racing madly, about to jump out of his throat.

"You are that villager everyone is looking for, aren't you?" This came from another dark figure standing somewhat apart, his silhouetted hands crossed over his chest, inappropriately calm as opposed to his fellow night travelers. A few more figures were scurrying on the ground, getting up or helping Iciwata's initial attacker out of the puddle, he surmised.

"Why did you attack me?" he demanded, feeling victorious all of sudden, in a position to demand explanations. He did make quite a few of them splash in the mud, didn't he?

"You were sneaking here like the criminal that you actually

are," cried out one of those who seemed to just recently get up. "What were we to do with you?"

"I'm not a criminal!" It came out a little too loudly, an indignant cry. "Whatever the filthy warriors from the west say, I didn't do any crime."

"Except for killing one of them," contributed the man with crossed hands, still the calmest of the group. "Then running all over these woods, spying on us."

"I didn't..." he began, then realized the implications of the first phrase as it sank in his mind. "That man in the reeds, he died?"

"Yes, he did. Badly too. It took him a long time to start on his journey. And a loud affair it was."

Against his will, Iciwata shivered. "They attacked me. I didn't try to attack them or anything."

"Yes, you just spied after them, creeping all over those reeds. Just like you did now."

The openly patronizing interrogation began wearing on his nerves, that and this mounting misunderstanding. He wasn't spying on anyone. Well, back in the reeds, he did that, yes, but it was a good thing, to spy on the enemy, learn about their war canoes and their weaponry, yet he didn't do anything of the sort now.

"I wasn't spying on you and I didn't creep all over these woods," he said firmly, trying to push away the wave of familiar anger, that building-up fury that made him do stupid things back at home often, the source of all his troubles. "I came down here looking for you. That's why I wasn't moving carefully!" The realization that they may have flattered themselves with the idea of catching him while he was "creeping around," frustrating his attempts to spy on them, made his struggle against the fury yet harder. Just who did they think they were! He made another desperate effort to keep his voice calm and his limbs glued to his sides, not an easy feat. "You could have asked what I'm doing here instead of just attacking. That was the stupidest thing to do!"

"Watch your tongue," growled someone, but the man with the linked hands shifted slightly, for the first time displaying that he was not a statuette carved on a stone pipe.

"Do you know us? Why were you looking for us?"

The reasonableness of the tone helped. "I saw you passing here before, with all those baskets of yours. I wasn't spying!" he added hastily, realizing how his words might sound. "I was trying to figure out what to do, how to return back without the western scum knowing about it. I bet they still want to put their hands on me."

"Do they," muttered the man who had attacked him first, mud dripping down his face, visible even in the darkness. The moon was again hiding behind the thick veil of clouds. "Everyone wants to put their hands on you, villager."

"Why?" he asked, mainly to break the silence that was becoming ominously heavy. It was clear why everyone wished to put their hands on him, these people included. He would have been the first one to hunt such a criminal down if in their place.

"Why would this town wish to pay for your crimes?" Again that calm tone, the voice of reason. But did he hate the reasonableness of those words.

"You can't force me to go back. No one can." He wished his words sounded confidently tranquil and not angry and challenging as they came out. "I can beat you all off again, then disappear for good. The easiest deed." But for his people who came here with him, his own sister, Nara, and the others, even that annoying Tcumu. He tried not to groan aloud.

"And leave your fellow villagers to the pay for it, eh?" The man was peeking into his thoughts, apparently. The filthy skunk!

"They will escape too!"

"How?" They still didn't dare to come closer, surrounding him in a halfhearted circle, easy to get away but for their threats. What would they do to Ciki or Nara? What payment would they try to extract?

The black wave was back, threatening to make him attempt more stupid deeds. He felt his teeth creaking from the force he clenched them with. His jowls felt as though they would never manage to move again.

"What do you want?" It came out like a groan, not an intimidating sound at all, professing no strength.

Another spell of silence prevailed. The night was reclaiming its normal tranquility, filling with usual sounds of life, of scurrying rodents and barking coyotes, the buzz of the mosquitoes and other night insects familiar, rejoicing in the storm but also recovering from it. If only there was a way to recover from the happenings on the shore, to forget all about it as well.

"Why did you come looking for us now? To send messages to your folk in the town?" The man with the crossed arms was again the first to break the uncomfortable silence, a practical man.

"I saw the western scum, their warriors. They are waiting for you by your wall, near the opening. Sitting there and waiting." Tiredly, he pointed at the rustling greenery of the incline. "I saw them from up there, most clearly. Loitering near the opening in the wall. Waiting."

Another heartbeat of stillness. "For us?"

He rolled his eyes, a wasted motion in the darkness. "Who else? You were the ones to hide something out there in the woods. Things you don't want to pay the tribute collectors," he added on the spur of a moment, beginning to see possibilities. Maybe, somehow, if they felt grateful enough... Would they at least let his sister slip away? Her and the other two women. Who knew what the western scum would do with them. The memory of the shore and the words the loitering men near the war canoe said about the local foxes made his stomach tighten painfully, with too much rage. Loathsome scum!

"You saw them from up there?" This came from the man he had fought, a matter-of-fact inquiry, with no previous hostility or disdain.

"Yes. You can go and look for yourself. There is a deer track all the way to the top."

"I know *that*!" An impatient exclamation. Then the man calmed again. "Come with me." Curtly, he motioned at one of the muddied figures, then nodded at his leader-like peer. "We'll go and take a look. Will you have trouble keeping an eye on him?"

The man with the linked arms laughed. "No, we won't. Our honorable visitor will go nowhere. Will you, man of valor?"

Iciwata ground his teeth in reply.

CHAPTER 7

She looked different in the moonlight, pleasing the eye even more than back upon the shore, all dimples and soft angles and shy, hesitant smiles. There were no smiles now and no chattiness, of course; still, even in the darkness and the remnants of the drizzling rain, her glance, timid and daring at the same time, made Ahal smile to himself, his tiredness and frustration retreating, if only a little. He was right once again, of course he was, spreading the trap, placing bait like a good hunter, not forced to wait long before the game came. A pretty doe this time, even if he needed her for no playful purposes.

The square was lit generously, the body of the dead warrior spread upon a platform, ready to be buried with the next dawn in the woods, his face and body cleaned of the remnants of the uneasy death, ornamented with decorations provided by the locals with no argument this time, his weaponry by his side, to be buried along with basic provisions, again supplied by the frightened locals. The fires were still glowing strongly, illuminating the towering mass of the higher pair of mounds, casting wild shadows. The other side of the enclosure sank in the darkness, flanked by prolonged line of embankments of no definite purpose, with no crowding locals save the suspected villagers confined to that corner.

Earlier, when the rain weakened, they had put the body up for quick preliminary rites, the warriors spreading their blankets, intending to sleep on the square, not trusting the locals and their hospitality, not after what happened. Following his instructions, Ahal's men nestled close by, just in case, and, completed by the town's elders and various dignitaries lingering around as well, paying respects, not daring to retreat to their homes, the entire enclosure looked as though a celebration was held there. A misleading impression. No one celebrated a thing, and the gloomy mood made the night seem darker than it was, despite the fires.

Fighting his tiredness, the monotonous thumping at his temples annoying, making his eyes hurt, Ahal spent his time talking to the elders, softening the lead warrior's angrily insulting remarks, wishing he could have retired to one of their homes as was customary, to enjoy just a little bit of rest and some sleep. Oh, but he needed it after such an eventful day, full of strenuous rowing until after high noon, then the arrival – docking, dragging the canoes out, supervising the activity of landing, never trusting his underlings or Utawah's men to see to various details – then the flowery politeness on the shore, estimating their prospective hosts, trying not to lose ground even before the negotiations began, the more serious talks in the town cut short by the murder back by the river.

There was no one single calm moment ever since, running back and forth, talking until his throat went hoarse, interrogating, convincing, arguing, then interrogating some more. Given a choice, Utawah would slay half of the town, then punish the surviving half with confiscating everything they had. At the same time, given a choice of their own, the locals would brush the whole incident aside, blaming the visiting villagers and taking their goods if not their lives in their turn, while sending Quachil Thecou delegation off with baskets of fine promises and flowery endorsements. And it all boiled down to his ability to make them all do what he, Ahal, felt fit, a perfect compromise between the opposite attitudes, and without resorting to force. Not an easy feat.

Toward the dusk, the wounded, suffering greatly and screaming in a dreadful voice, died, which made the lead warrior more tractable for obvious reasons. Utawah was not a man of mindless impulses and deeds, if nearly a moon of a journey was any indication, not an unpractical man, even if his temper did snap easily and sometimes with no warning signs. It was possible to handle him without resorting to threats and reminders of his, Ahal's, more senior position. Still, he was relieved to see the man talking reasonably, with no shouting or threatening the hapless locals, a considerable change. They all knew that if the culprit, the filthy villager of bad temper and treacherous disposition, was not found soon, they would have to reach an agreement as to the size and the nature of the compensation that would be given in addition to the amount of goods to be paid as a regular tribute, the amount of which Ahal still had to determine. How much did this town owe to Quachil Thecou as a regular contribution? Talks with the elders and a peaceful evening spent in the town were supposed to help him arrive at the conclusion. Murders and general unrest did just the opposite. He refrained from grunting aloud.

The other side of the square was lit by uncertainly flickering fires, relatively quiet, deserted but for the unfortunate villagers, huddling together, miserable and afraid, the nicely dimply young woman included, now frightened into lack of chattiness and smiles. Herded at the town's square and confined to it, they were side-glanced and looked askance upon, not allowed to go anywhere until their fellow criminal had been found or came back of his own free will, the filthy piece of human excrement that he probably was. What gall! To assault a warrior escorting Quachil Thecou tribute collectors, then run away leaving his fellow villagers – his own sister among them! – to fend for themselves and pay for his crimes. What a lowlife. And yet, the young woman claimed that he wasn't.

He sought her out with his gaze, not willing to be obvious about it. It was not the time for frivolous thoughts, not in the face of the mourning rites that were to be held for the dead warrior, dying in such tortured agony, a terrible death. It still made Ahal shudder, the memory of the screams. Not to mention that if the criminal wasn't found, his word would be the one to decide the fate of the others, an impartial judgment he intended to make, not colored by lusty considerations or thoughts. There were people who enjoyed benefits of such high positions, pleasing themselves freely, expecting to be bribed with gifts consisted of goods of flesh, but he was above any of it. The town would pay what it was supposed to, then add a compensation for the life of the warrior.

Unless Utawah insisted on paying the problematic village itself a visit, to try and hunt the culprit down all the way to his home and thus teach the entire region a lesson. There were merits to such an idea, and Ahal had considered it already, trying to think its advantages and downsides through. The elders of this town, when asked casually, were eager to tell the tales of pearls the villages upstream their so-called Good River produced, plentiful and of a good quality, the jewelry made with it delicate, worthy of trouble sailing after it, even fighting for it. It was plain that the town's elders saw the possibilities to wriggle out of this trouble relatively unscathed, even rewarded maybe. The greed he didn't begrudge them or held against. People were people, everywhere. *Miche-quipy*, peasants, nobles, *considerates*; they all needed means to get along and try to make the life as easy for themselves as they could. The way of life.

Shrugging, he glanced at the woman once again. She was watching him, covertly, but she did, huddling around one of the fires with her fellow villagers, not looking as miserable as one would expect. Perturbed, yes, uncomfortable, hating to spend the night outside and under everyone's accusing eyes surely – who wouldn't? – but not visibly frightened, not haunted.

He made his way toward them, motioning at his followers, some of his men and two warriors assigned to him by Utawah since the afternoon events to stay behind. Violent villagers or not, he could take care of himself, certainly with the womenfolk that made up almost half of their group.

"Are you confined to this part of the enclosure by the word of the town's authorities?" he asked curtly, careful to sound distant but not threatening, wishing to put them at ease.

They froze momentarily.

"Yes," said one of the men after the silence lasted for too many heartbeats, threatening to turn glaring. "We are to wait here until... well, until this matter is settled." He shrugged, then spread his hands to his sides, palms up, telling it all in a simple gesture of acceptance.

Ahal nodded somberly, liking the man's directness almost against his will. "What was your business with this town? Did you come to trade goods?"

"Yes, we did." Politely, the man moved, clearing a space for their guest to squat comfortably, motioning his younger peer to move as well. "We brought goods to exchange for foodstuff, seeds and dried meat." He seemed to be the spokesman of the group, older than his only male peer, a mere youngster by the looks of him and the only one to look frightened. Ahal watched him for another heartbeat, wondering what he knew. The criminal was reported to be a young man as well, maybe a friend of this one. His eyes drifted to the criminal's sister again. Another one to fish for information, definitely. Nothing to do with her looks.

"Did you finish your trade by now?" Appreciating the gesture, the basic politeness of it, Ahal nodded but did not follow the invitation to sit beside their fire as he might have had they been locals of a respectable status. "Were you about to leave?" It was easy to remember the woman's words back upon the shore, informing him cheerfully how her brother had talked them all into staying.

"Yes, we did!" This came from one of the women, a middle-aged matron, respectable looking, the agitation not sitting well with her generously-wrinkled face. "We should have left on the day before instead of listening to the hotheads among us!" A glance she shot at none other than the sister of the culprit could not be mistaken. Oh yes, it was just like the girl told him. Good!

"We traded all we brought here, yes, Honorable Leader." The spokesman took the lead again, this time remembering to add the correct title. Curious, reflected Ahal. They didn't fear him and they didn't remember to talk to him with appropriate humbleness, oh yes, like the girl back on the shore, as though unaware of their different statues. Small village or not, they should have known better. The man seemed to realize that, but the women didn't. Curious, indeed.

"You will do better thinking where your fellow villager is wandering now," he said mildly, hoping his tone projected earnestness and a hint of good will. Their cooperation would certainly reach further if they thought someone was on their side. "Your situation will improve immeasurably when he comes back to confess to his deeds. Maybe to explain and make it all clear," he added as a concession, needing their cooperation but wishing to detect undercurrents as well. The way the young woman winced, turning her face away from the others, her mouth quivering lightly, told him what he needed to know. Disagreements were there, oh yes. Did they actually know where the villager was hiding? Did she? Her eyes dropped and stayed there.

That did it. "You. Come along."

They shifted uneasily, then one of the women, a fleshy matron with joyfully round face, now screwed up in an unbecoming frown, looked up. "What do you want with her, warrior?"

Not your place to ask me such questions, you filthy miche-quipy, he thought but didn't say it aloud, not wishing to scare them into lack of cooperation, certainly not the girl. She was a cute little thing, even now enlivening his mood, making some of the tiredness lift.

"I wish to speak to her, ask her questions." He glanced at them sternly, then shrugged. "She will come to no harm at my hands." She was still squatting, glancing at him from under her brow. He motioned her curtly. "Come."

The darkness was thicker at the edge of the square, with no fires and no steady hum of loud exchanges, quiet talks or too many figures drifting around, restless, uneasy, agitated, warriors and his men. Slowing his step, he glanced at her, satisfied with the litheness of her walk, her step light, disclosing no tension.

"We can talk here," he said, not certain what he wanted to talk about, but pleased to face her without hundreds of eyes upon them, following. What did he want indeed? What help? What cooperation? The murderer was not that important, whether he got caught or managed to escape, heading back home to await the arrival of their forces. But was there a point in the continued progress against the current? They were already more than half a moon of sail away from Quachil Thecou, with one delegation loaded with goods and manpower sent back home by now. Should this town provide them with two, three canoe-loads of goods and enough sturdy men, he might have considered the mission completed, fulfilled to his satisfaction, with no need to continue into the unknown, unless tempted by the promise of rare goods. Pearls, oh yes. The town's elders mentioned those several times in connection with the upstream settlements, didn't they?

"What about?" She slowed her step and was peering at him with touching sincerity, like back on the shore, with no inhibition or fear, no visible understanding of his superior status. Interesting, he thought. Didn't she realize that he held her and her people's fate in his and no one else's hand just now?

"Your brother."

This time, she winced and he regretted the curtness with which his words came out.

"I wish to help you. All of you. You are in trouble, you and your fellow villagers. This town's authorities will not let you go away without paying for his crimes, even if we decided to overlook what happened."

Her eyes dropped, then darted over the dark mass of the prolonged earthwork that was towering close by, arresting their progress. "It wasn't his fault." Her voice trailed off into almost a whisper. "You have to understand. He is not a bad boy, not a malicious person. He has a temper, yes, a hot temper, but he doesn't wish to harm or do bad. He just can't control his temper at times."

"Does it happen to him often, such violent misdeeds?" He wasn't truly curious, not about a wild villager that would be hunted down soon, paying with his life for what he did. Trust Utawah to see to it. Yet, if she kept talking, feeling at ease, then hopefully, she might yield pieces of useful information, chatty thing that she was. "Is he a violent man?"

"No, no! He never killed anyone. No one of our village would do something like that." Her hands pressed to her chest, eager to convince, her eyes boring at him, imploring. Large and nicely spaced and tilted, they dominated her face, the prettiest of sights. "Our men, they are not like that at all. And my brother, he isn't hurting people. Only when he loses his temper, and he never intends to do that."

"He bested two warriors and another two of my men," said Ahal mildly, in the habit of stating the truth. "He must have some experience fighting people. Warriors, or at least hunters. Even the locals who watched from the cliff said he fought like a wild forest beast."

Her shoulders lifted desolately, defeated. Fragile, pleasantly helpless, her eyes clung to him, pleading for help. He suppressed a shrug. There was plenty of help he could offer her, if he wished to do that. It wouldn't be difficult to prevail upon this town's authorities, to force them into letting her and her fellow villagers go with or without compensation, ample or not. Even her brother could be spared brutal execution when he got caught. A strong youth good with his hands could always come handy in the mound-building projects, such as the one he was requested to supply workers for. More than two dozen were sent on already, and additional half a dozen men about to be collected, but an exceptionally strong villager from the faraway side of the river, an exotic addition, would certainly not be turned away, if he could be trusted to behave. A big "if."

"Back on the shore, you said he was the best hunter, didn't you? The strongest, the fastest..." Oh yes, the young criminal could round the count of requested men, unless impossible to handle. A fair assumption. He wished she went away for a little while, until he thought it all through.

"He is, oh yes! He is the best in everything." She nodded vigorously, her eyes opening impossibly wide, their innocence spilling, not pretended or exaggerated, not as far as he could judge. "It is no wonder he managed to escape these men. He is the strongest, oh yes. He killed a giant bear. Alone, and with nothing but his spear, he faced the forest monster just a few dawns ago. He took it down with one single throw. He is *that* brave and his spear or his bow never err." Her smile was back, as wide and as uninhibited as back on the shore, adorning her cheeks with two dimples, like Lallak's, one more pronounced than the other.

"He is that good, eh?" Shaking his head, he tried to think it all through.

Utawah would make trouble, but he could handle him, squeeze

a worthwhile compensation out of the town instead, pacify the lead warrior for the time being; well, to a degree. Letting these villagers go could be a part of the general settlement of this round of tribute. He could prevail on the elders in this matter, oh yes. And then, if decided so, they would proceed up the river and toward the pearl-producing village itself to collect additional goods and maybe more compensation for the life of the dead warrior. The wild villager, if he had fled this area by now, would be rushing back home, wouldn't he? Where else was one to flee? And then, after laying their hands on the young criminal, it would be up to him to decide whether to let the warriors take his life as a payment or trade it off for a labor of a few moons. The new mound could use additional hands, especially of strong willful peasants who would have no choice but to behave, knowing that the lives of their family members were to be forfeited otherwise. Unless the young hothead didn't care for anyone but himself, which his current actions actually hinted at.

He looked at her again, aware that she was talking, praising her criminal of a brother, her face animated, the dimples again on full display. A smile threatened to sneak out against his will. "Are you always that talkative?"

She paused abruptly, her eyes opening yet wider, the smile quivering, threatening to dim. "What?"

"You are talking and talking." He grinned mainly to keep her from closing up again. "You never stop. Are all you villagers upstream like that, lively and bubbling?"

This time, she giggled. "No, no. Of course not."

He nodded solemnly. "Thought so." There was no need to force his smile into staying; it was widening all by itself, the sight of her dancing eyes and the crinkling lines of laughter around them helping along. "So back in your village, is that what you do? Talk and giggle all day long?"

The dimples multiplied. "Not only."

He glanced at the darkness spreading behind the earthwork's wide base, plastered with damp grass and the brown mass of the muddy earth. Beyond it, the dwellings of people would spread, or maybe another square, the way toward the palisade, a possible opening in it, not the one leading toward the river. The forest spreading behind it would be now hostile, soaking-wet, inimical. Not a place to stroll in the company of a pretty girl, to enjoy her allure. He had no leisure for that anyway. It was certainly not the time, and she might come to expect special favors, better terms for her countryfolk, leniency for her criminal of a brother.

"Do you know where your brother is now?" he asked more curtly than intended, glancing at some of his men who were lingering nearby, the torch one of them held glimmering brightly, freshly made, well oiled. "It is imperative that he came back of his own free will, confessed of his deed. If he does that and if he is as strong and as good as you claim, then he may not need to pay with his life for what he did. Maybe," he added carefully, not wishing to give out firm promises, not yet. She would have to do with a mere possibility for now. After all, it wasn't she who would be taken back to Quachil Thecou, expected to slave for quite a few moons and to do so humbly, with no violent spells of hot temper.

"I don't believe that he left," she was saying, her words gushing again, the smiles and the dimples gone. "He wouldn't have done that, not to us. He is not cowardly. He wouldn't run away just like that. Not him." When earnest and pleading, she looked not nearly as pretty, with no dimples or crinkling lines of laughter around her eyes. Still, the wish to comfort her was there, warm in his chest. "It must have been an accident, you see? He must have tried to get away from these men. Because he wouldn't have attacked them just like that, for no reason and with no weapons. He is not violent in this way, and we never see warriors or... or the others... Your people, they never visit our village. Red Horn town only, once in many seasons. And this one..." Her voice was trailing off, dissipating in the surrounding darkness.

"Your village was never visited, eh?" He shrugged, reminded of his own tiredness. "You must help us find your brother. Think of ways to do that. If you have found him and let him know that there are ways to pay for his crimes, not necessarily with his life or the freedom of you and the other villagers, it might help." He shrugged again, liking the way she was peering at him, with unabashed attentiveness. "If he isn't a coward, he must come back, face his fate. If what you say about him is true, then he will."

"But how do I find him?" Her forehead, high and free of hair, which was tied on her nape somewhat carelessly, with occasional fringes fluttering in the cold breeze, creased. "How would I make him know? And also..." Her eyes narrowed for the first time, suspicious. "What will you make him do? How will he pay for... for what he did?"

The conversation was turning tiring and purposeless. He wasn't here to bargain with lowly villagers. "He will pay with work. It is the only way. Unless he has plenty of goods to offer stashed back in your village." *And now go back and think of ways to locate him,* he wanted to add, annoyed with the wish to linger some more, to prolong the conversation. It was ridiculous, wasn't it? And unnecessary, a waste of time. "What do your people do besides farming and fishing? And hunting bears alone, armed with spears."

That made her smile return promptly. "We do plenty. We aren't lazy or as poor as some town-people would love to think we are."

That was more like it. "They certainly think that you have nothing but deerskins and some dried meat to spare." He spread his arms wide, palms up. "That's why they are so upset with you now. They think they will have to pay for what your brother did, knowing that you have nothing to offer in compensation."

"They said that?" she cried out, the smile gone again. "But those are lies! We came to trade our goods with them just now, beautiful decorations, necklaces, shirts. They are the ones to pay us with food for those. Not the other way around!"

"Simple jewelry, they said." It was too easy to lead her on. He felt a prickle of irritation against the stupid feeling that it wasn't worthy or right to play games designated for crafty elders with her. "Nothing as beautiful as pearls. Only some polished bone."

"Pearls?" she cried out so loudly, the people with torches who had gone toward one of the fires in the meanwhile looked back at them. "They said we didn't bring any pearls?"

He shook his head noncommittally.

"Oh, but those are lies, open lies! Our pearls are most beautiful and the people of this very town are eager to exchange plenty of goods for them. Not only here but other villages downstream are asking to get our decorations. Kayina makes the most beautiful earrings and bracelets and necklaces out of her pearls. Everyone wants to wear them. Not only her pearls, but the decorations she makes out of mussels' pieces too. They took everything we brought on the day before." Again too loud of an exclamation. "Everything!"

Ahal nodded to himself, satisfied. "I see." By the pair of the strangely curving mound, Utawah's stocky figure was pacing impatiently, unmistakably his, a torch in his hand flickering angrily.

What now? he wondered, knowing that he should be there with his men, calming the spirits, or better yet, retiring to one of the elders' houses for a good rest. Even though the results of this side conversation were rewarding, confirming their next destination, justifying the chase of the criminal should the young hothead turn out to be successful at getting away. It was better for everyone that he came back and confessed, sparing them the trouble of chasing him down or making an example out of the rest of his countryfolk. This young woman did not deserve to take the brunt, did she?

He pushed away the wish to ask her more questions. "Go back to your people. While resting, think about the ways of letting your brother know."

She watched him from under her brow, then nodded solemnly, as though satisfied with making her point. He refrained from shaking his head or smiling too widely. No Lallak that, not a petulant creature. What was this girl's name anyway?

"Will you go after him all the way to our village if he doesn't come back?" she was asking, walking beside him, her head down, deep in thoughts.

"Yes." There was no need to let her know that they would be going upriver now regardless, after what she said. The crafty elders of this town didn't lie about the pearls. "A crime should be answered for, any crime, let alone something as grave as a murder. Do the elders of your village let killing of people or stealing or maiming go unanswered?"

"No," she whispered, her head hanging miserably now, defeated.

He fought the urge to touch her in order to reassure, wishing she would return to her previous chattily enthusiastic state. The fire of the villagers was in their sight again, as weakly flickering as the other flames that were blazing with might and challenge, as though reflecting on the general mood.

"He won't be forced to pay with his life. I already promised you that."

Her nod was as listless as her last words were.

"You can't ask for more than that." Irritated, he found himself laboring on, annoyed with himself for being cornered into the need to justify something as simple and to a common village woman, even if as attractive as this one. There was no time to even fool around with her if she was willing – an unclear prospect so far – and if he himself wished to do so. There were too many problems to solve. "Your brother's troubles or not, your village still needs to pay the tribute. Every settlement along our Great River, or what you call Good River, pays. It has nothing to do with your brother or his misdeeds."

But why was he doing it, justifying his mission before this village woman? The wish to turn around and let her find her own way back to her people and their miserable fire welled. There was too much to do and she had served her purpose, hadn't she? And why was she trailing behind now, falling out of his step.

"I didn't thank you before," she was saying, halting for good, the frown upon her face fitting this time, clearly visible in the light of the fire, not looking out of place. "You were so good to us, from the very beginning. I thank you for that. I truly do. And if I sounded complaining before... Well, no, I wasn't complaining. Not at all." The smile was back, beautifully wide, open, causing only one of the dimples to return, enough to make his insides warm again. "I thank you for everything you did for us."

"It's nothing," he said, forcing a smile, his eyes following a few tendrils that escaped the simple leather band that tied her hair on her nape in no intricate fashion. If back in the relative privacy of the curving earthworks, he might have reached out, to push away the unruly hair, or maybe take her into his arms. The temptation was strong, surprisingly powerful.

"Honorable Leader." One of his men was nearing them hurriedly, his arms spread forward, palms up, as though warding off an unwarranted accusation of intrusion.

Ahal glanced at the girl. "Go back to your people. If the local authorities bother you, let me know."

Before turning to go, he noticed that the villagers' fire was surrounded by more than the original six silhouettes, the newcomers, at least two more figures, standing instead of squatting, looking ill-at-ease.

CHAPTER 8

The darkness was at its thickest when the locals came back and went away again, only two men this time, soaked as though the storm was still raging. It wasn't, but the wet trees shed plenty of drops, and Iciwata knew that he himself did not look any better.

Starved and exhausted, he had huddled in the space two thick trucks had created, alert to every possible sound of movement, knowing that for now he had been turned into prey for every living creature bigger than a squirrel, from forest predators to people, all eager to catch him and tear him apart given half an opportunity.

Well, he wasn't about to offer them anything of the sort, but the waves of tiredness didn't help, the rambling of his stomach the only thing to keep his eyelids from turning to heavy, from sliding down and staying this way. What an annoyance!

The locals he had managed to talk into helping him, grateful for his timely warning that they were, had gone back to the town and didn't seem as though in a hurry to keep their promise of coming back or aiding his fellow villagers to escape through the same back openings they had intended to use in order to slip in. Apparently, they had been sneaking out certain costly valuables the filthy westerners might have wished to lay their greedy hands on. Why argue about the amount of goods to be handed over when those same goods could be made disappear, not raising any questions at all? The tribute collectors did not bother them for a long time, he had been told, so no one remembered what amounts were to be handed over, and with the backing of so many warriors, the greedy westerners might turn yet greedier. One never knew with those men.

Why didn't they fight the annoying lowlifes? he had asked angrily, appalled by the very idea that not only could people come and take what they liked, but that they could change the amount of the "owed" goods at their will. But what gall! The rare instances when some tribute collectors were rumored to visit this or that settlement came to plenty of flowery talks and little goods handled over, or so the visitors from such places boasted at times. As far as he knew, nothing was smuggled away and into the woods. Unless the talkative travelers missed those particular parts of the story, or he himself did not pay much attention, being still too young when the last reports came through, or too indifferent. Well, now he did care, enough to manage causing damage.

He cursed under his breath, too spent to do so loudly, afraid to draw attention. Stabbing a warrior to death while fighting off two more of the filthy lowlifes, weaponless as he was, improvising with rocks or canes, might have been a brave deed, worthy of a hunter of his caliber, the bear slayer, but for the unfortunate circumstances surrounding it. If not for the rest of their people being trapped behind the clay-covered fence, he would have been gone already, heading home, to boast his deed and warn his village against the coming of the filthy enemy. They could have prepared a worthwhile welcoming, couldn't they? Trap those war canoes while they were busy paddling along, shoot at them from both sides. Why didn't the cowardly locals attempt to do that here?

There was no point in trying any of that, claimed his unasked-for companions, growing angered with his questioning, taking those personally as they actually should have. Warriors were no people to try and best with hunting bows and spears. Besides their war canoes and their viciousness, those people had clubs and longer flint javelins, quite vicious weaponry and not just hunting tools. And moreover, they knew how to wield them against human foe and not just a herd of a fleeing deer. To confront the warriors from the west was the peak of stupidity, and didn't his own experience teach him that much?

To counter that with the claim that he had actually killed a warrior and with no worthwhile weaponry at all – not even his "hunting tools" as they had called their bows and spears with such annoying disdain – did nothing to calm the spirits. However, by this time, they were all making too much noise, and the older among the locals motioned them all to shut up and go back through alternate openings in their impressively high, strangely plastered palisade, drawing no attention to their return, empty-handed or not. There was no need to raise questions from their distrustful guests, their suspicion made obvious by the warriors patrolling the gates. Although, of course, the warriors might have been waiting for him and not the wandering locals at all, eager to lay their hands on their fellow warrior's killer.

The gazes Iciwata had received served to sober his mood, no matter how heroic he privately thought his deed was. The instinct of self-preservation kicked in, a rare thing to happen, and he had tuned his tone down, drawing the older man, the one who seemed to be in charge of the entire group, aside. What did he think of this entire situation? he had asked as humbly as he managed, making a conscious effort to sound unassuming, even afraid. What would be the consequences of his deed for the town itself, and not only his fellow villagers? Did he land any of them in trouble?

His stomach fluttered at the effort, hating it all, them and this entire situation, and the need to humble himself, but somehow he managed to make the man listen, promising to repay everything these people might have been forced to hand over because of his deed, every single bracelet or foodstuff, every extra ear of maize or the smallest among the additional tools.

And now, here he was, waiting at the designated place, wavering between confidence and despair, not certain of his next step. What if the locals did not believe him, did not feel grateful enough for his previous help to repay him by passing word to his fellow villagers, aiding their possible escape? What if moreover, they had let the enraged invaders know and so their ferocious warriors were now on their way here? Could he trust them? And how was he to repay them if they did keep their word and helped them all escape? Would he manage to talk the elders, Father and others, into letting him have so many goods to hand over? If the western scum was to head on up the river, they might be arriving in their village as well, and then there would be no goods to repay left anyway. What a stupid predicament!

The forest rustled loudly all around him, the wind strengthening, the darkness thickening, promising more rain. He tried to listen, huddling against the rough bark, frozen to his bones. It didn't feel like the end of hot moons at all.

Shivering, he considered climbing the tree, or any other silhouetted trunks towering all around. It might give him an edge if someone came here trying to surprise him, as well as keep him well away from the howls of coyotes, too numerous for his liking, resounding through the darkness, a piercing hoot of an owl making him jump with its pronounced mournfulness. But what spirits were now lurking in this forest, what deities? The knife felt slick in his palm, the wet bark of the tree hard against this back. To climb it would be a desperate solution. He would tear his skin all over and would probably fall down anyway, breaking his limbs as a reward for the try.

Busy thinking of his possibilities, he nearly missed a deliberate plopping in the mud. And then all other considerations fled his mind, and he was clawing his way up, clinging to the cruelly sharp bark with everything he had, his hands, feet, his entire body. The lower branches, too thick to cling to comfortably, tried to get in his way, but the noisy breath behind his back gave his limbs yet more power. And the smell, oh that unmistakable stench of foul breath and wet, smudged, muddied fur!

He held his breath, not daring to make additional sounds. The racket he must have created while storming that tree must have been more than enough, and they could climb, not grizzled bears, but the others. Oh yes, they were climbers! Better than the two-legged creatures, swifter and more agile when on the ground or above it.

His heart was thundering in his chest, interfering with his ability to listen. Had the monster gone up the same tree already? Or was he just sniffing the ground, taking his time? The noisy snoring let him know that the latter must be the case. His palms tightened around their precarious hold, the knife's handle cutting into his skin, somehow still there, clenched between his sweaty fingers. If worst came to worst, then... Then what? What could he do with a knife and nothing else, blind in the darkness, with no surprise of the initial attack and nowhere to run, to retreat, to climb, or jump?

He clung to the slippery branch, not daring to pull himself up in order to perch more comfortably. What would it help if the monster went after him, surely seeing better than him, at home in the rain-soaked darkness.

The sniffing went on for some time, accompanied with ridiculous grunts. He wanted to laugh hysterically, knowing that his precarious perch wouldn't hold should he succumb to an inappropriate fit of mirth. The beast might appreciate an easy meal, but...

His heart came to halt once again, detecting other more distant sounds. Cracking of branches and voices, oh mighty spirits, but someone was walking the foot of this hill, heading toward him. More locals smuggling out goods? Warriors combing the woods, hot on his heels maybe, if the locals did betray him after all? Oh yes, yes, please let them come here, straight into the beast's claws. A perfect solution!

The bear stopped wheezing and seemed to be listening too, as hopeful maybe. Oh yes, warriors would be a decent enough challenge for the old sticky-mouth. Unless...

His heart missed a beat once again, then threw itself wildly against his chest, causing the wet branch to nearly slip from under him. Unless it were his fellow villagers, Ciki and Nara and the others, coming here just like he wanted to, having managed to escape the accursed town. If the locals passed on word just like they promised to do, then it might be them, and then, oh mighty spirits, but then they would be in a grave danger.

He tried to slam his mind into working. The distant creaking stopped for good, but the bear did not resume his sniffing around. Instead, he froze, obviously there, but keeping his quietest. A crafty beast! Iciwata didn't dare to draw in a breath.

A heartbeat passed, then another, then ten more. He counted them, finding nothing better to do. The bear under his tree began breathing noisily again, clearly returning to its previous activities. There must be something tempting there, something delicious, like an anthill or a heap of sweet roots. Just his luck to have the old sticky-mouth that busy under his tree.

Again muffled sounds drifted in with the renewed gust of wind, coming from closer proximity now, maybe halfway up the hill. Some creaking, then voices, unmistakable now. People were walking not too far away in the dampness of the woods, among the continued trickling. The rain had stopped for so long now, but the forest enjoyed recreating it, its spirits busy at work. He wished to have a fire at hand, one of those well-oiled torches the dwellers of this town sported with easy wastefulness, at their homes and outside, on the night before. What riches!

He tried to see through the darkness, hoping to detect the flicker of a distant light moving, wishing there would be none. If the locals betrayed him, the warriors looking for him would be certain to carry torches, and the bear was still there, clearly interested in the happenings all around, not in the mood to retreat before the unknown.

"Iciwata!"

The faint cry made him catch his breath: weak, distant, but unmistakable. His name! Someone was calling him in the darkness, a female voice, familiar even from such a distance. His insides quivered with excitement, then shrank with dread. Ciki? Coming here – *just like he wanted, following his word!* – straight into the danger of the wandering bear.

Another repeated cry sounded stronger, oh yes, heading in his direction, reinforced by an additional voice. A male this time. Still, not nearly enough against the bear, whatever its size or age was. If only he could determine that! With no surprise on their side, people were powerless against the rulers of the forest unless in large, well-organized groups set on a planned out hunt. That was when the old sticky-mouths got edgy, trying to run away instead of attacking sometimes. There were ways to make them run, oh yes.

The new thought made his skin prickle. Tricky and dangerous, but what choice did he have? Judging by the beast's placid behavior, it didn't seem to know someone was up that tree; or maybe it managed to forget it somehow, or just didn't care. And if so, the element of surprise still might be on his side, if he jumped down just like that, out of nowhere, landing in the darkness and making plenty of noise. Such a deed might cause the forest master get frightened and flee, mightn't it?

The voices drew away, then intensified again. No more calling of his name, but they were talking, their words muffled, carried by the wind. The bear was growling quietly, as though warning them to go away. If it wanted to charge, it would have gone in their direction already. He willed them to go elsewhere, not daring to pray, remembering his lies concerning the old grizzly he slew – he didn't pray while hunting it, didn't address its spirit after besting it. He lied about it and now he was paying the price.

The decision arrived, a foolish one, but he found no better one. Clenching his teeth, he bettered his grip on the slippery branch, then concentrated, listening to the bear and not the cracking of nearing footsteps. If walking their own woods, unafraid of being detected, they would have spoken loudly now, warning the forest creatures such as the one huddling under his tree. That was what people did if forced to wander the woods; however, this time, they were not legitimate walkers themselves. The warriors and some other locals might be on the lookout for them.

The bear growled again, this time more loudly, and the creaking stopped abruptly, as did the muffled halo of a faint light. So now they paid attention. Good for them. He didn't wait for the encounter to develop. Pushing the branch he perched on away, disregarding his instincts that urged him to cling to it against the decisions of his mind, he did his best propelling his body away from the location of the growling, yelling as he did this, hitting too many obstacles on his way, all those sticking out sprigs. But how high did he manage to climb before? The racket his fall created should have disturbed spirits living in another world. So much noise!

He tried to protect his vitals from the fall, flogged by the sticking out twigs with no mercy, curling into a ball while hitting the ground, which plopped wetly, softening his fall with its soaked, muddied touch, not nearly enough but more than nothing. Disoriented, he tried to get a grip, spitting the mud out, in the corner of his mind remembering the need to make noise. An easy feat now. The howl of pain that accompanied his leap back to his feet must have been deafening in its genuineness, better than anything he could have hoped for. Busy gasping with pangs of agony that shot through his stomach before he took his weight off one of his legs, he wondered where the beast was. Should he dash around some more? Go on screaming? With his ears ringing, plugged with mud, it was difficult to tell.

Then, just as he leaned against a half crooked stump of a tree, his head reeling and his body feeling too battered to support his one-legged stance, more cracking and plopping erupted and he sought his knife frantically, aware that it wasn't there anymore, grabbing a twig that wasn't nearly thick enough to fight off an attack of a toddling baby, let alone angered bear. Curse it all!

The light pounced on him, illuminating the cozy enclosure, a mess of twisted roots and rocks and broken branches and saplings. The marks of the bear were everywhere, unevenly round footprints and torn pieces of bark, one of the trunks bleeding sap from its long vicious gaps. He didn't wish to think of the creature's size.

Instead, he put his attention on Nara's gaping face, followed by Ciki and one of the locals he found easy to recognize. Then the realization dawned and he whooped with joy, forgetting that now, with the bear gone, it was wiser to actually keep very quiet. It didn't matter. The victory was clearly his again, and what a victory it was!

"What happened?" panted Nara, while Ciki threw herself at him, hugging him fiercely, her hands wandering in a not entirely sisterly fashion, feeling his injuries out. She was always like that, the big sister. He felt like laughing hysterically.

"Was there a bear here?" Nara was still blinking stupidly, his torch flickering, surprisingly well oiled. The local who probably was holding it in the first place gripped a nice-looking club, clutching it with both hands.

"What do you think?" He pushed his sister's hands away,

needing to come to grips with the reality himself. "He was growling and growling, trying to warn you, but you kept walking here with not a care in the world."

"And where were you?" cried out the local, clearly offended.

"He was busy falling out of the tree," giggled Ciki, releasing him but not stepping back, just in case. "Right on top of the old sticky-mouth."

"I did it on purpose!" he protested, offended by her lack of appreciation for what he did. It was brave, wasn't it, another one of those deeds no one could boast but him. "Otherwise, he would be busy tearing you all apart now."

They acknowledged it with an appropriate bout of silence.

"Tell him what you came to tell," said the local finally, shifting his club into one hand while motioning at Nara to hand the torch over. "We don't have time for storytelling here."

Iciwata clenched his teeth, angered by such a dismissive telling off. Just who did this man think he was?

"What?" he demanded, making a point of ignoring the armed local with his fancy torch. "Why only the two of you here? Where are the others?"

The glances Nara and Ciki exchanged made him forget the annoyingly haughty local.

CHAPTER 9

"I know where Iciwata is hiding."

The man looked furtive and afraid, to Ahal's new bout of suspicion. The spokesman among the villagers, he had noticed that one before, lingering in the darkness, not daring to come near the doorway and into the light the fireplace in the middle of the elder's dwelling cast.

Making himself comfortable on the widest, most padded of the wall benches, a place of honor for the exalted visitor, Ahal had pushed his tiredness away, his mind swarming with plans, needing time to think it all through, not thrilled with the need to maintain conversation, to respect the elder whose hospitality he had accepted out of politeness, preferring to stay on the square with his men. Who knew what developments he might miss on such an eventful night, but the elders had been adamant, refusing to leave the square before the most respectable among the visitors did. The rules of hospitality were apparently the same everywhere. Briefly, he glanced at the doorway once again.

"Tomorrow, with the dawn, we shall have a feast," the elder was saying, flanked by a few more respectable-looking men and some women rushing in the background, spreading additional pelts and blankets upon various banks or clanking with their pottery. It was nearing midnight, but under current circumstances, no one seemed to be about to retire to sleep. The whole town was alive with dots of flickering fires. "What happened on the shore was a most unfortunate interruption, an incident that should never have happened."

"It is," agreed Ahal, wishing nothing more than to be left alone, to enjoy the privacy to think it all through, catch up on some sleep maybe, talk to his people, or the warriors, or maybe the villagers, in case they found a way to send word to their fellow young criminal. That girl was vigorous, and seemingly practical; she might have managed.

The old eyes were studying him, brimming with wisdom. Reading his thoughts? He pushed irrelevant musings away. Maybe when reaching her village…

"The unfortunate incident aside, your hospitality is beyond reproach, Honorable Elder. I shall report it as such back in our glorious capital of the Great River."

Idly, his eyes followed a young woman whose decorated skirt clanked with soft ringing of birds' claws, enhanced by the vigorous sway of her hips as she passed him, heading toward the doorway, following a curt command of an older woman. This one was staring at the opening, her frown pronounced.

"We are honored to receive visitors of your importance, Honorable Leader," the elder repeated, talking empty politeness for quite a long time. *If you are so honored, then you won't make trouble in contributing goods toward Quachil Thecou's wellbeing,* thought Ahal to himself, knowing that flowery talk had usually nothing to do with any actual deeds.

The pretty thing by the doorway was talking hurriedly, exchanging hushed-up sentences, addressing the man who was trying to peek in, of that Ahal was certain. When the argument peaked, even the elders began glancing her way.

"What is it, Daughter?" their host demanded finally, his wrinkled features set in a hint of displeasure.

The young woman hesitated. "The villager, he begs the honor of addressing your guest, Honorable Father."

All faces turned to Ahal, as though by a prearranged sign. He made sure his nod was deliberate, expressing no eagerness to know. It was about the villager, wasn't it? And it didn't come through Utawah or one of the warriors, who wouldn't hesitate to enter this or any other dwelling.

"I'll see him," he said coldly, returning his gaze to his host.

But the visitor refused to come in, and more loudly whispered exchanges took place before Ahal could allow himself to be persuaded, fighting the urge to rush out right away. Inappropriate for the man of his status, of course, but for the afternoon happenings.

To a certain sense of disappointment that irritated him with its unreasonableness – he didn't expect the village girl to come after him in the middle of the night, did he? – the man who dared to request a clandestine audience looked only slightly familiar, the one who had spoke for his fellow villagers, a person of average looks, his face as weather-beaten as that of a typical peasant, stout and hardy, another one fit for lifting heavy baskets. His expression was the only one to stand out, troubled, furtive, even afraid.

"I know where Iciwata is hiding."

Ahal watched him for another heartbeat, letting his gaze turn piercing. Was that the villager's name? Iciwata? A mighty strong name by the sound of it.

"Where is he hiding?" he asked, leaving his unasked-for informer to disclose all that he knew before revealing his knowledge or the lack of it. He should have inquired with the girl about her brother's name. And her own, for that matter. "How did you come by this knowledge, villager?"

The man tensed visibly, expecting maybe a warmer reception of his clearly promising news. "I… I will tell you all that. Honorable Leader," he added somewhat hastily, again not sounding practiced at using titles at all. "But you have to promise… I will ask you to promise, that is… to promise that the rest of our people aren't harmed or prevented from leaving this place."

Through the depths of the painful frown, it was easy to see the man's tension; and his fear. Oh yes, this one knew he was out of his depth and possibly getting himself in trouble.

Ahal pursed his lips. "You are in no position to bargain for terms, villager," he said coldly, not raising his voice, but actually lowering it, knowing the effect of a slow, low-toned speech. At times, it made people's fear grow worse than a thundering roar would. "The information you have – and the ways of you receiving it! – might be already in my and my lead warrior's possession. And the missing parts of it might be beaten out of you easily. Do not try playing games with me!"

By the end of his growling tirade, the man was terrified enough to take a step back, then another, his nape pressing against the nearby pole, with nowhere to retreat unless opting for turning around and running into the darkness. Something the frightened informer might have been contemplating actually.

Ahal moderated his tone. "Tell me what you came to tell me."

A heartbeat of paralyzed silence let the hushed voices around them fill the night. Oh yes, not many slept snugly, not tonight.

"Tell me!"

He didn't take a step forward, but he made it look as though he might, marking the man's looks in case this one fled after all and he would have to give the warriors his description.

"One of the locals came…" The man licked his lips hastily, then coughed, clearing his throat. "He said that Iciwata is out there, in the forest. Hiding. On the hill facing the back of this town's fence. Halfway down it. He is hiding there."

"From our warriors?"

"Yes."

"Why did he send a local to let you know that? Why you, of all people?"

Why not his sister? he asked himself. Or his friend she had mentioned? Unless this man was the mentioned friend, and then the villager displayed poor judgment in choosing his confidents.

"Me?" The man looked genuinely surprised. "No. The local man came to talk to us. All of us. We were sitting by the fire out there. On the square. Where you came to talk to us and Ciki. The local came there."

Ciki, thought Ahal. A cute little name, as cozy and as rounded as she was.

"What did he tell you?"

"He said that Iciwata is hiding out there. Out there on the hill. Behind the opening in the fence that does not lead to the river."

Ahal nodded again. "Come along."

"Where to?"

"Along!" He squashed the man with his gaze, aware of his continued dislike, puzzled by it. There was something about this villager, something shifty, an exact opposite to the girl's naïve honesty. "Why did they send you to talk to me? Why you in particular?" Hastening his step, he made sure the man following a few paces behind, wary and openly fearful again. What was he so afraid of?

"I... well... I suppose... I don't know why me. Any one of us could have come, yes." The words barely managed to overcome the muffled rustling of the night, trailing off pitifully.

Ahal felt no compassion. "Not everyone among you was so eager to sell off his own countryfolk, eh? Some of you must have better principles than that."

Did she argue against it? he wondered. What did she propose to do with this unexpected knowledge of her brother's whereabouts? The question made him uneasy.

"I'm not selling off my countryfolk," the man was protesting, gathering enough courage to talk in a stronger voice. "Iciwata is the one who doesn't care for anyone but himself. That young hothead is always this way, thinks himself to be better than everyone, cares for no one. There are six of us trapped here because of him, about to pay for his violence and stupidity. It isn't just to expect us to pay while he walks away as though nothing happened. "

There was the truth to this statement. Ahal shrugged. "If he cared for no one but himself, he would be running back home with no one the wiser." It was ridiculous to defend the stupid villager and his possible motives. He motioned the man to walk faster, still wondering why the girl did not volunteer to find him instead of the shifty man of dubious looks.

The warriors were milling next to the fires, most of them awake but not daring to spread around the town as they might have done under regular circumstances. Ahal beckoned one of them.

"Bring word to your leader. Tell him..." He hesitated, suddenly not certain he wished to involve Utawah. The fierce warrior might prove difficult and he did promise the girl to have her brother paying with work, not his life. "Tell your leader I wish to speak to him here, and with no delay." The proud lead warrior might not take it kindly, such ordering about. He might ignore the presumptuous summons, and thus, leave him, Ahal, to deal with the trouble all by himself and as he saw fit. Good!

His informant was still there, chewing his lips, looking more uncomfortable with every passing heartbeat. "Where is the local who told you about the villager? Bring him here. Or better yet, take me to see him. Is he still around that fire of yours?"

The man shook his head helplessly.

"Where is he?"

"Gone, I think. Well, he may still be around. I... I'll go and see if he is." At that, the man actually tried to dart into the flickering darkness behind the warriors' fires, but Ahal was faster, grabbing his shoulder in an uncompromising grip, making his victim whirl around too sharply, nearly losing his balance in the process.

"You are going nowhere until I say you are."

The man was staring at him wildly, still wavering, spreading his hands in order to maintain his balance, not looking helpless or afraid, not anymore.

"Tell me what you didn't tell me until now and do it fast." He motioned at another spearman. "Get half a dozen of your fellow warriors ready. In no more than a hundred heartbeats. Hurry!"

"What for, Honorable Leader?" The warrior looked more bewildered than the assaulted local, blinking in quite a stupid way.

"Do as I say!" growled Ahal, not pleased with such challenging of his authority, certainly not in front of the local whose cooperation he needed, out of fear or respect—it didn't matter. "Hurry!"

The spearman fled away and toward the fires.

"Now tell me what you didn't tell me before, villager. Or your guts will be covering this square while I ask the same question your other fellow villagers, getting faster answers. Talk!"

The color was gone from the round, homely face, and for a wild moment, he wished the man would faint so he could proceed with his threat of going on to question the others. The girl's tales would be surely more comprehensive than that.

"I told you everything, I did," mumbled the man, wincing when Ahal's fingers dug into his shoulder, still gripping it, with all his force now. "The local youth, he told us... There were two of them, but only one stayed to talk to us. I'm not making it up!"

"Come with me." Shoving his victim ahead, he turned toward the darker side of the square and the miserable fire of the villagers, the one that gave little light or warmth.

"What for?" The man resisted the continued pull, struggling to break free now. Ahal shoved him again too sharply, this time causing his victim to crash down and into the muddied earth.

"What you are not telling me?"

"I... I..." This time, the interrogated villager pushed himself up with surprising agility, on his feet again and looking as though ready to put out a fight. "I'm telling you everything. But the local, he isn't here. He might have gone back to the woods."

"What for? To warn the villager?" He heard his voice piquing and made a conscious effort to bring it back down to reasonable tones. "Who else went back into the woods with him?"

The suspicion surfaced, too unwelcome to let it in just like that. The girl! But of course. Being the criminal's sister, worried as she was, defending her brother's actions as she did with him before. And also, hadn't he told her to try and think how to locate the wild villager, how to make him know that he wasn't going to die if he came back and confessed. If she was in the woods now, it might be because of him.

"Who else went out there with the local? Talk truthfully. If I found out you didn't, you will pay with your life for your lies, villager!"

Now the man looked genuinely miserable. "Some of our people. Ciki, she is worried. And Nara—"

"How long ago did it happen?"

"Some time. Not very long." The man looked at him hopefully, his face furrowed with troubled lines. "I went looking for you the moment they left."

The raising voices back at the warriors' fire drew his attention, letting him know that the events were going out of hand again, rapidly at that. Utawah's voice, impossible to mistake, was rasping with curt commands.

He charged back toward it, dragging the local along. "You tell him whatever you told me about the villager, but not about the others going out and into the woods. Is that clear to you?"

There was no need to look at the man to understand his answer. A wise person that he probably was, he wouldn't implicate the rest of his countryfolk, not unnecessarily. That was why he must have come to him in the first place. To try and reason and make it right for those not implicated in the crime, even if connected to the criminal by the unfortunate ties of a neighborhood or a family.

"What is this all about?" demanded the lead warrior, his scowl rivaling the dead of the night. "Why did you summon me here, Ahal?"

"The locals might know where the murderer is." Regretting using a strong word like that, he grimaced, then hardened his gaze. "We will take a dozen of your warriors. Surround the place where he is hiding. It's on the hill opposite to the back of their fence. Or so the locals claim. This man," he pushed the villager forward, not releasing his grip on his victim's shoulder but now keeping it for the sake of communication, in case he needed to signal a message, in case the man started blabbering. "Tell the Honorable Warriors' Leader what you know."

While the man talked haltingly, openly afraid, he thought his possibilities through, realizing that if the villager indeed hid on that hill, trying to contact his people instead of abandoning them, then maybe she was right and he wasn't so bad or hopeless. There was certainly merit in keeping a strong, well-adept person alive to use accordingly. Sent back to Quachil Thecou along with the goods collected in the local settlements, the village of the exclusively made pearls included, he would bring more good than if executed hastily out there in the woods; or ceremonially in the middle of the town's square, for that matter.

But what about the girl? If she was with him out there now, betraying his, Ahal's, trust, what was he to do with her? Kill her? Take her along for his personal use? Let her go? Depended on what she was doing out there, he decided, irritated with the awareness that he cared. She was just a village woman from one of the most backwards hamlets, even if a surprisingly honest, uncomplicated, attractive-looking thing.

"Bring torches. One for every other man. Spears for those who are not carrying torches, in addition to clubs." Utawah's roar brought him back from his reverie, the lead warrior waving his hands, sending his men scattering in several directions, carrying the indicated equipment. "We'll go openly, with plenty of light. If he is there, he has nowhere to run or hide."

Ahal nodded in agreement. "Have someone bring me my spear." His hand was still locked around their informant's upper arm. "And have the warriors round up a few locals to lead us out. This one is of no use but as a witness. He'll be coming with us in this capacity."

But the man winced and then actually tried to twist out of Ahal's grip. "I can't!" His eyes were huge, exaggeratedly round in the light of the flickering torches, pleading with strange desperation that wasn't there in the placid features before. "Please!"

"You can't what?" For a heartbeat, Ahal found himself staring, taken aback. "What are you talking about, villager?"

The man licked his lips, then pressed his hands to his chest, imploring. "They shouldn't see me... I don't want them to know... Please!"

"What is the *miche-quipy* talking about?" demanded Utawah, coming closer and towering above, intimidating. "What's wrong?"

Ahal scowled, understanding too well, incensed with the shifty man worse than before. Not every betrayer would find enough courage to face people he betrayed.

"I won't be able to show my face back in the village," he pleaded. "I will never be forgiven. I came to you in good faith!"

Utawah shook his head. "Do you need him out there or not? Decide before we head out." In another heartbeat, he was already away, storming toward the group of returning warriors.

"I can be of use to you later on too, Honorable Leader. If you come further upstream... Or if you stay here... Please!"

Ahal fought the urge to strike the man, or at least push him hard enough to make him fall. "I'll decide before we go out." To storm away as well seemed like the best of solutions. He didn't wish to vent his frustrations on pitiful or unworthy targets.

The forest behind the town's fence greeted them with a glaring lack of amiability. Groaning with chilling gusts of wind, the trees swayed all around, sprinkling passersby with drizzling clouds of drops, as though welcoming the chance to make someone else uncomfortable. The torches flickered, struggling to keep their flames. Quite a few needed to be rekindled, time after time.

The villager must have had it quite badly, whether still lingering around or heading away already, wandering the wet woods, reflected Ahal, shivering in the cold squall.

"Out there," one of their guides was saying, pointing in the direction of what looked like a thicker grove. "It must be this hill."

Two locals pressed into guiding them claimed to know nothing about fleeing criminals or the townsfolk cooperating with them. The loudness of their protestations could be heard on the other side of the river, quite a heated denial. Utawah was losing his patience, about to resort to violent means, but Ahal prevailed to leave it at that. As long as there were enough volunteers to lead them out and into the suspected hills, it was enough to let the matter go. For now. There was no point in wasting their time on harassing the innocent townsfolk who clearly did not cherish silly ideas of cooperating with the criminal foreigner, not the majority of them. The villager might be surprised into captivity if they hurried.

And so here they were, trudging through the damp, wind-stricken night woods, ruining their shoes and their well-deserved rest, getting more furious and frustrated with every added step.

"Does the trail lead all the way to the top of the hill?" demanded Utawah curtly, talking in an unusually quiet voice, glancing around while gesturing to a pair of warriors that followed their leader close behind.

The rest of the men, three more pairs armed with either clubs or spears, slowed their step, clearly ready for more wordless orders. Ahal bestowed them a curious glance despite the need to keep his attention on his step and his weakly flickering source of light, impressed. His own men, four in all, the ones he decided to bring along because of their skill in scouting and handling a club, treaded the wet ground noisily, with no particular coordination or heed. He himself did not feel especially warlike in the wet, cutting wind, the nagging question as to what were they doing there surfacing again and again, prying, nagging as to why was it more important to catch the silly villager than to rest and get ready to tomorrow's dealings.

"Spread around," the warriors' leader went on, as quiet and as matter-of-fact as before, not his aggressively loud usual self. "You two stay over there. Wait for a signal." A pair of warriors melted in the drizzle to their left. "You two, the other side." Another pair disappeared as wordlessly in the opposite direction.

Ahal said nothing, waiting for instructions, under circumstances not opposed to being told what to do. The lead warrior clearly knew his craft when it came to hunting people down.

"Put your torches out." This time, the man glanced at him and his following, motioning the local to move aside. "Leave yours on, Ahal, but be ready to cover it if I tell you. Have your men follow closely and keep theirs ready to be lit."

He found nothing better than to nod in response, for the first time feeling out of his depth, with nothing to offer in reply, neither suggestion nor critique.

"Put your torches out," he hissed at his men, displeased with their lack of appropriately quick reaction, their looks that radiated nothing but bewilderment. "Follow close by and do whatever the warriors' leader says."

With only a few remaining torches, the thicker grove greeted them with eerie murmuring, its natural inhabitants active and alive, relieved to have the storm ending for good. The chirping of the night insects was calming, but various rustling and creaking accompanied by distant howls of wolves or coyotes, and closer hooting of several nocturnal birds, suggested to keep one's guard up.

Larger animals roamed around, Ahal's ears reported to him, catching the gist of a heavier cracking, occasional but there, brought with each new breath of wind. Which actually wasn't as strong as back on the more open ground, a mercy in one way, a hindrance in another. It wasn't as cold now, but the suspicious sounds did not reach them as readily, more difficult to decipher or understand.

A glance at the two locals let him know that they were worried as well, even if the broadness of the lead warrior's back did not relay any misgivings. Ahal shrugged to himself, bettering his grip on the club he chose to bring over his favorite spear, but counting on the warriors' fighting skills nonetheless, even if they didn't feel at home in the night forest any more than he did.

"Are there many bears around here? Mountain lions?" he asked the nearest townsman, motioning at his followers to keep close, not to leave the relative safety of his flickering light, which without a constant drizzle and gusts of wind flamed quite merrily, casting plenty of light. At least that!

The local just nodded, edging closer to the circle of light. At this very moment, the night erupted with ear-splitting screeching of creaking branches, of bushes breaking or maybe whole trees snapping in two. Roars and yells filled the air somewhere up the trail and to their left, howls and yet louder clatter.

In another few heartbeats, the avalanche of the ominous cacophony neared, rolling their way, now undoubtedly, lacking in yells but reinforced by more growling and rasping. Darting away out of an instinct rather than a thoughtful reaction, Ahal slipped in the slough of mud, his shoulder crashing against a rough trunk, hands groping for its hurtful support, managing to let him remain upright, somehow. His club plopped in the mud with a deafening thud, but the torch was still there in his gripping palm, its flame miraculously alive, flickering wildly.

In its unsteady light, it was easy to take in the hubbub of scattering and faltering figures, and the monstrous form that broke through the dark greenery, huge and misshapen, foul-smelling, its smudged fur swaying madly, caked with twigs and whole pieces of shrubs, looking grotesque, a bad spirit of the forest.

Paralyzed with dread, he watched it halting abruptly, slipping in the mud, struggling onto its hind legs, the roar already there, emanating from the gap of the foul-smelling mouth, a blood-curdling sight. It was turning whichever way, but Ahal's torch must have caught its attention as the monster froze for a moment, then roared again, louder than before. Being in the center of the light, it was easy to see even the details like the small darting eyes pausing, focusing, filling with purpose. Then the monster was again on all four, charging, and Ahal's frozen limbs came back to life with a start, his body throwing itself sideways and into the bushes, their tearing touch preferable to the terrible claws, the huge paw already sweeping above, breaking his unsatisfactory cover.

To scramble to his feet felt hopeless; still, he tried to do that, his hand with the torch, now extinguished and helpless, lashing out, stabbing at his attacker rather than striking, the impact hurtful, encouraging until a new sweep of a powerful paw sent him back to crush the bushes amidst an outburst of acute pain. The shrubs' hurtful touch became the least of his worries.

There was yelling and screaming all around, and with his mind darting frantically, seeking for avenues to escape, refusing to accept the inevitable, the torch still there, oily and scorching his skin, he struck out again and again, until the realization dawned. The roaring was still there, thundering, but in no immediate proximity, with no stench to wash his senses as before.

Scrambling back to his feet, he tried to understand, the illumination of the surviving torches flickering madly, jumping all around. The bear was roaring, on its hind legs again and turning every which way, as though in a bizarre ceremonious dance. The silhouettes of people jumped all around in fitting grotesqueness, some waving clubs, others scattering. A spear flew, missing its target. It landed temptingly close by, just a few paces from the broken chaparral, and as the bear roared and lashed toward another madly wavering light, Ahal took his chances by darting toward it, stumbling on the broken shrubs and somehow managing to reach the weapon, even if on all fours together with another pair of hands. His contester, who seemed to burst through the broken bushes the bear left in its wake while first falling upon their party, managed to get a better grip, and for a heartbeat, they actually fought for its possession, until a howl of pain distracted Ahal, his eyes darting away, following something dark cutting the air, a figure of a man, flying like a tossed straw doll, in a ridiculous manner.

Utawah's voice was thundering somewhere, distributing orders, but attacking the monster as well, leading his men. The bear was bellowing deafeningly now, charging blindly, sending those who tried to oppose it scattering. Again, Ahal's instincts took over before his mind did, giving up on the struggle for the contested spear while rolling back into the deceptive safety of the underbrush. Fairly adept at throwing javelins, invited to participate in the official spear-throwing games of the city, the rolling stone disk being a more difficult target than a crazed darting-around bear, he was not about to fight for the contested weapon's possession. Whoever wished to face the monster with the only adequate weaponry, they had had his blessing to do just that. For a fraction of a heartbeat, he wondered who the man was, realizing that he didn't seem familiar, none of the warriors or the guiding locals.

Then his attention drew back toward the roaring beast, who lashed out after another stumbling figure, while the silhouette of the man who beat him to the spear seemed to be bolting for a darker shade of a bent-down tree, its trunk nearly fallen, touching the ground. Not bothering to dive under its readily offered coverage, the man straightened up instead, his legs wide apart, the hand holding the spear already raising. There was no mistaking his intention, and Ahal caught his breath, like a spectator watching an important contest, his eyes glued to the spear but trying to see the target as well.

The bear was turning around swiftly, as though sensing the danger, having struck down yet another clubman – the warriors' cudgels were no contest for the beast, that much was obvious. The warriors' leader? There was no time to wonder about it, as the beast clearly having seen the standing man, was already charging toward him when the spear pounced in a powerful lunge, meeting the monster halfway.

His heart racing madly, Ahal watched the long shaft nearly disappearing in the mass of the smeared fur, so deeply it buried itself, with such finality; which didn't stop the onslaught, not right away. The beast charged several more leaps, determined to reach its new assailant, who was already safely away, darting toward the darker cluster of trees, as agile as another forest dweller.

For an additional heartbeat, the bear clawed at the half fallen tree, crazed with pain, his roaring turning into a gurgle, then some frightening rasping sounds. Then it all became eerily quiet.

A few tension-filled heartbeats passed, then some more. The groaning of the wounded broke the silence, quite a few voices, too many for anyone's comfort. The regular forest sounds returned as miraculously.

Incredulous, Ahal pushed himself into an upright position, pleased to feel his limbs firm, offering sufficient support. Enough to make his way toward the fallen giant, now a revolting mass, a mound of wet, stinking pelt.

The man who had taken the giant down was already at work, pushing the tangling limbs away, trying to make the limp pile turn over, desperate to get to the spear. It was easy to guess that. Why? wondered Ahal numbly.

"Who are you?" he rasped, catching the slippery shoulder, his throat not working properly, not yet.

The man pushed him away, then doubled his efforts to reach the protruding shaft. It was buried so deeply, the flint tip must have been coming out of the bear's back. Other footsteps and voices broke the darkness, the unharmed warriors probably rushing to help their wounded comrades. Absently, he wondered if Utawah was hurt. It was not like the warriors' leader to take time coming back to his senses.

"Stop that!" This time, he grabbed the man violently, suddenly knowing even before his mind could try to confirm the suspicion, ready for a fight. "Tell me who you are."

The young man did not resist the pull, but as they straightened, his body twisted, one shoulder shoving into Ahal's chest, pushing him away, his leg lashing out with a vicious kick. Had he not been alerted, expecting something of the sort, the combination might have sent him sprawling, releasing the man for enough time to get the spear, or maybe just dart into the woods and try to disappear there.

As it was, a veteran of handling unarmed people however strong or desperate, Ahal didn't give way, twisting from the worse of the kick, using his assailant's momentarily one-legged stance to shove his opponent down, his entire body dedicated to that purpose. His hands didn't give way either, loosening their previous grip in order to let it slide down the upper arm, locking above the elbow to twist it firmly, making his victim whirl. In another heartbeat, they were both back in the revolting slough, with Ahal on top of his rival, mounting his back, not letting the man even think about moving, the twisted arm ensuring obedience.

By now, many feet rushed about, splattering mad. They crowded the fallen giant and the arena of new fighting, their voices loud, bordering with hectic, the light of the torches stronger again, rekindled on quite a few of the extinguished beacons apparently. Someone actually tried to attack him, if a lashing out first or maybe a pair of hands that tried to grab him and pull him off his victim were to judge by. A woman's scream followed by another explained some of it, not the grip of unmistakably male hands but the possible cause of anyone taking the villager's side. His warriors seemed to take care of the problem quickly.

"Get a rope," he rasped at one of them, busy catching his breath, his nerves still taut, ready to react to the moves of his captive, who was indeed trying to break free despite the possibility of his arm coming out of its shoulder as a result. Muffled shouts that could be nothing but curses dissolved into the muddy earth. "Something! Anything that we can use to tie him with."

A few faces melted away.

"Who is it, Honorable Leader?" One of the men knelt next to Ahal, taking hold of the sprawling captive helpfully, frustrating more attempts to break free.

"The villager," breathed Ahal, shifting to ease his aching shoulders, certain of his conclusion. Who else would be there, running around rain-soaked woods, killing bears and fighting warriors? A fierce, violent piece of excrement, indeed.

As though eager to reinforce his last conclusion, the villager lurched wildly, sensing the lessening pressure on his twisted arm probably, not about to miss a chance. Frustrating Ahal's attempt to recapture his grip, he rolled over, kicking viciously, shoving his original captor away, while actually grabbing the warrior, who was attempting to hold him before, yanking hard. The man crashed into the mud with a loudly plopping sound, and a brief skirmish that followed saw the villager springing up before his adversary, momentarily victorious.

Fighting to keep his own balance while lunging at the man, not thinking it all through, Ahal felt the yank on his girdle, and then a knife – his knife! – was slashing at him, and he twisted to escape its touch, successful if only partly.

The ragged flint brushed against his torso, slicing his shirt. It made him lose his balance and crash into the mud in his turn, ready to withstand another attack, or rather escape it, still disbelieving that it was his own weaponry turned against him, his exclusive dagger, presented to him by the leading priest of the Raven Temple. How did it happen?

The villager did not try to attack him again, but his attempt to dart away and into the darkness did not crown with success, not with so many warriors surrounding them, rushing to his, Ahal's, aid. Struggling back to his feet, his hand pressed against his torn shirt, not encouraged by the warm dampness that could not be attributed to the thrashing in the mud alone, he saw the wild man escaping a thrust of a club, then wavering as another managed to reach him, sliding against his side. Additional blows sent him crashing into the muddled pelt of the slain monster, but by then, Ahal was on his feet already, rushing toward the fray.

"Don't!" he shouted, seeing the man still struggling, his face glittering with blood, fighting like a crazed bear he had just killed, resisting as mindlessly. "Don't kill him. Just disarm him. Make sure he is tied properly." He ground his teeth, firm on his feet and not dizzy but worried by the suspicious wetness under the palm pressing into his side. Damn it! "Knock him unconscious if you must, but don't kill him. I want him disarmed but alive."

CHAPTER 10

The moment they were gone, Iciwata allowed his muscles to relax, the temptation of sliding against the shaky wall too great to battle. His whole body felt like a piece of clay put into the fire pit for too long – fragile and stiff, and about to crack into dozen little pieces. He didn't even start to wonder where he might have been hurt for real and where it was just the pain of simple scratches and bruises. Curse it all!

The memory of the fierce night storm and the bear made the waves of hectic excitement return, causing his body shake in violent tremors and his back break out in a new bout of sweat despite the cold of the night. It was incredible, wasn't it, better than killing that other bear back at home. The first time, it was a hunt, a brave daring hunt of a person not afraid to face the old grizzled monster all alone, a courageous thing to do, but not like this time. Oh, no! Nothing matched jumping down the tree to scare the sniffing beast off, then chasing it, *actually* chasing it, bursting into the scene of so many armed warriors, useless each and every one of them, besides that other man maybe, the violent piece of rotten meat who had somehow managed to lay his hands on him afterwards. What gall! The man wasn't useless, but still, he, Iciwata, had beat him to the spear, impaled the crazed beast on it while other armed invaders were hopeless and harmed. That man who the bear hurled like a corn-husk doll, but he flew quite a long distance, didn't he? Must have gotten hurt for real. And yet, he, Iciwata, did not hesitate, didn't not slink into the safety of the darkness. He had grabbed the warrior's spear, had challenged the master of the forest with it, had bested him so very thoroughly, killing him in one single thrust.

Oh, but it was wild, incredible, invigorating, so very thrilling, to relive again and again until the memory faded like they always did. It was worth falling into their captivity, the dishonorable pieces of human waste that they were. Fancy to bother a person after such fight, to interrupt his moment of privacy with the fallen giant. He might have been muttering a prayer, talking to the fallen animal's spirit for all they knew, asking for acceptance, guidance, forgiveness. He didn't do any of it at the time; he was too busy trying to lay his hands on the fancy foreign spear that was now rightfully his. Still, they couldn't know that, could they? The violent piece of excrement he managed to cut deserved that for his lack of most basic manners. But for this man, he would have been free now, back in the woods, away from this mess, armed with the captured spear too and a tale of a new glorious deed behind him. Ciki and Nara were there, weren't they? Having run after him toward the noises of the fighting, they must have seen what had happened, at least some of it. And they didn't even see how he had made this bear flee in the first place, saving their stupid hides.

Again he tried to shift into a better position, the rope securing his hands cutting into his wrists, killing the idea of trying to sneak away. In his current state, he could not possibly hope to make his ties loose before they came back, even though the darkness and the relative privacy of this place were tempting. Fancy throwing a person into this or that storage room. Who did things like that? And who erected special houses for storing? Back in the village, people stored what they had in their own homes. And yet, it was clear that he was surrounded by various tools now, plenty of large containers, even the outlines of several boats piling one on top of another, unmistakable shapes. The locals' vessels or the intruders'? Were the filthy invaders afraid someone would try to steal their boats?

He chuckled darkly, remembering the shore. It would have paid off if he had tried to do that, steal one of their fancy canoes and boated home instead of getting in trouble with their force and the entire town hosting them, spineless lowlifes that they were. How hard would it be to fight off this fancy little fleet, their spearmen or not? He had killed one of them with a stupid piece of broken cane; and back with the bear, they did not display much fighting skill either. Besides the lowlife with the knife. Was that the leader of the delegation? And if so, did he manage to slash his stomach or chest enough to wound the man for real? Oh, all the great forest spirits, please let it be so!

For another heartbeat, he reveled in the glory of the thought of killing two warriors, one of them a leader, then tried to wriggle into a sitting position, his head exploding with pain along with plenty other parts of his body. But did the pieces of human waste go wild with kicking and punching! Ferocious beasts. It was good for them that he went into the dream worlds for a while. Otherwise, they would have never managed to keep him down or restrained. He would be away and in the woods now, heading off for good, this time for certain. Curse it all!

The noises outside were hushed, coming and going away, drawing closer, then shuffling off, voices and footsteps. Not many had slept in this town tonight. He chuckled grimly, then settled to rub his ties off. If they forgot him here for some time, he would manage to get away. And then, once outside, he would decide what to do. Find Ciki and Nara, still waiting in the woods, hopefully, and not trying to do something foolish like coming here in order to help him escape. They could do that, couldn't they?

He muttered another briefly inappropriate plea to the spirits, to make his sister and his friend stay away from here, wait in the same place where they had met and where he spooked the bear from, dragging the carcass of this same old sticky-mouth there maybe. It was his rightful spoil, wasn't it, the pelt and the claws. It wasn't right for the stinking westerners to lay their hands on his prey.

Several new outbursts of voices and footsteps passed, however, when the heavy piece of bark that shielded the entrance moved, he didn't hear anything suspicious besides the regular night rustling. Or maybe he was just too immersed in working on his ties. The wall he had rubbed his wrists against creaked atrociously, being as shaky as it was, made of interwoven branches like back home but of a low quality, with no density a good wall should display.

Catching his breath, he grew very still, his heart leaping to a wild start, his eyes having difficulty seeing, even though one of the newcomers held a torch. It flickered weakly, giving more smoke than light; still, it offered enough illumination to see that there were two silhouettes there, one male and one female. Why female? His heart kept making wild leaps inside his chest and he refused to wonder at her familiar smallness and roundness. No, no, his sister was safe out there in the woods; worrying about him, yes, but safe out there with Nara, ready to escape should the things go bad for him here...

"Wait by the doorway," said the man's voice, another familiar sound. The lowlife of the spear. So this one wasn't cut badly, not enough to prevent him from running around, distributing orders. Too bad. Iciwata ground his teeth and wished his ties were torn off by now. The stinking westerner wouldn't expect a renewed attack, would he? But to have this man's knife in his possession again.

The torch left a glimmering trail in the darkness as it neared him before thrusting close to his face, making his eyes water with the suddenness of it. Unaccustomed to the light, even if meager, Iciwata blinked, tossing his head backwards out of instinct, making the shaky wall tremble with the suddenness of the bump. Not a hard surface, the hit resonated in his aching head, not helping his blurry vision.

"So you are awake. Good." The torch drew away to stay beside the man, outlining him favorably, a confident figure, not tall but well-proportioned, very much leader-like, having an authoritative air about him.

Iciwata just stared, his strength spent on the attempt to do so without blinking, even though it must be difficult to tell in the darkness. He certainly couldn't see the newcomer's features or what his gaze held, but after the previous shameful lurch, it was essential to profess his lack of fear, his determination, even if the darkness wasn't on his side in that.

"Now we will conduct a quick talk, villager," went on the man, his voice annoyingly calm, lacking in expression. It was as though they sat around a campfire on some obscure hunting trip, taking unimportant differences out. "Unless you are still not in a talkative mood. If violence and fighting are still on your mind, then I will leave you here and you will not live to see the upcoming dawn. Think this over carefully, if quickly, and let me know if I would do better retiring to sleep for the remaining part of this night."

The sound of the dispassionate words died down, but he could hear Ciki breathing noisily by the dark entrance, gasping at the ring of the last words. It irritated him to no end. It was enough that his sister's mere presence put him at dire disadvantage, made him vulnerable to all sorts of threats and nasty surprises. How did she manage to fall into this man's hands?

"Well?" repeated his captor, standing there like a tree, unmoving, even the flame of his torch not daring to flicker, or so it seemed. "Answer fast. Are you smart enough for a civil talk or lashing out then running away like a coward, not staying to face your deeds, is all you are good for?"

Now it was his turn to gasp. "I killed one of your warriors and I killed the crazed bear that was throwing you cowards all around, helpless like little children!" He heard his own voice rasping, low and ugly, more of an animal growl. He didn't care. "I'm not a coward! You are!"

"Keep your voice low," said the man, unimpressed. "There is no need to wake this entire town up with your yelling about your crimes or other deeds. Keep your anger in control and listen!" The last words rang stonily, a clear order.

Iciwata didn't care. "I will yell as much as I—" The rocky palm slammed against his mouth, shoving his head backwards to crash against the woven wall and make the entire construction shake. It set the clubs pounding inside his skull to assault it with new vengeance, but as painful as it was, he didn't pay it much attention, busy fighting for breath, the rock-hard fingers smothering his nose as well, not letting the air in.

He fought fiercely, wriggling and kicking as best as he could, succeeding only to slip down, pinned more helplessly than before, with nowhere to move and his rival now sitting on his chest, making the struggle for breath so much worse.

"Your last chance to behave reasonably."

The hated voice was coming in waves, as though needing to overcome an invisible barrier, something misty or maybe watery. It didn't even shake or gasp. The ragged palm didn't move, and for a moment, he considered biting it, sinking his teeth into it savagely, like a cornered animal, which he actually might have been, in a manner of speaking. Still, something in the overly calm presence made him pause, as did the sobs that were beside them now, not at the distance of a doorway. Those annoyed him into more reasonable thinking. It was not Ciki's place—

"Good." The voice seemed to react to his thoughts, the strangling hand relaxing its grip, not moving away but not smothering as before. "Stop that. He isn't hurt, not yet. If he behaves reasonably, he won't be." Those words managed to cut the sobs that now, with the world steadying gradually, began to be more distinct, assaulting his senses worse than before. "Stop crying! If you wish to help, talk to him. Explain his situation yourself, in your tongue. Maybe he'll listen to you more readily." The man shifted slightly, the pressure of his weight going away with him, not entirely but some. Another relief. "We don't have time. The boats for Quachil Thecou will be leaving some time after midday."

That made Ciki's whimpering subdue for good. "Iciwata, please. Please, you must listen to what he says. Please!"

The sobs threatened to return, so he wriggled to free his mouth some more, pleased with this small success. "Stop wailing!" It came in a grating rasp. He tried to clear his throat, glad to have no fingers crushing his face. "How did you come to be with this lowlife?"

"He is no lowlife," she whispered hurriedly, her breath hot upon his ear, her nearness not reassuring. "Don't talk like that, please. You must listen to him. He is a good man. He is the only one who doesn't wish to kill you. He is..." Her voice broke again, lost its regained clarity. "They are all after you! All of them, this entire town and everyone! They want to kill you, but this man, he doesn't let them. Please listen to him and do as he says. Please!"

He tried to process this information, hard put to do that while spread on the earthen floor with too many objects jutting against his back, his tied hands being one of the obstacles, twisted unnaturally, hurting as though about to break. "What... what are you talking about?"

For some reason, the question, grating and barely intelligible as it was, made her calm down. "Iciwata, listen, just listen. You are in trouble. And so are we, the rest of us. We came to tell you that out there in the woods. What you did before... that warrior you killed out there by the river... Well, they make this town pay for it, and they, they won't let us go until our village pays. But now that you are here... this man..." He could feel her shifting uneasily, as though turning to look at the violent piece of dirt who, as expected, just hovered there, again a motionless slab of stone. "He is so very kind. He says you won't have to pay with your life. He says you will have to go with them, pay with your work. Work out there, in their cities, you see. Just for some time. Not forever. A few moons, he said. This... this will pay for the life of that warrior, you see. And they won't have to kill you or to make our village pay!" At this, her voice began climbing up to unpleasantly agitated tones again.

Iciwata wanted to groan, not even understanding her flooding of words properly but already knowing that it was something bad, something with no way out. They wanted him to pay for the life of that lowlife by the river, not with his life, yes, but with something as nasty. They were lowlifes like that. And yet, she said that otherwise their village would have to pay; to pay while learning the extent of his crimes, the humiliation of what was happening to him. Oh mighty spirits!

"You must do as Honorable Ahal tells you. You must!" Her sobs were back, more irritating than ever.

"Stop that!" It came out as a groan. He ground his teeth, then tried to pull himself up, an impossible feat under the circumstances. "Tell your honorable-whatever to let me up. Then we'll talk."

The slab of stone came to life without the need for her explanations or translating services, his rock-hard palm grabbing

Iciwata's shoulder, jerking him upwards and sideways so suddenly, he felt like losing his senses for good, his head reeling, the pain in his twisted arms bursting with vengeance. When his back slammed against the wall once again, he welcomed its hurtful support, ridiculously relieved.

"You don't offer your consent to talk as a favor, wild villager," said the man curtly, his tone again mild but grating, relaying a message. "Not a criminal like you. I'm offering you what your sister said as a favor to her and other decent people of your village. They do not deserve to have all their goods taken from them on account of your deeds, their entire food supply and their valuables. This is not the tribute we came to collect, but it will happen if you refuse to pay for your crime." The pause was brief if heavy, filled with the faint sounds from the outside, the rain returning, rustling softly on the roof of the storage hut. "Your running away was dishonorable enough to put you outside the law, any law of respectable human beings. But your village should not suffer instead of you. If you have any self-respect left, you will do as your sister says. Your choosing death may be an easy way out, but it wouldn't be an honorable way and it will not ensure your place in the afterlife, will not help you to cross the narrow plank. Just the contrary is true." The voice hardened again. "Make up your mind and do it fast."

He tried to slam his mind into working, the words pummeling like pelted stones, each one a missile, so deviously distorted and yet all true. He did kill that man by the river, fighting his attackers off, yes, but still, a man was killed, with him, the culprit, fleeing ignobly, running for his life, leaving his fellow villagers to answer for his crimes. Did he think they wouldn't know who did this? How stupid and unworthy. Of course they found out easily, and his own sister and his friend and several others among his fellow villagers, annoying pieces of rotten meat that some of them were, were now held here, expected to pay for his crimes. And what if...

The new thought hit him like a blow in his stomach, with no need for actual violence to make him gasp for breath. What if those war canoes sailed to his village, *actually* sailed there. Did the man say something to this effect, about his village paying with all their goods, all the foodstuff? Oh mighty spirits! If something like that happened and because of him, oh, but he would never manage to live this shame down, never!

"Yes, yes, Iciwata, please." His sister's continuous sobbing didn't help. She was kneeling beside him again, clutching him with her arms, not helping the suffocating sensation. "You must do as he says. You must!"

He pushed her away using his shoulder, then glared at the man, a mere silhouette in the darkness. Still, he couldn't help hoping that his rival sensed his fury, even if he could not see it.

"You are lying. Those are all lies!" It came out satisfactorily firm, with matching quietness of the tone, matching deadliness. "You want something from me and this is why you distort everything that happened to make me look unworthy. My sister, she has nothing to do with it. Let her go!"

A pause lasted for less than a heartbeat; still, it made him feel victorious, even if for a brief moment.

"Your sister is not a prisoner here. You are. It was her will to come along and try to talk sense into you. If she wishes, she may leave any moment."

Ciki stopped sobbing abruptly and what might have come across as a mercy before now promised nothing but more ominous threats or revelations.

"Honorable Ahal is not deceiving you or trying to trick you into something," she said, twisting the words in the manner the filthy westerner did, her voice ringing with familiar firmness. Ciki could be like that at times, strong-minded and determined. At times. "He is the one who is trying to help you out. To help all of us out!"

Iciwata ground his teeth. "You are silly, sister. Go away. Leave your honorable invader and the robber of our people to his dishonorable deeds. Let him kill me with no witnesses, then go and rob our village of its goods with or without the lies about my deeds." That came out so well, he felt his lips twisting on their own, forming a nasty smile. Too bad they couldn't see it in the darkness. "When his war canoes come to our village, don't let them lie about me and my deeds. That warrior attacked me back by the river. There were two of them, and they were armed, and still I killed one of them and harmed the other badly enough. They won't admit that, but that is the truth. Don't let them lie about me to our people."

Her gasp tore the darkness, but the silhouetted head of the man shook with what looked like open derision.

"I will not be executing you myself, criminal, even though I have the authority to do that. A backward villager like you can be excused thinking in such simple terms, but this is not how the justice of the great sun cities works." This time, the pause held a curiously satisfied ring, as though the unperturbed slab of stone was pleased with himself. Like a predator sensing the scent of fresh meat. Iciwata clenched his teeth. "You will be taken to your village with us when we sail there having completed our talks here. Tied for good measure, as it is clear that you could not be trusted to behave reasonably."

The rain was beating stronger now, seeping through the cracks of the sloppily thatched roof, giving a proper background to the dread welling in his chest. But it couldn't be true, it just couldn't. They could not drag him back home, tied and beaten and accused of cowardly running away. Not after what he did, killing that warrior, impaling the crazed bear. Those were brave deeds, worthy of respect, but if presented otherwise, in the light of his flight, yes, and now this. But no, it couldn't—

"Your elders might be able to advise, might help me, the head of our delegation, to decide," went on the calm voice, and he noticed that Ciki stopped sniffing with her clogged nose and was listening with what felt like bated breath, mesmerized. He couldn't get enough air. "The lead warrior of our escorting forces wishes to execute you, yes, but I do not see the merit in taking lives as means of revenge. I do believe you can pay for the damage you have caused with hard work and maybe some brave deeds. After all, you did slay the crazed bear, alone and single-handedly, did keep some of our men from harm or at least saved us plenty of unnecessary fighting in the night forest. Such feats cannot go without acknowledgment. I'm not in the habit of overlooking positive deeds."

He wished to close his ears and stop listening, the measured words hurting, even though all of a sudden they held a hint of praise, an admission. The man was aware of his bravery out there in the woods, not about to rob him of his achievements, even though he could have done that. Suddenly, he knew it for certain. He was in their hands, an outlaw according to everyone's custom, his village included. The elders would be appalled, Father before anyone. And the others, those who wished to see him humbled, that filthy Tcumu, even a shadow of a man like Hikua, even the girls; oh yes, that spicy Uruna would make the most out of his allegedly coward behavior, and Kayina would know now for certain that she had been right in avoiding him, preferring nobodies like Hikua. As for the others, those who had followed him and did what he said, would they turn their faces from him with words of derision? There was little doubt about the answer to this.

"Please, Iciwata. Please!" Ciki was back to her sobbing and pleading, but he closed his ears to her words, pushing the panicked wave back with such an effort, his forehead broke with a new bout of sweat, even though the chilliness of the night was bursting in through the gaping opening and the cracks in the wall, swishing with the moaning wind. The storm was not about to fade or go away.

"Go away, Ciki." He heard his own voice grating again, not a pleasant sound, barely human, if at all. "Leave us!"

She fell silent for a moment, then started to protest, her words not reaching him, their teary tone assaulting his senses.

"Go away!"

He lurched from her groping hands, so terribly clumsy and uncomfortable, but not caring, the splashing anger helping, encouraging in a way. It was better than the bottomless fear, the sensation of falling into the pit, of being buried under the weight of his own deeds. A terrible sensation.

"Leave us, woman." This time, his tormenter actually came to his aid, his voice still impartial but holding a hint of peculiar warmth, a curiously comfortable familiarity. "Do as your brother asks. Go. Go now."

It was easy to feel her hesitating, then suddenly relaxing, as though a burden was taken from her. Another heartbeat of indecision and the persistence of her grip was gone, leaving him alone yet not relieved, not heartened. The cold wind was back, chilling him to the bone. If only there was a way to shake off his ties, to curl around himself and try to make himself warm again. Or better yet, to spring to his feet and be gone. Where to? He had nowhere to run, nowhere to hide until this particular storm passed. Back in the village, they would know what he did, as soon as the filthy westerners took off. As soon as they finished the talks here, the man said. And then, his people would be forced to pay for his crimes, and he would never dare to show his face back home again, never! Even if they allowed him or forgave.

"Why did you want her gone?" With no Ciki around, the man's voice returned to its cold, stone-cutting edge. Still, there was something conversational about the question, a flicker of affability.

Iciwata unclenched his teeth with an effort. "What do you want me to do?" It came out like an ugliest of grunts. He tried to clear his throat but ended up choking on the cough, not realizing that he was holding it in before. "I... How do I pay?"

The faint flicker of light moved with the man stepping closer, squatting not far away, making himself comfortable. It was easy to guess that, even in such an inadequate illumination. The moon outside the gaping opening wasn't there anymore, hiding behind the screen of the monotonous drizzle. In spite of himself, Iciwata strained his eyes, desperate to catch at least a faint glimmer of its natural light, anything really.

"You pay with hard work. This is how it's done in the Revered Sun's cities of the Great River. Everyone comes to work, to erect great mounds, to please our divine patrons and those of their descendants who watch over us and our wellbeing."

A pause lasted longer this time, but it gave him an opportunity to relax a little, to try and organize his thoughts. When the man shifted, then rustled with some bags or tools he might be fiddling with, it resulted in a stronger flicker of flame, making the night horrors recede, if only a little.

"It is hard enough work and you will have to display more patience and good sense than you did so far." In the faint illumination, it wasn't possible to see but the general outline of the strong face, the sharpness of its angles, the prominence of the long aquiline nose, slightly misshapen, as though broken once upon a time, the patterns of suggested tattoos, plenty of intricate designs. Not a reassuring view, but somehow, it took the edge off his nervousness. "You will have to work hard to do that. Those who supervise *miche*—the workers, foreign or locals—are not the people to pick fights with." The outline of the pursed mouth seemed to press tighter. "The warrior you managed to kill was caught by surprise. The outcome of our own skirmish back in the forest just now should have shown you that you are not good enough to engage armed people who know how to fight."

That brought him back from the brink of a briefly gained calm. "I didn't lose to you! I cut you thoroughly enough to have you fallen, to have the others coming to fight me instead of you." The twisted grin facing him held open condescension. "It was your own knife turned against you!"

"It was indeed," agreed the man calmly, making Iciwata wish to have the aforementioned knife once again. If not tied, he might have tried to lash out, to hurl himself at his captor, and maybe, if lucky, to hurt him for real, even at the price of being dragged back home, to face his father and the rest, accused of every crime possible. The recollection of the last threat made his thoughts clear of anger, an unfamiliar feeling.

"Not a badly executed attack," went on the man, squatting comfortably, unperturbed once again, the torch in his hand not wavering, held firmly, only its flame alive and dancing with gusts of wind. "You do have good instincts and a strong body. You may certainly learn to become a warrior. However, first you will work to pay for your crimes. Then I may help you along, if you earn the right to receive my help." The lightness and surprising chattiness of the voice was gone, and even though impossible to see in the semi-darkness, he knew the man's eyes were boring at him, stern and foreboding once again. "You will journey with our canoes that are heading back to Quachil Thecou along with this town's tribute and other goods. The men I will charge with responsibility for you will be your masters until you arrive." The voice grew sterner and colder. "You will obey every order of whoever will be made responsible for you, and you will not offer any violence in response. Is that clear to you? Say so!"

He thought his jaw would crack from the force with which he clenched it, his stomach constricting violently, painfully, as though he had eaten something bad. "For how long?" he managed to squeeze out in the end, the words coming with difficulty through his clasped teeth.

The wide shoulders lifted in an unmistakable gesture. "Until the end of the rainy moons at the very least. Until the first frost. Maybe more."

"But it's two or three moons away!" It came out in quite a shout. The dread was welling again, threatening to choke him. To work days on end, answer some lowlifes' orders and commands and for nearly three moons? No, he wouldn't do that. Death was preferable, a dozen times more preferable! And yet, he wasn't offered such an easy solution. Oh no! What he had been offered was as intolerable, more so, the disgrace of having been dragged back home like the last of the mindless criminals, accused of cowardice among other things. Was it better to bear the humiliation of working until the cold came? Build some stinking mounds, like the man said, with no shape and no likeness of a sacred animal, no purpose. Like the strangely curving mounds of this filthy town, filthy excrement-eaters that they all were.

"Yes, it is. But I might have more interesting work in mind for you. When I return to the city, I will see to that. Maybe. If you behave with enough gratitude and none of the insolence you keep displaying."

"Where will you go?" It came out almost on its own, a desperate attempt to take his thoughts off the dreary life ahead, even if temporary. Two or three moons, until the frost came. Only until then.

The man rose to his feet, exhaling through his boldly carved nostrils, clearly not amused or sympathetic, not anymore. "This is exactly the insolence you will have to get rid of, villager," he said coldly, a small bag attached to his wrist swinging, the torch flickering, struggling against the additional breeze its owner's movement created. "I'm far above the status of an average denizen of Quachil Thecou. As for the villagers like you..." A shrug made the small flame flicker fiercely, about to die down for good. "You will address me by a proper title from now on, with correct obsequiousness you will be taught to use. I'll leave instructions to this effect. Whether I decide to help you out or should I choose to pay your fate no more attention, you will work obediently on whatever task you will be given and you will offer neither argument nor trouble. Any display of disobedience or silly deeds will cost you your life in the best of the cases." Before diving into the warning shrieks of the wind, the man turned back once again. "Remember that it is not only for your own good that you agreed to the conditions I outlined for you. Your fellow villagers and their elders will not be made to pay for your crimes unless you do not keep your word and your side of the agreement."

In another heartbeat, he was gone, disappearing into the raging darkness, leaving worse turmoil behind. Iciwata closed his eyes, then slid toward the earthen floor, curling around himself as best as he could. To think about it all was too much, so he let the waves of pain and exhaustion lull him into a semblance of sleep. It was better this way. At least until the dawn came.

CHAPTER 11

Uncle Ahal was back in the city!

Tucking her own smile away, Sele shifted in her carried seat, excited like back when she was a little girl and her mother had allowed her to be taken to the market square for the first time. Back then, her mind felt like exploding from within, and her heart beat three times faster than after racing her siblings up and down her father's estate. She was all eyes and nerves and wild expectations, and now it felt almost the same.

To leave the Royal Mound and descend the city, at long last! And in what state, carried in one of the royal palanquins, a prettily done seat that could host three of her type at the very least, even though she wasn't as slender as before her elevation in life. How could she be, with so many delicious snacks and nothing else to do but to gorge on them. Revered Sun enjoyed drinks and buns sweetened with honey, always around, ready for the demand. It was easy to develop a taste for them.

Squinting against the glow of the sacred deity, the direct ancestor of her powerful husband, she tried to look important, not to gape around like a silly child. It was imperative to present a respectable façade, fitting the status of a favorite wife to the great ruler. The palanquin was so much more comfortable than the one her mother used on occasions, upholstered with prettily woven mats, and she was glad that this time she gathered enough courage to use all her old tricks, having pled with her powerful husband in the artfully female way, frightened at her own forwardness and yet proud of herself at the same time, aware of her power. To think that Revered Sun himself was not proof against her charm was invigorating. The powerful ruler of Quachil Thecou could not tell her "no," could he? A thrilling sensation.

She shifted upon her upholstered seat, slightly bored but trying not to show it. The spearmen upon the wide, perfectly flattened field were preparing for yet another round of throwing, clutching their javelins, the muscles upon their bare torsos bulging, straining visibly, their tension on display. It thrilled her to no end in the beginning, such a display of virility and strength, of remarkable marksmanship, of pure physical power and skill – a beautiful vision.

Still, now, half a morning later, she felt like shutting her eyes and drifting away, preferably in the comforts of the royal dwelling, away from the scorching mercies of the powerful sky deity. The flying spears or those who had cast them looked all alike after a while of watching them. Beautifully powerful, yes, both the weaponry and those who hurled it, but after half a morning, they became nothing but a blur of a movement.

A girl in the neighboring smaller, not as richly padded seat clapped her hands and squealed with excitement, bringing Sele's attention back to the happenings upon the plaza, the roar of the townsfolk crowding every possible side of the vast enclosure beside the elegantly elevated ground reserved for the royalty and their closest of followers rising like a squall of storm wind. It matched the mighty hiss so many spears cutting the air at once generated, and against her indifference, Sele shielded her eyes, wishing to see where the carved disk was rolling, toward which one of the hurled lethal missiles and their apparent landing place. It was so difficult to predict at times. Uncle Ahal told her once that many different things could influence the course of the rolled pellet – its size and maneuverability, the smoothness of its surface, the strength with which it was sent to roll, even the wind and its power and direction – the players had to take it all into account in the shortest span of time, after the disk was already rolled and before they had to throw their spears or chance missing the timing to do that at all and thus shame themselves before the entire city. He had participated in such contests aplenty, Uncle Ahal.

Her stomach twisted with anticipation, because even if the rumor wasn't true, he would be returning back soon anyway. It had been nearly two moons since he had left, just as she had been elevated in life, and it would be good to see him again, to boast her exalted new status. He would be pleased to hear that she had done so well. He would swell with pride in her, even if he would try not to show it. Uncle Ahal was so very transparent at times.

"Stop making that silly noise, Hekuni!" Another young girl in her own padded seat burned the one who had clapped with her gaze, her pleasantly round face screwing in an unpleasant grimace. "You yell like a silly *miche-quipy* down there by the field." Her gaze encountered Sele's and turned yet colder; however, this time, she kept her peace, evidently satisfied with mere staring.

Sele retaliated with a likewise cold glaring topped with climbing eyebrows, which had been plucked prettily only this morning into a perfect arch. Most of the celestial family members were possible to handle or interact with if not forced to do it daily, not all of them malicious snakes, turning into such only occasionally and only if provoked. By now, she knew how to handle them. While living away from their quarters and in the protective shadow of her celestial husband, it wasn't difficult to do that. No one but his exalted sister, the royal lady *Quachilli Tamailli*, Female Sun, could flare at her and talk nasty. However, by now, she knew who would have done all this and worse should she slip from her favorable position in the Royal Hall, all divine spirits protect her from that! This same Tehale, for one, the first daughter of Tattooed Serpent, another exalted sibling of her husband, his younger brother and the head of all warring and civil affairs in the city and outside of it. Always around the top of the Royal Mound, in and out of the main temple and the Royal Hall, the man looked foreboding but not nasty, not like the royal sister was. Still, some of his female offspring were as intolerable as they came.

"Oh please!" cried out the girl who was clapping before, a nice little thing, a daughter of this or that royal cousin, with enough divine blood to warrant her occupying the women's quarters of the lower terrace but not enough summers as yet to be handed out in marriage. "If one is not sitting as straight as a temple's pole, one is not turning into a yelling *miche-quipy*. That is the silliest thing to say, Tehale."

"The silliest is to yell and clap your hands like a market woman," parried Tehale, her lips turning thin in the haughtiness of her inverted grin, just a hint of it, a perfect imitation of the royal sister's arsenal of venomous smiles. "You may be just the youngest daughter of our Revered Sun's cousin, but you still carry this family's blood and you should conduct yourself accordingly."

Oh please, thought Sele, burning the annoying bag of primness with her gaze, but not daring to sound her mind like she would have with her own half-siblings, putting them in their place. Here she was an outsider, a pushy intruder, a lucky visitor from lower classes. The purity of her blood, noble on both sides, did not interest divine offspring. She might have been a *miche-quipy* woman from markets and fields as far as the dwellers of the Royal Mound were concerned, basking in their own divinity, even those who could boast barely a sprinkle of it, like the cute, easily-excited Hekuni, maybe the youngest daughter of the ruler's cousin twice removed, but a female cousin, which made all the difference. The female blood was the one that counted, not the male one, even that of the most direct offspring, even the children of Revered Sun himself. On that count, the haughty Tehale lost badly, having a divine father and not a divine mother, and she knew it. Sele did not try to hide her smirk.

"The youngest daughter, pah!" Evidently, Hekuni reflected on the same realization, basking in the frustration of the other girl, secure in her own better position, her own unimportant mother as opposed to Tehale's all-important father or not. "You will be married off the moment your bloods finally come, if it'll happen at all. And either way, it will be farewell our Royal Mound. Out there in the city, you are invited to behave as royally as a temple's priest. I'll be watching you from up there, making sure you do not shame our divine heritage." The crystal bracelets clanked with the enthusiastic wave of the girl's delicate hand, indicating the Royal Mound towering behind their backs, dotted with watching royalty as well, the denizens of the lower terrace mostly. Only certain royal family members were allowed to join the descending procession of luxurious palanquins, a few females among them, none of them wives. She was the only exception, and it wasn't easy to convince her powerful husband. It took an effort, but it was worth it. Oh yes, it was!

He was feeling relatively well for quite a few dawns, growing stronger with no fits of terrible fever to torment him, his face filling out and his gaunt body allowing him to walk about and not only to summon advisers and hear them out in the spaciousness of the Royal Hall. He fell into a habit of summoning his palanquin to be taken to the temple of the Royal Mound's lower terrace, something he couldn't do when feverish and weak, so the idea of visiting the city for the spear-throwing competition did not come as an utter surprise. As did his increasing ardor in the privacy of the royal bed, something she didn't greet as readily as the rest of the aspects in his improvement, but maybe it was due to this that he had deigned to listen to her sweet and well-calculated words of begging. The spear-throwing contest, oh but she couldn't live without watching it, could she?

Paying no more attention to the quarrelling girls who were going at each other with much spirit and spite by now, she glanced at the cluster of more impressive-looking palanquins and other seating arrangements at the edge of the incline, with servants dashing between them like a bunch of spooked mice, carrying trays with refreshments. The delicately worked hides adorning her husband's chair, a wide intricately carved seat he always occupied while receiving visitors or advisers, brought here by several servants with much care, moved with the slight breeze, a net of black threads supporting his brilliant red diadem, embellished with beads and seeds, with white feathers weaving around the back of his head, making him look majestic indeed. He had drunk his medicine later than usual in the morning, and she hoped that he was still feeling well, not succumbing to renewed shaking or fever.

Unable to see more than the back of his shoulders, his nape concealed by the brilliance of the white feathers sliding down his headdress, she let her eyes wander, pursing her lips at the sight of the royal sister's palanquin, flanked by their powerful third sibling, the mighty war leader and adviser Tattooed Serpent. They were talking, the two of them, leaning toward each other, looking immersed. What about? wondered Sele. Tattooed Serpent was a tall man, with wide enough shoulders but strangely narrow hips, which looked disproportional when he stood upright. A foreboding person, not someone one felt safe looking at idly. Out of the three sacred siblings, only her husband was a nice man. She thanked all mighty deities for that, then took her eyes toward the royal sister again, safe in doing so as the woman's back was turned to her, with only a glimpse of her profile outlined boldly against the glow of the actual sun.

The highest most revered lady of the land, Female Sun, the mother of the heir, the next Revered Sun, the nasty arrogant power-hungry sneak that she was, notorious for her temper and not very subtle interference with the governing issues. Even Sele herself could see that, inexperienced girl that she was, adviser's daughter or not. Her husband's sister felt that she was the one fit to rule Quachil Thecou and the lands surrounding it; she thought no one knew better than she. As if!

She snorted to herself, then remembered another juicy gossip, the powerful woman's appetite for fit-looking *miche-quipy*, the more muscular the better. The insatiable woman picked servants that pleased her eye like goblets or plates, or so her own serving girls whispered, to use and discard afterwards unless they pleased her enough to be kept as her personal guarding warriors. There were plenty of such well-built spearmen to be seen escorting the woman indeed. It was hard at times not to stare at the Female Sun's following.

Tossing her head high, Sele let her gaze stray back toward the plaza and the spearmen competing there, readying for another round of throwing. The spot the lesser ladies occupied was not a bad one, with a clear view of the entire plaza, but away from the comforts of erected sunshades that protected Revered Sun and his following. Still, from their less privileged vantage point, one could see not only the spearmen and the surrounding crowds, but also a nearby mound in the process of building, with the procession of sweating *miche-quipy* walking back and forth, carrying their heavy burdens strapped to their backs, as unclad and as enticing to watch, some of them, with their glistening bodies looking like figurines carved out of polished stone. A decent competition to the spear-throwers, come to think of it. The mere frivolity of this thought made her chuckle.

The day was scorching hot and the sun beat upon the earth and the people walking it with no distinction, even though, of course, *miche-quipy* who trod the uneven incline of their partly erected mound, squashed under the weight of their huge baskets, had it the worst, them and those who stood by or ran around, coordinating their actions. Safe in doing so, as back upon the field the new bout of spear-throwing generated plenty of screams from the crowding spectators, signaling that the stone disk the throwers were to precede with their throws was about to be rolled, Sele let her eyes rest on the working men, their muscular figures brown and glistening in the sun, a delightful sight, more than the players, truth be told, their bare torsos and limbs smeared with streaks of mud and drier patches of earth, curiously pleasing the eye. Even their faces, or what she had managed to glimpse of them, screwed-up in what looked like a panting scowl, facing the ground they were treading, frozen in grim determination, did not look repulsive. On the contrary, she found herself craning her neck in an attempt to see better, the man with a light long-sleeved shirt covering his torso, various tools clutched in his hands, rushing between them, yelling something from time to time, accompanied by a few sullen spearmen who clearly preferred to be on the field or watching, not treading among the sweating *miche-quipy*.

A few were finishing their ascent, reaching the higher ground she could still glimpse from her elevated vantage point. It didn't look like a future sacred earthwork, nothing but a badly ruffled mound of earth, and they seemed to be having a harder time now, forcing their way through the rumpled dirt.

Sele motioned one of her personal serving girls. "Are they going to just pour it there? Those baskets they carry."

"Yes, oh yes!" cried out the girl, delighted to be singled out. "They are carrying those things back and forth all day long. For many dawns. I watched them just the other day when sent to bring fruit from the traders."

Sele grimaced, not pleased to be reminded that lower class women like that serving girl could go down the Royal Mound and ran around the city whenever they wanted to. Or at least whenever sent to do things. While she, the favorite wife of Revered Sun and the daughter of an important adviser, had to nag and plead and use all her wits and charm to be allowed to do something as simple as a descent of three dozen stairs. Sometimes it seemed better to be something as common as all those people running around Quachil Thecou.

"Hard to believe this would turn into a sacred mound one day," she said, mainly in order to take her thoughts off the familiar light resentment that she never allowed herself to formulate in words. Her life was the envy of the entire city, wasn't it?

"Oh yes!" Another enthusiastic response made the servant's braids jump. "They say they will try to finish it before the cold moons."

"Who says that?"

"Everyone!" The braids jumped again, with even more vigor. "They brought plenty of new *miche-quipy* from some very faraway places. Canoe-loads of them!"

Sele took her eyes off the two men who were watching the procession, shouting every now and then, pointing their javelins as though trying to reinforce their words. Their bodies were not as vividly glistening as those of the men with the baskets, but their muscled limbs pleased the eye even more. Or maybe their poses did this, straight-backed and not bent and tottering, their legs spread wide in an impressive manner.

To ward off inappropriate thoughts she forced her attention back to her chatty converser, deciding to forget the girl's lack of proper address. But this one was gossiping as though talking to her fellow serving maid.

"How do you know so much about the building of sacred

mounds?" she asked, motioning another girl, the one who carried a fan of bird feathers but didn't seem to be concentrating on her mistress's needs enough to notice that she might need relief in the accumulating heat. Another one caught in unseemly staring. But those men drew everyone's eyes, not only hers, didn't they?

A glance at the simpler palanquins of her fellow noble female watchers and the men rushing further up the incline, around her powerful husband's palanquin, confirmed a different conclusion. They all seemed to be fascinated with the game or conversing between themselves, even the refreshed-looking ruler. He was sitting straighter in his decorated chair, addressing a group of *honorables,* her father in their midst, his hands moving along with his words. Unable to see from the distance of quite a few dozen paces, she could bet that his gaunt cheeks retained a hint of coloring, his eyes glittering with healthier glint than its regular feverish glow.

"Oh, oh, there is this man who comes to report up the Royal Mound every now and then. He said that they can't dig and carry when it's raining or the earth is hard because of the cold. He said the tribute collector was told to bring foreigners from all around, canoe-loads of those!" Her enthusiastic informant was shaking her head in another spell of excitement, her hands burdened with several flasks of sweetened water and fruit too busy to come to her words' aid. Which was a good thing, decided Sele irritably, motioning the girl to calm down. Too much agitation might draw attention, might make the gossipy fowls look her way. "Another delegation came in only this morning, or maybe on the evening before. They brought plenty of things from the far, far east, where no one visited before they say!"

Sele felt her stomach tightening painfully. "The head of the tribute collectors is my uncle, and he might be out there, among the *considerates.* Go and see if he is around. Let him know that he might wish to pay his respects to me."

It came out well. She nodded at another servant to take the trays away, her stomach thrilling at the mere possibility. If back in the city, Uncle Ahal would be there, in the thick of the city's happenings. He never loitered in his home, like other *honorables* and *considerates* did, a wild nomad that he was at times, according to Father's complaints. He had only one wife, and she was not a nice person, not like some of Father's spouses. She scanned the crowd down the mound-like construction they occupied once again.

The swaying feathers of the fan cooled the unseemly heat that washed her face at the mere possibility of meeting Uncle Ahal, actually meeting him and talking to him. She was allowed, wasn't she? Oh, but it would be good to see him. And coming back from the journey in the mysterious far east, weathered, darkened with sun and full of stories, handsomer than ever. He would be surprised to see her as a woman now; and far above his status too. That would show him.

The smile threatened to sneak out on its own. The last time he was amused when they talked, when she was still in her father's house, a silly girl, readying to embark upon the journey toward the blinding glory of her new life. But she wasn't anything of the sort now, was she, and he would be impressed. He wouldn't dismiss her words with mere laughter this time, not the words of Revered Sun's favorite wife. He would never dare.

Amused by the thought, she slipped out of her luxurious seat without thinking, tossing her head in a challenge at the appalled gazes of her remaining maids. She could stretch her legs, couldn't she? It was tiring to sit for half a morning without moving at all. She wasn't breaking any custom, not glaringly. Even Revered Sun's sister was seen strolling the mats her maids hurried to spread so she wouldn't mar her delicate royal feet clad in annoyingly fancy shoes with ridiculously low edges. Sele tossed her head higher, then strolled in the opposite direction, stepping carefully on the uneven earth. After two moons at the Royal Mound, she forgot how normal un-flattened ground felt.

The procession of *miche-quipy* was easier to observe from her new vantage point, now heading down the crumpling pile of earth, some of them, the huge baskets previously strapped to their backs clutched in their arms, their straight-backed poses radiating relief. Only one of the men had his container still hanging over his back, thrown over his wide shoulder carelessly, different from the others. It was easy to see how tall he was, and broad-shouldered, the outline of the muscles crisscrossing his legs, glistening in the sun, his forehead high and not as flat as accepted, as though his mother did not bother to bind his head when he was an infant. Some foreign communities out there didn't have this custom, Uncle Ahal once told her. They were that backward!

Curiosity-consumed, she peered at the man, able to make out his features, enjoying the sight of his protruding chin, clean of facial hair, even though *miche-quipy* did not always take care of their appearance in such a way. Certainly not the ones carrying buckets of earth for days on end. Or did they?

The man slowed his step, and her heart made a strange leap inside her chest, because it was easy to see him raising his head, then proceeding to stare at her, her in particular, his eyes narrowed with unsettling intensity and no shame. Or maybe it was just because of the sun. No working *miche-quipy* or even the city commoners crowding every vacant ground around the plaza dared to raise their eyes toward the royalty upon the elevated ground, but the lowly foreign worker did just that, stared back at her with what looked like annoying intensity, maybe even a challenge. From the distance of the route the loaders treaded and the incline she stood upon, it was easy to tell, helped by the way he had slowed his step, nearly halting in the evenly progressing flow.

The motion of the feathered fan became a blessing, cooling off the burning of her face, which must have burst into the worst of coloring, but she felt none of it for a moment, mesmerized, frightened, her stomach turning as though she had eaten something bad. It was so hot, so annoyingly humid, the air sticking to her throat, refusing to move down. Even the roaring from the field, the noise of so many people jumping and screaming or talking all at once retreated, penetrating her ears like a distant rainstorm. The strangest of sensations.

"Honorable Mistress!" The voice of the serving girl with the fan was annoyingly real, assaulting her hearing, unwelcomed. "Are you feeling well, Revered Lady? You should return to your palanquin; it isn't allowed —"

"Yes, yes." With an effort, Sele took her eyes away, the man still staring, his jaw protruding more prominently than before, as though challenging her too. His chest was thrust forward, wide and well-muscled, smeared with streaks of muddy earth and adorned with scratches, like a carved figurine on the pipe back in the royal dwelling, brown and slick, inviting to touch. One of the men who had run back and forth along the column of working *miche-quipy* seemed to be yelling at him, motioning him to move on, she surmised, her mind in a daze, trying to get a grip.

"Would you like to drink something sweet, Mistress?"

Her heart fluttering, Sele nodded, welcoming the distraction this time. It was the strangest, most unpleasant sensation, and she had to fight the urge to look again, to consciously restrain her eyes from drawing back toward the sun-beaten route the workers walked.

Accepting the promptly filled goblet of exquisitely painted pottery, she glanced at the site of construction again, with no regard to her conscious decisions. The insolent worker's eyes were not on her anymore, his head turned toward the gesturing overseer, his back relaying as much insolence and challenge as his face did, his head held high. In another heartbeat, he joined the rest of the descending men, glancing at her again briefly, making her stomach turn once more. What an annoyance! Sele clenched her teeth against the unwelcome fluttering in her stomach.

"Who are those men up there?" she asked as nonchalantly as she could, taking a sip from the offered goblet, not tasting the sweetness of the beverage it held. "The ones who are carrying the earth. Are these the *miche-quipy* of our city?"

The girl with the fan shook her head helplessly, displaying her lack of knowledge. However, another one, a plump little thing who was entrusted with the flasks when Sele's chosen maid was sent to ask about Uncle Ahal, cleared her throat shyly. "They are coming from out there, most of them, Mistress," she volunteered. "Our tribute collectors bring them from the villages."

Tribute collectors! Sele's gaze leapt back toward the crowded plaza, hopeful, but the outburst of shouts caught her attention, coming from the working *miche-quipy* this time, the direction she tried to avoid looking at. The foreigner, as expected, slowed his step once again, staring with no shame, somewhat closer and easier to see, passing below the colorfulness of the royal palanquins' congregation.

However, this time, not only the overseers of the construction site did not take well the insolent man's frivolous gazing or change of a pace. Several spearmen guarding the progress of the work clearly had had enough. Before she could decide how to react herself, to look away with all the dignity she could muster or to squash the pretentious intruder with the fury of her own gaze, one of the warriors rushed toward him, his javelin balanced evenly in his hands, to be used as a pushing device, or maybe like a stick to strike down the insolent onlooker. Uncle Ahal had said once that the royal warriors preferred spears for just these tactics, that there was no need to harm or even kill disobedient citizens, that to push or strike them away and thus display possible consequences was more than enough in many situations.

Well, maybe disobedient people of Quachil Thecou could be pushed away or into any other desirable action by the less harmful side of a spear if need be, but it didn't seem to be the case with the foreign *miche-quipy*. Her breath caught, she watched the man turning in time to meet the advance, twisting away from the blow of the first nearing guard, pushed by the bland edge of the spear but not badly. Wavering momentarily, he did not seem to fight hard to maintain his balance, his hands tearing the strapped bucket off his shoulder, hurling it at his attacker with astonishing accuracy, as though it was a missile, to collide with the surprised warrior's face and make him waver. In another heartbeat, the rest of the man's body followed suit, pouncing, colliding with the surprised guard, sending him crashing down.

Aghast, Sele watched them hitting the ground together, in the back of her mind expecting the foreigner to land on top of his rival, not surprised with this development at all. His hands looked like paws of a ferocious animal when they locked around his victim's throat, and it took a few overseers to drag him off and kick him into obedience. Or try to do that. It was difficult to see in the melee, but somehow, the fierce *miche-quipy* was on his feet once again, wrestling with another royal guard, somehow escaping the thrust of a spear that this time meant harm, its flint point pouncing toward the disobedient worker's exposed torso. It drew a line across the glistening skin plastered with mud, but yet again, the foreigner didn't give up, grabbing the sturdy shaft and yanking hard, careless of the barbed flint adorning it.

The fan was not moving anymore, bringing no relief in the heat, but Sele didn't even notice, her eyes glued to the fighting men, her mind running amok, refusing to understand. There were gasps all around and outcries, the noble girls in their palanquins turning their heads to gawk as well, Sele's own maids crying out, the plump one with the flasks gasping in an annoyingly loud manner, sounding fake. But for her own need to see, Sele would have liked slapping the silly thing hard, if only in order to silence her. As it was, her mind was too busy struggling with the wild whirlpool inside her own chest, aghast, wishing the guards to apprehend the wild beast, willing the fierce *miche-quipy* to succeed. Succeed in what? There was no answer to this question, the crimson lines crawling down his side, where the first spear left a glaring print, making her heart try to jump out of her chest. It looked beautiful and bad.

There were more guards rushing toward the scene, where the foreigner, now armed with a javelin he managed not only to wrestle from his rival's hands but also to turn against his attackers, was standing hunched forward, whirling whichever way, not letting anyone near.

"Shoot him," roared someone, an authoritative voice from among the *considerates* who were nearer to the developing drama, crowding the same side of the incline the royal women occupied, away from the royal dais. "Doesn't anyone of those guarding the mound have a bow? Useless men!"

This made the commotion among the armed men intensify. More shouts erupted all around, while the foreigner down the incline made a move as though about to charge, which caused the armed men and the overseers surrounding him to jump backwards quite a few paces. Someone's javelin pounced toward him, leaving its owner's hand on the off chance of hitting its target, but the handsome *miche-quipy* was quicker, jumping away, then pushing the flying missile with his own newly acquired weaponry, deftly at that.

Sele remembered to draw in a breath, apparently having held it in for too long, daring not to move or blink, for that matter. If she blinked, that man would lose, she knew, would get hurt, impaled on the pointed javelins. A ridiculous notion, but it felt real enough not to give it a try. Even the maids around her stopped their stupid whimpering. But of course they did. It wasn't just a relief from boredom, not anymore. Somehow it became important. How?

She didn't dare to think about it, watching the cornered man charging again, whirling his long-reaching weaponry as though trying to keep his attackers at bay, probably the case. He didn't dare to cast his javelin or to attack any of the surrounding warriors, not separately and with the others ready to pounce on him the moment his weapon was entangled and busy. Even she could understand that. What hopelessness. The pit in her stomach deepened some more.

Another group of armed men came running down the incline and from across the other side of the plaza, pushing their way through the congregating city dwellers who seemed to transfer their fascination from the spear-throwing contest as readily. Even the dignitaries crowding Revered Sun's palanquin began sneaking glances, their frowns easy to surmise.

At this very moment, her eyes caught sight of the familiar broad shoulders and the weathered sun-burned face, and her heart made a wild lurch inside her chest. Uncle Ahal! Square, solid, reliable. She caught her breath, watching him clearing his way toward the commotion, single-minded in his determination, knowing what he was doing. Always the case.

Back in the circle of spearmen, the foreigner managed to make one of his attackers fall, landing his spear against his victim's temple as though it were a club, with what looked like a resounding thud even from a distance. His victim went down at once, helped by an additional blow, less well directed than before.

With admirable quickness, the victorious *miche-quipy*

straightened his spear so the correct end was facing his fallen rival; however, the rest of his attackers seized on the opportunity, several spearheads pouncing toward him, lethal and unerring. Still, somehow, he managed to avoid a thrust of the nearest javelin, but when another blunt shaft crashed against his side with much force, he collapsed as decisively as his previous rival, doubled over and gasping, to disappear in the fury of lashing out shafts.

"Don't kill him!" The shout resonated easily through the crowd.

Her heart going still once again, Sele recognized the voice before her eyes confirmed the conclusion. Uncle Ahal was already up the uneven slope, shoving his way through the congregation with his typical calm authority, not about to be stopped, even though he wasn't even armed but for his girdle that she knew would contain his prettily decorated knife, a solid, long-bladed affair of ragged flint and a beautifully polished antler handle. She was always craving to hold that treasure, never daring to ask. Uncle Ahal used to spoil her rotten whenever he could, but such a treasure was off limits; even she knew that.

Solid and dangerous-looking, his movements guarded but uninhibited, relaying confidence and not a hint of uncertainty, he was already talking to the guards, and what he said made them pause. It was easy to see that despite the distance and the yelling of the surrounding people, because their clamor went down as though on its own, and she knew everyone watched him with as bated breath as she did, knowing that, whatever his goal was, he would manage where the others failed. He always did!

"He doesn't even have a club, this man! Or a spear," cried out the girl with the fan. "Why do they listen to him? Who is he?"

"Quiet!" hissed Sele, not taking her eyes off the growing commotion, noting that the rebellious *miche-quipy* was still very much alive, pushing himself up stubbornly, with no visible effort. Uncle Ahal glanced at him only once, as far as she could see, motioning him to stay where he was. Did he know this man in particular?

"What is he telling them?" another girl was chirruping in a

dramatically loud whisper. "Why doesn't he let them kill that worker?"

Sele ground her teeth, desperate to hear at least a word of what had been transpiring down the slope. "Quiet, all of you. One more word and I'll have you all thrown out of the Royal Mound!" But for the entirety of her attention being on the spearman and Uncle Ahal, with more important people strolling down the incline, joining the argument, she would have slapped the no-good fowl and other of her chatty followers painfully enough to silence them. She never did this before, but now it felt like she might, a welcome idea too, almost tempting.

A terrified silence that followed gave her a moment of satisfaction, but it didn't compensate her for missing the exchange at the scene of the fighting. There was so much noise all around, people's voices subdued but not enough to let her hear her uncle's words. He was standing so firmly, unwavering, his legs spread wide, arms linked across his decorated chest, his entire stance radiating solidness, durability, sense of security, a person certain of his course. It was obvious that what he said was important and calm, making even the violent *miche-quipy* listen, who, despite an obvious order, leaned forward, blood trickling down his side, which he clutched with one hand, the other still gripping the spear, clearly ready to use it if need be. Still, it was clear that even he listened to Uncle Ahal's curt, measured words. A wonder!

"What is he telling them?" murmured the fanning girl, forgetting her breeze-creating device once again, as well as the previous tongue-lashing, apparently. Still, this time, Sele didn't mind. The girl was articulating her own thoughts.

The wild *miche-quipy* shifted defensively, his spear thrust slightly forward, clutched for dear life, of that Sele was sure. Uncle Ahal was talking to him now – actually talking to him! – half turned toward his previous audience, as though afraid they would act with no accordance to his words. When he reached out, clearly demanding the weaponry in question, she stopped breathing again. Wounded or not, this man was dangerous and Uncle Ahal wasn't even armed himself! To her relief, the other spearmen seemed to be ready, but her uncle's curt gesture had them staying motionless, not pouncing on the dangerous man.

"Why is he doing this?" Another ardent whisper had her nearly jump. "What is he saying to the wild worker?"

To her own slight surprise, Sele found herself snickering. "Stop waving this spear, it's dangerous. Go back to shovel the dirt, be a good boy. That's what he says," she whispered, giggling somewhat hysterically but needing to say it, to share the incredibility of it all.

The snickering of her maids made her feel better, even relieved. Squinting against the glow of the fierce midday sun, she watched her uncle indeed stepping closer, receiving the javelin after another heartbeat of hesitation, then turning to face the surrounding men, talking rapidly now, in quieter tones. It was easy to surmise that. Relieved beyond measure, she puzzled over the way he stood, as though shielding the criminal *miche-quipy* with his back, as though defending him against his own peers now. Why would he?

"What is he doing now?" She heard herself saying it and wished to push the words back, not needing the silly serving girls' opinions.

"He doesn't want them to kill that *miche-quipy*," reacted the flask girl promptly. "Who is he? Must be someone of importance."

"He is my uncle," said Sele testily, incensed all over again. "He is important. Very much so. The stupid flask girl was supposed to find him when I sent her to do just that. In fact..." She hesitated, eyeing the circle of armed men growing, tightening instead of dispersing, with Uncle Ahal still shielding the foreigner, who looked tense and ill-at-ease, clearly ready to pounce again, weaponless as he was now.

A group of decorated dignitaries was pushing their way through, the lavishly dressed figure she recognized in the lead, honorable Anksheah, the Royal Mound's head guard. Briefly, she wondered where her father was. He could lend his younger brother support, couldn't he, whatever Uncle Ahal was trying to do. He seemed to be arguing with some of the warriors, repeating himself, judging by the mildly irritated expression she knew so well. Even from the distance, it was easy to read that grimace of his.

"Take me down there, where the other dignitaries are crowding," she said firmly, motioning her seat-bearers, appalled by her own gall but knowing that it was now or never. It was her chance of meeting her uncle, and she wasn't going to miss it, not this time, not if she could help it.

CHAPTER 12

When he glimpsed the heavy figure of the Royal Mound's lead guard descending the incline, he knew he was in trouble.

Busy trying to talk to too many people at once while keeping an eye on the wild villager and the spearman who were still eager to impale the dangerous piece of work on their javelins, Ahal tried to cajole his mind into inventing at least a semblance of a plausible excuse for what he had done.

The exhaustion, made worse by the splitting headache that attacked him while crowding the better side of the field, watching the selected few among the city players displaying their skill, made his thoughts scatter all of a sudden, and just as he needed his presence of mind. To burst out in the way he had done when recognizing the wild villager being again in the heart of violence and insubordination was stupid, to say the least. He had no right to stop the royal guards from doing their duty and the wild foreigner did manage to harm at least one of the warriors, seriously enough to have the man still lying on the ground, out cold. Not dead, hopefully, but who knew. The villager's count of killed warriors was going up, the damn stupid man! Still, it was not Ahal's place to interfere, or make such a public scene out of it. He was not one of the advisers, not a person Revered Sun relied upon, or even knew by sight. Had he been something of the sort, he would have known better than to act as he acted. Curse it all!

Gathering his thoughts hastily, he turned toward the villager, who was standing erect and seemingly unafraid, despite the blood trickling down his side, the sharpness of his cheekbones ruined by distinct swelling, his prominent forehead matching, already changing its coloring to a darker shade. Still, the man looked fit to fight on, his eyes flashing wildly, their determination and lack of fear on display.

"Take him to the edge of the spear-throwing court and wait for me there," he said curtly, trying to appear as authoritative as though still back on the journey, the highest authority among the travelers, not the case here in the city. "Keep an eye on him and don't harm him." A glance at the wild man reassured him, the look in the narrowed eyes focused, boring at him, full of wary intensity. Good. He answered the piercing glare with his own, then held it for a fraction of a heartbeat. "Go with them and do whatever they tell you, villager. Do not make any more trouble. I will come to inform you of your fate shortly."

A promise he wasn't certain he would be able to keep, but the man needed the reassurance. Again he reflected that it was a mistake to send this one ahead with the goods and the rest of the working hands instead of keeping this particular captive by his side, delivering him here personally, supervised and looked after.

Back on the night of the storm, the villager promised to behave, and his men promised to keep an eye on him without pushing this one too hard or stomping too much on his pride. The villager had more than his share of it, but this was something Ahal actually appreciated. Better a fierce man made to serve you out of his own free will, or at least as a reasonable necessity, then a mindless crowd of obedient nonentities. Or so he believed. However, he was not in the position to dictate his beliefs or make people follow them, not here in the city, not when it came to the circles that mattered.

"Tribute Collector!" The heavily decorated figure of the lead royal guard Anksheah, followed closely by other decorated men, was already upon them, clattering with his copper and clay necklaces and armbands, creating a racket that might have pleased the ear under different circumstances.

Ahal took his thoughts off the troublesome foreigner, glad that the spearmen obeyed with no hesitation, already at a respectable distance, not about to interfere, not before their time. One less worry for the moment. "Greetings, Honorable Chief Guard."

"It is you, Ahal, the Head of the Tribute Collectors," drawled the man, a hint of a smile reflecting in his closely set eyes, their friendliness concealed but not too deeply. At least that. He might have expected the man of such status feel irritated at being dragged from the royal incline with an uncalled-for errand. "Greetings. Did you have a fruitful journey?"

The necessary politeness. Ahal hid his grin, despite the disturbing fluttering somewhere there in the pit of his stomach. It was stupid what he did, stupid and unnecessary. The villager had proved to be trouble despite his promises. He should have let him die, if not back in the provincial city, then here and now. Why was he concerned with the wild man anyway? What did it matter if one less foreign *miche-quipy* was to work on the new mound? He had brought enough manpower as it was.

"Thank you, Honorable Anksheah. My journey was indeed satisfactory, with plenty of goods that were due to be paid to our glorious city, plenty of workers to help us in our building undertakings."

"Plenty of workers indeed," muttered the man with a telling grimace and a glance at the group surrounding the troublesome foreigner. "Some of the *miche-quipy* you brought do not seem to contribute but to confusion and disorder."

"Some of the foreigners need to learn our ways in order to contribute to our prosperity, Honorable Leader." Marveling at how smoothly it came out, as he didn't manage to prepare any such claims in advance, Ahal took a deep breath. "I apologize for the disorder this particular *miche-quipy* has caused. He has potential to turn into a useful worker. I believe he can be tamed and used to enhance the glory of our city. His fighting skills are admirable, as you can see, and I have seen him fighting and killing a forest giant, a huge forest bear crazed into attacking our warriors. We were having a hard time with the maddened beast, but the foreign *miche-quipy* challenged it with a spear, killing the mad monster alone and unaided before more of our people were hurt." He shrugged, reliving the moment. "I mention this incident in order to explain why I undertook bringing this man to our glorious city. I believe he could be of use to us and not only as a simple worker carrying baskets of earth."

The heavyset man frowned thoughtfully, then shook his head. "What you believe is of little importance, Ahal. It is not your place to supervise the workers you bring to the city. Your interruption was unwarranted and it caused our Revered Sun and his loyal advisers certain inconvenience, interfering with the procedures of the important competition our sacred sovereign honored with his hallowed presence. Do not take upon yourself duties you were not honored with."

He tried to will his heart into more reasonable beating, his throat dry, palms tingling. "I'm grateful for your advice, Honorable Leader. Your words honor me and I do take a heed of them, always! However," he paused, not daring to draw a deep breath, which he needed badly, if for no other reason than to enhance the transition from politeness to practical talk, "if allowed, I shall dare to offer an argument on this particular matter. As a person who collects such working power, the *miche-quipy* that came from the provinces and are needed in our glorious city for various tasks, construction being only one among those, I do believe that sometimes my opinion on the matter of particular workers might be worthy of sounding. This certain *miche-quipy* I selected personally from among his fellow villagers for his physical strength and his fighting skills. My belief is that he may contribute to our glorious city given a little time and some training. If allowed, I would keep him under my personal care, tame him, and make him prove himself, Honorable Chief Warrior. Our city will benefit from differently gifted people like that. And now that what needed to be sound was sounded, I apologize for offering an unasked-for advice, Honorable Leader."

Various expressions seemed to be challenging each other, peeking through the customarily impenetrable mask of the lead guard, reflecting in the depth of the eyes boring at Ahal, from displeasure, the most prominent visage, to what seemed to be a puzzled surprise. When the massive head shook, he wished to let out a held breath. The man did listen. At least that.

"You have your share of courage, Ahal. Something that may be construed as insolence and presumption, but for your reputation, my brief acquaintance with you, and, more importantly, my close association with the distinguished head of your family." The massive head kept shaking as the narrowly set eyes stared at Ahal, cold and calculating, not relating the philosophical tone of the words. "Come with me." The stone bracelets rang dully with the wave of the beefy arm, reinforcing the summons. "If Revered Sun, Revered Tattooed Serpent or any of their advisers wish to listen, you will have a short time to state your case. I do not wish to have our revered ruler conclude that I wasted his time with unworthy denizens of this city. Should it happen, I will not be as favorably inclined toward you as I was until now. Is that clear to you, Tribute Collector?"

Ahal nodded hurriedly, his heart beating too fast to try and react in a more eloquent, or at least appropriate, manner. To summon the spearmen guarding the prisoner with a curt wave seemed like his only option, the wide back of the lead guard already upon him, drawing away, not waiting for his reaction, polite speeches or otherwise.

He motioned at the spearmen to hurry, then, reassured, tried to rush what had been said through his head, appalled by his own brazenness more and more with every passing heartbeat. Did he actually presume to push himself into matters that had nothing to do with him, important royal matters? Did he argue just now with the head of the royal guards? He did all that, didn't he, and in a forward fashion too. And why? For what purpose? What end?

The dry earth crumbled under their feet as they headed up the incline and toward the dignified clamor surrounding the divine ruler's dais. Such a colorful congregation. Ahal felt his shoulders straightening on their own. Whatever was in store for him, it was thrilling to be allowed near the sacredness of the royalty, the direct descendants of the Sun Deity itself. It never happened to him before.

He willed his heart into a calmer pounding, glad that even though he had arrived only this morning, with no time to visit his home but to head for the gathering upon the Grand Plaza, as the official who had greeted him and the remnants of his men and his warriors insisted, he still had enough time to have one of the aides sent to fetch his personal servants with clean clothes and appropriate decorations, necklaces and armbands, and that his outfit still looked presentable despite the commotion the damn villager caused. What to do about that one?

He shook his head once again, knowing that the sensible thing was to let the unruly, violent foreigner die, the sooner the better. The mess he had caused now or back at the eastern town was more than enough, his promise to the pretty village girl, the foreigner's sister, notwithstanding. Ciki, he thought with a twinge of a pleasantly light longing. As agreeable as her short, nicely easy name, pleasing, delightfully uncomplicated, accommodating, infectious with her lightness and cheerful, easy ways. She was the reason he had stayed in that gods-forsaken village for a whole two dawns instead of one single span of the sun's journey it took them to collect piles of pearls and pearly decorations among this village's possessions. Such a forsaken place, and yet not so insignificant. The single strangely-shaped mound covered with grass this eastern settlement sported did not impress him in the least, an old embankment, not very high or distinctly in use, just a hill really. The locals claimed it was a sacred mound, left to them by their legendary ancestors who ruled this part of the land once upon a time, flourishing, an important cultural center that they were.

Well, maybe it did happen once upon a time, a long time ago; however, now the forests around the village looked wild enough, untouched by cultivation besides the obvious patches of clearly sown and about to be harvested earth, not too many of those, as of course the village was pitifully small, spreading around their ancient mound, surrounded by a basic palisade, with no larger construction than the multitude of regular huts. And yet....

When the dusk was nearing and the village's elders, relieved to have no edible goods demanded but only pearly adornments that this place had in surprisingly large quantities, promised to have the demanded goods amassed in the town's square by the middle of the next day, Ciki, as lively and chatty as she had been from the moment of their acquaintance, before her brother's deeds unnerved her into hysterical behavior on the night of the storm, led him outside and along the prettily pastoral trail climbing up the nearby hill.

Full of more anticipation than he had experienced for some time, he had followed, enjoying the walk, expecting an evening of an idle pleasure. Not arguing when she insisted on following the trail all the way to the top of the hill, he had found himself gaping in surprise at the view of the ancient mound that had opened to his eyes, the sight of the giant bird, probably an eagle, or so the girl claimed, its wings unfolded and spread, small and sketchy, leaving much to the imagination yet unmistakable, its giant body and smaller head rough likenesses as well, again merely suggested but enough to make one think that he saw what he saw. An Eagle Mound, impossible to guess unless looking from far enough away and above.

He had found himself staring for a long time, eyes fighting the thickening darkness, outlining the obvious shape, suddenly knowing that this village had more to it than what met the eye. A different place, not to be judged by the regular standards, this land and its denizens. No wonder the wild villager behaved differently, with a generous measure of self-respect, ready to pay what had been demanded as long as he had been spared the humiliation of going back to face his family and his people, a respectable trait in a person one wouldn't expect to encounter in an uncouth land-working *miche-quipy*. Who were these people?

The night spent on the hill, warmed by the camp fire and the cozily intimate affection of the easygoing Ciki, every moment delightfully warm, full of laughter and coziness, even the lovemaking itself, didn't answer the question. She was special as well, in a way, uncomplicated but not like a backward village woman. Her ardor was real, her affection not indifferent or forced, free from natural greed of regular women who expected to be paid for their favors. None of that. Nothing but lightness and joyfulness. He had made his men stay for another night, even though the pearly jewelry and adornments were promptly collected, handed over by the early afternoon of the next day. Still, the prospect of another night in her company and on the magical hill and in the view of the giant eagle made him delay their departure. They were late to return to Quachil Thecou as it was, but this was to be the last of delays.

Shaking his head to get rid of irrelevant memories, he concentrated on his step, regretting nothing. The canoe-load of pearly wonders, quite a few crammed baskets, were already received with enough enthusiasm by the city officials, making him plan another journey to these regions later on. The eastern lands did owe Quachil Thecou some additional goods, and even though she was nothing but a cute village-girl, infinitely beneath him and his status, he would bring her a present, some city adornment she had never seen or imagined in her entire life.

He motioned at the spearmen once again, the sight of the plaza and the contesters crowding it giving him a clearer direction. "Bring the foreign worker to the edge of the plaza and keep an eye on him until I came to relieve you."

They glanced at him gloomily, not pleased at being ordered about by a mere official who had nothing to do with the fighting forces. However, the broad back of the chief royal guard was still close enough, drawing away, motioning Ahal to keep up in his turn. A clear sign. None of them was in the position to argue with the protégé of the influential head of the royal guards.

"Remain here until summoned, Ahal."

Upon reaching the guarded part of the incline, the heavyset man motioned at the dignified gathering that crowded it, those allowed to near the royal seat doing so delicately, backing away when dismissed without turning their backs to the seated figure, others milling at a respectable distance, sneaking glances or talking in a quiet manner, accepting food or goblets from the rushing-around servants. Such a glaring difference to the throngs of *considerates* he had spent his time among until now; brighter, flashier, the clattering of the clay and copper adornments pleasing the ear, hurting the eye in the light of the midday sun, which was now hiding behind the clouds again, bringing relief in the heat. An atypical day for this time of the early autumn, but not unwelcome. Still, something seemed to be wrong in the sky, something that made his nerves prickle.

Trying to hide his apprehension, unused to moving in circles that were so glaringly above his status, his brother's company notwithstanding – family was family and they didn't meet on official occasions and ceremonies – Ahal turned to watch the plaza and the spearmen strolling it, enjoying a break in the competition. From this vantage point, the flat patch of land spread before his eyes comfortably, at a perfect distance, allowing the view of the entire field and every competing man. If forgotten to be summoned or sent back, he might enjoy observing the next bout of spear-throwing in the manner he never did before. But for something like that to happen.

The nagging worry was back. What did the head of the guards wish him to tell and to whom? Not Revered Sun himself, surely. It would be out of place, inappropriate, uncalled for. He wasn't ready for such an august reception, his garments respectable but not in the league of the true nobility. Even the serving *miche-quipy* were clothed in fine material here, their torsos and limbs covered, clattering occasional jewelry. What riches!

One such nicely clad maid, a pretty little thing, openly playful, seemed to be sneaking glances at him, no tray in her hands to suggest a good reason for her insolent scrutiny. To hide his uneasiness, he motioned at another servant, the one whose tray was loaded with flasks.

"Greetings, Tribute Collector." One of the men, a lean, gaunt-looking type, an official responsible for organization of public feasts he remembered, passed his hands over his face and his chest, offering a customary greeting. "Is it you, my friend?"

Ahal responded with a matching gesture and words prescribed for such situations. The man was not a friend or a close acquaintance. Just someone who deigned to acknowledge him in these august surroundings despite his clear lack of belonging, someone who might need something from him.

"You have been brought here by Honorable Anksheah, have you not?" After more flowery exchanges, the man got to the point.

"Honorable chief of our glorious guarding forces wished me to sound my opinion on a certain subject, yes."

"Oh." The man nodded reservedly, then turned toward one of his peers, another lesser master of ceremony, this one clearly a

Royal Mound's frequenter, his clothes a celebration of adornments.

Out of politeness, Ahal let his eyes wander back toward the plaza.

"Honorable Master." The voice of the girl was timid, and he knew it was the curious serving maid even before deigning to look her way.

"What do you want?" he asked more curtly than intended, unwilling to let his thoughts stray from their purpose. When faced with an important dignitary, polite talk was necessary. Not so when accosted by a silly serving girl.

"I..." The girl blinked helplessly, as though about to burst into tears. "My Revered Mistress, she told me to... to find you and let you know..." At this, her voice broke and her eyes dropped with no pretended humility, not this time.

"Your mistress?" As always, the compassion was there, making him regret his previous coldness. "Who is your mistress, girl?"

"My mistress, oh!" Clearly encouraged, she looked up, her gaze wet but glittering with hope. "Our Revered Sun's favorite wife. Your niece, Honorable Leader. She says she is you niece, and she told me... she told me to find you, to send you word..."

Sele? He blinked, then let his gaze wander toward the royal family palanquins crowding the other side of the incline, trying not to appear as though staring openly, not at the lavishly dressed female members of the royal family occupying their carried seats. "Is my niece there among the royal ladies?"

"Yes, oh yes!" The girl's eyes sparkled excitedly, with no previously displayed distress or concern, almost conspiratorial. "She was most anxious to see you and she ordered her palanquin to be taken down there." The prettily round arm waved in the direction of the plaza where the players were again gathering around its edge, watching the stone disk being prepared to be rolled forcefully, their spears ready to launch. "She wished to talk to you urgently. She told her palanquin-bearers to take her toward the plaza—"

"The plaza?" he asked stupidly, not understanding. "Why didn't she send me word earlier?"

Why indeed? He stopped himself before uttering any more silly nonsense. What could he have done had he known that she was around, spending her time in the royal company she belonged to now, a part of the divine ruler's following, not a location he had been allowed to show his face at until these very moments, and thanks to none other than the wild villager. He glanced at the edge of the incline, hoping that at least that one managed to pass a short span of time without getting in trouble.

"Go and tell my niece that I shall try to see her before the last competition is over. Have her return to her proper surroundings until it happens." The girl was gazing at him, wide-eyed. In the corner of his eye, he could see the broad arm of Anksheah waving him to approach the thinner crowd surrounding the royal sitting arrangements. "Go!"

Her paces were light and hurried, and for another heartbeat, he watched her running down the incline, pleased with the sight of her swaying hips. Only the prettiest were chosen to serve the royal family, that much was clear. And Sele was among those, the prettiest and chosen, even if for a much higher position, but still only to serve, to pass her earthly blood to the divine ruler's offspring by her, to never be one of the sacred family, not even through her children. And if Revered Sun's health was failing him... Was it?

The question that was answered, even if partly, shortly thereafter, when the curt gesture of the head guard invited him to bypass another thinner and more luxuriously clad gathering, allowing him into the view of the massive seat covered with painted hides of intricate designs, made out of what might be a solid wood, difficult to tell under so many decorations. The divine ruler was also somewhat difficult to make out under the magnificence of his outfit, his shoulders covered with a cape of matching designs, his legs adorned with multitude of peltries, his face nearly hidden under the grandeur of a heavily ornamented headdress, a net of black threads supporting a brilliant red diadem, embellished with beads and seeds, white feathers weaving around it, some loose and differently painted, some bunched and decorated with beads, a magnificent vision.

Tempted to stare, Ahal lowered his gaze hastily, uttering an appropriate noncommittal greeting, a short cry everyone was required to make before daring to enter Revered Sun's vicinity, even the closest of his advisers. Three obligatory exclamations to let the divine ruler know of one's presence, invited and expected as it might be, allowing the sacred offspring of the sky deity an opportunity to respond with either greeting or silence if he wished to do so, thus politely refusing the visitor or the petitioner. A strict and an uncompromising custom, a wise one.

The heavily ringed eyes rested on Ahal, not about to refuse his admittance. "It is you, Head Tribute Collector." The customary greeting sounded strange coming off the colorless lips. The mighty ruler of Quachil Thecou did not know of his existence in most probability, not until now.

"It is me, oh mighty Revered Sun," uttered Ahal, his throat dry, craving a gulp of water, suspecting that none was offered, not in this vicinity. Only flasks of sweetened mixtures servants with trays seemed to press on the visitors, the mere thought of which made him nauseated and thirstier than before.

"You are bidden to step closer, Tribute Collector."

He knew better than to near more than four paces, of course, a distance no one but the Sun's family was allowed to close. Still, the closer proximity allowed a clear, even if a brief peek into the mighty ruler's face, a shocking contrast to the finery of the colorful garments, the sunken, heavily ringed eyes, the hollow cheeks, the skin hanging loosely, almost in folds, the strangely folded mouth appearing as though no teeth were there to support the frame of the flesh. He was not an old man, Quachil Thecou sovereign, not by his count of summers, and yet he looked like an ancient elder. Ahal pushed the renewed wave of worry away.

"They say you are the younger brother of my esteemed adviser," went on the man, frowning lightly, his eyes, even if sunken and slightly feverish, concentrated and thoughtful, relating no infirmity.

"Yes, Revered Sun. I have the rare honor to belong to the family of your faithful adviser, the father of your youngest of wives."

"Oh yes, my youngest of wives." This time, the empty lips stretched into a hint of a smile, a gesture speaking of contentment. An encouraging sight. So there was no dissatisfaction there. Good for Sele. "Your family serves me well, Tribute Collector. It is good that people like you constitute the backbone of our glorious city."

"It is an honor to serve you, Revered Sun." The sounds of agitation among the watching nobles were growing, as did the more distant roars of the excited spectators near the less prestigious side of the field. The players must have been casting their spears again. He thought about the villager, hoping the man was watching along with everyone else, wiser than to quarrel and make trouble again, or just too busy for that.

Another spectacular headdress turned toward them, not asking for permission to near, a majestic figure covered with intricate markings and strangely bright garments, the upright feathers adorning it rustling in the strengthening breeze. Recognizing famous Tattooed Serpent, a full sibling to the divine ruler and the second most powerful man in Quachil Thecou, Ahal caught his breath, noticing that clouds that suddenly rushed to cover the sky did so in perfect accord with his own mounting apprehension. It was unusual for the sun to yield its dominance at this time of the day and the season, so close to the harvest ceremonies. Not the time for the rains to fall, yet it suddenly felt as though it might happen.

"So, one hears you've been eager to offer advice on matters that have nothing to do with bringing goods or people to our glorious city, Tribute Collector." The tattooed leader did not waste his time on customary greetings, neither toward his powerful sibling nor their lower class company. Even the head of the royal guards, lingering nearby, clearly allowed to be a part of this particular interview, did not receive as much as a casual nod. "Our Chief Guard claims that you've been offering him advice. Is that true, Tribute Collector? Have you been presuming to speak on the matters that are outside of the realm of your duties and responsibilities?"

To draw in a quick breath became a necessity. He could feel the presence of the lead guard, listening avidly, ready to contribute.

To support or to harm? A question that had to remain with no immediate answer.

"I regret if my actions displeased you or caused trouble, Revered Tattooed Serpent." His voice rang satisfactorily steady, just a little higher than usual, strained but in no visible way, or so he hoped. "I have nothing but the best interest of our glorious city and its divine ruling family at heart. My actions are marked by this sole goal and purpose."

The feathers flowing down the sides of the royal diadem rustled lightly, swaying with the sovereign's thoughtful nod, the wave of the bejeweled hand barely visible, yet enough to arrest any more words or accusations. "Tell us about the disobedient *miche-quipy* you've been protecting, exempting the lowly foreigner from well-deserved punishment."

Ahal didn't dare to pause, not even in order to organize his thoughts. "I offer my abject apologies if my actions caused harm, oh mighty Revered Sun." Now that the issue was in the open, he felt better, calmer, ready to face the charges or challenges, whatever came first. "The disobedient *miche-quipy* is a foreigner from the distant villages of the east, beyond the point where our Great River is joined by another mighty flow coming from the barbarian north. He doesn't know our customs, but he came here ready to serve our mighty city, to participate in erecting yet another sacred earthwork in honor of our gods."

The eyes were boring at him, maybe ringed and weary, but very much in control, not about to accept meaningless words or excuses. No one cared for hundreds of *miche-quipy*, local or foreign, flooding the fields and the market alleys, carrying baskets of earth when a new sacred mound had been constructed, serving the *considerates* and the higher nobility, even the Sun Family, taking care of the city and its needs. Of course they were there to serve. That was what *miche-quipy* existed for. He never questioned such reality himself.

"The man I brought here, Revered Sun, Revered Tattooed Serpent." Hastily, he glanced at the other man, not certain if he was supposed to address both sacred family members, out of his depth on the accepted protocols of behavior that ruled the Royal

Mound's dwellers. "The foreign *miche-quipy* possesses certain warring skills that I believe could be of use to the greater glory of our city. Every *miche-quipy* can carry a basket of earth. Not every one of them can handle a spear or challenge a warrior or a forest beast with great skill and no fear."

The ringed eyes narrowed slightly, then shifted toward the decorated warrior. Ahal did not dare to breathe with relief.

"What do you think, Chief Guard Anksheah?"

The heavyset man moved his head noncommittally. "It may be useful to single out men of special skills among the *miche-quipy* brought from faraway places, Revered Sun. As long as it serves our glorious city, there might be merit in using various foreigners' skills and abilities."

The ruler nodded again, then glanced at his brother. For a brief moment, Ahal wondered how such an evidently sick man could remain so regal, managing his intricate headpiece, an obviously heavy symbol of power that allowed him nothing but a strictly straight posture, with even such a simple gesture as nodding becoming a complicated maneuver to proceed with carefully. It looked so hefty, this arrangement of feathers and decorations, beautiful and more exquisite than anything he had seen before, but cumbersome, challenging to handle.

Again the feverish gaze was upon him, piercing. "What is the special ability of your foreigner, Tribute Collector?"

"He is fierce and resourceful, skilled with a spear. If you wish me to, Revered Sun, I will be honored to take it upon myself to find out what else the foreigner could do and with what weaponry. Villagers of remote provinces are usually adept with bows in addition to spears, Revered Sun, but not the clubs our warriors put to an admirable use."

"What precisely do you intend to do with this *miche-quipy*'s possible warring skills?" This came from Tattooed Serpent, a curt and somewhat unfriendly demand. "You can't thrust a filthy foreigner into the ranks of our spearmen serving the city, and with our provinces quiet and no enemies bothering our forests, what would you do with a *miche-quipy* who can wave a spear against a bunch of surprised guards, a violent barbarian that he is? Of what use could the insolent villager be to us besides the amusement of watching him trying to best our guards, the value of sheer entertainment such a sight can bring to my brother's revered eyes?"

"There is always a need in armed people who could use weaponry and are not afraid to do so, Revered Tattooed Serpent." He tried not to glance at the watching sovereign, feeling the scrutinizing gaze almost physically, the penetrating quality of it. "Our traders are traveling far and wide, and so are our tribute collectors. A cluster of armed and trained commoners can spare our warriors escorting duties of such expeditions."

A momentary silence let him collect his thoughts, sensing other dignitaries moving closer, still outside of hearing range, as required, yet curious, wishing to approach their ruler, to talk to him or offer refreshments. The spearmen upon the plaza must have been preparing for yet another bout of casting, even though their sovereign did not show signs of desire to watch.

"What you are proposing is outside the realm of our customs, Tribute Collector." The royal sibling was talking slowly, as though measuring his every word. "You have the audacity to—"

The hand of Revered Sun was as skinny as a dry stick, its gauntness enhanced by the multitude of bracelets encircling it. Still, its sway cut the words of the tattooed leader short.

"His *miche-quipy* has challenged our warriors, hasn't he?" To Ahal's surprise, the mighty ruler, while not interested in the happenings upon the field, did not seem to be listening to the conversation regarding customs either, his gaze remote, wandering. "And he is still alive, isn't he?" The ringed eyes were upon him, glittering with professed amusement. "How many men did he manage to hurt?"

"Well, yes, Revered Sun. He managed to knock one spearman down and damage a few of those who attack—who tried to restrain him." He felt the sweat gathering upon his forehead, similar rivulets trickling down his back, an understandable thing in this midday heat. Still, it was unseemly to perspire, not while the divine ruler honored you with a private, extraordinarily unofficial conversation. "The man is still wild and untamed, still unaware of the proper ways, Revered Sun. However, even his natural violence could be channeled into useful directions. I believe I can make him contribute more than as a mere worker, to serve our city and further its glory, Oh Revered One. I apologize if I have been inappropriately forward in offering unasked-for advice."

The colorless lips stretched into a one-sided grin, showing the hinted lack of teeth, an unsettling vision. A thoughtful nod followed, while the narrowed gaze kept wandering, as though listening to its owner's inner thoughts. Then they focused on the lead guard. "How many rounds of spear-throwing remained to the end of the competition, Chief Warrior?"

"About half a dozen rounds, Revered Sun." The head warrior was frowning, seemingly as puzzled as Ahal was. "If you wish to shorten or lengthen their performance, Oh Revered Sun, it will be done promptly."

"We shall not deprive the people of Quachil Thecou of the well-deserved entertainment they were awaiting since the previous moon's festivities. I enjoy watching our warriors' skills and prowess as much as they do, as you all do. However..." The twisted grin was back, not fitting the man's gaunt looks, the paleness of the face and the feverish flicker of the ringed eyes. "However, we may wish to enliven the traditional competition. Speaking of challenging the accepted customs, eh, Brother?" This time, the gaze flickered toward the tattooed leader. "Enrich it, one might say. Our innovative tribute collector suggests changes to our ways. Do you think your divine ruler cannot be allowed to do so as well?"

They all stared, momentarily lost for words. It was easy to see that. Ahal felt a snicker sneaking up on him, inappropriate and uncalled for. The royal sibling's eyes were opened so widely for a change.

Revered Sun was the one who let out a chuckle, clearly pleased with himself, a surprisingly human reaction in the man Ahal always thought of as a remote deity along with the rest of this city's dwellers, those who weren't allowed in the divine offspring's proximity. A dry cough cut his musings short.

"Are you well, Revered One?" The head guard was leaning forward, chancing to trespass the permitted four-paces distance. Tattooed Serpent motioned one of the servants, snatching a goblet from his hands angrily, offering it to his divine sibling, supporting the trembling shoulders as the ruler drank.

"You wish to add to the entertainment of our spectators, Revered Brother," he said, making his words a statement. "In what manner do you wish to do that?"

"In an innovative manner." The cough was subduing gradually, leaving the man drained of the last of his color. It was touching to see him struggling not to succumb to the sickness. Ahal held his breath. "His *miche-quipy*... he is a fighter, or so our tribute collector claims." Another pause, another gulp from the rapidly emptying goblet. "Let him fight our spearmen... those who compete out there. Let us see who comes a winner out of such competition."

"Oh!" The head of the guards' eyes widened, then sparkled with excitement.

Tattooed Serpent raised one of his bushy eyebrows. "An interesting idea, Revered Brother. But it will be a short bout of fighting. No filthy *miche-quipy* can stand up to even one of our fearless and skillful warriors."

"He already fought with our warriors, according to our lead guard and the tribute collector." Another bout of dry cough was subdued quickly this time, with what seemed like a stony resolve. "He stands a chance to last for more than a few heartbeats, doesn't he?"

All eyes were upon Ahal again, even those of the lead guard. He swallowed hastily. "If you wish it so, Revered Sun."

He tried to think fast, not liking the idea in the least, the cruelty of setting a man in a deliberate fight against... how many seasoned, practiced warriors? One, two, a dozen? What chances did the wild villager have to make it out of such a contest alive? No contest but slaughter, unless the fight was with poles that were usually thrown at the rolling stone disk instead of the actual spears, for something symbolic maybe, until the man was subdued. A glimpse of a smile tugging at the ruler's lips disabused him from silly assumptions. *Miche-quipy* were many and expendable, the show of real fighting resulting in bloodied death rare.

He suppressed a shrug, not liking to be a direct cause of the wild villager's death. "The *miche-quipy* in question does have a chance of fighting back for some time, Oh Revered Sun. I hope he will please you with his fighting."

The feathers of the magnificent headdress rustled lightly, following what looked like a satisfied nod. "Go and prepare him. Both of you." The head of the guards received an additional nod. "Pick the best among your men. Three or four would be enough, I believe. What do you say, Brother?"

The tattooed noble shrugged. "Probably one would be more than enough, but I do hope that his *miche-quipy* is half as good as the tribute collector claims. We do deserve a refreshing diversion many among our nobles would adore. Our Divine Lady Female Sun has been complaining of certain boredom inherent in traditional competitions. This will provide a refreshing new pastime, Revered Brother. My admiration for your innovative thought knows no bounds."

To prepare him how, wondered Ahal, backing away without turning his back, as was customary, following the lead guard's example, not difficult to see now without the sun shining into his eyes. It was hiding behind thicker clusters of clouds, coloring the day in the gloomy hue, as though not pleased with the proposed activities as well.

Strangely perturbed, Ahal glanced at the sky, his sweaty back welcoming the suddenly cooling surroundings, yet his skin prickling with a sense of foreboding. Something was wrong. But what?

CHAPTER 13

The unexpected relief in the heat came as a welcome surprise, with the sun not doing its best to scorch the earth and everyone walking it all of a sudden. Still, it made Iciwata feel peculiar. There were plenty of clouds to veil the shiny deity, yes, and the strengthening wind brought nothing but relief; yet, his instincts of a hunter warned him of something, something bad, ominous. Something to keep away from, to look for shelter. But what?

Forcing his eyes back to the gushing incline, he tried to push the bad feeling away, having enough trouble to deal with as it was. The spearmen crowded him, burning him with their glares, the flint tips of their javelins glittering with a bloody promise, impressively massive, sharpened to perfection. The sight of them made him regret giving up on his lawfully captured spear. That man, Honorable Ahal, or just Tribute Collector, as everyone kept calling him, had no right to demand that, did he? And yet, what could he do but to yield the contested weaponry, with the man shielding him from all those who were spoiling to pounce on him, making them stop and obey. So much authority! Just like back in that filthy town down the Great River, wielding too much power, personal and the one belonging to his high status, but not eager to flaunt it, to force people into obedience. Would the man come back in a hurry? It felt safer with this one around, a hard truth to admit.

Again, a glance at the colorful crowding rewarded him with a glimpse of a strange figure seated upon something incredible, an elevated construction of what looked like skins full of intricate designs he hadn't seen but in the woods and river banks, such vivid hues! The moving-around men, some strolling with dignity, some rushing quite humbly, the less colorfully dressed ones among those interfering with his ability to watch, challenged the eye as well, the feathers upon their garments and an occasional headdress breathtaking and not looking real, oval things that might belong on an especially large eagle but for its coloring, again so much vividly glowing red and blue.

The cooling air was a blessing, and he turned toward the gusts of the strengthening wind, wondering about it, knowing that back home, at this time of the season, one couldn't hope for any such mercies, aware that to stare at the richly dressed lowlifes was to seek trouble. That much he had learned from the insanity of this particular day. The brutes with the spears were touchy and easy to provoke. Too easy. The others who had been supervising the stupid earth-shifting activities he has been forced to do since arriving here were prone to yelling, waving their hands but not doing anything with them, neither violent nor productive. Stupid skunks. They were called "considerates" as he heard the other men who were forced to carry the annoyingly heavy baskets tied to one's back and forehead in an intricate manner referring to those who didn't carry a thing but just looked after those who did. It often came with a sneer they were careful to conceal when those same aforementioned "considerates" were in sight. Another bunch of stupid skunks!

Keeping his back straight and his shoulders upright, despite the pain in his bruised side and the burning in the cut that at least stopped bleeding, he tried to locate his former captor again, the only familiar face. It had been the seventh dawn since his arrival in this monstrously huge place of mounds and houses and squares, walled in the fashion that put even the town where all his troubles began to shame, with a sturdy wall one couldn't dream of climbing or breaking through. Compared to this means of defense, their palisade back in the village looked like a cluster of sticks playing children had planted when bored. An annoyance. Compared to this place, his entire village looked like a playground of silly boys. How did they build all those mounds and walls, crowded squares, plazas stretching so far one's eye had difficulty locating its other edge?

The question that was answered, if partially, at the very first moment of his arrival. Plenty of things could be built if you managed to force others to do that for you, a great number of others, with him among those, not the one to do the forcing. Filthy lowlifes!

And it was not that it had been so bad back on the journey that was commenced indeed on the day after the terrible night of the flight and the bear. Once over his initial rage and despondency, with his various cuts and bruises not giving him more trouble than necessary, he had found himself glancing around with curiosity, even if quite against his will. He didn't wish to communicate with these people, the filthy rats who had managed to force him into such coerced traveling, may all their canoes drown, turn over, crash against the rocks, fall into vicious cascades, the smaller canoes loaded with goods, in one of which he was put – a part of the loot! – and the long, massive monstrosity the men armed with spears navigated and guarded, maneuvering alongside the smaller vessels, protecting them. They were chatting among themselves, the pair of men in his canoe, sharing jokes and occasional tasty treats. When offered one of them, he refused proudly, even though his stomach was rumbling badly after a long day of sitting and doing nothing, his body stiff and feeling as though about to break. Did they intend to let his ties loose, at least at some point? Was he to make his needs in the boat, right where he sat?

When with dusk they had camped in a cozy-looking inlet, the spearmen from the long vessel made a fire, then sprawled in comfort, letting the men of the smaller boats do all the arrangements, gather the needed firewood, pluck cooking devices, then busy themselves around them. The spearman did bother to drag him out and into the nearby grove, so he was not to make his needs upon himself and into their precious vessels apparently. He snorted in disgust, even though by that time, his head reeled too badly and his legs did a half-hearted job supporting him, too stiff to react after squatting in the same pose for the length of an entire day. The smells of the cooking meal were tantalizing, but he held his head high and kept looking at the river, turning his back toward them. Still, when later on, one of the men from their boat came with some pieces of dried meat and a plate of what looked like cooked beans, it turned difficult to say no, certainly not upon the repeated offering.

"You can't starve yourself to death," the man said, shrugging. "Honorable Ahal told us to bring you to Quachil Thecou well and unharmed. If you keep refusing food, you will get there all skinny and weak, useless to anyone, yourself included."

"Why would I want to get there, well and unharmed or not?" he grunted, fighting the spasm in his stomach, the hope that they would have to untie him in order to let him eat splashing in force. "It's you who need me there well and unharmed, you and your honorable whatever, the slave capturer that he is. I don't want to get there in whatever way."

The man shrugged again, rolling his eyes. His snort was loud enough, telling it all. "You are wild." His back was bare, weathered, crisscrossed with muscles.

Iciwata fought another spasm in his stomach, his mouth, so hopelessly dry until now, suddenly nearly drooling, overflowing with saliva. "If you untie me, I'll eat."

Derisive laughter was his answer.

The next day went by faster, because he was too dizzy to brood or fume, or pay attention to their progress for that matter. The sun was high, beating mercilessly on the backs of the rowing people, the forested banks flowing by. He didn't notice arriving in yet another resting place, but when one of the warriors was yanking him hard, nearly throwing him over the side and into the muddy shallows, he noticed that the dusk was nearing again. To fight his way back onto his feet in the marshy slough turned out to be an effort. He did so mainly in order to escape the murky water from choking him, not bothering to go further than a sitting position. It didn't really matter at this point.

The warrior who had shoved him out cursed, his fingers crushing in their uncompromising grip, yanking him up and actually supporting, insisting on keeping him upright. He cursed back, but faintly, his throat too dry to produce worthwhile sounds.

"You either feed him or throw him overboard and tell the tribute collector he fell out without intent."

One of the men from their boat, the one who was more talkative than his peer, rushed to their side, grabbing Iciwata's other shoulder, helping him up the slippery slope. Iciwata cursed again, this time audibly enough to have their attention.

The supporting hands pushed him away. "Shut up, you filthy bag of human refuse."

To hit the ground once again was actually relieving despite it being harder than the muddy slough of the riverbank because his head spun too badly and the need to vomit the non-existent contents of his stomach was turning unbearable. Not that his miserable retching produced anything more than a strangled cough.

"Do something about him." The voice of the warrior was drawing away.

He pushed himself up stubbornly, wishing to yell something terribly offensive, settling for spitting in disgust.

"Drink."

A pottery vessel was thrust into his face, ridiculously welcomed. He finished it in what seemed like a single gulp, some of the water running down his chin and his body, adding to a surprisingly refreshing sensation, the bout of additional cough not tearing at the inside of his throat as badly as before.

"Easy, villager. Don't make yourself drown in this thing." The man took the flask away, then shook his head. "Will you eat this time?"

He was too busy coughing. Still, the question lingered, challenging. The respectable thing to do was to refuse with appropriate words of pride and contempt. They could drag him wherever they wanted, but they couldn't make him cooperate, could they? And yet, the drink felt like a life giver, sweeter and fresher than anything he had drunk in his life, and his throat was anyway too tortured to offer any more worthwhile insults. He could do it, of course he could, curse them and fight them if let free, but later, after he stopped feeling like dying on the spot. A nod was not a betrayal of his principles, was it?

From that moment on, the journey turned bearable again. A spare meal, then another one, restored his health in a miraculous manner, so quickly even his captors were made to give him puzzled looks. With the next dawn, while setting off, one of his fellow canoe raiders commented that if their prisoner was so perky, he might as well take a paddle, contribute to the mutual effort, a weighty addition to their vessel that he was. The prospect set Iciwata's spirits high, the mere possibility to be rid of his ties. When set free and armed with a paddle, he could do plenty to harm them, or even just get away, slip overboard on some difficult passing and be gone. Oh, but for such an opportunity!

The warriors in their fancy long vessel didn't like the idea, their own progress lighter and swifter, unchallenged by additional weight or uncoordinated rowing – that much he had noticed about their party through the previous two days of sail, blurry and wandering as his mind was, the way the warring boat was speeding, unhindered by baskets of goods and pushed by a mutual effort of half a dozen men rowing as one. Massive and monstrously long that it was, so many skillful rowers were no match for a pair or a trio apiece every smaller boat, loaded with cargo and additional riders like him. Still, when he promised he would row and make no trouble, warned that a mere funny move would see him dead and in no quick or painless manner, the warriors agreed, and the third day of the journey went by in delightful freedom of movement, in the familiar satisfaction of mere physical work as opposed to enforced idleness and despair. They still tied him for the night, but a few dawns later, even that changed, although by that time, he had had enough leisure to think it all through, to remember that he did give his agreement to the man who had captured him, that the stone-cold lowlife was in his village at that very moment, taking goods and doing whatever other evil deeds, ready to let them know about his, Iciwata's, blunders and crimes, ready to make them pay, unless he did what he promised, namely paid off with hard work, slaving somewhere out there, in the big filthy towns of the west. Curse them all!

Reassured by his continued good behavior, casting suspicious glances at him but only occasionally, looking ridiculously relieved when he took the paddle every morning anew with no argument or resentment, the men in his canoe chatted away between themselves, talking about that city, clearly happy to be heading back there. Quachil Thecou, they called it, Lesser Sun City, a curious name. He had wondered about it, himself feeling ridiculously unconcerned considering his circumstances, almost elated. Food and drink did this, of course, freedom of movement, physical exercise as opposed to the state of being starved and tied and about to die. Still, at the rare moments of being honest with himself, tottering between sleep and awareness at nights, he had to admit that there was more to it, that it was interesting to travel so far down the Good River, that he had never dreamed of going so far, and that while rowing, it felt as though he had been doing it of his own free will, traveling far and wide, visiting strange places.

When free from this filthy imprisonment, having paid off his debts, he would do just that, he promised himself, would sail on his own, head wherever he wanted. Maybe even to this same Quachil Thecou city, but as a free man. Like a trader. He could collect goods, couldn't he, hunt more bears and have their precious pelts to offer in exchange, trade for other things, tools or weaponry or Kayina's prettily pearly necklaces, then sail with them to the big towns of the west, enjoy the journey, come back enriched with something rare and precious, to be held and admired back in the village more than before, to have this same Kayina stop dropping her gaze every time he approached her, or just passed her by.

What were they told about him back in the village?

The question would surface every time anew, ruining his mood in an instant. So he would row even more vigorously, forcing his ears to listen to the chatter of his captors, venturing questions occasionally, never fond of solitude, even when principles were involved. One had to talk to people sometimes, even when those were filthy invaders set on forcing him into some filthy work out there, erecting mounds only ancestors knew how to build. He didn't believe them that readily. There could be no crowded cities they were describing, with towering mounds and plazas spreading so far one could barely see their opposite side. Of course, there were no such things.

Or so he thought, until the moment of their arrival.

Shifting to make himself more comfortable, he tried not to snort, remembering the last day of the journey, when the river turned busier with every passing heartbeat, more difficult to maneuver without chancing to bump into this or that vessel, many dozen canoes springing from everywhere, in a hurry and uncaring.

Grateful that the paddle was out of his hands by this time, he watched with no interruptions, his uneasiness growing. The warring boat sped away and out of their sight with the first light of dawn, leaving the remaining vessels to make their own way, navigating in the growing commotion. Were they not concerned with the safety of the carried goods anymore? The realization that only increased the foreboding sensation, the tightening in his stomach that he tried not to acknowledge. It was so crowded, the river near the low bank they were sailing as well as the shores, teeming with people, their shouted exchanges and cries carrying over the water, disturbingly loud. All those people clustering over mats spread on the flatter shores, sometimes shadowed with what looked like hides stretched over poles, made him stare. What were those gatherings? And where did so many people come from? It didn't seem possible that so many were living along the banks of any river!

By the time the huge silhouetted earthworks appeared to cut into the blue of the sky, he was beyond wonder, not excited in the least, feeling threatened and cornered, even though no glances lingered on him. They were too busy to stare; still, the towering monsters of mounds alone, drawing closer, bearing down on him, were enough to make him wish to jump overboard and try to swim away whatever the cost. They did exist after all, those huge man-made earthworks. And probably all the rest too, those "market squares" his fellow riders were in the habit of mentioning with longing, the plaza with "festivals" and "royal palanquins," whatever those were. Crowded to choking like the shores? Full of shouting people? He feared that it would be like that and worse, and the monstrous place was drawing closer and closer, whether he felt ready to face it or not. Which he wasn't! Not yet.

Their canoe was lurching now more often than not, its sides brushing against similar vessels, the water of the river barely visible, if at all. The shore they tried to approach teemed with more running-around figures than ever, and they had stayed in the water a long time, pushing a little closer on every opportunity, usually when someone gestured or shouted an instruction at them. It seemed that there were men there, dressed in ridiculously long clothes with sleeves, who were trying to make an order out of the great swarm of canoes. How, he couldn't surmise, as all he could see by now were the sides of the boats pressing against theirs, their riders as impatient as his unasked-for companions, exchanging heated arguments or observations, pushing closer every time it seemed possible to gain another free spot in the agitated water, yet not going against the gesturing men, following their instructions.

And it didn't get any better as the day progressed. Once on the dry land, he had been elbowed and shoved, almost losing sight of his fellow boat riders, trying to keep up against any better judgment. They seemed to know what they were doing, locals that they were. It was safer to stick with them, at least until he was out of this impossible human hubbub, not crushed, smothered, or trampled under too many hurrying feet. Such thoughts alone made his body go limp with unseemly fright. If one fell in this insane congregation, one would be helpless, like a person stuck in the way of a fleeing herd of deer. Worse than that!

He shook the memory off, glancing up the mild incline once again, seeking the colorful garment of the man whose word had brought him into this insanity. Honorable Ahal was his name, wasn't it? People who had worked on digging and shoveling the earth beyond the half-built construction, packing it all in huge baskets for others to carry, talked about this man too. Apparently, he was quite famous here, the cold-blooded beast that he was, but after what happened here earlier, it felt safer to have this man around. While digging and shoveling for the last half a dozen days, he didn't have to face filthy warriors or their ready-to-explode violence. A small mercy, apparently.

The spearmen who were told to keep an eye on him were busy talking between themselves, or peering at the colorful gathering themselves. *Considerates*, beyond doubt, curse their evil eyes into the worst parts of the bad swamp. Why was he forced to wait here now? No barely clad workers like him were anywhere in sight. The stares he drew could burn holes in his skin.

Stubbornly, he kept staring. The crowd uphill was so colorful it hurt the eye, the rustling of the people's clothing and the clacking of their decorations – so many! Those who held prettily ornamented javelins seemed to be simpler dressed, not allowed near the extravagant gathering. Others, more heavily clad individuals, seemed to manage pushing their way closer, uttering strange cries when nearing, backing away without turning their backs on the strange wooden construction and the majestic silhouette seated there, hidden under too many feathers and gild. Even this same Honorable Ahal did this, when bidden to near, not right away, far from it. He seemed to be relatively humble as well now, unsure of himself. An interesting observation, even if hard to tell from the distance. It was difficult to imagine this man outside his cold, unperturbed, authoritative bearing. Did the magnificence of these surroundings humble this one? It didn't seem so. Back under the incline and when telling the filthy lowlifes with spears off, the man looked exactly like back in the Red Horn town, domineering and calm, making everyone listen. Even while on the ground and struggling against those stupid pieces of rotten meat and his own uncontrollable rage, it was easy to see that.

He felt the anger returning, threatening to take him again, worse than before. But how dared they, filthy pieces of human waste! Enough that he had trod back and forth upon this stupid incline since the first light of dawn, making it bigger with the enormous amounts of soil he had been made to dig up and carry along. Seven dawns of slaving like that, without a murmur, biding his time, looking around, trying to be patient, not to do something stupid, not yet. Later, yes maybe, when despairing of getting away. Was he destined to trudge back and forth, squashed under the great weight of the cursed baskets and buckets until the cold moons came and went? It was barely the beginning of the harvest time!

Still, he had managed not to get into trouble, not even with his fellow other diggers or carriers of earth, plenty of those, from all over these land, apparently. They were chatty, those people, bored before the exhaustion of the later part of the day would kick in, speaking different tongues, some of which he didn't always manage to understand. The locals spoke clearly enough, even if with a funny way of pronouncing the same words. Yet, it wasn't the case with some of the other foreigners. A wonder.

He straightened his shoulders once again, feeling the eyes upon him, too many gazes, all brimming with curiosity, measuring, probing. At least that. Until now, the rare looks he received in this enormously crowded city were filled with dismissal and scorn, too obvious to miss, unconcealed. This morning, it was the first time someone looked at him with anything but scorn. That beautiful vision upon the edge of the terraced incline, the reason for his brawl with the spearman, but did she stand there and stare.

Against his will, he sneaked a glance at the cluster of carried seats further up the colorful incline, away from the flattened ground covered with grass, a sprawling field upon which many dangerously armed lowlifes strode, talking between themselves, sneaking glances of their own. Still, further up, the colorful feathers of swaying fans suggested a prettier congregation than the one surrounding the figure on the luxurious seat. The hum of the higher-pitched chatter confirmed the conclusion and he knew that the beautiful vision was there, with her intricately interwoven braids defying the wind unlike the rest of her flying draperies, airy and washed with the golden light, her face as though chiseled from the most polished stone, belonging to the world of the spirits, the goddess of the moon, an ethereal creature. Her eyes were the only ones to disclose her earthly belonging – such outright gaping. She was staring at him, him in particular, and he must have felt her gaze before, the intensity of it, as there was no need to look up despite the atypical commotion all around, the deafening roars and cries coming from the vast field, the commotion that wasn't there on the previous days. It touched his curiosity, but not enough to spend his energy on looking up or around. Until her gaze made him do that, so wide-eyed and intense. Of course it made him stop the stupid treading about, defy the annoying overseers, and then the spearman. He shouldn't have done it; of course he shouldn't. There was no way to succeed in such an undertaking. And yet, she was so beautiful and even though her stare was like that of the most unsophisticated girl, she was clearly a divine creature, like a goddess surprised by a human apparition. They could be surprised, couldn't they, the creatures of the unearthly world.

Then the irrelevant thoughts drained from his mind all at once. The tribute collector was coming back, nearing in his forceful stride, walking down the incline, having finished backing away without turning apparently. Another burly man, a dangerous-looking type loaded with decorations and weaponry, walked beside him, talking rapidly, his scowl one of the direst.

Iciwata held his breath, the tightening in his stomach painful again, not letting any air in. The armed man looked even more important than his original captor, more prominent and displeased. The way he talked, waving one of his hands, gesturing with it, told of indignation, but it was his current benefactor's troubled expression that filled Iciwata's stomach with ice. The tough piece of rotten meat never looked that perturbed, not even when facing the crazed bear in the night rain-soaked forest, not even when knifed.

"Don't stare, you ignorant foreigner!" A push in his side was vicious, accompanied by a lighter blow to his head that he didn't manage to anticipate, busy doing what he has been accused of, namely staring. "Ground! Look at the ground, you filthy worm!"

Fighting for balance, he tried to whirl at the spearman, who apparently remembered to put an eye on him as originally instructed, having chatted with the others to his heart's content until now. The attempt to reach for the once again lunging shaft of the spear – but did they have a habit of using the wrong side of their javelins! – might have crowned with relative success but for the important men being already upon them, with the tribute collector inserting himself between him and his attackers, shielding either him or them, firmly at that, blocking any next possible blow.

"I will take it from here," he said curtly, again in the familiar chilly fashion that reassured Iciwata greatly this time. The man was still in control, still listened to. To force his senses to focus turned out difficult enough, his blood boiling, but his mind gripping for control, knowing he would not survive another skirmish. Not with so many of them, all armed and brutal and spoiling for the kill. What *was* wrong with these people?

"He is eager to fight, eh?" The overly armed and decorated dignitary was among the enraged spearmen too now, the round plate adorning his chest sparkling, hurting the eye. It was carved with intricate designs, and for a heartbeat, Iciwata was tempted to study them, to put his mind to something that did not require the need to cope and survive anew every single heartbeat. "Good. Get him ready and let us hope Revered Sun would not be disappointed with his performance. I'll instruct my men to go easy on him in the beginning, to have him last for some time."

"Yes, Honorable Leader." From such close proximity, it was again easy to see that the tribute collector deferred to this man, did not seek to tell him what to do as he did with the others. Iciwata felt the pit in his stomach deepening once again. "Let us meet and discuss the exact rules of the fighting after I talked to the foreigner."

"Of course. Bring him to the nearest edge of the plaza. I'll determine where the fight will be taking place until then."

In another heartbeat, they were left with only the company of the violent spearmen.

"Come along." Now the man was addressing him, motioning with his head curtly. "Hurry."

To walk as proudly as he could wasn't easy, the new blow causing his side to resume its painful protests, the warm trickling down his ribs reminding him of the spear that had grazed him in the first skirmish. It stopped bleeding for some time, but now the lazy trickling was back, tickling his skin. Bother this!

"Now listen to me and listen carefully." The man was walking by his side, his paces long, enviably steady. No newly received wounds and bruises, not for this one. Iciwata did his best in suppressing a grunt. It wasn't the time to pick fights, not with the man who seemed to be busy keeping him from harm through this particular day. "We don't have time and your chances of remaining alive are not promising as they are. So just listen to me and try to do your best."

The need to keep with the briskness of the pace turned challenging, keeping Iciwata's mind from focusing on the demanding words. The spearmen upon the field looked at them curiously, then took their eyes away, not daring to return the fierce glare of his formidable companion. Still, the broad back of the other man with decorations and weaponry was there too, gesturing at certain warriors, sending them running toward various destinations. It made Iciwata breathe with relief when they stopped a few paces short of entering the actual field of the neatly cut grass, the spearmen's realm.

"Bring here a bowl of water and clean cloths." In his turn, his companion motioned to the group of simply dressed people, the trays they held loaded with flasks of various sizes. "Give me your vessel." The first man to near was relieved of his burden quite forcefully. "Drink." This was tossed toward him. "Not too much, just to relieve your thirst. You don't want to be heavy or dizzy. You will have to do your best without those drawbacks."

"My best at doing what?" The phrase left his mouth before he could judge if he wished to say it aloud or not, the resolution to keep his tongue between his teeth challenged again. It was annoying, the way everyone now ran around him, full of purpose he didn't know a thing about. If it was about him, he was allowed to know, wasn't he?

"Your best at doing what you tend to do most of the time," said the man testily, his eyes suddenly on Iciwata, sparkling with anger. "Pick fights and challenge warriors. Well, this time, you shall do so with the blessing of everyone around."

"Challenge warriors?" he repeated stupidly, then shook his head to make it work. "How?"

The wide palm cut the air, jumping up, cutting his words short. "Listen to me and listen carefully. Revered Sun, the sacred ruler of this city, wishes to see you fighting against his spearmen. Not everyone at the same time. I will make certain to convince the head of the royal guards against such an idea. However," the air hissed, drawn forcefully through the widening nostrils of the man's prominent nose, "you will have to fight for your life even if your rivals will come against you one by one. You will be given a good javelin; I sent a man to bring a few spears for you to select from. I don't believe your rivals will carry additional weaponry, but be prepared for surprises. Our Revered Sun wishes to enjoy a different completion than the regular spear-throwing contest. He may decree to change the rules, maybe even halfway through the fighting. Be prepared for that and do your best. Do not glance around, stare at the nobility watching you, or do anything but fight and try to harm your rivals while coming to less harm yourself. I do not know if you'll be required to fight to the death. The more impressive your fighting is, the more chances of it to be stopped at some point." The wide shoulders lifted in a shrug. "This is the best advice I can give you. Follow it and you may live."

He tried to take it all in, frightened by the foreboding tone and the man's scowl, troubled rather than direful, the piercing gaze concentrated, as though trying to think of all possibilities. Possibilities of what? The prospect of having his pick of fancy spears to fight off some of the violent lowlifes, the same arrogant rats he wasn't allowed before to even look at, let alone fight, wasn't that bad. He was in worse situations than that since meeting the western invaders, this man in particular.

"Am I to have a spear of my choosing?" he asked mainly in order to say something, but also to make sure. "Any javelin I choose?"

"Any javelin out of the ones that will be brought here. Do not make trouble on this account." The stern tone returned, cutting like polished flint. "You don't seem to be concerned with your life or the possibility of throwing it away, but this time, you will be watched by the sacred ruler of this city and his nobles. Any more

blunders like staring at the people who are above your status –
which is the lowest, if you didn't notice – or offering insults or
even just arguments in reply will result in your death without the
dignity of fighting back, and with me in no position to interfere,
not this time. Do you understand?"

In spite of himself, he shivered, then accepted the flask thrust
into his hands, drinking thirstily, blessing the freshness of the
water and its relative coolness, the pottery ware heavy and
familiar, like the utensils back home, curiously reassuring.

"Now clean yourself."

Another man rushed toward them, carrying a tray with a pile
of bright cloths of the quality he never saw before. So soft! He
tried not to wince while rubbing the dry and fresh blood off his
cuts, wishing someone else did this. Who liked cleaning one's
own wounds?

"Your face, your hair, everything. Clean him and make him
look presentable." This was tossed toward the man with the tray,
two more similarly dressed types hurrying to come to his aid,
summoned with another curt nod.

"Am I allowed to harm them, or just to strike them down?" he
asked, feeling better by the moment, the sensation of cleanliness
as always lifting his spirits. It was better than to dig or carry
massive containers, splashing in your own sweat, breathing the
dry earth until it made you cough.

"You are *required* to harm them. Otherwise, they will harm
you." The stern gaze turned thoughtful once again, flickering with
the hint of appreciation. "But if you can render someone
weaponless and unharmed, you do not have to kill him. Unless
ordered so. Be attentive to what they are telling you, Honorable
Anksheah, the Head of the Royal Guards, or anyone else who
might be around and directing. If they tell you to kill your
opponent, do it with no arguments."

He wished there was another flask of water available, his
mouth growing dry once again at the images his mind began
painting vividly, too vividly. Would it feel the same to plunge a
spear into a person and not a mad raving bear? Would it *look* the
same? He wished the tightening in his stomach wouldn't be so

painful, so annoyingly strong.

"Will you be there too? Giving orders?" He didn't plan to ask that, but suddenly, it became imperative that the answer was positive, even if accompanied by more stern instructions or admonitions.

A pause lasted for more than a heartbeat. He felt the gaze boring at him, maybe measuring, maybe angered. He didn't wish to meet it. What the men with cloths did gained the utmost of his attention.

"I'll try to remain involved." Another pause that followed held a comforting quality, the tone of the words less distant than before. "If I can be of help, I will be."

He clenched his teeth tight, not liking the sudden trembling in his jaw. It felt loose, about to fall off. A strange sensation.

"You will do well starting to remember the proper address, foreigner." The tone grew sterner again, still ringing with the previous lack of distance, but now having a thread of admonition in it. "Honorable Leader will do. Make certain to use this title while speaking to anyone who is in the position to give you orders. It will make your stay in Quachil Thecou more bearable by far."

Under different circumstances, he might have wished to suggest to the giver of such snotty, unasked-for advice to stick his "honorable leader" up his honorable haughty behind. It was tempting to do that. He clenched his teeth, then forced out a nod, not straightening his gaze, busy watching the clear water in the bowl for cleaning turning murkier with each dip of the cloth. There was plenty of mud to scrape from his body, wasn't there? Why didn't they let a person to do a sensible thing like going down the river banks and wash quickly and properly? Fancy marring those wonderfully soft cloths. His instincts told him that more people were heading their way, the filthy spearman to be sure. He didn't need to glance sideways to assert that. Still, he couldn't help it, shivering against his will.

The decorated piece of human waste was leading that group, heading toward them with a heavy pace of a person certain of his status and rights. Bother this! But how was he to fight all those men? And would it be like the tribute collector had told him, not all of them upon him, but one by one? But for this man to stay around, if for no other reason than to make sure they didn't just swarm him all at once. Maybe he should have answered the demand of honorable-something with words and a title added and not just an offhanded nod. He needed this man's goodwill, didn't he?

"What are you doing here?"

The exclamation made him nearly jump, his attention still on the armed men, relieved to see some of them turning to head up the incline and back toward the prettily dressed gathering around the sparkling seat. Some, but not all.

Hastily, he glanced at his benefactor, not yet ready to meet his gaze, but needing to know what made the man cry out in such surprisingly human reaction. Whatever this one did, until now he was a talking stone, sometimes warmer, sometimes colder or presumably angered, but still an emotionless rock. But not anymore.

A brief look rewarded him with an image of wide-open eyes and the amount of creases upon the frowning forehead doubling themselves, a few other expressions chasing each other across the surprisingly open face, something between worry and bewilderment, maybe even an open surprise. No wonder really. Following the puzzled gaze he had found himself staring as well, another strange-looking construction of a seat carried by people nearing them, hosting none other than the beautiful vision that had landed him in trouble at the first place, now composed and not staring, her head held challengingly high.

"Greetings, Honorable Uncle." Her voice was deep, slightly husky, as though she had been shouting for some time. It pleased the ear, this surprisingly low sound. He had expected such a creature to chirrup like a singing bird. "I wished to greet you in person. Didn't my maid tell you that?"

"Yes, she did." The tribute collector seemed to gather his senses and the unbecoming astonishment left his hardened features. "You are surely not allowed to leave your current vicinity, Sele."

The girl's nicely full lips twisted indulgently. "I am allowed to do many things, Uncle. I can certainly greet my family members if I wish to do so. Unless they don't wish to be greeted." The last phrase came out with less aplomb, openly reproachful. Then her eyes shifted to him, filled with familiar challenge. The way her head straightened, not that it was lowered before, reminded him of the previous incidents with other haughty inhabitants of this city, so much fire and most annoying indignation and scorn. "Who is this, Uncle? Why does he dare to stare at me?"

His anger splashed as suddenly as back under the incline, her nearness feeding the flames. She was no goddess, this petulant creature, as nasty as they all were, looking down on him, thinking him to be nothing but dirt.

"I can stare all I like—" he began, but the man grabbed his shoulder, his rocky-hard fingers pressing, relaying a message. It was not the time, and the decorated leader was upon them again, accompanied by several spearmen carrying more weaponry than they seemed to need. Iciwata tried to will his heart into slower pounding.

"Go back to the royal ladies, Sele," repeated his benefactor with the old familiar authoritativeness. "I shall find you there later, after the games."

The armed dignitary motioned at the men carrying two javelins in each hand. "Have your *miche-quipy* choose his weaponry, Tribute Collector. Our revered ruler and his following shall send word and then we shall begin at once."

He could feel her there, lingering, not doing what she was told, namely taking off and away, back where she belonged, upon the incline sparkling with too many bracelets and necklaces, with her snotty *considerates* or *honorables,* or whatever the richly dressed pieces of rotten meat were called. To put his attention back to javelins came as an effort. Under the heavy gazes of the dignitary and his warriors it was anything but an easy feat.

"Choose your spear." The tribute collector's voice served again as an anchor, something to cling to and make an order out of the wild whirlwind his thoughts swerved at. "Try each one."

He didn't need to be explained to like a child. Of course one didn't pick a weapon by just looking at it; and yet, how was one to know what these people allowed or expected, the violent westerners with their grand way of doing things. The warrior who carried the javelins tossed them at his feet with such animosity and contempt, he felt like grabbing the first one and putting it through the filthy piece of refuse.

"What will be the rules of the fight?" asked his benefactor, frowning as the other dignitary's gaze suddenly shifted toward the carried seat, clearly appraising its beautiful rider, appreciating what he saw. One could not mistake that basic masculine glint. Iciwata fought the urge to follow the man's gaze.

"A simple fight, a contest. Each man having a spear, using it to the best of his ability." The man shrugged, his gaze back upon his peer, brimming with meaning. "Depending on your *miche-quipy*, it will last for some time, or it will end fast. If he fights as well as you claim he does, then our revered ruler and his nobles will enjoy a worthwhile entertainment."

The tribute collector pursed his lips. "Will they aim to kill each other?"

"Of course." The gaze of the armed dignitary grew slightly colder, boring at his converser, measuring, in a way. "Had you in mind suggesting that they fight like angered *miche-quipy* at the market stalls, waving fists or sticks?"

Now it was the turn of Iciwata's benefactor to clasp his lips tight. "I had no such suggestions in mind, Honorable Leader." The air hissed, drawn forcefully through the boldly carved nostrils. "Will they fight one on one? I strongly suggest that such rule should be observed."

"We shall see what Revered Sun or Revered Tattooed Serpent wish to say on this matter." This time, the heavily lidded gaze turned toward Iciwata, for the first time acknowledging his presence but with no flicker of recognition one pays to another person. It was as if he was a commodity, an inanimate object to exchange for some other goods. "He looks strong. If he is skillful, he may hold against a few of my men. At least for a little while."

"I can fight against as many of them as you wish!" It burst out in an angered exclamation, too loudly and with no accordance with his will. Still, the moment the words were out, he felt better. The suddenly concentrated, narrowing gaze of the armed piece of refuse did this, the recognition, even the angered one. The next words that escaped his mouth did so without his mind's acknowledgement as well. "Honorable Leader."

The tensions lingered for another heartbeat, then visibly lessened. Without daring to look his benefactor's way, he could imagine the man nodding his approval, invisible as it might be.

The decorated leader grinned with one side of his mouth. "Eager to fight, aren't you, foreigner? Well, it shall be arranged. With 'as many of them as you wish.'" Then his gaze returned to his peer. "Have him brought to the edge of the plaza nearest to the royal dais. When it's time, you will be signaled."

"Pick one of the javelins."

This came from one of the spearmen, all of them huddling together, eyeing him darkly, with no good-natured enthusiasm their superior displayed last. Iciwata felt it safer to busy himself with picking the weaponry, even though to tell them off and in no polite words was tempting.

Still, he would have his chance to hurt them, he decided, curbing his anger, snatching the nearest spear, a long perfectly polished pole adorned with the most impressive flint spearhead he had ever imagined, two times larger than the one he had lost back in the filthy town where his troubled began, or his original weaponry back home, the one he had killed the old bear with. Did it happen less than a moon ago? It seemed as though a whole span of seasons had passed.

He straightened up without checking the rest of the spears, not wishing to remain on the ground, not with those lowlifes near and watching. It made him feel defenseless, almost submissive, as though already defeated. Also the girl was still there, another one watching. His senses told him so.

Against his will, he glanced at the hovering seat, still there, oh yes, lingering. The men who held it up in the air looked as though they wished to disappear under the earth, the way their backs sagged and their eyes drilled holes in the ground around their feet. As opposed to them, their cargo was leaning forward, her eyes on the conversing leaders, listening unashamedly, her face a perfect oval, like as a pearly shell, the ones Kayina would pick to work into a pretty ornament, so perfectly smooth it gleamed with different colors. The girl's face didn't gleam, but it felt like it might if put under strong enough sun, the upper part of her intricate seat casting a shadow, enhancing her decisively high cheekbones, the soft angle of the narrowing chin, the slightly opened full lips, all attention and an attempt not to miss a word, again not an annoying haughty fox but a creature from other worlds. He felt his fingers tightening around the smoothness of his new spear's shaft.

As though sensing his scrutiny, her gaze shifted toward him, even though the rest of her body didn't move, not even her face. Only her eyes did, wide open and huge in the gentleness of her face, not angered or petulant and haughty, not at all; mesmerized like back on the incline: gaping, wondering, expectant.

The pit in his stomach widened, then tightened but not painfully this time, rather with matching expectancy. It lasted for another heartbeat, then another. Or maybe plenty of such. It was difficult to tell because his heart was thumping quite madly. When the moment broke, he could feel the silence becoming heavy again, and her gaze darted back toward the speaking dignitaries, first bewildered, about to become angry, then turning frightened.

"Take her back to the royal tent." The voice of the tribute collector tore the silence, stony and cutting like back in the beginning, with no affability to it and no promise of leniency. "Hurry!"

The sweaty carriers jumped as though yanked physically, with too much strength, making her seat waver precariously. He could see her grabbing its edges with surprising agility he would not expect in such delicate creature.

"But, Uncle!" she cried out, clearly taken aback, not used to following orders, not an outlandish creature like her.

"Do you as you are told!" This came out even more freezing cold. The curt sway of the head indicated the carriers again. "Take the royal wife back where she belongs."

Iciwata tried to make his mind work, the stares of the spearmen and the twisted grin of the decorated dignitary unsettling, but not like the stony gaze of his benefactor, the man who had kept him safe and alive through this afternoon.

"You!" The cold glare bored into him, making him wish to take a step back. Or maybe even several such. "Come along, foreigner. Offer no trouble." There was not a hint of friendliness in the man's voice, no flicker of affability, no sensation that he was safer with this man around. Not anymore.

Clenching his teeth against the new wave of rage and that persistent flicker of fear he wasn't ready to admit, not even to himself, Iciwata swallowed any possible response, all appropriate or rather inappropriate words – every word coming out of his mouth would be inappropriate at this point – clasping his spear tighter, relishing the feeling of being armed. At least that. If they attacked him now, any of them, the spearmen or their fat decorated leader, or his former captor, for that matter, he would give them all the fighting they wished to see, more than what they had bargained for.

CHAPTER 14

The wind was strengthening, a welcome diversion against the feeble sway of her feathered fan the girl responsible for it barely bothered to move. Her hair was in no danger of turning disarrayed, even though when earlier the mean-spirited hag, Revered Sun's revered sister, yelled at her own fan-carrying maid, slapping the girl hard enough to make her nearly fall for being overly zealous, causing a few tendrils from the lady's intricate clusters of braids to escape and flutter across the divine face, Sele did worry about her own hair if briefly.

In all the wild happenings of this day, her coiffure was most likely already messed beyond repair, but until returning to her current dignified surrounding of the royal ladies, it didn't bother her, didn't even reach the forefront of her mind. There were more important happenings to think about, to puzzle, or worry, or fume. Like Uncle Ahal's unceremonious telling off, sending her back and away as though she was a disobedient child, a silly girl who used to run after him once, long ago, and not Revered Sun's favorite wife. Next he would be smuggling her tasty snacks, teasing her before yielding his treasures. Unacceptable! She was higher in status than him now, much higher.

As for his insolent *miche-quipy*, the violent foreigner who didn't know his place, staring at her as though she was a simple girl from the city's alleys and pathways, picking fights with the warriors who were most correctly making him cease and return back to work... She strained her eyes, glad that from her old vantage point she could see the happening upon the nearest corner of the plaza beneath their feet most clearly, the men fighting upon it, *actually fighting*, fencing with spears instead of throwing them, set on killing each other.

Her stomach, already squeezed by what felt like invisible but brutal fists, twitched some more, making her nearly gasp. The insolent *miche-quipy* twisted out of one of the javelins' range a mere fraction of a heartbeat before it cut across his stomach, wavering but not falling, not like it happened to him several times until now. When attacked by more than one warrior at once, there was little he could do at times but to duck and fall down and roll away from all this barbed flint. Even she could understand that. He did so well enough, avoiding the worst of the blows time after time, but his torso and limbs were covered with crimson patterns now, and each new such addition made Sele's stomach spasm worse than before, her heart tumbling down every time anew, threatening to slide into her belly and stay there, squeezed and of no use.

"Oh gods, look!" squeaked an especially silly high-pitched voice belonging to another one of Revered Sun's cousins, a stupid talkative pest, dancing an exaggerated attention on the royal lady while giving her, Sele, freezing looks full of disdain.

"Keep quiet, little sister," whispered Hekuni, back in the best of spirits after yet another spicy exchange with the ever-bitter Tehale, who was also staring now, all eyes, too busy to sneer at anyone or give ice-cold looks. It was good to escape the etiquette and the sharpness of the Sun family's eyes, even if for a little while, but now, and thanks to none other than Uncle Ahal, she was back at the worst of it, greeted with the warmth of the deepest winter moon, looked upon askance. An annoyance.

"But how," went on the empty-headed royal cousin, nearly falling out of her decorated seat. "How is he still alive?"

The handsome *miche-quipy* indeed not only managed to avoid yet another stab into his side with an impossibly twisted maneuver, but actually launched an attack of his own, and what an attack! Not bothering to sway his javelin in the elegant way his assailants did, either trying to stab or cut or just hit with the sturdy shaft, he leapt backwards and away, escaping renewed assault, then hurling his weapon as a missile, in a beautiful arch that seemed to be one with his body, which tilted in a surprisingly graceful manner, as though about to fly after the javelin as it left his hand.

Her heart going absolutely still, Sele watched it reaching one of the warriors, then doing something her mind refused to analyze even though her eyes insisted, trying to look away, unable to do so. The spear went through the man's body with such ease, like a sharpened stick entering a pile of earth, with incredible smoothness and no visible difficulty.

The collective gasp went out of so many throats it seemed as though thunder rolled over the clouded sky, which actually fit the persistently gloomy surroundings, the lack of sunlight that kept lingering, as opposed to the brilliance and the heat of before. Absently, she thought about it, wishing to glance at the sky, refusing to process what her eyes relegated to her mind, the way the impaled warrior staggered, thrown backwards and into the ground, his limbs jerking strangely, as though having forgotten how to go about getting up again but trying to do so nevertheless. No wonder really. How could one get up or move around with the sturdy shaft stuck in the middle of one's body, protruding from its sides at an impossible angle, not belonging.

Holding her breath, her throat constricted, which was a mercy as the delicacies she had sampled before seemed determined to travel in the wrong direction, she heard the warriors down the plaza yelling something, rushing toward the fighting men, who stood there momentarily frozen in the same stupor as the rest of the watchers, the wild foreigner included. He was poised like a stone statuette carved on a pipe, still leaning forward as though about to throw another projectile, one leg ahead of another, planted widely, supporting his pose. To stay thus forever?

In another heartbeat, the illusion shattered. As the other men bore on them, the group around him came to life at once, and she saw him leaping forward and toward the fallen man, failing to reach him due to someone's thrust, changing his direction halfway, ducking the blow of another spear. It seemed to brush against his shoulder, and it was easy to see him losing his balance, clutching the assaulting shaft with one hand while going down, as though determined to stabilize himself.

Fascinated enough to forget her horror at the sight of the impaled man, who was still moving in an eerie dance of jerking limbs amidst forceful sprinkles of disturbingly vivid crimson, she watched the melee growing, more people joining the fray. For a heartbeat, it all turned into a blur of running figures and flailing limbs and spears, and unable to keep still, she pushed the serving girl with the fan out of her way, jumping from her seat, even though it didn't give her a better vantage point, needing to know somehow, to do something.

The clamor of female voices all around her, some high-pitched, some hysterical or just squeaking excitedly enveloped her, reinforced by the agitation of nobles around the royal dais. Then her eyes caught the figure of the foreign *miche-quipy*, back on his feet and somehow armed again, holding a spear in his outstretched hands, waving it wildly, with no visible purpose. Trying to keep his attackers at bay?

She felt the unpleasant sheen of perspiration breaking over her back despite the wind and the unusual chill it brought. In the middle of the day and through one of the last summer moons, it didn't make any sense, as did the darkening air as though the dusk was about to descend. Too busy to think any of it through, she tried to push past the crowding palanquins that were getting in the way of her vision, their owners' agitated cries and outright squealing making her wish to shut her ears.

"Stop that!" The angered voice overcame the commotion, making even the loudest among the shrilling girls lapse into momentarily frightened silence.

Her heart in her throat, Sele caught the glimpse of the haughty royal woman, her palanquin still hovering near Revered Sun's dais, yet now turned toward their little cluster, a few paces closer than before, its rider's face calm, its chilling expression unchanged, this perpetual haughtiness and scorn, the coldly quivering edges of the thin mouth. The lady Female Sun didn't even need to raise her voice despite the distance of quite a few paces, a dozen at the very least.

"Stop yelling. Compose yourselves, all of you!"

Unable to think of anything but the happenings upon the plaza, Sele blinked, feeling the veiled gaze pausing on her.

"Go back to your little carried seat, my brother's little toy." At that, the woman motioned at her own palanquin carriers, indicating the edge of the incline, about half a dozen paces removed from the royal surroundings, presenting another angle to view the happenings upon the plaza. "On second thought, come along, adviser's daughter."

Dazed by too many strange happenings occurring all at once, Sele stared for another heartbeat, rooted in her place, unable to move, shivering. It was getting strangely cold, as though the night was nearing. It was turning darker as well.

"Look!" cried out one of the girls, a familiar voice, Hekuni most probably, the silly chatter of the others resuming their lively if now carefully hushed gushing. They were referring to the strange occurrences of getting colder and darker, she somehow knew, but a servant was already hurrying toward her, ready to guide her to the indicated spot, make her obey the lady Female Sun's wishes, and as much as she wished to turn around and flee back to her palanquin, the rising clamor upon the plaza made her hurry to comply. She *needed* to see what was happening!

The man with the spear stuck in his body was lying motionless, in an unnatural pose of bizarrely spread limbs, the crimson pools around him not as vivid as before, as though losing something vital as well. It made her wish to gag, but her eyes kept darting, seeking the violent *miche-quipy* who had evidently gone down in the meanwhile, with the commotion surrounding him seeming to be at its highest, now with Uncle Ahal being a part of it as well, shouting something, clearly arguing with the warriors who weren't busy assaulting their prey but looked as though they might be tempted to dive in.

The man facing Uncle Ahal, a broad-shouldered leader she remembered seeing upon the Royal Mound often, the head of the royal warriors or something, was arguing too, motioning at Uncle Ahal, then at other armed men. By this time, the foreigner was up again, bloody but striking out with as much spirit as before, somehow managing to escape several more lashing out spears, his back pressing against one of the supporting poles, hands clutching his ill-gained weaponry. His face was turning whichever way, but she was sure he was glancing at Uncle Ahal, hoping for help, and somehow, whatever her uncle's thing was with the strange outlander, she found herself hoping that he would find a way to stop it, at least for a little while. He was brave, that violent insolent foreigner, even if he dared to look at her with no shame like before.

"I wonder how much longer this one will last. An interesting type. Good-looking and so very virile."

The words made Sele jump, reminding her of her dangerous company. The royal woman was leaning slightly forward as though fascinated by the happenings, speaking to no one in particular, even though several other members of the royal family who had drifted after their female sovereign tore their eyes off the fighting and gazed at Female Sun dutifully, ready to answer or respond, or do her any other bidding. Even the silly cousin with her squeaky voice was bouncing in her own smaller seat, glancing at the sky, her plump round face creased with an obvious thought process, puzzling.

"Look!" Evidently feeling Sele's gaze, the girl glanced at her, then pointed, her voice satisfactory low this time, not wishing to invoke the royal lady's displeasure. "Isn't it strange?"

There was no need to squint when looking at the sky, even though the clouds did not conceal the sun, not anymore. It was there, glaring brightly but only when one looked straight at it, its glow somehow subdued, the perfection of its circle marred, not as round as it should be, as though missing an edge. Even the strengthening wind, rushing filmy clouds across the direfully frowning sky, felt out of place, enhancing the eerie sensation. It made Sele shiver with dread she couldn't even explain.

"What is happening?" she heard someone whispering and it took her a heartbeat to understand that it was her who had uttered the words. "What—?"

"Fight the lowly foreigner two warriors each time." The voice of Tattooed Serpent rolled over the incline, overcoming the clamor up and down the plaza easily, as it always did. "This is the wish of our mighty Sun."

Always intimidating, all warriors' markings and foreboding looks, the man did not need to use his august sibling's name to be obeyed. Still, Sele's eyes leapt toward her husband's seat, barely visible under the heavy magnificence of his tiara, his pose more straight-backed then she ever remembered, leaning forward as much as his headdress allowed, animated in an atypical way. Oh yes, it was his wish to see the foreigner fighting, killing more warriors maybe, impaling more men. The crawling of her skin was back, making her shiver in the new gust of cold wind. The sun, she noticed, did not return to its regular size. If anything, it seemed to shrink even more, with a whole edge of it turning darker, hemmed by some ominously black verge.

Down at the plaza, the warriors regrouped, not daring to contradict the new orders. Two men, one armed with a spear, flanked by his peer carrying a club, with more clubmen hovering nearby, ready to join the fray, came forward, motioning at the foreigner, who didn't hurry to obey, looking cornered and not at his best, streaks of brown and red covering his body, strangely appealing yet frightening at the same time. He was as good as dead now, with even Uncle Ahal unable to protect him. No one could, not against Revered Sun's wishes.

"Do you intend to have him put to death, Revered Brother?" The royal woman's voice again rang with too much force and abruptness, reminding Sele that she did not belong in this immediate royal vicinity, certainly not standing like a maid and not reclining on appropriate sitting arrangements. Even the silly cousin who kept glancing at the sky was sitting in her carried chair like a lady of her status should. "What if he kills more of your warriors? How many would you consider enough?"

Revered Sun did not turn his head to look at his illustrious female sibling. "The man must die, Sister," he said curtly, his voice distorted by a short dry cough. Despite the turmoil her senses were in, Sele wondered if he needed to drink his medicine now. "He is not destined to live. Not after he killed one of my spearmen."

"At your request, Brother," said the woman tersely, but did not go on persisting with more arguments. A certain novelty. Every dweller of the Royal Mound knew that Female Sun thought herself to be above anyone, her sacred sibling and her son who was to follow in his uncle's footsteps included.

Down at the crowded plaza, the fighting was already in progress, or rather the attack on the foreigner, who, following something Uncle Ahal clearly shouted at him, left the relative safety of the wide beam, but did not progress much further, holding his spear like a club now, trying to fend off the approaching cudgel. Something that didn't seem too difficult at first, as both warriors lunged at once, and by Sele's estimation, were getting in each other's way, not bothering to coordinate their actions.

Darting away from the thrown spear, the foreigner somehow managed to escape the shorter range of the swishing club, parrying another onslaught with his own long-reaching weaponry, managing to deflect the descending cudgel but not to stop it for good. Gasping, Sele saw the smoothly rounded tip crashing against the smeared bloodied shoulder, sending its owner flying sideways, slamming into the same column he was not so eager to leave before.

At the same time, the spearman, in possession of his javelin once again, pounced like a hungry predator, a huge forest cougar as she would imagine these magnificent animals should be, closing the distance in one single leap, the flint tip already descending, diving toward the sprawling man.

Her breath caught, Sele saw the foreigner struggling but weakly this time, maybe trying to get up, or maybe to turn around or roll away. It was difficult to tell. The spear was coming down, and this time, it was going to impale him just like he did to that other warrior, to make him do a terrible, disgustingly bloodcurdling dance of limbs. It didn't seem to pause at all.

Despite the choking wave the memory of the previous ghastly death brought, she kept watching, her mind strangely detached, noting the details; the way the spear plunged with no hesitation, unerring and beautiful in its vicious determination to take life; the way it shuddered in the end, twisting while pulling its holder along, to crash on the top of its victim and remain there in a pile of struggling limbs.

To crane her neck didn't help. It was so messy, so difficult to see, the people around talking or shouting, the nobles on their incline and the gushing lake of the city dwellers crowding the entire perimeter of the plaza. They sounded agitated, maybe even scared, but she didn't have leisure to look at them, not yet. The two men upon the ground gained the entirety of her attention. They were still sprawling, both of them, but what did it mean?

"The warlike *miche-quipy* added another slain guard to his count, Brother." The royal sister's voice rang with a certain amount of satisfaction, almost gleeful, as arrogantly calm as always but not as cold. There was a purr to her words, surprisingly human satisfaction, even a hint of sibling rivalry, a sister happy to prove her brother wrong. "How many more will it be before you see the obvious?"

She could hear her husband grunting something in response, her eyes glued to the men on the ground, the spearman shuddering, then going eerily still. In a strange accord, the foreigner did not try to scramble up either, sprawling there beside his new alleged victim, not even reaching for the contested weaponry that somehow seemed to roll away and was lying there, discarded. Was he also dead or dying? Sele strained her eyes, the palanquins and their bearers crowding around, setting her nerves on edge, some of them pointing at the sky instead of watching the bloody show, gasping in awe.

"Do not kill this man." The voice of the royal sister stopped the warriors, who came out of another momentary stupor and this time pounced like hungry predators, set on killing, their spears ready. "Bring him here!"

She could hear Revered Sun exhaling loudly, again inappropriately unofficial, an exasperated sibling. "Stop that, Sister," he said tiredly, then cleared his throat. "Dispose of this man!" This came out in a surprisingly strong voice, resonating like the shout of Tattooed Serpent before, steady if hoarse. "Kill the foreigner."

The warriors upon the plaza hesitated, taken aback by

contradicting orders. Or maybe it was the strengthening wind, the cold and the deepening twilight it brought. *What was happening?* People were crying out in outright fright and even the warriors were staring, forgetting their duties.

Still disoriented and as though in a haze, Sele followed their gazes, appalled to see the sun glowing in a meager half a circle, like a drawing upon the sand, an inaccurate sketch. That black edge, she remembered, her mind numb, refusing to comprehend its possible meaning. It was just a simple black line along the sun's edge, but now almost half a sun was missing, swallowed by a terrible bleakness, something ominous, scary, something one could only dream about. What *was* happening?

Amidst growing cries and shouts, and even outright wails of terror coming from among the women in palanquins but not only – the *miche-quipy* crowding the edges of the ceremonial field were yelling and pointing worse than before – she glimpsed Tattooed Serpent rushing toward the royal dais, where her husband sat as though in a daze, staring at the sky, his mouth agape. Such an unbecoming pose!

Despite her own welling terror, Sele couldn't help a light splash of embarrassment. Revered Sun was not a well man, oh yes, but he was the sacred sovereign of this city, the younger sibling of the Sun Deity itself, the same deity that was now harmed somehow, disappearing bit by bit, being devoured by the darkness.

The terror splashed anew, worse than before, and she rushed toward the dais as well, bumping into people, nearly pushing a maid with a tray off her feet, then spending some time fighting for balance, unaccustomed to running anywhere, not at a neck-breaking pace.

By the time she managed to get her bearings, Tattooed Serpent was there, helping his divine brother out of his seat and toward the edge of the incline, holding on to his arm firmly, either supporting or guiding, probably both. The darkness was spreading more visibly now, and a glance at the sky informed her that the situation with the sun hadn't improved. If anything, it got worse, with the glowing side of the sacred deity yielding more of its surface to the crawling darkness.

"You must address our revered patron, our Father and Elder Brother," the voice of the royal sister resonated firmly, with no hesitation and no fear. "Come, Brother. Talk to our Revered Ancestor, our Patron and our Elder Brother. Ask for his mercy and his benevolence. Promise our gratitude. Promise!"

Her senses on fire, dazed and panicked at the same time, Sele clung to the steadiness of the woman's voice, managing to stay where she was without another headlong run, peering at the pinched sharp-angled face she had resented so much until now, feared and actively hated, wished it harm. Now it felt as though the woman was the only safe haven, her hand waving firmly, directing her august siblings toward the edge of the incline and the priests that were huddling there, darkly clad and foreboding, muttering at the sky, the blackness of their loincloths setting them apart. The rest of the Sun's family members and following were crowding nearby, each in a different stage of hysterical fright.

An annoying voice was whimpering next to her, persistent fingers clutching her hand. She tore it out of the slippery grip, nearly pushing the girl off her feet, that silly chatty royal cousin, the last person she wished to share her welling dread with. It was better to be next to Revered Sun's sister, not pleasanter but certainly safer. That woman knew what she was doing.

Again she glanced at the sky, hoping to see the blackness gone, disappeared, the shiny benevolent deity who watched after Quachil Thecou and its dwellers, all of them, the high and the low, who gave of its light and its warmth every dawn anew, without whom no food would grow and no mounds would raise, with the night spirits and demons taking over and... No, no, it could not be gone, not like that. It couldn't!

Unable to contain her dread any longer, the monotonous chanting coming from the priests wearing on her nerves, the voice of her husband lacking in firmness, more of a broken whisper, addressing the sky dwellers with his arms spread wide, not an impressive gesture, not in his case, she glanced around wildly, then, seeing a small opening between the crowding nobles, dashed toward it, diving into it, not thinking it all through. The masses of people were yelling and screaming, terrified all of them, frightened to death. All but one person.

She didn't stop to think, not for a heartbeat. Uncle Ahal! He was here, down the nearest corner of the plaza, only a few dozen paces away, and he would not let something dreadful to happen. Not him!

CHAPTER 15

He tried to see through the simmering twilight, not certain where he was, or why, for that matter? What was happening? The nasty blow to his head was to blame. Or maybe the rest of the fighting. Insane that he was still alive, plain insane, but maybe he wasn't. Maybe he died already, and it was only his spirit that floated around, refusing to leave. People's spirits were in no hurry to do that at times, were they?

To try and remember something like that proved difficult, the effort of directing his thoughts through the soft soggy moss that seemed to fill his head from the inside. If only people would stop running all around, thundering with their hard-soled moccasins and yelling or crying out. Enough that there was plenty of wailing and screaming coming from somewhere further away, somewhere where it wasn't so suffocating and crammed. Or maybe it was as bad everywhere. That heavy stench emanating from the man lying next to him was annoying. He needed to escape that before he retched all his insides out. It couldn't be that foul-smelling everywhere, could it? The cold and the darkness and the stench, oh but he needed to escape those. None of it made any sense.

"Oh mighty deity, oh benevolent sun… Oh mighty…"

So many voices were repeating that. He pushed himself up, or rather sideways, because of a bout of blinding pain somewhere around his left shoulder, not something he was ready to deal with, not in such an unsteady world. It swayed worse than before, but he clung to his newly gained height of a semi-sitting position and the sense of victory it brought. No, he wasn't going down, not again. One time was more than enough. Not one, but several. But what a wild thing this fighting was! These people, they were insane, plain insane. Except the tribute collector, the only reasonable person; well, to a degree. Where was he now? Running all over, screaming like the rest of them?

He strained his eyes, trying to see. All those milling-around legs. It was a wonder no one stepped on him or trampled him for good. But he needed to get up, at least that. Or maybe even flee. It could be possible, couldn't it? They were all so busy running and screaming.

A renewed attempt to get up did not crown with success, not this time. It seemed that even the wind joined the effort to hinder him, to keep him where he was. It tore with renewed viciousness, chilling as though it was a night of a deep autumn, bringing a hint of a nearing storm, making the darkness deepen. But how long had he been lying there, dead or alive? The night was not even near when they began that bizarre fighting. Or was it? Did they leave him here for dead, forget all about him?

The cry of an owl confirmed that conclusion. But if it was already night, why were they all still around, this stupid multitude of people, all those who watched him fighting, yelling their hardest, assaulting his ears, but not like now. Didn't the city-people retire to sleep at night? Oh, but he needed to make the best out of this mess, to get away, somehow, somewhere.

"Oh mighty sun!"

"It's disappearing, oh mighty benevolent sky deity!"

"It will be gone for good, unless..."

The last voice sounded somewhat familiar, belonging to one of the warriors, maybe, those whom he fought. Oh yes, they were still around. Too bad.

For what felt like a heartbeat, or maybe plenty of them, he tried to decipher their features, but the thickening darkness was making it nearly impossible, and the buzz inside his head didn't help. He needed to get away from it all, somehow. The world was going mad and he couldn't stay like that, swallowed by the eerie darkness or trampled to death. Even the birds that were chirping quite loudly before, enough to overcome the hum of the multitude of gathering people at times went quiet, them and the day insects.

Only the owls remained. And people. So many! One wouldn't imagine so many existing in the entire world, let alone herded together, to watch some spearmen throwing their javelins at the rolling piece of stone. Or fighting him, one by one, and then all at once. What lowlifes!

"Revered Sun is praying. Look!" Another hysterical shout erupted, too close for his peace of mind. If only he could reach that pole that supported something, a roof or anything. It must be somewhere around, mustn't it? Leaning on something like that he might manage to gain an upright position. To crawl around among the madly running feet wouldn't do, not in this darkness and the unsteady wavering world that was turning colder with every passing heartbeat.

The villager wasn't at the scene of the fighting, even though his fallen victims were, discovered Ahal, clearing his way through the throngs of the berserk people, forcing his thoughts off the terrible happenings up in the sky and all around. Was the world ending, falling apart, sinking in the premature darkness for good?

It certainly looked that way now, with the moon-like crescent glowing where the full circle of the sun had been shining in the perfect early afternoon fashion only a short time ago, as it did every day of every season. It was inconceivable, and but for his other senses and the terrified crying of people all around him, he would have refused to believe his eyes. It couldn't be, it just couldn't. The most revered deity, the sacred patron of Quachil Thecou, let alone the Great Sun City of the west, the benevolent sky deity watching over the Great River valleys, it could not abandon them like that, could not die in front of their eyes, devoured by the ominous darkness.

Fighting for breath, his stomach squeezed by an invisible ring, not allowing more than a gulp of air in, Ahal struggled to get a grip on his senses, not to succumb to the all-consuming panic, the wild urge to run, anywhere, somewhere, to hide or escape, to flee the world that was sinking into the terrible glum. Anything but that!

On the edge of the incline hosting the watching royalty, he could see the silhouetted figure of Revered Sun, turning toward the diminishing crescent, his hands spread wide in a silent address. More figures crowded him, the headdress of Tattooed Serpent impossible to mistake, all those tall upright feathers. He remembered facing the man such a short time ago, bidden into the royal presence for the first time in his life. An incredible honor, marred by the dubious circumstances of the wild villager's creation. Where was the man? Still alive or already dead?

The need to look around and maybe try to clear his way in the mayhem of running and screaming people helped to concentrate, to make a semblance of order out of his thoughts. The cruel fighting the divine sovereign had ordered, an unheard-of entertainment that had even his warlike sibling, the militant Tattooed Serpent, frowning in doubt, put him, Ahal, in the worst of positions, responsible for the performance of the foreigner destined to die, associated in the eyes of the mighty ruler with something as dubious, certain to harm his stance for the times to come. Still, he could not abandon the villager. The man was his responsibility, his current fate more than anything. And he wasn't a bad man. Violent, wild, unruly, yes, an untamed spirit as the man's own sister had put it, a promising youth according to her words. Well, siblings' love aside, the man did hold promise, and it was a waste to have him killed in such a cruel, hopelessly slow and brutal way. It wasn't right and maybe the mighty sun deity was showing its displeasure, turning its face from its favorite progeny, looking away in disgust.

The stony fist was back, squeezing his insides, and he looked around resolutely, forcing his thoughts to concentrate on the new challenge, to think where the man might have gone to. He was wounded, there could be no argument about it. All smeared with blood, sprawling after a club sent him down, unable to get up. He had to grab the cutting edge of his new attacker's spear to try and do something against the impending kill. The hair-raising sight of such a powerful will to live, or maybe a bloodthirsty need to kill,

kill, kill, even when unable to get up anymore. The villager was an enigma, a puzzle.

When the spearmen had gone down instead of impaling his victim, Ahal held his breath, hoping against hope. It was inspiring, in a way, and he felt his heart racing, eyes trying to see better, refusing to believe, hoping against hope. That other spearman thrashing with his limbs, then going motionless, and the villager still moving, as though about to start getting up. Was he charmed by unknown magic of the east? Was that why the foreigner didn't seem overly concerned with his prospected fate when told about the fighting, greeting it with enthusiasm, earning an almost amiable nod from the head of the royal guards with his recklessly brave declarations?

Back then, he had assumed that the man did not understand the implications, did not comprehend the strange fighting-to-the-death concept, unfamiliar to them all as well. Well, there was no point in trying to enlighten his charge. What would it change, besides making the prospective victim to feel bad, dispirited, doomed before his time? And maybe somewhere deep, he might have hoped that if the villager held on, fought as best as he could, did not get hurt too badly or succumbed to the might of his attackers otherwise, Revered Sun might change his mind, might decide to let the man live and be of use to Quachil Thecou.

A futile hope. The moment the villager had gotten into his fighting mode, cornered and played by the spearmen who felt their superiority acutely as it was, he displayed nothing but mindless ferociousness, no different than a cornered beast – brutal and fearless and not completely sane. When he impaled one of the spearmen, ran the man through with his javelin in the most gory of manners, unfit for the city denizen's eyes, it was clear that he would not be allowed to live now no matter what. And still, he, Ahal, found himself trying to do something, to prevent an outright killing, getting into another uncalled for altercation with the head of the royal guards. It was not right, what was happening, not right and not just. And yet, what could he do about it? When another warrior was killed and Revered Sun himself shouted his will to execute the culprit, angered by the slaughter, even though it was his will, his decree to have the fighting commenced, he knew that the villager was doomed, and but for the sacred sky deity's predicament up there in heavens…

Clenching his teeth, he glanced at the sky, the ring around his chest squeezing tighter, the splash of panicked fear near again, welling. The diminishing crescent shone brighter than before, as though sending its farewells while being overrun by the dark forces, eaten away. Strange strips of light were darting across the plaza, and it was filling with more and more people, with the multitude of *miche-quipy* rushing into forbidden zone, forgetting their fear of authorities at the face of a greater fear. The priests' chanting did not overcome the loudest clamor, but they all knew the gods' servants were praying now, begging forgiveness of the disappearing deity, imploring of it to stay, or be strong, not to succumb to the dark evil forces. Revered Sun was of the celestial family. He could surely speak to his worshipped elder brother, couldn't he?

Trying to hide his own desperation and fright, Ahal pushed several men out of his way, then spent a heartbeat stabilizing a woman who collided with him, shoved violently and about to fall under everyone's feet. It wasn't easy to free his arm from the desperation of her grip. Again his eyes darted around, then caught the sight of someone wavering next to the pole supporting a sheltered construction, clinging to it as though it was the only means of surviving the world sinking into darkness.

His legs took him toward it without giving it an additional thought, shoving several people out of his way, colliding with one of the spearmen, not spending his time on muttering polite apologies, neither of them. It was not the time and the rising wailing and screaming didn't leave room for unnecessary exchanges anyway.

By the time he reached his destination, the villager wasn't upright anymore, huddling next to the supporting beam's base in a heap of limbs, clinging to it with his previous determination but no visible results. Ahal reached him with another forceful shove through the renewed surge of figures, every face turned upwards or toward the chanting priests, all but his. To grab the wounded's shoulder and pull hard turned out to be a difficult business. The violent foreigner resisted with surprising readiness, lashing out with his free arm, jamming his elbow into Ahal's ribs, putting it all into an attempt to break free.

"Stop that," breathed Ahal, shoving the man into the rough wood of the pole, using his entire bodyweight to pin him to it, tempted to use his fists. "Stop fighting or I'll knock you senseless, then leave you here to die under everyone's feet."

The attempts to break free did not grow less spirited; however, the man clearly had no more strength left to rely on, slippery to hold on to, smeared with too much blood and dirt. His rasping breath tore the darkness, brushing against Ahal's face, overcoming the hum of the wailing and hollering. The darkness was almost complete now, full of lamenting silhouettes. He didn't have time to get frightened by it. The body his own was assaulting sagged against his grip, even though the attempts to break free repeated themselves, feeble but there.

"Stop it," he repeated, trying to sound calm, a ridiculous attempt under the circumstances. "I'm here to help you. Have you been hurt badly?"

With no ready answer forthcoming, he dared to take his attention away, glancing at the sky, taking in the diminishing crescent, a beautiful vision despite the terrifying meaning of it, with strange longish shadows dancing across it, as though a part of a sinister ritual. The hoot of the nocturnal birds coming from the direction of the wall and the river behind it had his blood freezing in terror. The night spirits were out, ready to harvest their terrible spoils.

"What... what is happening?" The man's words, faint and heavily accented, not belonging in the luxurious plaza of Quachil Thecou, reached him in time, pulling him off the brink, helping to concentrate on something not related to the disaster that was happening all around. The chanting of the priests, but was it turning louder now, more desperate?

"I don't know." It came out surprisingly steadily, with firmness that encouraged him himself, ridiculous as it was. "Now, can you stand on your own?"

The answer provided itself the moment he tried to act on his words, eager to pull away, not enjoying too close a proximity with another man, certainly not someone smeared in so much blood and gore and smelling like that. The man collapsed like a straw mat put on its side. The attempt to recapture his grip did not succeed, and just as Ahal knelt on order to check his charge's condition, hysterical sobs reached his ears over the splashing waves of dread, penetrating the general mayhem of shouting and wailing around him, distracting in their familiarity.

His eyes darting wildly, his heart going off again to a wild start, he leapt to his feet. The darkness was nearly complete now, the cold most perceptible, the shadows darting violently, alternating with strips of light sweeping across the perfectly swept ground. People stopped wailing and were staring at the sky, and he didn't have to rush more than a few paces away to locate her, her sobs guiding him, or maybe it was some instinct heightened by the disaster.

She was on the run as well, also unerring despite the crowding and the darkness, crashing into him before he managed to stop the collision, throwing herself into his arms, again nothing but a little girl to save and comfort. This alone made him feel infinitely better, helped to battle his own bottomless desperation and fear.

"Uncle Ahal," she sobbed. "Uncle Ahal! Wh-what... what is happening?"

He pressed her firmer, containing her trembling, succumbing to the need to process her questions, unable not to watch now. The dark circle where the sun should have been was still there, silhouetted by a beautifully glowing aura of light, a breathtaking sight despite its ominous meaning. The people around them grew quieter and it pleased him, ridiculous as it was, helped to achieve a semblance of tranquility. Even the resumed chanting seeping from the direction of the royal dais sounded calmer, less frantic than before, more appropriate as an address to the displeased or maybe somehow assaulted deity, even though Revered Sun himself was nowhere to be seen now, not even his silhouetted form. Instead, the eerily orange glow was spreading above the Royal Mound, hair-raising and dreadful, its beauty sinister, promising destruction.

"What is happening, Uncle?" repeated Sele, peeking out like a small animal, wary and ready to dive back into the safety of his chest. Poor little thing. "What will happen to us?"

He winced at her climbing-up tones, then pressed her firmer, trying to relay the calmness he didn't feel. "I don't know, little one. But stay where you are. I'll keep you safe."

How? The reassuring words did not help, the realization that his own family was out there in the city, in the pretty neighborhood with spacious houses and towering mounds, safe from wandering commoners but not from the disaster of the disappearing sun. Were they terrified out there like the rest of the people around him, crying and panicked like Sele, but with no one to comfort them and promise to keep them safe, his children so much smaller but more vulnerable because of that.

"That man who f-fought," whimpered Sele, squirming as though about to free herself. "The *miche-quipy* who fought... Is he dead? Did it happen because of him, because of what he did?"

"No." He could not take his eyes off the bizarre glow, now stronger on the other side, opposite to the previous advance of the dark circle. He pushed the thought of the villager away, unable to take his eyes off the terrible sight. The man would have to fend for himself now, and what did it matter anyway when they were all to disappear along with the world swallowed by darkness.

The wave of panic was back, and he pressed his niece closer, determined to shield her from the worst of it. The silence, but why was it deepening with every passing heartbeat? Were the people around them already gone, dead, disintegrated?

"Uncle!" Sele's voice helped to pull him off the brink of panic again. "Look."

The glow on the opposite side began to dim as though the dark circle shifted, the sliver of light seeming to grow, imperceptibly, but it did. He didn't dare to let the sudden splash of hope soar. Could it be? That sliver, did it mean that the sun was coming back, winning its fight against the darkness or just deciding to stay?

The collective gasp, like a breath held for too long in too many throats at once, went up, bringing the darkness surrounding him to life. They were all alive and still well, the denizens of Quachil Thecou, and maybe, just maybe…

"It's coming back!" squeaked Sele, tearing herself from his grip but not stepping away, her arm pointing upwards. It was easy to guess her pose. "The Great Sun, he is coming back!"

Other people were echoing her words, some breathing them out, some yelling at the top of their voices. The commotion piqued again, but not like the terrified chaos of before. This new uproar was all cries of joy and elation, and he didn't fight his own jubilation anymore, seeing the sliver of light growing, definitely now, the sacred deity escaping the darkness, slipping from the other side of the black trap, invincible. But of course it was!

The yells and the shouts threatened to deafen everyone in hearing range, but he didn't mind, joining the victorious cries, not caring in the least how he sounded or how inappropriate their current company might be, all those city *miche-quipy* from their observation spots around the plaza, not allowed into more hallowed surroundings like these ones but for what happened. Upon the incline with the royal seat and the palanquins, the figure with its arms spread toward the sky became more visible along with the returning light of the benevolent deity, its pose encouraging, its straightness and the obvious firmness of its stance, the sound of its powerful chanting.

"It's Tattooed Serpent," murmured Sele, standing separately now but gripping his arm in hers, not about to let go, not yet. "He is speaking to the Great Sun. Thanking him!"

"Not our revered ruler?" he asked, eyes on the orating royalty, but his mind already thinking, questioning, worrying. What was the better timing to ask? "Your husband, he isn't well, is he?"

He could feel her shrugging with one shoulder, and there was no need for further inquiries. Still, the man was well enough to attend the spear-throwing contest, well enough to order an unheard-of fight to the death. Couldn't he stand on his own, address his own divine ancestor?

The thought brought another and he caught her shoulders, pulling her along, guiding her through the crowding forms that were turning more and more visible. The villager! Was he still alive out there?

"Uncle, where are we going?" she asked, not resisting his pull, as nimble as a slick little fish in the river, helping his progress rather than hindering. "Back to the—"

He didn't have time to answer, the pole where he left the wounded easy to locate, to push his way toward it. With the retuning light, it was no challenge. "Wait here."

Guiding her near the rough wood, he knelt next to the huddled form, wondering if the man was alive and what he was to do with him if so. Was it not better to fake forgetfulness, to take his niece back to her royal gathering as was his duty and his right? This was his way to achieve another admittance into the noble presence, to try and make a better impression, to separate himself from the wild foreigner and the bad mark the association with him had probably made.

"Are you alive?" To grab the man's shoulder turned out as challenging a business as before, the touch of his skin slippery, smeared with plenty of gore. "You..." He tried to remember the man's name, something with the word mountain lion in it, surprising because unlike other easterners, it had the sound of their own western tongue. "Iciwata!"

The man shuddered, then muttered something, making a movement as though about to try and break free. In the brightening air, it was easy to see in what bad shape he was, covered with sheen of blood and dirt, with too many alarmingly twisted cuts still glistening with too fresh of a crimson, still bleeding. The glimpse of the lifeless face provided Ahal with a view of the disproportionally swollen side of the forehead and the veiled bleary gaze, the cracked bloodless lips moving, struggling to produce something coherent, or so it seemed.

"Keep an eye on him!" Back on his feet, he caught Sele's gaze, holding it, willing her to obey. "I'll be back in a heartbeat. Don't let anyone get to him."

She was staring at him, wide-eyed, clearly shocked into temporary lack of argument. He motioned her toward the sprawling wounded, then scanned their surroundings.

The man nearest to them did not look like the type to carry anything as worthwhile as a flask of water, a simple fellow from the riverbank, his lack of clothing besides a muddied loincloth testifying for him. Another group huddled in the distance of a few paces, as unpromising-looking, their unburdened hands waving in the air, as agitated as their voices were. Better dressed people flanked them, mixed in an atypical manner, not a view one would expect on the plaza facing the Royal Mound.

Shrugging, he rushed toward them. "Do you carry water on you?"

The plainly dressed *miche-quipy*, clearly of a higher status than simple workers, several women among them, stopped yelling for a moment, staring at him in the same manner Sele did before, shocked into lack of response. His penned-up irritation welled like never before.

"Answer me!" His advance toward the nearest man gained him more wide-eyed stares. "Do you carry flasks of water on you?"

"Yes, yes, honorable *considerate.*"

Apparently, the air brightened enough to give them an indication of his status as well. A glance at the sky reassured him once again, even if briefly, the sun's growing crescent, spilling its murky light, banishing the darkness for good, or so he hoped.

"Give me your flask." He didn't like to rob people of their goods, certainly not with so much aggression, but there was no time for politeness. The sight of the spearmen gathering around the broad-shouldered figure of the head of the royal guards relayed the urgency of his own actions. "You will be rewarded for that," he tossed, snatching the prettily painted pottery vessel, not a cheap skin flask he expected to receive. "I will ensure that."

Another glance at the gathering warriors made his worry increase. They were turning his way, certainly now. He rushed back where he left the villager and Sele.

Surprisingly, she was still there, having not only obeyed his hastily issued command, but actually expanded on her new responsibility by kneeling beside the sprawling man, attempting to support his head, or maybe to move him into a better position. It was difficult to tell, even in the strengthening light. Briefly, he glanced at the sun, elated to see the crescent promising to become a full half circle, the most welcome view he ever saw.

"Drink!" There was no time to check on the man's injuries, or let him come back to his senses at his own pace. He shook the bloodied shoulder forcefully. "Come. Wake up. Drink, you need to drink."

Not certain of what he intended to do once his charge stirred and maybe managed to get back to his feet, but knowing that he wished it to happen before the head of the guards or any of the spearmen who had fought him remembered, he shook the man forcefully. "Drink!"

"Let me, Uncle." As the wounded tried to fight off the flask thrust into his face, Sele reached to the neck of the vessel, shifting with surprising adeptness, managing not to let the lolling head she supported slip from the grip of her other hand. Her approach was infinitely gentler, winning the wild villager's cooperation, causing most of the liquid to slip between the cracked lips, with very little of it trickling down the bloodied chin.

For a heartbeat, Ahal found himself staring.

"Pour some water into my palm, Uncle." Her demand accompanied with the flask being pushed back into his hands, her tone as uncompromising as his must have been before, a matter-of-fact command.

Raising one eyebrow, he did as he was told, watching her brushing her newly wetted fingers over the wounded's face, causing the man to shut his eyes momentarily, then open them with more spirit than he displayed even while back up and fighting off Ahal's help before.

"Here, this is better," she was murmuring softly, striking her patient's cheek softly, caressing. "Now you must drink again."

"Where did you..." began Ahal, then thought better of it, handing the vessel back to her, getting up in order to keep them both safe from the trampling feet.

People were still rushing around, their shouts and agitated chattering shaking the brightening air, their talk gushing. *Miche-quipy*, *considerates*, even *honorables*, all mixed for a change, their difference in statuses temporary forgotten. The sight of the elegantly clad Sele, her exquisite clothes and beauty belonging on the Royal Mound, kneeling next to the bloody foreigner, supporting his head with the gentleness of a lover while cajoling him to drink some more, enhanced the strangeness of the situation like nothing else would. Where did she learn to be so efficient or caring?

Then the sight of the spearmen clearing their way toward them, purposeful as opposed to the mindless gushing all around, made him forget all such frivolous thoughts.

"Get away from him," he hissed at her, his eyes on the approaching group, quite an entourage, pale and wild-eyed but steady in their step. "Do it now!" His tone brooked no argument, and he knew she would obey this time, out of old habit and because she trusted him, her newly found and evidently enjoyed skills in nursing wounded notwithstanding. "Run back to your palanquin, the way you came." Another curt order he needed her to obey. Revered Sun's wife could not be caught wandering unattended and in dubious company, even if that of her uncle. She was of a higher status than he now.

"Honorable Tribute Collector!" The warriors were upon them before she managed to as much as spring to her feet, wavering lightly, having evidently saved the wounded's head from bumping too roughly against the ground, its new resting place. "The foreigner, is he still alive?"

Ahal made sure his back was as straight as it could be, expressing no guile. Their wide-eyed stares at his company that had nothing to do with the sprawling villager did not reassure him in the least. "He is wounded, dying. Who sent you?"

The spokesman among the spearmen squinted against the ground upon which the wounded was struggling into a sitting position with marked success, his timing bad, unhelpful. Where was the barely conscious heap of limbs? It was as though Sele's ministrations breathed life into the wild foreigner, giving him new strength.

"Revered Tattooed Serpent sent us." The man took his eyes off the villager but seemed to have a harder time tearing his gaze off Sele, who was standing quite proudly now, her head held high, beautiful and royal-like but for her hands and the hems of her exquisitely bright dress that were marred with plenty of bloody evidence. "The foreigner is to be brought before the divine family."

Ahal held the firm gaze for another heartbeat, hoping to will the man into further explanation, or at least a more respectful address. "Revered Sun's favorite wife needs to be escorted back to her palanquin." The stony tone helped to have his adversary lessen the intensity of his own stare. "Allocate an appropriate escort for the royal lady."

He could feel Sele shifting, and for a wild moment, he was afraid she would offer an argument, try to claim her right to stay, willful thing that she was.

"Do as my honorable uncle says, warriors." The imperious ring of her voice made the armed men straighten some more. "Have my servants bring my palanquin here in a hurry."

In the minor confusions her words caused, the lead spearmen turning to his men, talking rapidly, spitting instructions, Ahal squatted next to his unasked for charge again, wondering how to haul the wounded up without scaring him into more spirited resistance. It was clear that Sele's treatment did something to restore the man's life forces, his eyes focused enough, staring back, openly wary.

"Don't make any trouble. I'll help you up."

The intense gaze narrowed, then shifted as though looking for something, focusing on Sele, turning calmer at once. "Where... where to?" The cracked lips moved with difficulty, but the words came out clear and direct, relaying strong will.

"I don't know." Feeling the eyes upon him, too many, not only the warriors but plenty of onlookers, Ahal grabbed the man's unharmed shoulder, in the returned brightness finding it easier to understand why the villager was fighting his attempts to haul him up before, when the sun was still gone. "Lean on me."

"Help him."

The words of another warrior sent several spearmen to his aid. He waved them away impatiently, staggering under his burden, the wounded heavy, swaying like a tree in too strong of a wind, threatening to take them both down.

"Take care of the royal wife and her palanquin." His own words came out in a helplessly low grunt. He paused for a moment, drawing a deep breath, desperate to dominate them again, knowing himself to be at disadvantage now. "I'll bring the foreigner to the royal presence."

"My men will escort you." There was indeed an uncompromising edge to the lead spearman's words. "Let us go." That was clearly directed at the rest of the warriors.

Taking most of his charge's weight, Ahal concentrated on his step, desperate to show none of the sudden exhaustion that attacked him, the headache back, the wounded leaning on him heavily, washing his senses with the disgustingly sweetish odor of fresh blood, making him wish to push the slumping body away. The way to the pontificating figure of the royal brother seemed like a long one all of a sudden, the uphill tilt discouraging.

"Not very long now," he muttered, not certain if he was attempting to reassure his charge or himself.

The man didn't respond this time, reeling too badly to spend his life powers on anything but his next step. Ahal bettered his grip on the slippery torso, regretting the impulse to bring the villager all by himself and in such a state. What an additional impression he'd make when admitted into the royal presence once again, for the second time through this wild, insane day, staggering under the cut dying men, smeared in his blood, associated with something more dubious than before, not only the wild foreigner but the terrible event of the disappearing sun he might have caused. A bad prospect.

"Stay upright, as much as you can," he went on when the tilt of the ground made it clear that they were nearing their destination, the chanting of the priests growing, actually calming his nerves in its pleasantly monotonous softness. The voices of their escorts died away in a direct proportion. "Do not look at Revered Sun at all. If honored by an address from him, use his title and be humble. Do not look up or get up from the ground..."

It was turning silly. He didn't even know if the man was listening or capable of understanding, let alone implementing his instructions. He could almost feel the pain and the exhaustion, coming in waves, radiating from the body he was propping, the odor of sweat and blood making his own head reel. It was increasing steadily, wasn't it? The man might not even survive to be present before the mighty ruler, or not to be in a conscious enough state to go about making blunders like looking the divine descendant of the Sacred Sun Deity in the eye.

"Over here." To a certain sense of relief, the wide frame of the Chief Royal Guard blocked their way before the full view of the pontificating royalty was upon them. "You, take hold of him and keep him down until my signal." A few men rushed toward them, determined, and he felt the villager's fingers clinging to him with surprising strength considering the man's condition, painful in the desperation of their grip. "Remain here, Ahal. It is Revered Tattooed Serpent's wish."

"Of course, Honorable Leader." The warriors were still fighting to pry his burden off him, forcing him into impoliteness of turning away from the leader of higher status. "Where do you wish me to place the foreigner?" It was imprudent and outright stupid, but he couldn't help it, the desperation of the villager's grip combined with the openly pleading gaze he managed to glimpse forcing him to try and block the warriors' efforts. "I'll keep an eye on him as long as need be."

"Step aside and wait patiently, Tribute Collector." The clipped tone of the Chief Guard had no affability in it, not anymore. "Do not presume to argue or interfere with your superiors."

He moved away at once, his stomach tightening in such a painful knot, he didn't think he would manage to draw in a breath. "I apologize for offering unasked-for advice or assistance."

Was it his voice, still measured and satisfactorily loud, having only a slight touch of stridency to it? Numbly, he watched the warriors dragging their victim away, overcoming the fierceness of the villager's resumed struggle easily. But this man's resilience was remarkable, like so many other traits the foreigner had. It was a pity he was given no chance.

Following the curt gesture of the thickset leader, Ahal proceeded toward the edge of the incline, taking the indicated place among the nobles huddling there, the faces he glimpsed looking pale and haunted, badly shaken, a mirror image of the commoners flooding the plaza. He remembered the heads that were turned upwards, toward this very incline, pointing, observing, hopeful, trusting the divine ruler and his equally divine siblings to intercede before the powerful deity, convince it not to leave. It was unsettling to see that the actual entourage of the divine family seemed to have less faith than this in their celestial ruler, the younger brother of the benevolent sun itself.

Numbly, he sought the magnificent headdress of Revered Sun among the chanting silhouettes crowding the edge of the incline in vain, the tall if lean figure of Tattooed Serpent prominent against the bright glow of the returned sun, his hands spread in an appeal to the glowering deity. Other royal family members crowded the priests, some chanting, some imploring silently, their arms spread in a similar fashion. Even Revered Lady Female Sun, the Sun's sister and the mother of the heir, left her palanquin and stood behind the tattooed noble, straight backed and as proud as expected, not visibly shaken or even perturbed.

Against his will, he found himself staring, having never seen the famous lady from such close proximity, the person who was rumored to have the greatest influence over her divine sibling, ruling in his stead at times, or so the rumor had it. Surprisingly slender for a person of such reputation, unimpressively slight, she did not look like a dominant woman of ruthless, fierce disposition, even though her profile or what he managed to glimpse of it did suggest a great deal of willpower, the prominent nose and the protruding chin. Quickly, he took his eyes away, then realized what was wrong. Revered Sun, the powerful ruler of the city and the direct link to the powerful deity, was nowhere to be seen.

"Oh benevolent sun, our exalted elder brother and the revered patron of our people," cried out Tattooed Serpent, spreading his arms wider and higher as though trying to actually reach the sky. "Oh wonderful creator, guardian, and protector. We lie at your feet, humbled, defeated, afraid. Have we displeased you, offended you, angered you?"

Unable to keep his eyes on the ground, Ahal let his gaze dart toward the palanquins, desperate to understand. Revered Sun was not there to address the displeased deity, but how could it be?

"Oh celestial elder brother!" The pontificating noble's voice rose, picking a different tune. "Please guide us. Please let us know what you wish us to do."

His head swayed somewhat sharply, and in response, the warriors rushed forward, dragging the villager, who was sagging between them, displaying none of his previous fighting spirit, maybe unconscious, maybe just stunned. Ahal held his breath.

"What is your wish, oh benevolent almighty deity?" implored the tattooed man, his voice a singsong, droning the words out, not taking his eyes off the shiny circle, indifferent to the commotion his previous gesturing brought about.

The villager, thrown to the ground, was again giving a hard time to his captors, who tried to keep him there, fighting weakly but steadily, his blood marring the trampled grass. Nobles were craning their necks, trying to see better. Even the entourage of the praying royal sibling turned their heads in a wide-eyed stare. Revered Sun's sister's profile became more visible, with the lady tilting her body, glancing at the kneeling foreigner, her high forehead creased.

Only Tattooed Serpent remained immersed in his prayer. "Have us do your bidding, oh mighty all-powerful sun. Manifest your will."

A gust of wind came, rustling in the treetops down the incline. The light didn't dim, but everyone seemed to hold their breath all the same.

"Give us a sign!"

Another stronger gust seemed to satisfy the noble petitioner. His headdress massive, not allowing sharp movements or much body tilting, the pontificating man turned around, closing the distance of several paces in what seemed to be one single leap. His grip on the victim's hair was unerring, his yank fierce, bringing the struggling man up and to his knees, keeping him there despite the renewed attempts to resist. A nod at the group of unclothed, elaborately patterned priests summoned one of the painted men, a rope, a long, slick red-colored affair, held expertly in his outstretched hands.

"Oh benevolent sun," cried out Tattooed Serpent, his voice thundering now, not a petitioner but a giver. "Receive our humble offering of the one who offended you. Do not refuse our love and veneration. Do not turn your face from your humble worshippers again."

His stomach nothing but a wooden ball, clenched so tightly he didn't think he would manage to move its muscles ever again, Ahal listened, mesmerized now, his involvement with the villager forgotten, overwhelmed, craving to hear every word, to see every gesture, the majestically rolling voice making his skin crawl. The powerful deity would listen. It would not turn its face from Quachil Thecou and its denizens again. Not after such an address and the magnitude of the offering. It had never been offered a human life before.

"Receive our humble offering of the one who offended you." The rope wrapped expertly around the kneeling man's forcibly stretched neck, and as though understanding the sacredness of the moment, the foreigner stopped struggling and went still, a perfect part of the ritual, a significant part. If destined to die, wasn't this the best way, the most meaningful, most symbolic? The powerful deity would receive its gift with pleasure and gratitude, would smile upon the givers, the villager himself as well, would receive him in the afterworld, allocate him a worthwhile place that no foreign *miche-quipy* could ever hope to reach.

The moment shattered in the following heartbeat, as the rope tightened and the foreigner shuddered, as though awakening from a dream. His hands, not secured behind his back as it would have been upon similar rare occasions when revered suns' wives and retainers were made to follow their ruler in the afterlife journey, shot forward, grabbing the noose tightening around his neck deftly, yanking at it with incredible strength, pulling hard. Not propped by anything but the strangling rope, he should have gone down, but somehow, the man was still upright, maintaining his bizarre pose, shouting in the voice that matched that of the pontificating noble, not in its depth but in its loudness and clearness.

"You filthy pieces of human waste. You sickness-stricken coyotes, you scavengers, you excrement-eaters! I curse you! I curse you to die in pain, I…"

The thundering words grew fainter as the man began losing his struggle against the rope, unable to maintain his unnatural pose rather than failing to keep the noose from tightening again, of that Ahal was sure, gaping like the rest of the spectators, breathless, beyond words or thoughts. No additional sound escaped anyone's throat, and it was left to the wind to mourn, its gusts growing in frequency, tearing the air.

"Hold him!" cried out Tattooed Serpent, coming back to his senses at once, his face pale under the coat of paint, frighteningly gaunt. "Restrain him!"

"No!"

The short word tore the silence, and as though in a trance, Ahal followed it, watching the slender figure of Female Sun strolling toward the melee surrounding the unruly offering, with more priestly figures joining the fray, overwhelming their victim with their sheer numbers, pressing him to the ground, smothering.

"Don't you see, Younger Brother?" The woman stopped a few paces short from her magnificently clad noble sibling, her own attire as grand despite the lack of a matching headdress, her lack of height not interfering. Her palm was elegant and long as it pointed toward the sky, making every pair of eyes follow. The sun, still perfectly bright and round, was hiding behind a thin veil of clouds, fragile and unobtrusive, but there. "Our mighty ancestor does not wish to receive your offering. Return to talk to him in your words and not deeds."

It was easy to see the tall man's mouth tightening. For another heartbeat, no one said a word or dared to let out a breath, for that matter. The silence turned heavy and the priests looked ridiculous, piling upon each other, frozen in their assault upon the foreigner, now barely visible under their painted bodies, not moving as well. Already dead?

"You take it upon yourself the duty to interpret our benevolent patron and ancestor's will, Revered Lady," said the tattooed noble finally, the feathers upon his diadem rustling with the new gust of wind. "Is it your place to do so?"

"It is our Revered Sun's place to do so, Younger Brother, as it will be the duty of my son in due time," countered the woman sternly, in a freezing tone that sent a wave of chill down Ahal's spine. "As long as our divine brother is unable to attend his duties in this matter, you will cease pacifying our benevolent deity with innovative offerings of an unacceptable nature."

Another heavy pause ensued, through which the royal brother just stood there, as motionless as a slab of stone, with only the nostrils of his eagle-like nose widening with every forcefully drawn breath. "I shall bring this matter before our divine brother, Revered Lady," he said in the end. "I do not agree with your interpretation of our sacred deity's wishes."

The woman just waved her bejeweled hand, dismissing the veiled threat, her own sharply outlined features unmoved.

"Take the foreigner away, priests. Have the healers attend to his wounds." Her face was a stony mask as it turned toward the rest of the awestruck audience, presenting Ahal with the full view of not entirely unpleasant features, an agreeable sight but for the expression of cold haughtiness. "Return to your homes and families, subjects. Offer your private prayers and gifts to our sacred main deity in your local temples. Be generous about your offerings. Do not offend our sacred giver of life again."

A subtle blame-shifting, reflected Ahal, unable to take his eyes off the woman, shaken to the core. Oh yes, the *honorables* of this city had something to think about now besides the bizarre scene they had just witnessed.

"Tribute Collector." He didn't have time to turn away along with the general exodus, his limbs freezing at the sound of the even voice, so chilling, so calm. The woman was in her palanquin again, already lifted off the ground on the strength of the pair of sweating men, holding the entire constructions as though it was made of feathers. Her hand waved ever so slightly, motioning him to approach. "Go with the priests. Supervise their treatment of your foreigner. I shall hold you accountable for his recovery. Do not disappoint me, *considerate*."

He had to draw a quick breath in order to make his voice obey him. "As you wish, Revered Lady. I shall do as you wish."

The chilling gaze measured him for another heartbeat, appraising but veiled, keeping its inner thoughts to itself. "Good. I may find you worthy of serving me or mine."

Her carried seat didn't sway as its bearers were bidden into resumed movement by a light wave that accompanied the clacking of clay bracelets. They knew their trade, those particular carriers, reflected Ahal numbly, not daring to move a limb, not yet. And what precarious work they had.

CHAPTER 16

The light was annoyingly blurry, drawing away then coming back, persistent like a hungry mosquito, bringing along increased nausea and no comfort. Clasping his lips against the overwhelming need to retch, Iciwata shut his eyes tight, hoping to make the blur go away. It did, but not entirely as now colorful spots were having a wild dance, twirling around, making his nausea so much worse. The throb in his head was vicious, a pair of heavily weighted, perfectly polished war clubs pounding at his skull from the inside, determined to shatter it, to tear it apart.

What was wrong with them all? he wondered angrily, frustrated by helplessness, unable to escape. *Where was he?*

The voices floated above, another bothersome bunch of mosquitoes. As long as they kept hovering far enough, he didn't mind them, but sometimes they would draw nearer and nearer and then it would hurt. Bother this!

He had tried to push the prying hands away, or even simply squirm out of their reach, but it only resulted in more palms grabbing his limbs, pinning him with too much strength, not letting him escape the agony. But for the wildly swirling and twirling world, and all this pain and the nausea and the dancing lights, he might have managed to break free. They could not best him again and again, the filthy pieces of rotten meat that they were, curse them all into the worst pits of a stinking swamp.

"Stop that! Lie still," a familiar voice was repeating. "It'll be over soon. Stop fighting."

He tried to place the voice with a name, or maybe a face. Who was it? It wasn't the first time the man demanded something like that, to stop fighting, or do other things. The uncompromisingly firm grip was familiar as well. Somewhere, sometime, it happened before. Or maybe differently, but it did happen. The man was reasonable. He did not demand something shady or unworthy. He could be trusted. Or couldn't he?

The fragments of bizarre memories kept floating, popping like pieces of light wood in a river. It was all current and whirlpools, but sometimes there was something, something to cling to, to forget the agony and the pain. That goddess, the beautiful vision, watching him from the sky, or kneeling beside him, enveloping in her softness and her scent, something sweet and foreign, caressing one's senses, murmuring and making him drink, keeping safe from the darkness and mad screams and running feet. It had such wonderful taste, that water, a magical liquid that only a goddess could offer to a mortal. But of course it was. If only the beautiful vision would come back.

"Keep him still!" A harsh voice burst into the rosy memory, ruining his painfully achieved tranquility, bringing back the world of nausea and pain. "The swelling is bad and needs to be opened. Make him stay perfectly still."

"In what way?" inquired the familiar voice, reassuring in its unshakable calm. It was as though these men were discussing the possibility of a rain on a summer day, something worrisome but not overly so, their words jarring in the way they were twisting, but he didn't mind, not as long as the man was there. They all talked strange in this huge towering city with too many mounds and people and unreasonableness. He grew used to it, truth be told.

"Here and here." The torture stopped and he rejoiced in this small mercy, not minding their talking and talking, even though the one who was more grunting than speaking was certainly not a person he wished to stay alone with and at this one's mercy, not before he got stronger or at least managed to get up somehow. Still, it was not so bad to just lie there and float, even though the whirlpool of lights was bringing the nausea back and in force. He clasped his lips tighter and didn't bother to open his eyes.

"Hold that knife above the fire. Twenty heartbeats, then the other side." The words flew in a different way, as though shouted in another direction. "Hurry!"

The hands pinning him down were back, more uncompromising than before. He tried to push them away, their touch hurtful, bringing the agony back in force. If only it wasn't so blurry. He tried to blink forcefully, to make his eyes focus.

"Stop wriggling. It will be over soon. Stay still or it'll hurt worse." The voice was again reassuring in its familiar stern serenity, the formidable broad face silhouetted against the grayish mist, its tattoos enhanced eerily, such strange patterns and so many, the rough palms pinning him down uncompromisingly, with this same strength the man always displayed, not seeming that powerful from just the look of him. And what if he wasn't on his side, not anymore? He didn't stay around when the filthy spearmen came to drag him away. Again the need to break free welled. They were going to do something bad. That talk about knives being heated, it had something to do with him, didn't it?

"You, help the honorable tribute collector." The harsh voice of the second speaker brought another blurry form into his view, this one seemingly old, generously wrinkled. "Take hold of his legs."

More shifting about produced another pair of hands, frustrating his struggle for freedom, this time for good. How could he shake off so many men when the world wouldn't stop spinning?

"Did you heat it from both sides? Good. Now hold him tightly, all of you."

He made another effort to shake at least some of the pressure off, but when his head was pushed backwards, pinned to the firm surface as harshly as his body was, he didn't manage to hold the scream back. It was blinding, the pain, dazzling, overwhelming. He never felt anything even remotely similar before. No one had, probably.

The darkness was near, beckoning, still he fought it, afraid to sink in, to drown in the suffocating depths, terrified of being lost there, unable to crawl back. No pain there, yes, but no comfort either. It was better…

In another heartbeat, the pain exploded like never before. It made his heart stop and his limbs cramp in a terrible spasm. His head, what was happening to it? Or maybe it was his insides, his entire body. The grayish mist exploded with too many colors, ghastly in their harrowing beauty, and then the darkness was back, a merciful escape.

When he opened his eyes again, it was quiet and there were barely any people around, if at all. He could hear shuffling feet, but they weren't near him, and best of all, no hands groped his legs or shoulders, or his head, for that matter. No one touched him or pinned him to anything and the pain was still there, but moderately torturing, not gut-tearing or ripping his insides apart, not like before. The clubs pounding in his head must have been getting tired. About time.

For a while, he just lay there, relishing the feeling, afraid to move in case it would make the agony return. Also the voices, they were still there, floating too near for his peace of mind. If he moved, they might remember him and his currently unrestrained state.

"How long will he stay in the other worlds?" The tribute collector was back apparently, hovering somewhere near, again reassuring with his mere presence. What was it about this man? He fought to keep his eyes closed, the temptation to look overwhelming, the desperate need to move his limbs. It was so stiff, his entire body, like a pottery bowl left in the sun for too long. One bump and it would crack, fall apart in an outburst of sharp pieces.

The pause lasted for too long, accompanied by more shuffling. When something heavy, disgustingly wet and sticky, thrust at his forehead, he couldn't help the recoil. It was beyond his power to remain still, even though the pain was nowhere near unbearable, and the coldness of the wet cloth wasn't actually that unwelcome or bad.

"Stay still." The command, by now familiar, shot out accompanied by restraining grip, as expected. "He is alive, apparently."

The other voice just grunted, then drew away to the immensity of Iciwata's relief.

"Now, if you want to sit up, you can try. But slowly."

The hands were supporting rather than restraining now, and he clenched his teeth against the increasing dizziness and the pain that burst all around, with no visible pattern or sense.

"Slowly. Now lean against this thing." A painful pull had his upper back bumping against something narrow and hard, a support he welcomed eagerly, glad to escape the restraining grip but not trusting his own strength to keep him upright, not yet.

The blur was dispersing, presenting the hazy outline of a place, very spacious or so it seemed, crammed with objects and beams and strange-looking platforms; and people, too many for his peace of mind, squatting or crouching, all busy and purposeful. The aroma of sweet grass and other burning substances was suffocating, tickling his throat, tortured with thirst as it was.

"Drink." As though answering his thoughts, the man reached for a bowl, thrusting its nicely rounded edge to Iciwata's lips, wasting no time on verifying its welcome.

The water tasted good, and even though a generous part of it spilled all over his chin and torso, the refreshing sensation was there, making his mind and not only his eyes focus.

"You'll receive more soon. And the medicine. Do not make any more trouble, certainly not to the apprentice healer. Just do as you are told."

Sensible advice. He met the penetrating gaze, struggling not to drop his. It was never easy to face this man, back in the town where all his troubles had started as much as here, in this wild, insane, overwhelming place. Tough and evidently ruthless, yet decent, trustworthy, well, up to a certain point, the man was an enigma, impossible to understand. Why was he helping him, he who had forced him into this situation in the first place, to pay for his crimes, allegedly, and yet, why was he so decent, now and back at the fight, and in the place of darkness and screams?

"What... what is happening? Where are we?"

A mirthless, one-sided grin twisted the pursed lips. "In the temple of the lower terrace upon the Royal Mound, wild villager. At the holiest of places only the highest nobility and certain few *honorables* of this city are allowed to ascend."

"Why?" He didn't care for the explanations, or for the identity of some honorable lowlifes, but the talk helped. The clubs inside his skull were again pounding too strongly, threatening to explode from within, the rest of his body in no better shape, evidently, even though he could not check its condition, not without moving his head while chancing to make the pain overwhelm him for good.

"Why? It is a good question. I'm not certain I have answers to that." Shaking his head, the man grinned again, as mirthlessly and as briefly. The outline of his wide shoulders lifted heavily, with hardly any enthusiasm. "Your fate must be of an interest to our celestial patron, the great deity of light and warmth. I wish I knew what it all means, but I don't." The narrowed eyes bored at him for more than a heartbeat, their expression peculiar, difficult to stand. "You are not supposed to be alive. Through so many happenings of today alone, you were destined to die, slain for disobedience, killed in the unheard-of duels with the best of our spearmen, executed by the word of our Revered Sun himself just before his great ancestor in the sky disappeared, sacrificed as an appeasement to the returned godhead. Revered Tattooed Serpent himself decreed that, the second most powerful noble of this city. So many occasions that should not see you surviving, and yet, here you are, alive and asking silly questions, not understanding what happened to you at all, not appreciating those miraculous circumstances of yours." The one-sided grin was back, gloomier than before. "I wonder what it all means. To me, to my city, to its fate. Not to you. You have your own destiny, clearly something out of the ordinary, exceptional. But it is your destiny, and if I could disconnect it from mine now, I would have done it in a blink of an eye. It was a bad decision to bring you here. I wish I had the foresight of that back at the time."

Against his will, he kept staring, the man's gaze gloomy, difficult to bear. Still, it felt imperative to hear more, even though most of what had been said made no sense. If only he could recollect it all better, the fighting at the open oh-so-meticulously swept and cleaned ground where the armed lowlifes with their bad tempers were throwing spears before he managed to bring their wrath upon him by staring at the goddess upon the incline. It all started back then, didn't it? With the beautiful vision of color and light upon the vivid greenery of the grass. It was a vision, wasn't it? And yet, she came back to give him water and to shelter him from trampling feet and the screams when the darkness fell. This man did it too, didn't he? But not like her, not like...

"The woman with the water... the one who gave me water down there, where it was all dark..." His throat hurt badly with every uttered word, and the clubs in his head redoubled their efforts, pounding with all their might. The pain was everywhere, flashing like lightning in the middle a storm, threatening to engulf.

"What about her?" The words rang sharply, with no reflective pensiveness like before, catching his attention, taking it off the overwhelming urge to slide down or fall sideways and close his eyes.

He blinked to make his eyes focus. "I don't know... I don't think... Was she..." It was truly difficult to form words. The man's face was nothing but a blur, swaying nauseatingly. "I need to—"

In the next heartbeat, he was retching his guts out, prevented from falling over the platform he was apparently reclining on by his companion's hands again, not caring in the least. The agony was back, not the paralyzing spasm like before but close enough to it. It tore at his stomach, inside and outside of it, but the need to breathe made it into a secondary worry. Oh, but it was terrible, those continued spasms. He could not take many more of those, not for much longer. Even the bowl of water thrust to his mouth again did not taste as good as before. It had such an annoyingly strange aftertaste, and the revoltingly bitter brew that followed did nothing to relieve the vile flavor. But for the absolute lack of strength in his body, he would have fought them, making them all angry again. As it was, he just choked on the bitter liquid, annoyed with the skillful way they were pouring it into his mouth, gulp by gulp, not leaving much choice but to swallow, or to retch it out as well for that matter.

"He'll feel better soon." The words of the harshly spoken man with torturing tools – was that the healer the tribute collector was referring to before? – reached him almost against his will. He didn't wish to hear or understand what they said. He didn't wish to have anything to do with them.

"How soon?" His benefactor, as expected, sounded as though he was discussing the price of a shell bracelet after a restful day spent at leisure. "Will he be able to walk if required?"

"Oh well, I do hope so, Honorable Leader. I wouldn't recommend under regular circumstances, however…"

The pause that ensued had Iciwata gulping those much needed mouthfuls of air. It made his head spin a little less violently.

"Help me have him seated again."

The placid request resulted in more hands pushing him up, making him feel somewhat better. Not only did the world stopped reeling, slowing its sways in a merciful fashion, but the pain in his head turned bearable again, and so did the gut-tearing sensation all around his torso. He blinked to make his vision clear.

"He might need to be at his best and soon. Whatever you can brew, do it to make him better by the time Revered Lady sends for him. It is imperative that it happens, for you as much as for anyone else."

The healer, a surprisingly unimpressive type, thin and gaunt and not as old as healers should be, gave the tribute collector a nervous nod, then scampered away, his eyes brushing past Iciwata, holding no recognition, estimating him as though he was an object, a pottery bowl that was glued together, expected to serve its purpose again but not for certain. He didn't care. The ability to breathe and see and actually think clearly was too good to spoil it by stupid observations.

"Do your best, apprentice healer," the tribute collector was saying, his frown mirroring that of the older man but not in its direfulness. It was as though he was weighing his possibilities, troubled by doubts. "I'll remain here until it happens."

Another nervous nod and murmured reassurance reached them from the clouds of smoke where other figures were crouching or moving around near the dim rectangle of an entrance. It seemed to be quite a long way, and again Iciwata wondered how big this strange building was, how many people it hosted.

"Feeling better?"

He forced his thoughts off irrelevant wandering, concentrating on the man who was keeping him safe, trying to recollect what were they talking about before. Something about fate and his fights, or maybe important places no one was allowed to visit but them. It was difficult to remember.

"What... what is going to happen now?" Even his voice sounded almost normal, not high-pitched or squeaking like before. He rejoiced in this new tiny victory.

"I'll be taking you to a very revered lady when she requests you to be brought before her. The revered sister of our sacred ruler and the leading member of the divine family expressed an interest in your fate." There was again an ironic twist tugging at the man's lips. "Your life may depend on the impression you make, so you may wish to listen carefully when I tell you how to behave."

The thought of the beautiful goddess invaded his mind in as vivid coloring as before. "Who is she? What does she want with me?"

The man raised his thick eyebrows. "I'm certain she may enlighten you on the subject. But if you accost her with such insolent questioning, the work of this temple's healer and his apprentices may come to be a waste of time and an effort."

He clenched his teeth against the renewed splash of anger, hating this man and his unflustered arrogant superiority, but too spent to react to it. After the insanity of this day and far from being safe yet – the fact that this man was careful to point out again and again – he had no strength to deal with any more inimical altercations, chancing turning the only person who for some reason was on his side into an enemy. A frustrating realization in itself.

"When the medicine makes you feel better," his converser went on as though nothing interrupted his previous briefing, his gaze serene and only slightly chilling, disclosing nothing, "you will rest and let the healers take care of you. If requested to be presented before Revered *Quachilli Tamailli,* you will do your best walking on your own, even if with my help. When admitted in, you will remain with your gaze down unless told to do otherwise. You will venture not a word unless demanded to speak by the revered lady or any of her entourage. If so, you will keep your gaze down and your words will be humble and always with the title 'revered lady' accompanied to them. Is that clear to you, villager? Will you remember all that?"

He stood the penetrating gaze for what felt like a long eternity before forcing out a noncommittal nod of confirmation. What else was there to do? The man wished to make him behave in the way of these people, and truth be told, it was not an unreasonable demand, even though after the hardships of this day he wished to hate them all more venomously than ever. Yet, it wasn't the time to express any such feelings, was it?

The attempt to shrug resulted in a realization that his body was wrapped in a generous layer of tightly pressed cloth, sticky with ointments, disgustingly so. The same went for his head, he suspected, not daring to reach for it but feeling it awkwardly heavy. How was he supposed to walk somewhere, meet persons of importance, and why? Back in his village, they would let a person heal before dragging him out to be present before the elders. He tried to think of an instance like that, but nothing came to mind, no incidents of visitors who did not arrive on their own, let alone suspected foreigners. Compared to this huge crowded city, with its life bubbling like a current of the worst rapids, his village had no life at all, a forgotten little puddle somewhere there in the woods.

He snorted to himself, then chanced a glance at his companion, studying the prominent features set in the solidness of the broad face, adorned with those fascinating parallel markings, safe in doing so because the man was looking away, immersed in his thoughts or maybe listening to the sounds pouring from the outside, disquietingly steady creaking and then quiet measured words, no shouting or gushing insanity of the spearmen field. It was so eerily quiet.

"Remember what I told you." His benefactor's eyes were again upon him, their concentration back, relaying urgency, maybe even worry. A puzzling change in the unperturbed slab of stone. Iciwata felt his stomach twisting violently, not helped by sharp twinges of pain under various pressing bandages. But how was he...

The single torch fastened into the wall flickered as the partition at the far end slid sideways, creaking in a strange fashion. He didn't spend his time wondering about it. The figures pouring in did not leave room for idle musings. So many! The rough wood of the supporting pole was cutting into his back, the painful protests under the bandages bursting louder than before against his own lurch backwards, the retreat necessary, the only possibility but for the walls all around.

"Don't." His companion's rock-hard palm was reassuring as it fastened around his undamaged shoulder, pressing strongly, giving support. He did his best to follow its pull, staggering badly, not falling down on account of this much needed support. The dimly lit air spun nauseatingly, and he knew he would vomit again if it didn't stop, all over the important lowlifes who were pushing their way in, whoever they were.

"Make him stand properly." A distorted voice bounced around, then retreated, followed by several more similar-sounding demands. "Or better yet, make him kneel!"

"He can't be presented before the divine family member, not in his condition." The tribute collector's words rang strongly, the anchor to cling to, low and steady, and unafraid. "I do not wish to offend the royal eyes with inappropriate sights. Do any of you, Honorable Guards?"

The brief silence that followed was a blessing. Without the ricochet of their voices to assault his mind, he could try to focus, to push the nausea back in. Somehow he wasn't upright anymore and it was an additional blessing. The world spun slower now, in an almost bearable manner, filled with additional sounds of clanking and rustling, the new footsteps relaying worrisome confidence, too light to belong to warriors with spears.

Reassured, he tried to make his eyes focus, his head tilted at a strange angle, letting him see mostly the lower parts of their bodies, all those outlines of loincloths and leggings, such strange garments. The nearing silhouette was nothing but a swaying cloth adorned with something waving and clinking.

"Out, all of you!"

The words echoed between the dark walls, tearing the momentary silence. Spoken in a calm, unmistakably female voice, they carried such profound authority, he felt his fear returning in force, in a powerful surge. That voice, but he heard it before, somewhere, sometime, not long ago, when still squashed under avalanche of pain and fear and anger, unable to breathe.

The struggle back into an upright position took the last of his strength. He didn't care. To face this new menace was imperative. He couldn't sprawl half turned and helpless. The spearmen would have no trouble impaling him if he did.

"Tribute Collector, remain here until told otherwise."

"Revered Lady *Quachilli Tamailli*, it would be my honor to do as you wish."

He could feel the man's renewed grip, hurtful but there, steadying him against the swirling of the world, helping to lean on the familiar roughness of the pole his back grew used to. It helped to calm the mad pounding in his ears, his heart trying to jump out or maybe just hammer its way through his chest.

"Is the foreigner dying?"

The woman did not near, silhouetted next to the flickering lights that glimmered around her like a halo. Not the goddess from the place of the darkness. His senses told him that, even if his eyes couldn't.

"He will recover his strength, Revered *Quachilli Tamailli*. It might take some time, but the foreign *miche-quipy* will be as strong as before, if that is your wish. The healers of this sacred place assured me of that, Revered Lady."

"I see."

Another bout of silence had his heart relaxing its mad racing, the shimmering mist shifting to flicker in the corner of his eyes alone, not interfering with his vision, not like before. The curt gesture of the woman's hand sent one of the glimmering torches his way, a welcome advance until thrust into his face, making him choke on its smoky fumes. Backing away had his head bumping against the accursed pole, resounding in splashes of fresh agony. Still, he fought the hands that were once again restraining him, not trustful of the man who kept saving him through this wild, insane day, never entirely. He was one of them!

"A wild beast, isn't he?" The woman stepped closer, evidently watching with keen curiosity. Did she wish to see him continue fighting, like back with the spearmen or those other lowlifes with ropes? "Where did you unearth such a violent creature, Tribute Collector?" Another blurry movement had the torch move a little, allowing him to breathe and thus relax in his panicked struggle. "Are all the barbarians of the far east like this one, wild beasts?"

"They are different people, yes, Revered Lady; different than us." Relaxing his grip as well, the man straightened hastily, his authoritative tone subdued if not gone completely. "But no, they are not fierce. We faced no trouble collecting what is due."

"How many warriors did you bring to your journey to the east?" This time, the woman sounded ridiculously similar to the man she was questioning, the pronounced arrogance and amusement of her previous speech gone, replaced with crisp practicality. Iciwata pushed his craving for a gulp of water away, the pounding in his head growing worse but not enough to discard the words of the "barbarian east," not completely. Did this woman call his people that?

"I was honored with the trust of taking three dozen warriors along in my last journey, Revered Lady. They were of a great help. However, the locals cooperated with no need to resort to violence. They are reasonable people and their appreciation of Quachil Thecou is strong. Our glorious city's name goes ahead of us, all along the shores of our Great River. I can assure you of that most sincerely, Revered Lady."

The woman's silhouetted head nodded slowly, now easier to see, whether because the torch was not scorching his face but instead hovered helpfully halfway between them, or maybe due to his vision, which was focusing gradually, with no regard to the clubs trying to shatter his skull from the inside. She was a striking enough vision, not anywhere near the beautiful apparition of the hill or down there in the place of the darkness, but as ethereal, with her draperies flowing about her in no earthly fashion and her head crowned with long slender feathers instead of hair. A bird-woman? Did the deities of these western cities come to mingle with the mortals inhabiting them, ruled them maybe, took care of their wellbeing? That might explain the wondrous mounds and the walls.

"Supervise the healing of this foreigner, Tribute Collector," the woman was saying, apparently having satisfied her curiosity regarding the "barbarian east" while his mind had evidently been wandering. He tried to collect his previous anger, not about to be badmouthed or looked down upon, not even by their gods. "Before you commence your next journey against the current of our Great River, you will be invited to pay your respects. Your underlings, those whom you trust to manage a journey on their own, will collect what is due from the settlements of the south. Have the most trusted among those deliver our share to the Sacred Sun City. You will not sail in this direction again. Your purpose will be different now."

There was a moment of hesitation on the tribute collector's part, a fraction of a heartbeat filled with what felt like uncertainty. He could imagine the man licking his lips, or maybe swallowing hastily. Or just staring, speechless for a moment. It was easy to feel that. But for the new splash of agony that he knew waited to pounce on him the moment he dared to move his head, he might have sneaked a quick peek, curious to see the dominant piece of meat losing his unshakable confidence, his authoritative aplomb.

"I shall always do as you wish, Revered Lady," the man said before the pause turned awkward. "I'm greatly honored by your confidence and your trust."

He was afraid of this woman, reflected Iciwata numbly, welcoming the respite, wishing nothing more than to close his eyes and let the dizziness lull him into oblivion. The man said something about the medicine and the rest, didn't he? And about the proper way when talking to the "revered lady." They wanted him to walk to her, but the haughty piece of divinity came on her own; to call him an eastern barbarian and to make the tribute collector uneasy with her demands. But what did she mean by traveling against the current, back to his homelands maybe, the real world of the ancestral mound and not the towering earthworks with stairs and walls.

"Busy yourself with making your barbarian well for now. Teach him proper manners before you bring him before the divine family's eyes again." A curt motion of the feathered head summoned the torch to dance back toward the opening and away from him, sinking their side of the room into its previous semi-gloom. "Do not fail me, Tribute Collector. Honored by the divine family's trust, you will do better to remember where your loyalties should be lying. Remember the circumstances that elevated you, adviser's brother. Remember them well."

The words were twirling around, soothingly soft, lulling Iciwata's mind into letting go. Whatever the woman talked about, he didn't care, not anymore. As long as she kept speaking like that, nearly murmuring, telling things that made his companion tense and more uneasy than ever, clearly perturbed but daring not to offer an argument, he didn't care. Even the thoughts of his homeland somewhere there up the current of their mightily powerful river – in the barbarian east! – did not stir a reaction, not anymore. It was good to let go, to sink into blissful oblivion with no pain. The tribute collector would stay and guard him until he surfaced again. He could be trusted, that man. An enemy or not, he was a decent person.

"I shall do everything in my power to serve the divine family, Revered *Quachilli Tamailli*. I shall not fail you, Revered Lady."

The words splashed somewhere far, far away, and he wanted to chuckle at their pretended serenity. The man was lying now, pretending tranquility he didn't feel, something he didn't seem to do before, not even on the night of the storm and the bear. Why? The question faded before he managed to decide what to do with it, the flickering darkness beckoning, promising safety and rest. He didn't try to fight it this time.

CHAPTER 17

She saw Revered Sun's sister emerging from the dark opening of the temple, relieving her numerous following from their obviously agitated wait. Too many were crowding the typically low entrance and even though after the day of the terrible happenings one might expect every temple throughout the city to be crowded with visitors bringing offerings, the sight of the most revered lady in the land walking on foot, lingering in the less important temple of the lower terrace alone, unescorted and unattended, had challenged too many accepted rituals all at once. Not that Sele herself did not throw too many of those to the wind on this same bizarre, frenzied, terrible day.

Shivering, she hugged her elbows, chilled in the gust of the evening breeze, hoping that the darkness would not give her presence away. To venture an unauthorized, let alone unattended descent of a dozen stairs leading to the lower terrace was a feat of courage she would never have dared only on the day before this one. There were strict rules of conduct on the Royal Mound, but no one seemed to follow any of it now, and she needed to see Uncle Ahal. The knowledge that he might be somewhere around, on the Royal Mound of all things, sent there by the word of Revered Lady Female Sun out of all people – an unheard-of occurrence in itself – had enough to kill any notion of rest, even had the Royal Hall been all cozy and padded in nightly arrangements like it was every time the benevolent sky deity retired the world for its own night sleep. Which it wasn't.

This time, the royal dwelling was teeming as though the day was still upon them, lit by torches and shrouded in clouds of burning medicine and incense. Healers and priests and servants buzzed all around, and various nobles crowded the entrance, worried for their sovereign, preying upon every word they managed to receive like it always happened when her husband had these terrible bouts of fever. Only this time, it had been nothing but pretense.

Clenching her teeth against the renewed wave of anger and dread, she remembered herself pressing the customary cloth soaked with perfumed water to his high forehead under the line of the receding hair, the way she had done on so many times when he was sick and wished her to minister to him. Back at those times, the cloth would dry up with frightening speed, but now it just clung to the outline of his skull, serving no purpose. Still, he slumped on the furs and the patterned blankets of the royal bed, devoid of strength or maybe just drained, his eyes partly shut, his mind seemingly wandering. But it didn't. She knew the signs.

Daring not to ask questions, she had sat there at first numbed and frightened, sneaking glances at the old healer and his numerous helping hands, busy brewing yet another medicine, filling the spacious hall with an unpleasant aroma of burning herbs – no sweet grass that – squeezing the cloth without looking at it, practiced as she was in the art of caring for a sick person by now, relaxing gradually, daring not to face the unsettling thoughts. He wasn't as sick as he looked, her husband. He was pretending. But why?

The gazes of the nobles crowding the entrance were almost tangible. She could feel them penetrating the misty gloom, needing to know. No one forgot the terrible afternoon, the horror of it, the unparalleled dread. What was the dreadful omen all about? What had the benevolent deity tried to tell them by fading, casting the world into darkness and despair, leaving its denizens terrified and alone, devoid of hope? Was it displeased, demanding appeasement of the sort Tattooed Serpent was ready to offer the angered godhead?

Shuddering, she remembered the top of the incline and the bizarre happenings no living person and maybe even the spirits of the dead ones could imagine or understand. Wives and servants were made to accompany their sovereign into his afterlife. It was the fate that might very well await her and maybe not in the too far away future, a desirable fate that would bring nothing but dignity and a happy afterlife to her and considerable elevation to her family. But no other living person was honored with the ritual death of this sort, a strangulation by the highest priests of the land, offered to angered deities and on the spur of a moment, with no preparations and no due consideration and thought. It was bizarre, unheard-of, unprecedented. And yet, Tattooed Serpent was determined to do it, with Revered Sun slumping in his palanquin, overcome by sickness. Was he pretending back then as well?

She was too far at the time to know, having just been brought back to the royal surroundings, dazed and disoriented, overwhelmed by everything that happened, her clothes stained with the foreigner's blood, the memory of his touch while she supported him and made him drink lingering like a physical presence, as though he was still there in her arms. To see him dragged by the priests was terrible. He was hurt so badly, near death. Couldn't they see how wrong it was? Uncle Ahal tried to save this man and Uncle Ahal never did things that weren't right. They should have let him handle this matter.

Her heart going out of tempo again, she remembered that moment, the nearly physical pain it brought by merely watching it. When the foreigner came to life all at once, refusing to be strangled, fighting the priests like a wild animal, overcoming them as though he had no wounds at all and not a whole afternoon of fighting behind him, she felt like collapsing herself, the strain unbearable, tearing her nerves. Was he mortal at all, this man? Did the powerful spirits or deities enter him?

Shuddering at the dreadfully vivid recollection, she narrowed her eyes, concentrating on the gathering outside the temple, Revered Lady Female Sun not in a hurry to enter her palanquin, conversing with several nobles, exuding nothing but cold tranquility, her usual façade. It was easy to tell, even in the concealing darkness. What did she do inside the temple, alone and unescorted?

Sele willed her stomach to relax, its muscles cramped, squashed by an invisible ring. Uncle Ahal must be there. With his wounded foreigner that he was directed to make well again? For a bizarre moment, she wished it to be so. The man did not look as though destined to live, not after everything he had been through and with the decree of Revered Sun and his powerful brother still hanging above his head. And yet, the benevolent sky deity did interfere with the fighting, so maybe it wished him to live just like the most powerful woman in Quachil Thecou, its direct descendant, did. Everyone heard the words of Female Sun. The willful woman did not bother to soften the way she contradicted her brothers' will, both of them, the sacred sovereign himself and his war leader, the second most powerful man in the land.

Straining her eyes, she sought Tattooed Serpent's tall figure among the crowding nobles, remembering that the man was by her husband's side back in the royal hall but for a short period of time. He must have matters of importance to attend to. After such a day, who wouldn't, even though Revered Sun himself chose to succumb to sickness, real or imagined. What *was* wrong with his health?

The memory of the blood-covered *miche-quipy*, on his knees and struggling against the rope of the priests, his head yanked backwards just like his hands, returned, making her nauseated worse than before. Some wives would be required to follow Revered Sun into the afterworld should he succumb to his illness for good, his favorite wives and his most helpful of servants and officials. It was a great honor to be chosen, but the sight of the bloodied man on his knees was never a part of such stories. No one told her it might be like that, so hurtful and desperate, so hopeless. A great honor, yes, but not like this.

Her fear threatening to become overwhelming, she clenched her teeth until they felt like creaking, knowing that there was only one man who could be depended on to make everything right again, or at least to calm her and make the terrible memory go away; one man who must be in there, in the temple she was watching, herself hiding like a common *miche-quipy* woman in the carefully trimmed shrubbery priests were meticulous in maintaining, waiting for the impatient nobles to disperse. It had turned out surprisingly easy to sneak out of the Royal Hall, to descend the less luxurious set of stairs leading to the further side of the lower terrace, something she didn't dare to do on her own until now. And yet, she couldn't crouch in the bushes for much longer, could she? They were certain to notice her absence and she had no good explanation for any of it, no excuse whatsoever.

The royal sister was nearing her palanquin, stepping as though walking on an invisible line, straight-backed, gesturing with one hand. Looking as stuck-up as by the daylight, reflected Sele, desperate to suppress her fear. The woman was so nasty with her ever-royal poses, the torches surrounding her glimmering like a cloud of glowing fireflies on warm evenings, yet relating no peacefulness. The nobles crowding the carried seat looked anything but comfortable or at ease.

Involuntarily, she inched her way closer, creeping along the slender line of the shrubbery, feeling safe to do so in the almost complete darkness. Maybe if she came close enough, she would manage to sneak inside the temple without being noticed; maybe through the back opening. The crowding nobles were all so busy groveling before the haughty woman.

The thinly spread shrubs rustled with untoward urgency as she crept along the unsatisfactorily thin vegetation, watching the glimmering lights of the torches. The Royal Hall and the main temple adjacent to it had more than one opening, so maybe it was the case with this lower terrace's temple as well. Revered Sun always began the day by greeting his mighty ancestor as it rose in the sky, standing at the eastern entrance, sending words of a prayer wrapped in the sacred tobacco smoke. No one but him was allowed to use this entrance. The rest of the god's servants entered through the lower opening on the western side.

She tried to think where the side of the rising sun was, difficult to tell something like that in the darkness. The voices of the groveling nobles were uncomfortably close now, as was the palanquin of the royal sister. She tried not to think of the implications of being discovered. It was too dreadful even to imagine, the annoyingly uneven ground hindering her step, the stupid bushes rubbing against her unpleasantly, catching in the flimsy draperies of her dress.

"—ill again—not certain how bad—with the terrible omen—"

Some of the voices reached her, and this time, she winced with the realization that it was Revered Sun's brother speaking, his words floating on the light gusts of wind. Many paces away from the torches lighting both sides of the building, Tattooed Serpent's figure was still unmistakable, his overly straight pose of a warrior setting him apart, his height enhancing the impression. He was almost a head taller than Revered Sun himself, remembered Sele, her stomach fluttering as though winter winds were having at it from the inside.

"It was a bad timing," his companion was saying, her words carrying even clearer, less difficult to overhear. The royal woman again! But how did she... "His illness is coming back more often than of yore. The terrible omen might have something to do with it." She could see the silhouetted head tossing higher, the sharpness of the prominent profile visible even in the surrounding darkness. "Our sacred ancestor is displeased. The benevolent sky deity doesn't wish to see Quachil Thecou losing its power and might."

The shrubs were rustling all around her, making her wish to burst into a headlong run. Oh gods, but how did it come to her crouching in the bushes, eavesdropping on the most important dignitaries of the city, the mad racing of her heart threatening to give her presence away, the moving dots of the torches at the other entrance she was determined to reach before beckoning, if only she could have made her legs carry her on.

"Quachil Thecou is not losing power, Sister!" cried out the tattooed man, towering over his royal sibling, making her smallness look ridiculous with his rigid warrior's pose. "Our city prospers as it did from the times immemorial. We are not losing our power or our influence, and the terrible omen is up to our servants of the gods to decipher. Not to a single member of the divine family, however sacred and eager to rule, however ambitious!"

The silence that followed the heated exclamation had a

thundering quality to it. Even the nobles at the main temple's entrance seemed to go quieter, maybe wishing to overhear as well, sensing the currents.

"Oh, but you are silly, Little Brother." The woman, when speaking again, did not sound angered, her voice low, perfectly calm, more difficult to overhear. "You have not enough spirit or power to stand up against me, so I will give you some well-meaning advice. From an older sibling to a younger one. Do not misjudge your position or little influence you have among certain officials or lead guards. It is nothing, Little Brother. Female Sun is equal to none but our Revered Sun himself, and sadly, our beloved brother isn't well. And should his health fail him..." A pause seemed to make the night around them deepen. "You have enough ambition of your own to act wisely. I trust you to do that, Brother."

Forgetting her own fear, Sele strained her ears, desperate to miss not a word. They were discussing her husband's weakened state, weren't they? His illness and the bad timing of it. The royal woman was harping on it insistently, the filthy snake that she was.

"What is your game, Sister?" The tall man did not seem to be cowed by threats and intimidation. If anything, he stood taller, stiffer of back. "What are those challenges and demands you are talking about? What changed to make you so lively, so eager to discuss our revered sovereign's health?"

"What changed?" The woman raised her voice once again, and it was easy to hear every word shooting out of her mouth like javelin in a spear-throwing contest. "Our sacred ancestor manifested his will like he never did before, not in our people's memory. Is that not enough for you to pause and think? Was your only answer to the terrible displeasure of our benevolent sun a ritual slaying of the foreign *miche-quipy*, an unprecedented deed and of no worthy nature?"

The thundering of her heart was again threatening to give her presence away. It was racing madly, trying to jump out of her chest.

"So this is why you have interceded on behalf of the wild piece of foreign dirt!" exclaimed the tall man, his own fury so tangible it seemed to fill the darkness. "How are you going to use this one, Sister? Besides the most obvious use, how is the lowly foreigner connected to your concern with our sovereign brother's state of health? Was the tribute collector acting on your behalf all along? Is he doing your bidding with his insolent shoving into our Royal Mound's affairs, daring to push the lowly barbarian on us with utmost insolence and no regard to the customs, the unimportant *considerate* that he is? Is that why you have gone to visit him in this temple just now, sending your servants and followers away in most inappropriate of manners?"

Another bout of silence had Sele holding her breath, afraid of the revelations, terrified by the mention of Uncle Ahal, and with such anger and outright accusations. Accusations of what? It was difficult to tell, but the mighty war leader did not think good things about Uncle Ahal, not after today's happenings. And it was the violent *miche-quipy*'s fault, the strange foreigner who didn't behave like regular people, not even like the lowliest commoners from the parts of the city she was never even taken to see. Who was this man? And was he destined to survive his wounds?

"Oh, but you are insolent, Brother. Insolent and impudent." The woman seemed as though growing in stature, her back turning so straight it seemed to tilt backwards. "Better go and rest, and think about this city and its future fate. Its future and yours."

Her pose remained overly straight as she turned around, her steps dignified and unhurried, hand motioning the palanquin bearers at the further circle of torchlight, not about to strain her royal feet for more paces than necessary.

Sele didn't dare to let out a breath, not yet; not with the powerful war leader still there, standing rock-still, rooted in his place, his silhouetted profile rigid with fury. When he stalked off, heading away from the lights of the crowding and the silhouetted palanquin bearers, she stayed where she was for a long time, her back bathed with sweat, mind swamped and refusing to focus. The sacred family members quarrelling like her half brothers and sisters back home, throwing barbed accusations, fighting for domination? No, it wasn't possible, it just wasn't! And what did the royal woman mean about her husband's failing health? Did she truly think...

The furthest entrance of the dark building spat out another cluster of torches, the silhouettes carrying them seeming in a rush, fussing about. Still in a daze, she made her way closer, beyond caring. One of the outlined figures carried a torch, looking bizarre in the wild shadows it cast, his shape not that of a human or maybe a human with too many angles and limbs.

"Bring that here—that plank, yes!—anything flat—hurry—"

Her heart made another wild leap inside her chest, her senses telling her who it was before her ears managed to analyze the fragmented words, her legs already at work, taking her toward the hushed activity. "Uncle Ahal!"

He half turned as she reached them, and it was easy to see what was bizarre about his pose. The foreigner, sagging against him, provided just the right amount of extra limbs, standing on his own but barely, leaning on Uncle Ahal with most of his weight. It was easy to see that. For some reason, the sight of them making a many-limbed creature caused her to fight a hysterical giggle.

"What are you doing here?" groaned her uncle, wavering under his heavy burden. The wave of his free hand sent the two of his followers back toward the temple, rushing away with their torches flickering madly. "Anything flat, stretched skin or bark, or even several mats put upon one another," he shouted after them. "Hurry!"

Two more men holding torches remained nearby, squinting against the darkness, clearly trying to see who she was.

"There is no need to waste any more of your time, Honorable Servants of our Sacred Deities." Uncle Ahal's voice rang with its usual firmness, brooking no argument even when speaking to his indirect superiors, the servants of the gods holding a special status. It was strange to hear him talking so calmly, squashed by the weight of the man he had made so many efforts to save on this day. The words of Tattooed Serpent surfaced, causing her shudder in the strengthening wind.

"Go with our blessing, Tribute Collector." The taller among the priests shifted, his torch tilting dangerously, dripping oil. "Do our Revered Lady's bidding."

The second man lingered for another heartbeat before following the patterned back of his companion, his gaze boring at her, narrow with concentration.

Uncle Ahal stared after them for a short while, then shifted tiredly. "What are you doing here, little one?" he repeated in a softer tone, glancing at the darkness where the previous pair disappeared, carrying out his instructions. "You can't be here. No one must see you sneaking around. Run back to the wives' quarters as fast as you can. The darkness will—"

The wounded shifted, then groaned painfully, clearly struggling to straighten up, or attempting to do that, his success not impressive. "Where... where are we?" he mumbled, swaying with the attempt to look around, or so it seemed. "What is happening?"

Uncle Ahal staggered as well, clearly having a difficult time supporting his burden. "Keep quiet. You will be allowed to lie down soon. Until then, do your best walking." His tone was curt and not very patient. Blinking, Sele found herself staring, forgetting her uncle's silly assumption that she lived in some unimportant wives' quarters and the need to correct him on that.

"That woman... is she gone?" groaned the man, disregarding the demand to keep quiet but clearly trying to obey the command to walk, or at least to stand on his own. They both didn't seem in a hurry to start walking at all. "The woman... the one you are afraid of... is she..." Then his head turned slightly, halfway toward her, and Sele caught her breath, her stomach turning hollow, empty like a vacant pottery pot. "You... you are here... again..." The last words trailed off, dying in the night.

"Stop talking," grunted Uncle Ahal, his own gaze boring into the darkness where the two of his people disappeared a short while ago, following his orders. "If you have so much strength left, walk on your own, descend the stairs, and try not to roll all the way down." At that, he shifted as though about to start walking indeed, steering his charge in the direction of the grand staircase, but not making the rest of his threat true by withdrawing his clearly much-needed physical support. "Go back to the women's quarters, Sele," he tossed toward her, his tone as commanding, but not as curt or as cutting as before. "Do it now. It's not the time."

"But I must talk to you!" She was beside them before she understood what happened, her legs making her close the distance, acting on their own, her grip of her uncle's arm surprising her as well, nearly ruining their painfully maintained balance. "Please, Uncle, you must listen!"

The smell hit her nostrils, the revolting aroma of something sweetish and sour and acrid. A familiar one. It smelled as much and worse on certain days in the Royal Hall, when Revered Sun was feverish and unwell. She could feel the pain and exhaustion emanating from the foreigner, his body close like back on the plaza, sticky with all sorts of additional mixtures, worse than back then, wrapped in fragments of stiff, starchy material, and yet still somehow pleasing, inviting to touch, to trace the unfamiliar limbs with her hands. The most bizarre of sensations. She tried to think what she wanted to tell her uncle.

"What are you doing, Sele?" There was no more warmth to Uncle Ahal's voice and no more softness. His struggle for balance won this time, he half turned toward her and but for the need to support the wounded, he would have grabbed her and shook her hard, she surmised. He had never done this before, but she knew when he was angered for real. Uncle Ahal was easy to predict, if not as easy to fool or manipulate. "Go away. Now!" There was a growl to his voice, but the rustling of hurried footsteps burst upon them, heralding the return of the men required to bring "something flat." Or so Sele hoped, worrying about the distant voices drifting here all the way from the temple's main entrance more than about her uncle's wrath. Were the royal sister or Tattooed Serpent still there, still angry at each other; or at Uncle Ahal?

A glance at the nearing silhouettes reassured her greatly. No magnificently high headdresses, no overbearing statures. The men accosting them did so humbly and hurriedly, carrying something that looked like a platform rather than a lifted seat, a smooth surface stretched between two poles both its carriers gripped for dear life.

"Put it on the ground!" Uncle Ahal wasted no time on talk or verification. "You! Lie down. Quickly. Make yourself as comfortable as you can. Then keep quiet."

The foreigner, still wavering between the two of them, washing her senses with not only his smell but the sensation of his exhaustion and pain, tried to say something, but Uncle Ahal did not pause to listen, his hands dominating, pushing the troublesome man down with enough care, not letting his body come to too rough of an encounter with the stretched surface. It was easy to see that.

"Uncle!"

He was straightening already, wiping his forehead with the back of his hand, shifting his shoulders with visible relief.

"Uncle, please, you must listen. Before you go, I need to talk to you, to tell you something."

"What?" He looked at her briefly, then even in the darkness, she could feel his sharp features softening, losing some of their foreboding expression. Just the edge of it, but it was enough.

When he caught her shoulders between her palms, pressing them lightly, reassuring in the old gesture that was his and his alone, she felt her body relaxing at once, like a piece of expensive material that was stretched to its limits, about to tear. But not anymore.

"It's been a terrible day, little one. Terrible day for everyone, every dweller of Quachil Thecou and other people inhabiting our world; worse for you because of everything that happened down there on the plaza." His grip tightened and she sagged against him, suddenly drained of strength, the tears warm upon her checks, falling like rain on the moon of Wild Turkeys. "You've been of a great help, little one, and I appreciate that. But now you must go. You cannot act wildly, out of fear, or longing for home. You are not a little girl anymore. You are Revered Sun's wife, his favorite wife or so I hear. Which does not surprise me at all, Sele. Of course it doesn't. But now you must go. Act in accordance with your exalted status, girl. Do not do any more silly deeds.

Remember your status and its responsibilities."

"But, Uncle," she sobbed, clinging to him when his hands tried to steer her away from the wideness of his chest. "I can't… It's terrible! I don't want to. Revered Sun isn't sick, not for real, not this time. And the haughty snake, she talks as though he will die. And I don't want to… If he dies, I don't want to… not like that *miche-quipy*… It's terrible. It's not right. You must not let it happen!"

"What are you talking about, Sele?" His arms were pressing her again, gently, not pushing her or trying to get rid of her otherwise. He was Uncle Ahal, and he would not let bad things happen to her. The realization alone lent her enough power to pull away.

"I just wanted to warn you," she muttered, not daring to wipe her face, appalled at the thought of smeared ointments and paint that must be covering it now. How was she going to explain that when back upon the top of the Royal Mound? "You must know, just in case…"

"Know what?" His gaze pierced the darkness, suddenly concentrated, laced with suspicion. "What did you hear?"

She swallowed hastily, then drew herself together with an admirable effort, or so it felt. "Revered Tattooed Serpent, he is suspicious of what happened. He thinks you work for Revered Lady Female Sun. He talked about you with open anger." She swallowed hard. "I thought you should know that. That is the only reason I sought you out. To let you know."

His jaw tightened in a familiar fashion. There were times when he would argue with her father, his elder and exalted brother, the head of their entire family and not a person to offer an argument in response. Still, Uncle Ahal would, at times, and then he would look just like that, determined and not about to be cowed, not even by people superior to him. "What else did he say?"

She tried to recall the conversation in its entirety, her thoughts scattering in annoying disarray. "He was angry with his revered sister. He was insolent to her. He dared to accuse her of ambition and wish to rule." Shivering at the sound of her own words, she swallowed again, determined to hold his attention, to impress him with her helpfulness, the word she out of all people could bring him, no one but her, not even her exalted father, the adviser. "He talked about you in anger, said you were working for this woman all along. He was angry because you saved the foreigner. And because Revered Lady Female Sun backed you on that."

His hands were still pressing her shoulders, but with no warmth or reassurance now, frozen like the rest of him. The night lost some of its softer or pleasanter qualities yet again. However, before she could panic and maybe try to cry her way back into his embrace, he shook his head forcibly, turning toward the platform upon which his troublesome charge was slumping now, drained of his previous spirit or other signs of life, looking like a grotesque creature out of stories, all smeared and bandaged. In the brightening moonlight, it was easier to see that.

"I appreciate your telling me that, Sele," Uncle Ahal was saying, his earnestness returning, dominating his voice once again. "You are brave and loyal, and I will not forget that. But now you must go. Do not let them catch you wandering without permission. Or eavesdropping on the sacred family, girl. Those are matters you should keep as far away from as possible, little one. Even if those concern your own family members. Do not let yourself be drawn into their dangerous games." His hands tightened around her shoulders once again before letting go. "And now go. I will try to see you again, and soon. As you can see, I'm permitted now upon the sacredness of the Royal Mound." His grin was brief, but it lifted her spirits, its lightness and its momentary crookedness. "Go, little one, and keep yourself safe." Another brief squeeze and he turned toward his followers, taking a torch out of the nearest man's hand. "Lift him and be careful about it. Don't let him slip out or drop the entire length of the lower staircase. I will lead the way."

She watched the unsteady construction shifting unevenly, causing the man upon it to groan in pain. He was murmuring something, and on an impulse, she leaned closer, knowing all of a sudden that he was talking to her, needing her touch, her reassurance; the same comforting touch that Uncle Ahal just bestowed on her.

To reach for his forehead came as another impulse, his skin clammy where the rough bandages did not cover it, awash with perspiration. It did not revolt her at all for some reason. Instead she leaned yet closer, feeling his gaze, disoriented and bleary, but still full of wonder, something she could sense rather than see. It made her chest clench in a strangely warm wave.

"You will be well," she whispered into his face, not revolted by the smell, accustomed to it back in the royal hall. "Uncle Ahal is watching over you. He will not let you die. You can be certain of that."

His eyes were as dark and as enormous as huge lakes from Uncle Ahal's stories. They peered at her, and she could feel his hand moving, trying to raise, not very successful but determined in its struggle. She pressed it with her own, then moved away hastily, letting Uncle Ahal's men carry their burden without additional challenges. They were to take it all the way toward the dark stairs and then down those, a challenge in itself, a difficult task. But under Uncle Ahal's command, they could do nothing but succeed, couldn't they?

The smile threatened to sneak out, accompanied by a silly giggle. She didn't lie to the battered *miche-quipy*. Oh, no! Uncle Ahal knew what he was doing, always. And he would manage to keep her safe in case of all sorts of dreadful happenings. He had promised her that much.

AUTHOR'S AFTERWORD

The magnificent earthworks that are spread all around the North American southeast fascinated historians and archeologists for many centuries, culminating in plenty of research done on the most prominent of the ancient Mississippians' sites.

Even as far back as late centuries of BC, the dwellers of the Mideast built ceremonial earthworks of impressive proportions, mostly burial mounds that testify to the complex societies their builders must have enjoyed. Different cultures erected different earthworks, sometimes burial mounds, sometimes effigy embankments in the shape of sacred animals or birds. The most famous among the Mound Builders, the culture we know today as the Mississippians, those who erected most famous sites such as Cahokia, were certainly not the first to build imposing earthen monuments in the region.

As the centuries passed, the cultural centers grew or shrank in size, moved, or established new settlements. The Mound Builders became more skillful, culminating in the 12th century urban centers with magnificent mounds towering as high as world heritage pyramids, urban centers of impressive proportions and other marks of highly complex societies and an imposing style of living.

The most known among the Mound Builders' heritage is of course the Cahokian complex of mounds, with its greatest among the man-made earthworks of this continent towering over one hundred feet high, sporting four terraces and an impressively extensive base, with more than fifty other earthworks of different sizes and purposes dotting the site, many still under excavation or study, concealing their treasure of information. However, of course, Cahokia is far from being the only historical landmark to adorn the valleys of major Mideast and Southeast rivers. Far from it!

The decision to set this story in the lesser Mississippian city located on the Ohio River rather than Cahokia itself came as a result of extensive research and several historically documented occurrences, the main one among those being the full solar eclipse of 1205. In NASA's catalogue of such dramatic occurrences, the most relevant and most massive event of the sun disappearing from the sky in its entirety is recorded to occur on September 14, 1205, covering a wide area of the Mideast, yet not reaching Cahokia itself. Plenty of other archeological sites along the Ohio River had certainly experienced the harrowing event, reportedly impressive cultural centers of the 12th and 13th centuries that they must have been. For cultures worshipping the sun deity as intensely as the Mound Builders did, such an event must have had a profound effect, to say the least. However, the dwellers of the Sacred Sun City known to us today as Cahokia were not touched but by a slight, partial eclipse.

The city of Quachil Thecou is fictional, based on several archeological sites dotting the relevant southern parts of the Ohio River spread on the path of the aforementioned solar eclipse. The eastern and northeastern towns and villages featured in the story go as far as upstream of the Great Miami River, places that were certainly an integral part of the extensive trade network, according to archeological findings.

Whether the larger Mississippian cities of the west collected tribute from their smaller northeastern neighbors belonging to another culture known to us today as "Fort Ancient" with their smaller effigy mounds, we don't know, but there is a solid base to assume that this might have been the case. The entire Mideast and Southeast certainly engaged in extensive trading practices that reached as far as the Great Lakes of the north and the Gulf of Mexico in the south.

Another question and a part of the wonder concerning tribute collection is manpower. To build an earthen monument of such magnitude, the urban centers needed plenty of workers, planners, and overseers to make it all function. The construction must have progressed in continued stages, each supervised by those who understood the basics of engineering. No firm archaeological evidence of slavery as a concept seemed to be found, even though it is clear that there must have been a strict class separation among the Mississippians as proved by those who might have been their direct descendants – Natches, Taensa, Tunihkas, and other dwellers of the Lower Mississippian valley as described by the early French chronicles of later centuries.

For the lack of hard evidence concerning the concept of outright slavery, I chose to feature the practice of collecting manpower as a part of a tribute to be paid by surrounding lesser settlements as a temporary arrangement. After all, to build great mounds or dig impressively large barrow pits to turn into artificial ponds for extensive waterfowl breeding – a food source the city dwellers must have relied upon as much as on the regular agricultural production – an urban center needed to have a substantial amount of human power at its command. A willing or an unwilling human power? That would be another question to answer.

Out of the wish to present as authentic recreation of those times and places as possible, I avoided using names of rivers or towns, or rather archeological sites, as they are known to us today. Cahokia was certainly not known as Cahokia back in 1205. This name was given to it by the archeologists, commemorating people who had lived in this region at the time of the contact, people who probably had nothing to do with those who had erected those great mounds. We cannot know what was the correct name of this place, therefore I resorted to calling it Great Sun City, given the fact that the paramount sovereign of the entire region called Great Sun had resided on the top of the Cahokian largest of mounds, or so it seems.

Quachil Thecou, a combination of words meaning "Lesser Sun" in translation, as mentioned above, was composed from several archeological sites of the southern Ohio River. Needless to say, like in the case of Cahokia, we do not know what those places were called by their original inhabitants.

The Ohio River's name came to us from one of the Iroquoian languages, the name that surely was not in use by the Mound Builders who lived alongside it. I chose to have the characters call it the Great River, a term the size of this watershed certainly justifies. The same goes for the Mississippi and Great Miami rivers, whose current names are said to be derived from one of the Algonquin languages, and probably have nothing to do with the way they were called by the ancient Mound Builders as well.

I admit that it would have been easier to use names and titles familiar to us, but I felt that the authenticity of the story would suffer needlessly because of that.

What happened next is presented in the second book of the **"The Mound Builders"** series, **"Royal Blood."**

The story continues with

ROYAL BLOOD

The Mound Builders, Book 2

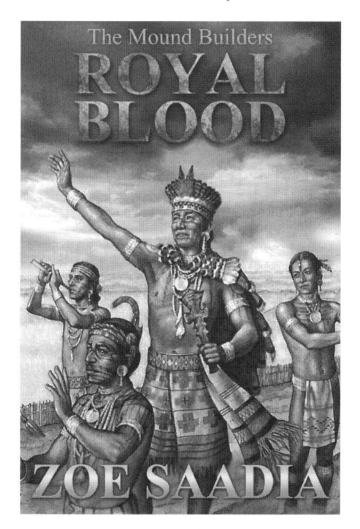

PROLOGUE

"Our revered brother seemed to recover rather fast from the illness the displeasure of our mighty sky ancestor had brought upon him."

The familiar piercing voice made Tehale's heart double its tempo, even though her limbs did not betray her, retaining their stillness, pressing against the temple's wall.

Sheltered by the outer palisade that separated this side of the spacious terrace from the fall of quite a few men's heights – the lower terrace of the Royal Mound was not as high as the sacred upper one – she held her breath, remembering her purpose. It hadn't been easy to escape her companions, but it had been worth it. Her empty-headed half-sisters and the chatty bird of a wife one of the royal cousins was forced to accept less than a moon ago, crowding the lower terrace's female quarters worse than before, were bearable company, but only for a certain amount of time.

She ground her teeth, then for the thousandth time, wished she could have lived up there, in the sacred surroundings of the real majesty and might.

"His spirit defeated the new illness, yes." She could hear Father's voice; low, unhurried, as though talking about regular matters. A brother of Revered Sun himself, the second most important dignitary in Quachil Thecou and the man responsible for all life and war matters, Father rarely displayed open anger. Even so, people knew better than to offer him arguments or dare to cross his path. Only Revered Sun was above Father in status. And Quachilli Tamailli of course, Revered Lady Female Sun, the full sister to both powerful men.

Her chest tightening, Tehale shuddered at the memory of her father and aunt quarrelling, nearly yelling at each other only a few dawns ago, on that dreadful day of the spear-throwing contest, when the Sky Deity had left their world, swallowed by a terrible darkness. A dreadful omen no living person ever witnessed or heard about. And yet, it was not the worst of it.

The benevolent Sky Deity returned after a while, taking pity on the terrified people, listening to their pleas and the desperation of their prayers. But it did not bring peace back to the Royal Mound. Even as the sun was hesitating, slipping back from behind the terrible veil of blackness, her powerful aunt had cancelled her powerful father's order and in front of the entire city, a fearsome occurrence in itself, not helped by Revered Sun's returned illness. The Quachil Thecou sovereign wasn't well enough to decree his will in the matter of the eastern barbarian and the offering of the foreigner's blood Father wished to make to the possibly angered godhead, causing a public disagreement between the two most powerful siblings of the sacred family, a disagreement that turned uglier as it carried on into the evening and the privacy of the Royal Mound's lower terrace.

Shivering again, she remembered slipping around the temple where the Royal Mound's nobility still crowded, those who were allowed to follow the revered lady Female Sun, flanked by Tattooed Serpent's own following. It was easy to sneak around this crowd, even though Tehale had praised herself on her ability to do that when no one was around but her prey of the day. Her skill of eavesdropping was a fruit of many summers of practice. One never knew when this or that secret knowledge would be practical or of use. She had happened to barter secrets for privileges until now, from servants responsible for women's quarters and from her fellow half-sisters and cousins as well. And yet, now she wished she hadn't managed to overhear the terrible quarrel her powerful father and her even more powerful aunt were having when thinking no one was listening to them, or just not caring anymore. They were yelling at each other, *actually yelling*, threatening each other openly. Well, her aunt was the one doing the threatening, while Father was busy accusing the power-hungry woman of being too power-hungry. Too ambitious, he said. Straight into her haughty face. Oh mighty deities!

"The spirits of the darkness did not manage to threaten his life," repeated Father's voice as though after a shrug. "Not this time."

Glad to take her thoughts off that dreadful evening, Tehale concentrated, wishing to hear what her powerful relatives had to say to each other this time. Scary as it was, she just needed to know. Father's important position, was it threatened now? Would his ever-domineering sister replace him with a new tattooed serpent when her own son Sothkoth ascended the throne? Impossible, but she could try to do that, couldn't she?

"They shouldn't have been able to endanger it in the first place," snapped her aunt, never in as tight a control as the male progeny of the family. The great Female Sun could afford that, of course. The certainty of her status warranted that, the flawlessness of her bloodline.

Tehale winced at the familiar wave of resentment, wishing so very badly to have this woman for a mother instead of an aunt; or at least, any of the lesser female progeny belonging to the sacred family. What a bright, happy future she might have had instead of being born to a man, even as great as her father was. What a cruel joke!

With an effort, she forced her thoughts back to the familiar voices, nervous at her own effrontery of daring to eavesdrop on her powerful family but used to it, having done that so many times before. What else was there to do around the Royal Mound, with no reasonable future in sight, except for being kicked down its stairs and into the household of this or that ambitious nobleman with a favor from the royal family to claim? She could not hide her monthly bloods for many summers to come, could she? They would discover that she had turned into a woman and then she would be married off as quickly as it took to say "Quachil Thecou." Quicker than that!

"Your son will occupy the royal hall of the upper terrace when it's his time to do that." Father's voice raised ever so slightly, its dispassionate ring gone. Would he yell at the powerful woman again, like he did on the evening of the disappearing sun? Tehale held her breath. "He is not ready, despite your wish that he were, Sister. He needs to learn, to expand his responsibilities, to start taking his future seriously. Chasing maids while gorging on food and invigorating drink in excessive amounts and with little to no restraint will not help him evolve into as great a ruler as our revered brother is."

A pause that ensued left Tehale with enough time to imagine every direful expression or glare her aunt must have bestowed on her father, a whole gamut of those. Still, when the woman spoke, there was no trace of the anger she must have been feeling while being reminded of her son's inadequacies. "Our brother was a good ruler before bad spirits had taken lodging in his body. He does not lead our city except in name now. When the darkness swallowed our revered Sky Deity, who was there to appeal to it, to offer our pleas and our prayers? Not Revered Sun of Quachil Thecou! It was you, Brother. Not our sovereign and our leader."

"You have not approved of my prayers and my offering." Father's voice again had a cutting edge to it.

"Indeed I haven't." Even in the peacefulness of the high noon, it was easy to imagine them glaring at each other, not about to break the developing staring contest.

Tehale wished she didn't sneak away and around the temple. In the women's quarters, it was louder but safer, and the silly new wife would make the maid she had brought along with her from the city prepare that sweetish drink for everyone to enjoy. She had her uses, this lowly girl, the daughter of this or that *considerate* from the other side of the plaza. They always had uses, those people. Even the stuck-up stick of uselessness, the adviser's daughter, Revered Sun's last and most silly of wives. What was that one doing, eavesdropping on the sacred family back on the eventful evening, slinking in the shadows?

"My son is not hopeless and he is not a boy of little summers. He is a fine man, capable of ruling our great city, open to the advice of his older and wiser family members." Her aunt's voice returned back to level dispassionate tones. "I vouch for that personally, Brother. You can trust my word in this matter. You know that well enough."

The silence that followed had Tehale's back breaking in a thin but disturbingly cold sheen of sweat. Despite the early afternoon, the air was too heavy, almost suffocating, the thickness of it. It made her think of bad spirits eavesdropping on the conversation alongside her, smirking openly, baring their sharp, pointed teeth.

"It is reassuring to hear that, Sister. However, as our revered brother's health is improving, I do not see the point in a continued conversation regarding this matter."

"Our Revered Sun's health may be improving, but our city's stance with its neighbors does not, the foreign delegation that is expected to arrive at the Grand Plaza before the sun completed its journey notwithstanding." *What delegation?* wondered Tehale, wincing at the tone of the speaker, the way her aunt's voice dropped instead of raising, became like that of a growling predator, something scary and out of wintertime tales. "Our brother's lack of strength is unforgivable. Even before his illness, he was not strong enough, but now..." The woman's voice rose, taking on a shriller tone. "What happened at the terrible darkness was a sign. Our sacred forefather in the sky is not happy. He is saddened and hurt. Our lack of devotion caused him to sink into the darkness before his time, and the reality of him taking mercy on us and coming back changed nothing. We should heed his kindness and his advice. We cannot overlook omens and signs."

A brief silence prevailed through which Tehale could imagine her aunt pausing for sheer lack of air, pursing her thin lips in displeasure under her brother's stony frown. Father was fond of those stony expressions. They made people fear him more than actual words.

"Or your interpretation of it," he said finally, too softly to understand his words with no effort like before. "You interfered in the sacred ceremony for a reason. The violent barbarian from the east is a part of your plans."

Another thundering pause reminded Tehale of the quarrel on the night of the omen more vividly than before.

"The uncouth foreigner is the part of the omen. Our revered sky deity frowned on the killings our brother had made him commence, and it did not wish to accept the offering of his life either. I was a mere instrument, heralding our sacred deity's intentions when you failed to understand those."

"Or so you claim, Sister." For some reason, Father did not seem to grow angered at the mention of the event through which his authority had been challenged and in front of the entire city. Tehale winced, remembering her own fright. The revered sky deity might have been devoured by the feral beasts of the darkness, but Father's anger at what happened afterwards must have been as terrifying when erupted.

"And he is a fearsome warrior, Brother; you must admit that." Evidently, the powerful woman did not fear Father's anger, not in the least, her voice now purring rather than growling, trilling with tease. "If I were you, I would have taken him into Quachil Thecou's warring forces. He had killed plenty of your skillful spearmen, and but for our revered sky deity's interference, he might have killed more. I may be sending my own guards to fetch the barbarian if he is still alive. The tribute collector should know."

"I have sent for the tribute collector myself." Father's voice rang with matching challenge of some acrid nature. "This man will be serving me now, Sister. Having just returned from the relevant areas of the east, he'll prove useful. And not as a toy for brief amusement of flesh."

Afraid that their voices would move toward her corner, the smoothness of the temple's wall not reassuring, not this time, Tehale slipped along the warm stones, retracing her steps.

"You sent for the lowly *considerate*? Interesting!" Against the breeze rustling in the temple's shrubbery, she could hear her aunt exclaiming. "Of what use could he be to you, Brother? One wonders."

Their voices seemed to be moving as well, fainter than before, as though progressing toward the entrance of the house of worship, but by this time, Tehale hurried to cross the open space, anxious to be where she was supposed to, in the midst of silly chatter belonging to her fellow other lower terrace dwellers, girls and women inhabiting several halls built for this very purpose.

There was no lack of female progeny in the sacred family, some destined to remain on the Royal Mound their entire lives, annoyingly lucky rodents that they were!

ABOUT THE AUTHOR

Zoe Saadia is the author of several novels on pre-Columbian Americas. From the architects of the Aztec Empire to the founders of the Iroquois Great League, from the towering pyramids of Tenochtitlan to the longhouses of the Great Lakes, her novels bring long-forgotten history, cultures and people to life, tracing pivotal events that brought about the greatness of North and Mesoamerica.

To learn more about Zoe Saadia and her work, please visit
www.zoesaadia.com

59781300R00184

Made in the USA
Middletown, DE
13 August 2019